D0439651

*Lord of the Deep*

# Lord of the Deep

## Dawn Thompson

APHRODISIA

KENSINGTON BOOKS

http://www.kensingtonbooks.com

APHRODISIA BOOKS are published by

Kensington Publishing Corp.
850 Third Avenue
New York, NY 10022

Copyright © 2007 by Dawn Thompson

All rights reserved. No part of this book may be reproduced in any form or by any means without the prior written consent of the Publisher, excepting brief quotes used in reviews.

All Kensington Titles, Imprints, and Distributed Lines are available at special quantity discounts for bulk purchases for sales promotions, premiums, fund-raising, and educational or institutional use.

Special book excerpts or customized printings can also be created to fit specific needs. For details, write or phone the office of the Kensington special sales manager: Kensington Publishing Corp., 850 Third Avenue, New York, NY 10022, attn: Special Sales Department, Phone: 1-800-221-2647.

Aphrodisia and the A logo U.S. Pat & TM Off.

ISBN-13: 978-0-7582-2179-7
ISBN-10: 0-7582-2179-7

First Kensington Trade Paperback Printing: September 2007

10  9  8  7  6  5  4  3  2

Printed in the United States of America

# 1

---

*The Isle of Mists, in the Eastern Archipelago,*
*Principalities of Arcus*

Meg saw the seals from her window, their silvery coats rippling as they thrashed out of the sea and collected along the shore. She'd seen them sunning themselves on the rocks by day and had watched them frolic in the dusky darkness from that dingy salt-streaked window in her loft chamber many times since her exile to the island, but not like tonight, with their slick coats gleaming in the moonlight. Full and round, the summer moon left a silvery trail in the dark water that pointed like an arrow toward the creatures frolicking along the strand, lighting them as bright as day. Meg's breath caught in her throat. Behind, the high-curling combers crashing on the shore took on the ghostly shape of prancing white horses—pure illusion that disappeared the instant their churning hooves touched sand. In the foaming surf left behind, the seals began to shed their skins, revealing their perfect male and female nakedness. Meg gasped. It was magical.

Her heartbeat began to quicken. She inched nearer to the window until her hot breath fogged the glass. The nights were still cool beside the sea—too cool for cavorting naked in the moonlight. And where had the seals gone? These were humans, dark haired, graceful men and women with skin like alabaster, moving with the undulant motion of the sea they'd sprung from in all their unabashed glory. They seemed to be gathering the skins they'd shed, bringing them higher toward the berm and out of the backwash.

Mesmerized, Meg stared as the mating began.

One among the men was clearly their leader. His dark wet hair, crimped like tangled strands of seaweed, waved nearly to his broad shoulders. Meg's eyes followed the moonbeam that illuminated him, followed the shadows that collected along the knife-straight indentation of his spine defining the dimples above his buttocks and the crease that separated those firm round cheeks. The woman in his arms had twined herself around him like a climbing vine, her head bent back beneath his gaze, her long dark hair spread about her like a living veil.

All around them others had paired off, coupling, engaging in a ritualistic orgy of the senses beneath the rising moon, but Meg's eyes were riveted to their leader. Who could they be? Certainly not locals. No one on the island looked like these, like *him*, much less behaved in such a fashion. She would have noticed.

Meg wiped the condensation away from the windowpane with a trembling hand. What she was seeing sent white-hot fingers of liquid fire racing through her belly and thighs, and riveting chills loose along her spine. It was well past midnight, and the peat fire in the kitchen hearth below had dwindled to embers. Oddly, it wasn't the physical cold that griped her then, hardening her nipples beneath the thin lawn night smock and undermining her balance so severely she gripped the window ledge. Her skin was on fire beneath the gown. It was her finest. She'd worked the delicate blackwork embroidery on it herself.

It would have seen her to the marriage bed if circumstances had been different—if she hadn't been openly accused of being a witch on the mainland and been banished to the Isle of Mists for protection, for honing her inherent skills, and for mentoring by the shamans. But none of that mattered now while the raging heat was building at the epicenter of her sex—calling her hand there to soothe and calm engorged flesh through the butter-soft lawn . . . at least that is how it started.

She inched the gown up along her leg and thigh and walked her fingertips through the silky golden hair curling between them, gliding her fingers along the barrier of her virgin skin, slick and wet with arousal. She glanced below. But for her termagant aunt, who had long since retired, she was alone in the thatched roof cottage. It would be a sennight before her uncle returned from the mainland, where he'd gone to buy new nets and eel pots, and to collect the herbs her aunt needed for her simples and tisanes. Nothing but beach grass grew on the Isle of Mists.

Meg glanced about. Who was there to see? No one, and she loosened the drawstring that closed the smock and freed her aching breasts to the cool dampness that clung stubbornly to the upper regions of the dreary little cottage, foul weather and fair.

Eyes riveted to the strand, Meg watched the leader of the strange congregation roll his woman's nipples between his fingers. They were turned sideways, and she could see his thick, curved sex reaching toward her middle. Still wet from the sea they'd come from, their skin shone in the moonlight, gleaming as the skins they'd shed had gleamed. They were standing ankle deep in the crashing surf that spun yards of gossamer spindrift into the night. Meg stifled a moan as she watched the woman's hand grip the leader's sex, gliding back and forth along the rigid shaft from thick base to hooded tip. Something pinged deep inside her watching him respond . . . something urgent and unstoppable.

Her breath had fogged the pane again, and she wiped it away in a wider swath this time. Her breasts were nearly touching it. Only the narrow windowsill kept them from pressing up against the glass, but who could see her in the darkened loft? No one, and she began rolling one tall hardened nipple between her thumb and forefinger, then sweeping the pebbled areola in slow concentric circles, teasing but not touching the aching bud, just as the creature on the beach had done to the woman in his arms.

Excruciating ecstasy.

While the others were mating fiercely all along the strand, the leader had driven his woman to her knees in the lacy surf. The tide was rising, and the water surged around him at mid-calf, breaking over the woman, creaming over her naked skin, over the seaweed and sand she knelt on as she took his turgid member into her mouth to the root.

Meg licked her lips expectantly in anticipation of such magnificence entering her mouth, responding to the caress of her tongue. She closed her eyes, imagining the feel and smell and taste of him, like sea salt bursting over her palate. This was one of the gifts that had branded her a witch.

When Meg opened her eyes again, her posture clenched. Had he turned? Yes! He seemed to be looking straight at her. It was almost as if he'd read her thoughts, as if he knew she was there all the while and had staged the torrid exhibition for her eyes alone to view. She couldn't see his face—it was steeped in shadow—but yes, there was triumph in his stance and victory in the posturing that took back his sex from the woman's mouth. His eyes were riveting as he dropped to his knees, spread the woman's legs wide to the rushing surf, and entered her in one slow, tantalizing thrust, like a sword being sheathed to the hilt, as the waves surged and crashed and swirled around them.

Still his shadowy gaze relentlessly held Meg's. For all her extraordinary powers of perception, she could not plumb the depths of that look as he took the woman to the rhythm of the waves lapping at them, laving them to the meter of his thrusts, like some giant beast with a thousand tongues. She watched the mystical surf horses trample them, watched the woman beneath him shudder to a rigid climax as the rising tide washed over her—watched the sand ebb away beneath the beautiful creature's buttocks as the sea sucked it back from the shore. All the while he watched her. It was as if she were the woman beneath him, writhing with pleasure in the frothy sea.

Captivated, Meg met the leader's silver-eyed gaze. She could almost feel the undulations as he hammered his thick, hard shaft into the woman, reaching his own climax. Meg groaned in spite of herself as he threw back his head and cried out when he came.

She should move away from the window . . . But why? He couldn't see what she was doing to herself in the deep darkness of the cottage loft . . . Could he? All at once it didn't matter. A hot lava flow of sweet sensation riddled her sex with pinpricks of exquisite agony. It was almost as if *he* were stroking her nipples and palpating the swollen nub at the top of her weeping vulva as she rubbed herself, slowly at first, then fiercely, until the thickening bud hardened like stone. She probed herself deeper. She could almost stretch the barrier skin and slip her finger inside, riding the silk of her wetness—as wet as the surging combers lapping relentlessly at the lovers on the beach. A firestorm of spasmodic contractions took her then, freeing the moan in her throat. It felt as if her bones were melting. Shutting her eyes, she shed the last remnants of modest restraint and leaned into her release.

The voyeuristic element of the experience heightened the orgasm, and it was some time before her hands gripped the windowsill again instead of tender flesh, and her gaze fell upon the strand below once more. But the silvery expanse of rock-bound shoreline edged in seaweed stretching north and south as far as the eye could see was vacant. The strange revelers were gone!

Meg tugged the night shift back over her flushed breasts, though they ached for more stroking, and let the hem of the gown slide down her legs, hiding the palpitating flesh of her sex. Her whole body throbbed like a pulse beat, and she seized the thrumming mound between her thighs savagely through the gown in a vain attempt to quiet its tremors and made a clean sweep through the condensation on the window again. Nothing moved outside but the combers crashing on the strand. But for the echo of the surf sighing into the night, reverberating through her sex to the rhythm of fresh longing, all else was still.

No. She hadn't imagined it. The naked revelers mating on the beach had been real—as real as the seals that frequented the coast. Selkies? Could the shape-shifter legends be true? She'd heard little else since she came to the island.

Meg didn't stop to collect her mantle. Maybe the cool night air would cure the fever in her flesh. Hoisting up the hem of her night smock, she climbed down the loft ladder, tiptoed through the kitchen without making a sound, and stepped out onto the damp drifted sand that always seemed to collect about the doorsill. Nothing moved but the prancing white horses in the surf that drove it landward. Waterhorses? She'd heard that legend, too: innocent looking creatures that lured any who would mount them to a watery death. Real or imaginary, it didn't matter. The people she'd just seen there having sex were real enough, and she meant to prove it.

The hard, damp sand was cold beneath her bare feet as she padded over the shallow dune toward the shoreline. The phantom horses had disappeared from the waves crashing on the strand, as had every trace that anyone had walked that way recently. There wasn't a footprint in sight, and the sealskins Meg had watched them drag to higher ground were nowhere to be seen, either.

Having reached the ragged edge of the surf, Meg turned and looked back at the cottage beyond, paying particular attention to her loft window. Yes, it was close, but there was no way anyone could have seen her watching from her darkened chamber. Then why was she so uneasy? It wasn't the first time she'd touched herself in the dark, and it wouldn't be the last, but it had been the best, and there was something very intimate about it. The man who had aroused her seemed somehow familiar, and yet she knew they'd never met. Still, he had turned toward that window and flaunted himself as if he knew she had been watching, exhibiting his magnificent erection in what appeared to be a sex act staged solely for her benefit. Moist heat rushed at her loins, ripping through her belly and thighs with the memory.

Meg scooped up some of the icy water and bathed the aching flesh between her thighs. She plowed through the lacy surf where the lovers had performed—to the very spot where the mysterious selkie leader had spent his seed—and tried to order the mixed emotions riddling her. Absorbed in thought, she failed to feel the vibration beneath her feet until the horse was nearly upon her. It reared back on its hind legs, forefeet pawing the air, its long tail sweeping the sand a *real* horse this time, no illusion. Meg cried out as recognition struck. There was a rider on its back. He was naked and aroused. It was *him*, with neither bridle nor reins to control the beast, and nothing but a silvery sealskin underneath him.

He seemed quite comfortable in the altogether, as if it was the most natural thing in the world to sit a horse bareback, naked in the moonlight. She gasped. The horse had become quite docile, attempting to nuzzle her with its sleek white nose as it pranced to a standstill. She didn't want to look at the man on its back, but she couldn't help herself. He was a beguiling presence. As mesmerizing as he was from a distance, he was a hundred times more so at close range. Now she could see what the shadows had denied her earlier. His eyes, the color of mercury, were dark and penetrating, and slightly slanted. Somehow, she knew they would be. And his hair, while waving at a length to tease his shoulders in front, was longer in back and worn in a queue, tied with what appeared to be a piece of beach grass. How had she not noticed that before? But how could she have when he'd made such a display of himself face forward? Besides, her focus was hardly upon his hair.

Her attention shifted to the horse. At first she'd thought its mane and tail were black, but upon close inspection, she saw that they were white as snow, so tangled with seaweed they appeared black at first glance. But wait . . . what had she heard about white horses whose mane and tail collected seaweed? A waterhorse! The phantom creature of legend that seduced its victims to mount and be carried off to drown in the sea . . . But that was preposterous. Nevertheless, when its master reached out his hand toward her, she spun on her heels and raced back toward the cottage.

His laughter followed her, throaty and deep. Like an echo from the depths of the sea itself, it crashed over her just as the waves crashed over the shore. The sound pierced through her like a lightning bolt. The prancing waterhorse beneath him whinnied and clamped ferocious-looking teeth into the hem of her night shift, giving a tug that brought her to ground. She landed hard on her bottom, and the selkie laughed again as she cried out. Plucking her up as easily as if she were a broom straw, he settled her in front of him astride.

"You cannot escape me, Megaleen," he crooned in her ear. "You have summoned me, and I have come. You have no idea what it is that you have conjured—what delicious agonies you have unleashed by invoking me." His breath was moist and warm; it smelled of salt and the mysteries of the Otherworldly sea that had spawned him. "Hold on!" he charged, turning the horse toward the strand.

"Hold on to what?" Meg shrilled. "He has no bridle—no reins!"

Again his sultry voice resonating in her ear sent shivers of pleasure thrumming through her body. "Take hold of his mane," he whispered.

His voice alone was a seduction. He was holding her about the middle. Her shift had been hiked up around her waist when he settled her astride, and she could feel the thick bulk of his shaft throbbing against her buttocks, riding up and down along the cleft between the cheeks of her ass. The damp sealskin that stretched over the animal's back like a saddle blanket underneath her felt cool against Meg's naked thighs, but it could not quench the fever in her skin or douse the flames gnawing at the very core of her sex. The friction the waterhorse's motion created forced the wet sealskin fur deeper into her fissure, triggering another orgasm. Her breath caught as it riddled her body with waves of achy heat. She rubbed against the seal pelt, undulating to the rhythm of the horse's gait until every last wave had ebbed away, like ripples in a stream when a pebble breaks the water's surface.

In one motion, the selkie raised the night shift over her head and tossed it into the water. Reaching for it as he tore it away, Meg lost her balance. His strong hands spanning her waist prevented her from falling. Their touch seared her like firebrands, raising the fine hairs at the nape of her neck. The horse had plunged into the surf. It was heading toward the open sea, parting the unreal phantom horses galloping toward shore.

Salt spray pelted her skin, hardening her nipples. Spindrift dressed her hair with tiny spangles. The horse had plunged in past the breakers to the withers. Terrified, Meg screamed as the animal broke through the waves and sank to its muscular neck.

"Hold on!" he commanded.

"I cannot," Meg cried. "His mane . . . It is slippery with seaweed."

All at once, he lifted her into the air and set her down facing him, gathering her against his hard, muscular body, his engorged sex heaving against her belly. How strong he was! "Then hold onto me," he said.

"W-who are you?" Meg murmured.

"I am called Simeon . . . amongst other things," he replied. "But that hardly signifies. . . ." Heat crackled in his voice. Something pinged in her sex at the sound of it.

He swooped down, looming over her. For a split second, she thought he was going to kiss her. She could almost taste the salt on his lips, in his mouth, on the tongue she glimpsed parting his teeth . . . But no. Fisting his hand in the back of her waist-length sun-painted hair, he blew his steamy breath into her nostrils as the horse's head disappeared beneath the surface of the sea.

Meg's last conscious thought before sinking beneath the waves in the selkie's arms was that she was being seduced to her death; another orgasm testified to that. Weren't you supposed to come before you die? Wasn't it supposed to be an orgasm like no other, like the orgasm riddling her now?

The scent that ghosted through her nostrils as she drew her last breath of air was his scent, salty, laced with the mysteries of the deep, threaded through with the sweet musky aroma of ambergris.

# 2

Meg groaned awake and opened her eyes to eerie green darkness. The sound of rushing water echoed nearby. She tried to raise herself, but her limbs felt weightless, as if she were floating. But she wasn't floating. Something was holding her down. She waved her arms about in the water . . . *water!* She was immersed in water. But it couldn't be. How was she breathing?

Frantically, she groped her body. She was naked. Where had her night smock gone? Oh yes, the selkie lord had flung it into the sea. But he couldn't have. That was just a dream . . . Wasn't it?

Something snaked its way between her legs, and she cried out. How strange her voice sounded under water. Why didn't she choke on it when it rushed into her mouth? Why hadn't she drowned?

She swatted at whatever was groping her thighs and cried out again when it probed the V of golden hair curling between, parting her nether lips. This was no eel . . . no creature of the deep, and sea vegetation did not move with the deftness of fingers. She shot her hand out and gripped a wrist . . . a man's wrist . . . *his* wrist!

His warm mouth covered her scream.

In spite of herself, Meg groaned as his pointed tongue plunged in and out of her mouth, filling her the way his penis had filled the woman on the beach. It felt like hot silk, moving with the same ebb and flow of the sea. She was dead; she had to be. She had drowned and this was the entrance to the Netherworld the elders spoke of, the purification by water the dead must endure that the shamans held in such high regard. But if that were so, why had he entered it with her, this enigmatic lord of the selkies?

Reason returning, she fought the human tether he had become. "Let me go!" she cried, slapping at his arms and kicking her feet. "Take me back. I will be missed. There will be reprisals. My aunt Adelia and my uncle Olwyn are shamans. They are mentoring me in the Witching Way. I am to become a priestess of the Isle of Mists! Take me back, I say, and no harm will befall you!" Why was the water so murky? Why couldn't she see?

He slipped one arm around her waist, threaded the other between her legs, and stroked her buttocks. "Every man, woman, and child on the Isle of Mists practices shamanism," he said. "They are nothing to me. You are in my world now, Megaleen, and here I am Simeon, Lord of the Deep. You summoned me, remember?"

"When did I do that?" Meg snapped at him. "How? I never summoned you. This is some wicked nightmare—some vicious trick of my subconscious mind. I will awake in my loft, in my bed of feather quilts, and you will be what you really are . . . a wet dream; a figment of my imagination . . ."

A deep gravely laugh lived in Simeon's throat. It resonated through Meg's body, sending little tingling shockwaves along her spine. She stiffened in his arms as his deft fingers traced the cleft between her buttocks. Her quick intake of breath rang in her ears as the finger slid lower, ever so lightly flitting over the taut pucker of her anus, then moved on to explore her virgin skin. The finger traveled higher, reaching for the tiny bud at the top of her vulva. Rolling it between his fingers, he pressed down upon her nether lips until he had exposed the hardened erection to his tongue, and he laved it until she cried out in excruciating ecstasy.

Meg gripped his shoulders. She should struggle—push him away. She could not. Instead, she threaded her fingers through his long wavy hair. Carried on the underwater current, it flowed about him like strands of silk. It was beyond bearing. Never had she dreamed such ecstasy existed. As if they had a will of their own, her hands fisted in that cool dark silk and held his head against the tender spot he nipped and laved and sucked until her body shuddered to a riveting climax.

The moan that left her throat echoed through the underwater labyrinth, through her body—through her very soul.

"This is only the beginning," Simeon murmured in her ear.

Taken with a sudden wave of remorse, Meg stiffened in the arms that pulled her closer. "I did not summon you!" she got out. Her voice was no more than a hoarse whisper. "Take me back! I beg you . . . Take me back to the Isle. . . ."

His deep throaty laugh shot her through with gooseflesh. She had heard tales of the selkies' hypnotic power over women, of their prowess in the art of seduction. What else had she heard about them? Why couldn't she remember? Why couldn't she think? There was more to the legend, so much more . . . But his hands were exploring her body again, playing with her nipples, just as he had played with the nipples of the woman on the strand—rolling them between his thumbs and forefingers, making them hard and tall for his lips to suck on, first one and then the other.

"Did you not come to the strand . . . and watch the seals . . . sunning themselves on the rocks?" he said between tugs upon her aching buds, meanwhile laving the pebbled areolas mercilessly. He was going to drive her mad. *Please the Powers, let this be a dream!* she prayed.

"The seals, yes," she said. "Many times, but I don't see how—"

"Did you not lament your lot, little fledgling witch? Did you not wish the kind of love your situation denies you, for you know no priestess of the Isle can marry, Megaleen?"

"I-in my secret heart, perhaps, but that does not mean—"

"Did your condemnation as a witch not make an end to your betrothal on the mainland?" Simeon interrupted. "You are not simpleminded. You know a witch of the Isle's mystery—her very power—lies in her maidenhead, in the taking of it by the shaman high priest in her right of initiation. . . ."

Meg had all but forgotten about that, and cold chills riddled her as she remembered what fate she'd resigned herself to when she escaped to the Isle of Mists. These traditions were eons old, rooted in the mists of time that gave birth to the Isle and created the mystical priestesses who ruled it.

Simeon's sultry voice cut into her thoughts. "Was that not the reason you were whisked away from your marriage bed before the conjugal quilts were laid out upon it?"

Meg gasped. "How could you know that?" she cried.

"We selkies are perceptive entities," he responded. His hands were everywhere, flitting over her skin, exploring every orifice, every crevice and fissure. It was as if he was memorizing every contour of her body with hands that knew just how to touch, to arouse, to tantalize in ways not even she had fantasized in her wildest dreams, waking or sleeping.

Whatever sea plant she was lying upon was as soft as satin, caressing her in places he could not reach since his hands were occupied elsewhere seeking out her pleasure zones. The broad, flat ribbonlike growth swaying in the water seemed an extension of him, as alive as he was and of like mind with his advances. How far did control of his water world extend, this

Lord of the Deep—even to the exotic plant life? She beat those thoughts back along with the nagging recollection of her destiny among the shamans on the Isle. Right now his control of her was paramount, for she was losing hers. Her only weapon was her tongue, and she used it like a knife blade, though it cut her as well.

"The only way you could have known that was if you'd read my thoughts," she snapped at him. The outburst left something to be desired, coming at the precise moment he had her on the brink of yet another climax. "And . . . and that is preposterous!" she flung at him. "Even if you did read my thoughts, I gave you no leave to act upon them."

He drew her closer. "Not your thoughts, Megaleen; your *heart*," he whispered seductively. There was a strange tremor in his voice that spoke of sorrows too terrible to probe. It passed in the blink of an eye. "Did you love him, your intended?"

"What does it matter?" Meg said wearily.

Simeon shrugged against her. He was aroused, his thick hardness throbbing against her middle, the velvety head probing her navel. "It does not," he said, "because all that is in the past. You cannot return to the mainland . . . ever, else you face sure and sudden death. If you remain with the shamans on the Isle of Mists, you will whither and die slowly . . . emptily. Celibacy is not for you, and that is what must be once you have become high priestess."

"How do you know what is and is not 'for me'?" Meg hurled at him. That was the wrong thing to have said. She knew it the minute the words were out. His guttural chuckle laced with derision testified to that.

"I saw, that is how I know," he said.

Meg lurched in his arms. "How could you have?" she cried. "I mean . . . I do not know what you're talking about." Hot blood rushed to her temples with the lie. Not even the cool water surrounding them could quell the fever in her cheeks. He had seen her! Somehow, he had seen her touching herself in the dark!

"Then I must show you," the selkie crooned. There was no mistaking his intent now. Again she strained against him, but it was a halfhearted attempt to free herself. How could she? Even if she did break his hold and escape, where would she go? How could she find her way back unless he showed her the way?

She would wake soon, in her bed of eiderdown quilts, and this delicious dream would fade away in the shadow of whatever glimpses her memory would allow. It was induced by what she'd seen from her loft window earlier, from her longing for a life she could never have. There was no other explanation.

"As I told you," he whispered. "You have no idea what you have unleashed by invoking me. So! Which shall it be . . . deflowering, then celibacy among the withered shamans on the Isle of Mists, or will you become consort of the Lord of the Deep? Decide!"

"You have other consorts, my lord," Meg snapped. "You hardly need me."

"Ah, but it is not what I need that has brought us to this pass. It is what I want, little witch, and I always satisfy those urges." He ran his hands over her body, following the contours of her breasts, her waist, her hips and thighs. "Why waste all this?" he said, his voice crackling with inner fire. "Why save it for naught but the moon to view as you chant your witching rituals. Will it pleasure you, your cold, dead moon?" He slipped his hand between her legs and stroked her vulva. "Will it enter you—fill you—give you what I have already given you even without this that you feel on your belly entering your exquisite body?" He rubbed his shaft against her quivering sex in illustration, and Meg lurched as if she'd been lightning-struck by the silky touch of its mushroom head against her erect clitoris. In spite of herself, she groaned. "Do not dare deny what you feel in my arms, little witch," he said, husky-voiced. "Your pleasure-moans betray you."

Meg could not deny it. She was no match for his prowess. Truth to tell, she didn't even want to be. What did it matter? It was only a dream, wasn't it—an escape from the cold reality of her very real nightmare? It had to be. No one could breathe under water. What harm to let him pleasure her? He was only a figment of her imagination.

It suddenly occurred to her that not once had she touched him as he was touching her now. Not once had she explored his body as he did hers. She reached for his erection. It was rockhard and massive, the ridged head fully exposed, veins distended. He shuddered as her fingers flitted across it, causing drops of something warm and thick to ooze from the tip. Meg drew her hand back as if she'd touched live coals.

Capturing her wrist, the selkie crimped her hand around his penis. "Touch it," he murmured. "See how my life lives for you, little witch. You have beguiled me. . . ."

The underwater fog had begun to lift. She could see him now. The silt their motion had churned up was settling again on the ocean floor. He rose to his feet and drew her up alongside. How magnificent he was, but then he would be since she had created him in her mind. His long dark hair was fanned out on the gentle water current that caressed them. His eyes, almond shaped with long dark lashes, shone like mercury in the eerie diffused light. How broad his shoulders were, how narrow his waist. Her hand still rode along his shaft. His Otherworldly eyes were riveted to it—to her fingers playing it the way a skilled musician plays a treasured instrument—cherishing, reverencing. His breath caught, and Meg hesitated.

"Don't stop . . ." he said. "Pull harder, little witch . . . work your magic. . . ."

Meg could feel the pulse throbbing through his erection. She quickened her pace, pumping him—milking him. He leaned into her caress. His hips jerked forward driving rapid, pistoning thrusts, and he groaned as the phosphorescent stream of his seed squirted into the water.

He drew her to him through the milky flow drifting between them, his breath coming short. "Take no comfort in what you have just done," he murmured against her hair. He drove her hand down to his sex again. "See?" he said. "See how it lives for you even now, little witch?"

"Any one of your handmaidens, the creatures I saw you with on the strand, could have done as much," she said. There was no use denying she had seen him now. He *knew.*

"Ah, but they are not pure," he pointed out. "They are cold, selfish vixens, like their sisters, the roanes, like the *Morganezed* and the sirens, even unto the Lorelei. They live in many worlds and fornicate with one and all. The sex act means no more to them than relieving themselves. I tire of their games. I want . . . more, and you did summon me, Megaleen, whether you want to believe it or no."

"I did not!" Meg insisted.

"The desires of all creatures' hearts ride the wind and reach the ears of all who would hear," the selkie said. "Your heart's desires rustle the beach grass and sail the surf. If you listen, you can hear the water sigh and moan as it reaches shore. And if conditions are just right, someone will hear and answer, as I have done. Do not trouble yourself with such mysteries. There are limits to the powers of the mortal mind—even the minds of witches. It is enough for you to know that your heart reached out, and I was here to answer."

With no more said, he swept her up in his arms and swam into a tunnel. Sea grass groped them familiarly as they passed, and schools of tiny fish flitted around them, nudging and nipping and tickling their skin, their scales gleaming like silvery shards of mirror glass as they streaked by. How strong his arms were, buoying her. His taut muscles were rippling against her naked skin. What an odd sensation it was, having been made weightless by the water, to feel those muscles flexing against her. She clung to him as they approached the threshold of a subterranean shelf, an air pocket where a coral palace stood. At least that is what it seemed to be, its sprawling architecture was only half visible from her vantage beneath the waves. It was enormous, glittering with reflected phosphorescence from the water and from the schools of silvery fish that had followed them through the tunnel. The effect was dazzling.

Simeon sucked the water from her nose and mouth, then broke the surface and carried her through the chambers to one boasting a raised bed made with quilts of sea moss and one slick sealskin, like velvet beneath her as he laid her down there and fell upon her. As he had done before, his fingers traced the outline of her nipples and flitted over every orifice from ear to anus, feeling for her sexual pulse. Meg scarcely breathed. *Please the Powers, do not let me wake here now,* she prayed.

The bed was wreathed around with odd white roselike blooms whose heads bobbed about as if they were humans sharing secrets. "What are those?" she asked, pointing.

"Um?" he grunted, gathering her against him. "Silt roses, they are called. They breathe like mortals breathe, and are quite annoying. Pay them no mind."

"If they are so annoying, why do you keep them, then?" Meg wondered.

"They purify the air, and they have a pleasant scent. All life in the sea has a purpose, little witch. Enough! Leave them to their tittering. Our time grows short. . . ."

He took her lips in a fiery kiss that seared her tongue. His skilled lips blazed a trail along her arched throat to her breasts, then between to the hollow of her navel. Meg arched herself against him, lifting her hips, raising her mound to receive his kiss. But he did not kiss her there. Instead, he dipped his fingers in a thick substance that filled a spinney conch shell standing on the chamber floor beside the bed. How curious that she hadn't noticed it before. It had a silvery sheen about it, and she stiffened as he slathered some between her thighs, parting her nether lips and rubbing it into her vulva, massaging it the length of her virgin skin.

"What is that?" she breathed, shrinking back as he stroked her. "What do you do . . . 'Tis cold!"

"It will be warm in a moment," he murmured, still palpating her sex. "It is a remedy eons old. It will dull the pain and give you much pleasure. I am surprised you are not familiar with pearl salve. The sirens grind the pearls with water herbs and rendered fat to bind them. The secret recipe is well guarded. It numbs the flesh slightly and heightens sexual urges. You will feel a pleasant tingle."

Meg spread her legs, writhing under his touch. All that he said was true. She was drenched in fire from his touch. He dipped his fingers in the salve again and rubbed it on his penis, then worked the silvery ointment into her nipples in concentric circles, rolling the aching tips between his thumbs and forefingers until they grew hard and she shuddered in anticipation. The substance had a pleasant aroma. It smelled of musk and ambergris—of him.

He mounted her. How she wanted him to enter her as he had the woman on the beach. She wanted him to fill her to the root of his sex, just as he filled that consort, in one smooth thrust riding her rhythm. That this act would put her in grave danger on the Isle, and the mainland as well, didn't signify in that wonderful, terrible heartbeat of time when he stretched her virgin skin with the head of his penis until it gave and admitted him to the seat of her sexuality.

A roar left his throat and spread through the air, like ripples in water amplified by the deep, as he filled her. The cry had scarcely left his lungs when it was answered by a sorrowful spate of siren song. Meg knew it well. She had heard the sirens singing on their rocks in the night. Once heard, there was no mistaking the plaintive, mournful wail of the siren song. But he was moving inside her, touching tender flesh never touched before, calling her back to the present. Just as he'd said, there was no pain, and she abandoned herself to the ecstasy of his volatile embrace.

Meg groaned with each of his thrusts. How strange it felt to have a man inside her. Was this what it would really feel like if the dream were real? His moves were fluid, like the water on the far side of the tunnel. His rhythm was the rhythm of the sea. He was the selkie now, moving to the pulse of the deep, and every place he touched, every inch of her tender skin, was on fire.

Her breath caught in her throat as he brought her to climax, then climaxed himself, filling her, emptying every last drop of his seed into her as her inner walls contracted and squeezed him dry. Groaning, he swooped down, covering her lips with his own. But it wasn't a kiss. He seemed to be breathing into her mouth again, blowing his sweet breath into her lungs. All at once she felt herself lifted. As if he couldn't bear to be parted from her, he hadn't withdrawn himself, and he carried her thus, with her legs wrapped around his waist, back through the chambers to the tunnel. Then they were surging upward. The sawing motion of his long muscular legs raising her up, swimming with her through the tunnel joined as they were, riddled her sex with unstoppable waves of orgasmic fire. Her loins, belly, and rigid thighs ached with it. Every cell in her skin was charged with sensation. Then just before they broke the surface, he sucked the water from her nostrils again, and everything went black.

Meg woke alone in her loft chamber. She was naked underneath the down coverlets. That wasn't unusual. She often slept in the nude. Her whole body tingled from her dream lover's touch. She was flushed from her burning cheeks to the tips of her toes. Sliding her hands the length of her body, her fingers flitted over her nipples, still hard and tall. She followed the indentation of her narrow waist and the curve of her thighs. Her skin was scorching to the touch, as if she had a raging fever. Her fingers probed lower, parting her nether lips, searching for her virgin skin. Instead, her fingers slipped inside the fissure that had always barred them. Something warm and moist coated her fingertips. She probed herself deeper, and adrenaline surged through her body, prickling her scalp with gooseflesh. There was no mistake. She was a virgin no longer.

Meg withdrew her hand and examined her fingers. They were smeared with blood and something else . . . the residue of a thick pearly ointment that smelled of the sea, of salt and musk and ambergris—*of him!* She sat bolt upright in the bed and winced at the dull ache in her genitals. Her erect nipples bore traces of silvery sheen, and the long sun-painted hair falling over her shoulders was tangled with seaweed. She gasped.

It hadn't been a dream!

# 3

Meg swung her feet to the floor. Her belly was swollen. And why wouldn't it be? The selkie was gargantuan. He had stretched her tight virgin quim to bursting. She padded to the window, where it had all begun, and gazed at the strand below. There were no revelers now. But for the gentle sighing of the surf as it rolled up the beach, all was still. Not even the phantom surf horses thundered toward shore. The waves had died, breathless and spent, as was often the case in the wee hours before dawn.

The moon was sliding low in the indigo vault above, its beams making a wider swath in the black water rippling toward shore. It lit the night to day. Meg snatched up her hooded cloak, lying just where she'd left it draped over a chair, and swirled it over her shoulders. She took no time to dress. What she had in mind to do must be done naked.

Climbing down the loft ladder, Meg paused. There was no sound save her aunt's loud snores. Aunt Adelia would sleep until first light if nothing untoward awakened her. There was no time to lose, and Meg quickly quit the cottage and padded toward the shore.

The damp sand along the hard-packed berm was like balm to her feet; they barely smudged the surface. She padded closer to the ragged edge the spent combers had left behind on the strand. Removing her cloak, she set it aside on dry land and walked naked into the water, into the docile waves lapping at the shore. Surf lace rushed through her toes, sucking the sand beneath them back into the ocean. She waded in to midcalf. Scooping up some of the cool saltwater, she bathed her genitals, washing away all trace of her virgin blood. The magical ointment the selkie lord had slathered over her vulva had lost its pain-relieving qualities. The salt would soothe the soreness after the initial burn, and she squatted down, spread her nether lips, and let the surf rush into her. Groaning in relief, she let the sea stroke her until the cold and salt and rhythmic strokes of the restless waves had numbed her aching sex.

Surging to her feet, she reached toward the heavens as the water cascaded down her body, over her breasts, her hips and thighs, returning to the sea. But for the sighing of the waves, all sound stilled around her. The waterfowl had not yet awakened to soar and sail and perch upon the boulders near and far that later selkie seals would climb upon to warm themselves in the sun. Would the Lord of the Deep be among them? Would he fornicate with his consorts—flaunt his prowess before her as he had done before. A pang of jealousy pierced her heart. How could she bear seeing him do to another what she had watched him do before . . . what he had done to *her?* All the fever the sea had drained from her body came rushing back, just as the waves rushed toward the shore. She had no right to him, this enigmatic creature of the deep. But somehow he had taken her beneath the waves—allowed her to see and feel and breathe where no mortal could. She had to see if she were still able. That was why she'd come.

Wading out breast deep, she sprang off the silt underfoot and plunged beneath an incoming comber. The ocean floor fell away drastically, a sheer drop in the coral reef. She entered the void. Her natural instinct was to hold her breath, and it took a moment for her to relax enough to free herself from old restraints, both mental and physical, to perform the test. Then opening her mouth and nostrils, she took a breath.

Water flooded her nose and rushed into her lungs. She couldn't breathe. Panic stricken she thrashed about in the water in a vain attempt to close her breathing passages. Her balance was gone, her rhythm broken. Her head felt as if it were about to explode. Ordinarily, she was a strong swimmer, but raw fright that she was about to die cancelled common sense, and she began sinking into the abyss.

White pinpoints of blinding light starred her vision. She was losing consciousness. The sick, queasy weakness that precedes a fainting spell overwhelmed her, nearly taking her under until, out of nowhere, something large and strong butted her in the stomach, driving the water from her lungs, propelling her toward the surface.

Stunned, she tried to grab on to whatever the creature was, but she couldn't get a grip upon its smooth, slick skin. In her anxiety, she lost what little grip she'd gained and started to sink back into the underwater chasm, but the creature butted her again, harder this time, and she broke the surface gasping for air, clinging to the long, bullish neck of a giant seal driving her toward shore.

Water spouted from the creature's nostrils, a fine spray blowing into the predawn mist as it parted the waves. A bestial outcry left the seal's throat as it nudged her to safety in the shallow water swirling around them at the edge of the strand. Coughing up seawater and gasping for air, Meg glimpsed the creature's eyes before it turned back toward the deep water. They were almond shaped, large, silvery black with red reflections. They were *his* eyes. In a blink, he turned and dove back beneath the surface of the water, but his scent remained behind—salt and musk and ambergris, not the unpleasant fishy odor associated with ordinary seals. It threaded through her nostrils arousing her—making her remember.

Tears welled in her eyes as she dragged herself up onto the shore. Kneeling, she pounded the surf with both hands balled into white-knuckled fists. He had made her his own. Why did he bring her back—twice! She should be grateful that he'd saved her life, but all she felt was abandoned despite the fact that she'd asked him—*begged him*—to do just what he'd done. Had she failed in some way—displeased him? It hadn't seemed that way when his life was living inside her. Whatever the cause, she felt downhearted as she dragged herself out of the water.

Taken with spates of wheezing and coughing, Meg tried to clear her throat. Her nostrils stung from the salt, and her ribs ached from the heaving. Staggering over the fine pebbles and seaweed to the safety of damp sand, she turned back, casting her glance toward the sea. The first rays of daylight had begun to blush the horizon crimson, but no sign of life appeared in the water or the salt-sweet air. A whiff of the dawn breeze smelled pleasantly of him. She drank it in deeply.

Climbing higher, she glanced about for the cloak she'd discarded earlier. It was a few yards off, and she padded toward it. Through the morning mist, she saw something lying on top of it, something white. Skittering to a halt alongside, she groaned and dropped to her knees. It was her night shift, neatly folded atop the cloak. Snatching it up, she held it to her nose. It smelled of the sea, of salt—of *him*. She sobbed into the soft lawn and blackwork embroidery, though her sobs were empty and dry.

"*Megaleen!*" Her aunt's voice knifed through the stillness. The sound of it must have roused the waterfowl, for Meg hadn't heard their morning calls until that moment. She leapt to her feet and wriggled into the shift, tossed her cloak over her shoulders, and trudged toward the hard-faced woman standing arms akimbo at the edge of the berm.

"Coming, Aunt Adelia," Meg called out. Her eagle-eyed aunt was the last person she wanted to see in that moment, when her sex was still pinging, swollen from the selkie's throbbing bulk inside her, that had filled her, stretched her to admit his gargantuan penis. She could still feel him hammering inside her, molding her sheath to his thick, curved contours. Her breath caught remembering, reliving his thrusts. The fingers of a blush crawled up her cheeks. Would Aunt Adelia know? Would she see? *She would have to be blind not to,* Meg thought, donning her most innocent mask. It would not be easy, when each breath she drew from the fiery dawn mist filled her nostrils with the haunting scent of the Lord of the Deep.

"Bathing naked in the sea?" Adelia scorned. "What can you be thinking, exposing your body in such a way for others to view?"

"I was hot, and I couldn't sleep," Meg said sweetly. "And there was no one to see."

"Um," Adelia growled. "And what of the scrying pool, eh?" she said. "You know the shamans gaze into it at dawn and dusk. Suppose one of the elders—"

"I hardly think they do so seeking me, Aunt Adelia," Meg said.

"You forget. Your initiation is soon. The summer solstice is nearly upon us, and you are not nearly ready to take your place among the priestesses. The shamans will be watching, have no doubts of it, niece."

Meg didn't want to think about that, not with the selkie's ardor still thrumming through her veins and moistening her sex. Would the throbbing never cease? How she longed to clutch her mons area to still the vibrations that threatened to betray her, but she dared not then, in front of her aunt. And there was something else . . . Would there be no end of splinters of thought nagging just beneath the surface of her consciousness to torment her? He had sent her back! Yes, she had begged him to, but that was before she consented to be his consort. What did it mean? How had she displeased him? Again and again the questions rang in her ears. Had he ruined her just to kick her aside? Was she nothing more than some mindless conquest? The selkies' insatiable passion for female humans was legend. Had she become just another casualty of the deep? She was loath to believe it, but there she stood, alone and deflowered in the aftermath of sex like no other imaginable, wearing the nightrail the selkie had returned to her neatly folded atop her cloak on the hard-packed sand. It could mean only one thing. He had spoiled her for any other. He had formed her sexual epicenter into the glove to sheath his enormity—custom fitted her to it. No other would suffice now, and he was gone! She was ruined.

"Why the sour face?" Adelia probed. "You are up to something. Do not think I cannot see it."

"I am not liking that I am spied on," Meg recovered, sulking. "I think I shall pour squid ink in the scrying pool. Let the shamans ogle me through that!"

Adelia threw back her grizzled head and laughed outright. She smelled of fish and peat and unwashed hair. Meg would not come too near. The foul-smelling woman spoiled Simeon's scent still rising from the fine lawn night smock underneath her cloak.

The old woman reached to take Meg's arm. "Come," she said. "There is no time for you to change. We are behindhand. Just because your uncle Olwyn is away does not mean the chores must stop. It is time to bait the eel pots. We have a business to run, or had you forgotten? Fie, such a face! I will help you, now come. . . ."

Meg trudged along beside her aunt. No, she hadn't fooled

her, but she hadn't betrayed herself either. She'd forgotten about the scrying pool. She would have to be more careful in future. But what future could she hope to have now? She needed to know more about the selkies—much more. Aunt Adeila would know something, certainly more than she. Deciding upon tapping that knowledge, she was glad Adelia had offered her help. It would give her just the opportunity she needed.

They had reached a small shack behind the cottage, and Adelia lifted the wooden bar and threw it open to the morning mist. A strong fishy smell laced with tar from the nets stored there rushed up Meg's nostrils. She grimaced. Inside beyond the threshold, the sandy floor was divided by wooden planks into three shallow bins, each housing a selection of horseshoe crabs at different stages of their development. Meg gazed down at the creatures with their horseshoe shaped shells, many legs, and long spinney tail-like appendages. Some were just babies, others just having molted once had been graduated to the middle bin, and then there were the mature ones, large and formidable looking, though they were quite harmless if one knew how to handle them. It was these that Adelia approached. Seizing one of the creature's tails, she swung it up on a wooden chopping block alongside and took one of the cleavers from its bracket on the wall.

"Well?" she said, glancing over her shoulder at Meg. "Grab a cleaver. There's room for two on this block. The eel pots should have been set at first light. What are you waiting for?"

"I . . . uh . . ." Meg stumbled over her words. Chopping up horseshoe crabs to bait the eel pots had never bothered her before. Now even the slightest injury to any creature that lived in the sea was repugnant to her. Uncle Olwyn had harvested the crabs along the strand after the spring mating and brought the females up to lay their eggs in the sandy floor of the shack, where they grew and hatched and molted until they were mature enough to kill for bait. She'd done it many times. She'd even come at sundown and fed the creatures worms and mollusks to fatten them up for the eventual kill. But now she could not force her hand to reach out for that cleaver in its bracket beside the door. "I . . . can't," she murmured, shaking her head wildly.

"What?" Adelia cried. "Have your courses come upon you again that you act so peculiar? Silly chit! You've never been squeamish about chopping *horsefeet* up for bait before, my girl. What ails you?"

Meg ignored the first of that, though it gave her a new worry. What if she were with child? Simeon had certainly reached far enough inside her to plant his seed. She rubbed her belly absently underneath her cloak. No! She couldn't think about that now—not with Aunt Adelia standing slack-jawed, cleaver suspended over the wriggling horseshoe crab. Clawlike feet churning, the poor creature was trying to right itself with its spinelike tail, which served it as a rudder for just such occasions. Meg couldn't bear to look.

"I . . . I'll fetch the eel pots," she said, darting back outside to where the semicircular traps of wood and wire mesh were stacked alongside the shed. As long as she didn't have a hand in the slaughter, she could bear it. What was happening to her?

The sound of the cleaver slicing through the horseshoe crab's hard shell ran her through as if the blade had struck her as well, and she took a moment to compose herself before returning carrying several of the eel pots. Two more trips and they began baiting the traps with pieces of the horseshoe crab and loading them into a wheelbarrow.

"Hurry with that," Adelia snapped. "And do not forget to bring back yesterday's yield. 'Tis market day. We will be set upon by mainland folk as well as our own before the sun reaches the zenith. Our customers want fresh eels, niece, and you know they will not come near the Isle once the sun begins to sink. Enough there! Come. I will help you load the skiff."

Meg pushed the barrow. "The pots should be set at night," Adelia grumbled, waddling alongside. "But I cannot risk putting you to the hazard out in that bay after dark, and I am too old to do it. Until your uncle returns, this is how it must be. The markers are hard to find at night, and besides, there are other dangers . . . creatures of the deep that frequent these waters. Women are not safe alone at night on the bay, let alone beyond the sandbar in the ocean, where the best pots are laid."

Meg's heart leaped in her breast. Her aunt had brought up the subject herself. It was more than she could have hoped for, and she pounced upon it.

"You always speak of the seal people . . . the *selkies*, is it, that frequent these isles?" she said. "You can't believe that all the seals we see sunning themselves out on those rocks are such shape-shifters?"

"Aye, I do," Adelia said. "The males are great seducers. They come ashore—especially during the full moon—shed their skins, and revel on the beach, fornicating and dancing their lewd dances long into the night. They will take down any willing female they find abroad, and few can resist their mesmerizing powers. Beware, niece. Keep off the strand after dark and never cry into the sea."

"Why not?" Meg asked, suppressing a smile.

"Do not smirk at me, Megaleen," Adelia snapped at her. "Seven tears cried into the sea will bring a selkie male. I need not tell you to do what."

Meg doubted that. She'd cried a river into the sea since it spat her out and she was still alone.

"And if you ever see a sealskin lying about, let it stay where it lays," Adelia went on.

"Why, Aunt Adelia?"

"She who possesses the selkie's skin possesses him as long as she holds it. Many husbands are gained thus by wily chits who long for the passion only a selkie can give. But the minute the selkie has the skin back, he will return to the sea, for it is his life force. While he is with his human mate on land, he never ceases to long for the depths that have spawned him no matter how beguiled he is by her."

"Myth, surely."

Adelia snorted. "Tell that to Mirabella Tupp, whose selkie husband walked back into the sea three years ago, or Elvira Sneed, whose paramour did also disappear last Midsummer's Eve. Aye, ask, niece. The selkie women do the same with mortal men and often slay the children they bear them. They can be treacherous, fiercely jealous, and vindictive; woe betide the gel who lays hands upon a mate of theirs. No, niece, and these are not the only dangers. Stay clear of the beach at night . . . especially when the moon is full."

Meg's hands trembled as she loaded the eel pots into the skiff in a little cove not far from the cottage. She had more questions, so many more, but she dared not ask them then and risk casting suspicion upon herself. Her aunt was already wary. A sidelong glance testified to that. Adelia was studying her closely.

"Why all the interest in selkies of a sudden?" Adelia said.

"You brought the topic up, aunt," Meg pointed out, climbing into the little boat.

"Aye . . . so I did," her aunt replied. "Well, take the lesson to heart. Go now, and hurry back while the tide is with you."

Meg didn't want the fresh baked bread and goat cheese Adelia thrust at her, having stopped at the cottage to fetch them, along with a wineskin filled with the last of the May wine. Taking up the oars, she propelled the little skiff forward, riding the gentle waves past the breakwater into the open bay. She was a seasoned sailor since a child. It was second nature to her. She loved the salt spray on her face, glistening like spangles in her hair, and the gentle thud of the waves slapping the bottom of the skiff as it glided through the water. Now and then a low-flying seagull strafed her, grazing her with its wings. Drawn by the eel bait, many came, circling the boat in anticipation of a treat. Meg had none to spare. She had a chore to do that should take her mind off the events of the past few hours, but it did not. Everywhere she looked there were reminders. Off to the east, seals were sunning themselves on the rocks along the shoreline. Was Simeon among them? If he was, had he come to gloat? She couldn't bear the thought that he might have.

She was alone on the bay. No other boats broke the horizon. She might have excused the whole episode as the dream she'd first supposed if it wasn't for the dull soreness in her nether parts, made worse by the hard wooden plank beneath her bottom that slapped her each time a gentle swell buffeted the little skiff's hull. There was no one to see her now, except the gulls, and she reached to soothe her aching crotch through the thin lawn shift. She'd longed to do that since she staggered out of the sea. At least that was her intent until, despite the soreness, waves of liquid fire surged through her core. She could no longer touch herself without thinking of him, the Lord of the Deep, whose scent and strength and massive shaft was still with her—in her—all around her in the very salt-drenched air.

She had reached the first marker—a little cork float tied with a strip of red cloth—and she shipped the oars, dropped anchor, and leaned back against the neatly stacked eel pots in the stern bundled beneath a tarpaulin to keep the birds at bay. Raising the hem of her shift, she exposed her genitals to the morning haze. Tugging the drawstring at the neck of her shift, she lifted her breasts free to the gentle breeze skimming the surface of the water and began rolling her nipples between her thumbs and forefingers, just as he had done. The gentle breeze rippling her pubic curls called her hand there, enticing her fingers to part the hair at the top of her slit and probe for the nub beneath. How strange to find no virgin skin to bar her way. Two fingers slipped inside riding her slick wetness; how inadequate those fingers were now . . . after *him*.

Meg shut her eyes. All things were tactile—palpable—then, especially the gentle breeze fanning the fever in her flesh, playing with her nether parts, whispering across the milk-white skin of her breasts, puckering the areola of her nipples, making the tall buds hard to the touch. They still ached from Simeon's kiss, from the sucking and nipping, and from bites just sharp enough to bring a twinge of pain that heightened the pleasure. The warm sun beating down and gilding her moist skin turned up the heat, making her whole body throb like a pulse beat— even her scalp. The tang of the salt-laced air seasoned the rest. She licked her lips, tasting it, tasting *him*. A groan escaped her throat. It was no use without him. He'd loved her so well. Why did he bring her back? Why did he abandon her? *Why?*

Meg opened her misty eyes to the seagulls circling the skiff—and something else. . . . Another winged creature that had been hovering with the rest suddenly soared high aloft—so high it seemed to ride the clouds. It seemed to have caught a zephyr, for it glided, its huge wingspan spread out from its body, but it wasn't the body of a bird. It was the body of a *man*. She blinked and rubbed her eyes, for the sun suddenly blinded her. When she opened them again the creature was gone. It had vanished.

Meg bolted upright, a cry upon her lips so shrill it scattered the gulls. A winged man? How could it be? But it was, and he had seen her trying to pleasure herself.

Groaning her embarrassment and utter frustration, Meg leaned over the side of the bobbing skiff, pummeled the waves that rose almost to the oarlocks with punishing fists, and shed her seven tears, and then some, into the bay.

# 4

Simeon paced the length of the bedchamber in his shimmering underwater palace, attended by six selkie handmaidens in human form. Fawning and hovering over him, they matched him step for step until he threw himself upon the bed made with quilts of sea moss and woven seaweed. That was unwise. No sooner had he touched down when the bed began to undulate with eager consorts thrashing about with all the lumbering aplomb of the seals they had sprung from. Alexia, who had been his main consort since time out of mind, barked at the others. She never could keep her entities separated, Simeon reflected; very unattractive. How was it that he never noticed the harshness of that bark until now?

She had hold of his cock. Alexia knew how to bring him to life. She knew how to stroke and suck and tantalize. Why wasn't she able now? Her skilled fingers were gliding over the long, curved length of his shaft, flitting over the mushroom tip. That always drove him mad, but not now—not even with the others mauling him, stroking his hard muscled chest, lapping at his nipples, fondling his balls. They had covered him like a blanket.

Time was when he would have had them all. He was a selkie, and a noble at that. Seduction was in the blood, and he was the Lord of Seduction—Lord of the Deep. There had been a time when he would have reveled all night with these mistresses of the sea. And now, nothing. Alexia had taken his cock deep to the back of her throat, and Risa, the youngest of the lot and the most inventive when it came to the sexual arts, had possessed his mouth, her skilled tongue gliding in and out, jousting with his tongue in such a way that only she had mastered. Still nothing. His cock was barely hard and showed no signs of coming anytime soon. Why weren't they pure? Why didn't they have long, pale hair that looked as if it had been painted by the sun? Why didn't they smell of honeysuckle and sweet clover, wet with the morning dew?

He took back his cock from Alexia and struggled upright through the press of naked bodies crowding all around him. "Enough!" he thundered, swatting at the hands that groped and arms that tethered him. "Leave me!"

"What? Before moonrise?" Alexia barked, making a grab for his member. "What ails ye, m'lord?"

"Nothing ails me, woman," Simeon returned, slapping her hand away. "Can a man not have peace in his own domain? Leave me, I say—the lot of you!"

Risa gave Alexia a vicious shove. "Now see what you've done, you old sea cow!" she railed. "You've spoiled it for all of us, with your pawing and pushing and crowding to be first."

Evidently in accord, the other selkie women joined the foray, fists flying. It had been coming for some time. Simeon had seen the telltale signs of insurrection for seasons—the jealousy, the competition for his favor. It had amused him until now. He had been able to handle it . . . until now. He no longer cared if they rent each other limb from limb, but he didn't need to stay to see it happen.

Surging off the bed, he left the snarl of battling females

pulling long dark hair out by the roots and tweaking tits. He stomped through the chambers, only to collide headlong with Vega, his half brother, whose many functions in Simeon's life included that of valet, the guise in which Vega approached him now.

"You have been summoned, my lord," Vega said.

"By who?" Simeon growled. Streaking toward the tunnel, he dove into the water with Vega on his heels.

"Gideon," Vega replied warily.

"And what would the dark lord want with me?"

"I'm sure I do not know, my lord. I am only the messenger."

Simeon stopped and began to tread water. "And was there a message?" he said.

"No, only that you should come at once," Vega replied. "That was quite clear."

Simeon loosed a string of oaths. "Fetch my clothes and see to me," he said. "If you value your life, do not go near my bed-chamber. The consorts are warring again."

"Yes, my lord," Vega said, his arched brow lifted. He was older, and a half-breed whose mother was mortal. That they shared the same selkie father was known by the rest, but not looked upon with favor, which was why Simeon kept him close, under his protection, as his father had before him. Such half-breeds were shunned, often outcast, and more often killed by the selkie purists who frowned upon the unions that pro-duced such creatures. There was a resemblance between them, but then a certain thread of resemblance wove through all the selkies. That they were half brothers was never spoken of in public, but it spawned a loyalty between them that could not be breached, and had done so for eons. It also gave Vega the privi-lege to sometimes step out of character, where another might have been slapped down for impudence, even to call Simeon by name when they were alone. This, however, with so many within hearing distance, was not one of those occasions. Vega always seemed to know when he should speak and when he should hold his peace. "Will you want your skin, my lord?" he queried, for he was keeper of the deep lord's sealskin while he went about in mortal form beneath the sea.

Simeon's head snapped toward him. "No," he said, "but keep it close. Do not let it out of your sight. I wouldn't put it past the vixens to try to make off with it like they did the last time they revolted, and I can ill afford to be at the mercy of any one of them now."

"You can count upon it, my lord," the valet said. "Will you be wanting Elicorn?"

"Yes. Ready him for me. I ride to the Dark Isle like a man."

"The surf is up, my lord, and he's frisky again . . . running with the herd on the shores of the Isle of Mists."

"Cut him out of the herd!" Simeon charged. "I don't want him anywhere near the Isle of Mists unless I'm seated on his back."

A new worry reared its ugly head. Megaleen would be haunting the strand now. Suppose the waterhorse were to seduce her from the shore and carry her off? She'd ridden in his arms on the animal's back. She would mount him, and if he weren't near to prevent it, the wily waterhorse would lure her to her death. No. He wouldn't think about that now—couldn't think about it. First, he had to see why Gideon, Lord of the Dark, wanted him in such haste.

It was barely twilight, dreary and cool, the color of sorrow, when the great waterhorse galloped out of the surf and deposited Simeon on the volcanic sand along the shore of the Dark Isle. Of all the isles in the Eastern Archipelago of Arcus, the Dark Isle was the most formidable. No one went there willingly, or to any of the Elemental Isles: Water, Air, Land, and Fire. Gideon, Lord of the Dark, Prince of the Night, was the most feared of the four Lords of Arcus who governed the principalities, the others being Marius, Lord of the Forest, Prince of the Green; Vane, Lord of the Flames, Prince of the Fire; and himself, of course, Simeon, Lord of the Deep, Prince of the Waves.

No outsider frequented the barrowlike labyrinth of caves that peppered the Dark Isle. To pass here was by invitation only, and even at that, a summons did not bode well. Gideon did not socialize. Whatever it was, Simeon was anxious to have it behind him so he could unwind his own coil . . . that of a certain little witch who had beguiled him.

Giving Elicorn free rein, for it was safe on the Dark Isle because Gideon was its only inhabitant, Simeon slapped the animal on the rump and watched while it galloped off to frolic in the surf. There was something undeniably sensual about the waterhorse, its muscular flesh rippling in the moonlight, wet and shimmering as it plowed through the spindrift and lapping waves, its aura spangled with crystal prisms in the fine spray carried on the wind. No wonder it was able to seduce unsuspecting females to their watery deaths. Its lure was irresistible.

Heaving a sigh, Simeon arranged his cloak over the garment beneath made of silvery eel skin that fit him like a second skin, then he climbed the coal black dunes to the petrified forest hemming the rise at the top of the strand. Looming from unwelcoming black swamps, the gnarled and twisted trees stood as sentinels, their branches clacking like bony arms and accusing fingers in the wind that never ceased to blow on the Dark Isle. Beyond lay the caverns, swarthy and deep. Vast, prohibitive caves, like a maze, stretched as far as the eye could see, the largest of which housed the Great Hall of the Lord of the Dark, fallen angel of the gods, outcast of the Celestials, deliverer of justice.

There was no door to knock on. Simeon didn't need to announce himself. Gideon would be waiting. Without a second thought, he entered the central cave, then hesitated. The darkness was palpable. It bore a living, breathing presence, an extension of the dark lord himself. It smelled of incense and musk. It had a pulse and seemed to sigh as a light farther along the tunnel blazed in welcome, albeit feebly. Squaring his posture, Simeon followed the shallow beam to an inner chamber, where he found Gideon waiting, arms folded across his broad bare chest.

How formidable he looked standing thus, the light of a smoking torch picking out the blue sheen in his raven-colored hair and dark eyes. Simeon couldn't recall when he'd last seen Gideon. However long it was, the dark lord hadn't changed. He never changed. That was part of his curse, to walk the Dark Isle, beautiful beyond handsome, the epitome of maleness, alone in seclusion throughout all eternity.

"I saw a sight today that troubled me," the dark lord said to Simeon's greeting nod.

"Which was . . . ?" Simeon returned as casually as he could manage. Adrenaline pricked at his scalp and raised the short hairs at the back of his neck. Something in the dark lord's tone flagged danger, or at the very least suggested ill boding.

"I was abroad today," Gideon began, strolling nearer. "Why the look? I am hardly confined here, Simeon. I come and go, just as you do, and enjoy what light I may. The punishment is crueler that way, in that I get to see what I am denied. Today . . . I saw something you have wrought . . . something that precipitated this interview."

Simeon's scalp drew back. His lips parted to speak, but common sense shut his mouth. Instead, he waited what seemed an eternity for the dark lord to continue.

"At first I didn't trust my eyes," Gideon went on, strolling back and forth in the torchlight. "So I flew closer. It was the lass you took beneath the waves—the golden one. From what I could gather, she was tending the eel pots of her shaman uncle in his absence, and she exposed herself—"

"To *you?*" Simeon interrupted him, shocked at the twinge of jealousy that shot him through like the sting of an electric eel.

"No, Simeon, not to me," the other said. "She did not even know I was there among the waterfowl circling the skiff, until the last. She thought she was alone . . . pleasuring herself with *you.*"

Simeon raked his hair back ruthlessly. He didn't want to hear this. He'd made up his mind to do the right thing, to walk away from the beautiful maiden on the Isle of Mists, while he still could.

"I don't know what you mean," he said warily.

"She has very beautiful breasts. She bared them to the sun and touched them . . . as if with your fingers, just as she touched herself below, as if her fingers were a cock—*your* cock. I heard her thoughts. I heard her heart cry out to you, but you did not answer, though you were there just below the surface, and then I saw her tears and her despair. What have you done?"

"What I should not have done," Simeon said flatly. "Not with her at any rate. And now the kindest thing I can do is let her go."

"Why not with her?"

"Because she is not like the others," Simeon hurled at him. "No plaything for a selkie lord. Her life lived for me. Her juices flowed for me. Sweet nectar I longed to taste and barely tapped. Thank the gods I had the fortitude to resist, or I would have been lost, old friend. She was slated to become a priestess. I may have spoiled that for her, but if there is still a chance, better that than the life I could offer her."

"So you leave her—just like that, to pleasure herself, or try to, for she failed—leave her for the wind to rape? Or worse."

"Or *you!*" Simeon realized.

"I have long dreamed of taking a consort, if the gods would turn their backs a while. I shan't deny it. She is beautiful, like a golden pear, sugary-sweet and toothsome—ripe for the taking. I would taste those juices myself. I would let her know my cock—let it live inside her. I would not abandon her to pleasure herself. I need to know your intentions."

Simeon's breath caught in a strangled gasp. "You want me to give you leave to take her?" He was incredulous.

"I hardly need anyone's 'leave,' Simeon," Gideon said. "I simply need to know your mind before I act upon my desires."

"Your 'desires' do not enter into it," Simeon said. "She is mine!"

The dark lord stiffened. In the blink of an eye and a whoosh of air, two great arched wings sprang from his broad back, filling the span. The torch flame writhed in its bracket from the wind they created in the close confines of the cave.

Simeon had forgotten the magnificence of the dark lord's wings. They appeared whenever he chose to use them in flight, or involuntarily, when he was angered or aroused. The hindrance they presented during the latter being one of the primary reasons Gideon had embraced celibacy. Simeon didn't need to wonder which emotion brought them out this time. The dark lord's eyes were smoldering with rage.

"Then finish what you've started," Gideon seethed through clenched teeth. "She is strongly sexed and ripe for conquest. Had another come upon her as I did, half-naked, her fingers where a cock should be, he would have remedied the lack of one quickly enough and ravished her."

"I have no right . . ." Simeon said, as if to himself. "What can I possibly offer her?"

"You *had* no right," Gideon pointed out. "Now, you have an obligation. You selkies are all alike: The great seducers. You take well enough, and then abandon. I see you divested of your precious skins, content to live above the waves. I see your kind sire offspring, which you leave behind along with your beloved mortal wives the minute your stolen sealskins are returned to you." He waved his hand in a rough gesture, ruffling his great wings. "All right, you cannot be faulted for these things, for it is in the blood, but that does not exempt you from reprisal. You have received fair warning. If I come on her thus again, there will be no more need of summoning. She will be mine."

"You make it sound as if I planned it all on purpose," Simeon said. "She summoned me, and I responded."

"In true selkie fashion."

"I am what I am, just as you are, Gideon."

"Do not bring me into it," the dark lord said. "I do not play the games of the Lord of the Deep."

Simeon heaved a sigh. "Midsummer's Eve is soon upon us. If she can dupe the shamans into believing she still possesses her maiden skin, she will be taken into the fold as a priestess of the Isle of Mists. Better that than consort of the Lord of the Deep. She would be safe—protected. If I were to take her below the waves with me, the others would kill her. Why, coming here, I left a rumpus in my bed. The jealous consorts pulling hair and tweaking tits, and the gods alone know what I'll find when I return."

"You had best be about it then," Gideon said, flexing his wings. "It is your coil to unwind, none of mine. My way is clear. You have been warned."

He turned away then, his magnificent wings drawn in, though they had not diminished. When he held them thus, their tips touched the ground. The interview was over. There was no more to be said. The deliverer of justice of the Principality of Arcus—usually a man of few words—had spoken more in this interview than he had in eons. Simeon offered a silent heel-clicking bow to the dark lord's winged back and melted into the shadows.

Outside, the wind had risen, ruffling his hair and billowing his cloak about him. The wind was always strong on the Dark Isle. The surf would be up, just as Elicorn liked it, but the magnificent animal would soon grow bored with no mortals to tempt, and Simeon quickened his pace. He could hear the roar of the breakers as he picked his way through the murky swamp among the dark waste of petrified trees that served as a forest. Sprinting down the dunes, he squinted toward the shore in search of the waterhorse. Dark clouds scudding across the moon only showed him the strand in brief glimpses, and he cupped is hands around his mouth and whistled as he approached the water's edge. Simeon strained his ears for Elicorn's familiar whinny, but only the thudding sound of the surf crashing on the beach met his ears.

Simeon's heart began to quicken. It constricted in his chest. Just for a moment, the veil of clouds parted and the moon showed him his worst fear. There, in the dark volcanic sand, Elicorn's hoof prints showed clearly, leading straight into the white-caped bay.

# 5

Meg strolled along the strand in fractured moonlight. It was just as well dark clouds had robbed all but the eerie phosphorescence coming from the water. She was hiding, even from the moon.

So much for seven tears shed in the sea summoning a selkie lover. There was no question that she'd been abandoned now. She had never felt more cast off than she did strolling alone along the strand in the soft semidarkness with a rainstorm looming.

The seals hadn't come tonight, either, and the waterfowl had long since sought shelter inland for the night. Once, she thought she saw something sail through the sky—something dark, like the giant eagles that lived in the mountains on the mainland. But it was only a fleeting glimpse before it soared off and disappeared in deep darkness. It brought to mind the strange winged creature she'd seen circling the little skiff that morning. But she'd convinced herself that creature was surely her imagination playing tricks on her. It had to have been. If it wasn't, that would mean whatever entity it was had seen her exposing herself to the salt-laced wind and hot sun, touching herself in broad, sultry daylight. Hot blood rushed to her temples as she imagined it.

Whatever creature it was she'd glimpsed soaring and gliding above, it was gone now, and her gaze returned to the strand and the tall combers rolling up the coastline, spilling froth on the hard-packed sand and spinning yards of gossamer spindrift carried on the wind. Though she was nowhere near the water's edge, her fine kirtle of mulberry homespun gauze was damp, clinging to her naked skin beneath, and her long, tousled hair was fanned out about her, combed by the gusts into spiral curls that teased her buttocks and framed her face with wild tendrils.

She was just about to turn back to the cottage before the rain came to further dampen her spirits, when she heard a familiar sound. Stopping in her tracks, she pricked up her ears and listened. It came again. She knew it now, the high-pitched whinny of the waterhorse riding the wind. Her eyes flashed toward the waves thudding on the sand, and her breath caught at the sight of the great white creature prancing through the surf, its high-flying forefeet pummeling the waves as it galloped toward the shore.

Meg's heart sank when she realized the animal was riderless, but she ran to it nonetheless. Could Simeon have sent it to fetch her? The waterhorse pranced to a high-stepping halt before her, puffing fine spray out of flared nostrils. It reminded her of the way the selkie seals spouted water from theirs. Tears misted her eyes, and she threw her arms about the stallion's neck.

"Have you come to take me to him?" she crooned to the horse. "Have my seven tears worked their magic, or are you naught but deep-sea glamour come to seduce me to a watery grave?"

The waterhorse snorted. It waggled its head noncommittally, Meg thought. She plucked some of the seaweed from its long wet mane. "I wish I had more knowledge of these mystical things," she said.

The horse's silvery eyes gleamed as it stretched its right leg out and knelt upon the other. Its message was clear. The animal wanted her to mount. Right or wrong, it took her only a moment to decide to climb up on the animal's back and less time for the horse to surge to its full height and bolt toward the water.

Hoping until the last that she hadn't made the wrong decision, Meg didn't panic until the waterhorse beneath her disappeared under the swells and brine threatened her mouth. It flooded her nostrils, and she knew. Simeon hadn't sent the waterhorse. It was acting in its own fiendish stead. It meant to drown her!

Saltwater rushed up her nostrils as the animal plunged deeper into the churning bay. Opening her mouth to scream did nothing but flood her throat with water. Frantically, Meg tugged on the horse's mane in a desperate attempt to coax it back above the waves, but the animal only sank deeper. She tried to climb higher—tried to stand on its back, tried to jump clear—but she couldn't. Her legs wouldn't move. Then, in that horrible terrible instant, she knew the secret of the waterhorse: once upon its back, its victims were powerless to save themselves. As though paralyzed, Meg was helpless to prevent the inevitable. A heart-stopping orgasm riveted her. She was going to die!

Simeon streaked through the water, his heart pounding so violently he feared it would burst from his chest. It was a good stretch between the Dark Isle, and the Isle of Mists—too far for a man to swim unaided. But Simeon was not an ordinary man; he was a selkie.

He had stripped off his eel skin garment and cloak and left them behind on the volcanic sand of the Dark Isle. He could swim faster naked. He knew where Elicorn had gone. If he knew nothing else, he knew the only thing that mattered was reaching Megaleen in time, for she would indeed die beneath the waves without his breath in her nostrils if the waterhorse were to take her under. Why hadn't he answered the dark lord's summons in his sealskin? He could have made much better time sheathed in the magical skin. How could he have thought he could walk away from the gorgeous, passionate creature who had stolen his heart, no matter how noble his intentions?

The Isle of Mists came into view at last, and not a minute too soon. Rain had begun to pelt down, slowing Simeon's progress. Through the horizontal splinters pockmarking the breast of the swells, he saw Elicorn plunge into the bay. Slipping beneath the waves, he parted them like an arrow until he came abreast of the waterhorse, within touching distance of Megaleen who was fused helplessly to the enchanted animal's back.

Simeon drew back his fist with the intent to pummel Elicorn to within an inch of his life. A hair's breadth from the animal's proud head, the selkie lord froze, his fist suspended in the water, as Gideon's words ghosted across his memory: *You cannot be faulted for these things, for it is in the blood, but that does not exempt you from reprisal.* The waterhorse was doing what his kind had done since time out of mind, just as he had done what his kind had been doing since the dawn of time when he seduced Meg. It was, indeed, in the blood.

But Elicorn was under his command, and he seized the animal's mane in both his white-knuckled fists and shouted: "Enough! Release her!"

The waterhorse obeyed, slipping away, and Simeon seized Meg about the waist and broke the surface of the water. The shower had passed, though more threatened, and the full moon showed its face through scudding clouds just long enough for Simeon to glimpse a winged figure silhouetted against it.

*Gideon.*

A spate of expletives parted Simeon's lips. Had the dark lord been there all the while, watching him struggle to reach Meg in time? Evidently. Cradling her against him, he raised his fist to the sky, and in a blink, the Lord of the Dark was gone. There was some depraved consolation in knowing that Gideon would never have let her drown, but not much. This was Simeon's reprisal. So be it! He would take that up with Gideon at a later date. Right now, Meg was clinging to him, her heart beating against his naked chest, the soft thatch of her pubic curls cushioning his hard cock through the flimsy billowed kirtle. Their eyes met for one brief instant before he breathed into her nostrils and spiraled with her down beneath the surface of the water.

His bedchamber in the palace was vacant when they reached it. There was no sign of the melee that had taken place there earlier. The rumpled bed had been restored—thanks, he had no doubt, to Vega—and the consorts were nowhere in sight. Laying Meg down on the bed, he climbed in beside her and took her in his arms.

"Why did you take me back?" she murmured. "Why did you leave me?"

Simeon crushed her closer, avoiding her accusing eyes. They were blue, a deep, shimmering blue. "I cannot keep you here, Megaleen," he murmured against her hair. It smelled of honeysuckle and of her own sweet musk. He inhaled deeply. "It isn't safe," he went on. How silky her skin was. As if they had a will of their own, his fingers could not resist touching, fondling the golden hairs that lightly furred her arms and overspread the V between her thighs. It held a great fascination for him, because the selkie females were hairless except for their long, flowing manes.

"I could not bring myself to keep you," he said. "I still cannot justify it, though I want you beyond bearing. You cannot exist beneath the waves for long periods. You are a daughter of

Eve. That you do so here now is only temporary, and I cannot exist long upon the land."

"Why not?" Meg said. "Others do."

"Not voluntarily, my love," he lamented. "Not unless they are tricked. It is the nature of the selkie to live in the sea, just as it is the nature of mortals to live upon land. We are what we are, Megaleen. As a priestess of the Isle, you will be safe—protected. . . ."

"You know what it entails, my becoming a priestess," she said. "You pointed it out to me, if you remember."

He could not prevent his hands from palming her breasts, his fingers from touching the tips of her nipples, bringing them erect. He was helpless to prevent his tongue from flicking the tawny buds and circling their pebbled areola.

"On Midsummer's Eve, I am to mate with the shaman priest who must take my virtue as part of the initiation," she murmured, writhing beneath his tongue. "There is more that you do not know, but it is not likely I shall ever see it. Once it is discovered that I am no virgin, instead of a priestess, I will become a blood sacrifice to appease the gods. That is how 'safe' I will be, Lord of the Deep. I thought you had saved me from a life that would whither my body and my spirit. Instead, you have condemned me to death. You should have let the waterhorse drown me. Such a death would at least have been kinder."

Simeon would hear no more. Bending, he took her lips with a hungry mouth, his tongue entwined with hers. His cock was bursting, aching for her fingertips to stroke it, throbbing in anticipation of those velvet lips wrapped around its veined shaft. She moaned into his mouth, and the sound resonated though his body as she undulated against him.

She was his for the taking. What was it about the sweet flesh of this mortal female that bewitched him so? He needed to delve more deeply into that. *Was* she the sorceress she'd been accused? He could think of no other explanation. Many mortals had aroused him. Many had become obsessed with him, but he had never been enchanted by a mortal before. It was not a comfortable thing.

He cursed Gideon, Lord of the Dark, under his breath. If only Gideon hadn't meddled. Simeon knew he'd made the right decision in returning Meg to the Isle of Mists. If the dark lord hadn't interfered, she would be preparing for her initiation into the sisterhood of priestesses now, and in time, she would have forgotten her brief interlude with the Lord of the Deep. Could she exist in his watery netherworld? She existed in it now only because the palace was part of one of the many subterranean air pockets that existed magically beneath the waves. It was only a pleasant fiction to believe it could continue indefinitely . . . Wasn't it? He was beginning to wrack his brain for a way to make that dream a reality.

His cock was so engorged he feared it would burst, and the pressure called him back to the situation at hand. Meg's exquisite body was arched against him, begging him to fill her. It was no use. Driving her hand down to his groin, he crimped her fingers around the thick, hard bulk of his sex. It leapt at her touch, the hot mushroom tip leaking fine pearly dew drops of precome. She had brought him to climax like no other the first time. He wanted to feel that again. He wanted to know again the riveting firestorm of drenching heat that rendered him all but senseless, that constricted his balls and gripped him like a seizure until his body begged for release. Not just any release. The blessed release of total surrender to a passion he had never known until now . . . Until the exquisite mortal beauty underneath him had opened the floodgates of ecstasy and drowned him in the depths of her innocent desire.

He parted the fascinating curls that hid her nub and began to fondle it. Meg writhed in his arms, moving against his strokes, showing him her need. Her moans filled his mouth as he tasted her deeply, savoring the flavor of her, like warm honey laced with the salt of the sea. How he thirsted for that sweet honey.

His fingers slipped inside her, feeling for the special spot that would bring her to rapture, the mysterious mound that when touched drove a woman mad. She bucked in his arms when he found it, her sex seizing his fingers, which he quickly replaced with his bursting cock, driving it into her to the root. She was his so totally then that he failed to hear the hushed murmur echoing along the corridor or to feel the cool influx of currents stirring the air that should have flagged danger until they were upon him, a swarm of female sea lions attacking from all sides.

Simeon withdrew himself unclimaxed in a valiant attempt to shield Meg from the onslaught of great hulking seal bodies slamming into them. She screamed and began to gasp and choke as one butted her in the belly with its head, another crashed into her from behind, and still another collided with her knees until they buckled—not to mention those attacking Simeon with intent to do bodily harm in that quarter. There were too many jealous female selkies to fend off without casualties, and Simeon was hard put to accomplish it.

In a mad rush to drive her out, the selkies rushed Meg along the corridor into the water tunnel. Her lips turned blue. She was losing consciousness. There was no question that they meant to drown her. They were driving her beneath the waves. There wasn't a moment to lose. Simeon would deal with the consorts later. So much for his pleasant fantasies of Meg existing with him in his world beneath the waves. Plowing through the hulking press of seal bodies, he loosed a bestial roar that reverberated through the water. It cowed the seals, turning them away as effectually as if he'd struck them a blow, though some still lingered on the fringes, milling about with the curious fish that had assembled there to observe the ruckus.

Seizing Meg about the waist, he raised her above the surface of the waves. Sputtering and coughing, she fought to breathe. The breath he'd blown into her nostrils earlier to allow her to exist under water had failed. Terror had broken the spell. Swooping down, he sucked the water from her nostrils and from her throat, then blew his breath into her again and plunged below the waves.

Streaking through the depths with her as he had done before, Simeon scattered the still lingering seals and fish as he plowed through their ranks. Meg had lost consciousness, and he didn't break the rhythm of his strokes until they'd surged through the heaving breast of the bay.

They surfaced off the coast of the Isle of Mists. The moon had disappeared behind a cloud bank, though the misty drizzle had stopped. Cool, rainwashed air rushed up Simeon's nostrils. Wet and sweet, it bore a marked difference to the scent of the sea he'd come from. *Please the gods, let her be breathing*, he begged the deities of the deep, meanwhile carrying her through the creaming froth of surf and silt, fine shells, and pebbles toward shore. Staggering up onto the hard-packed sand, he dropped to his knees and laid Meg down where they would be sheltered in lee of a jutting dune, well hidden from prying eyes. He dropped down beside her. Her kirtle had been left behind. He scarcely gave that a passing thought. Frantically, he felt for a pulse. It was there, albeit weak, and he gathered her against his hard-muscled chest and shook her until she coughed and sputtered and spat out seawater.

Relief overwhelmed him, and he crushed her close, rocking her in his arms, burying his hand in the fine-textured silk of her hair, inhaling its honeysuckle fragrance. After a moment, Meg stopped coughing and drew a deep ragged breath. Now that he knew she would be all right, he started to rise. He needed to get back to the sea and deal with the consorts who had nearly killed her. That could not wait. Besides, it wasn't safe for him alone, without the other selkies when he resisted on the Isle of Mists. Their presence had always earned the respect of the shamans. Alone, without the protection of his sealskin, he was vulnerable—especially considering his association with Meg. Where was Gideon now? The dark lord had always been an enigma but never more so than at this moment in his conspicuous absence.

"No!" Meg cried, seizing his wrist. "Don't leave me . . . I will never see you again!"

"You will," he said. "All that is past . . . But I cannot linger here alone. It isn't safe for either of us."

She seized his arm with both hands. He was aroused just by the sight of her lying there naked, her slick wet skin gleaming in the faint moon glow, her tawny nipples peeking through spirals of her wet, tousled hair. Simeon glanced about. All was still. The strand was vacant. It was still hours before first light. He hesitated, licking his lips in anticipation of his secret fantasy becoming a reality there to the gentle sighing of the waves lapping at the shore on that narrow stretch of mystical beach.

He reached to soothe his rock-hard shaft, but it would not be soothed. Instead, it leapt to life, its thick bulk throbbing, aching—demanding. Soothing became stroking. Meg's hand reached to take it from him, and it responded to her touch. It was more than he could bear, and he sank to his knees and gathered her into his arms.

But first, his fantasy.

He would fulfill the dream he'd dreamt waking and sleeping since he'd first set eyes upon the little witch of the Isle of Mists. It had become a palpable desire to savor all of her juices since he'd tasted her honey sweetness. This he could not experience to perfection under water, though he had taken a tantalizing taste that first night. To do justice to his appetite, it needed to be done at the palace, which was what he'd intended earlier, or on dry land, where nothing could dilute her succulence.

It began with a kiss.

His first taste was slow and deep, his tongue entwined with hers in a ritual that brought deep moans up from the depths of her throat, vibrating through his body. Building a little pillow in the damp sand beneath her, Simeon lifted her hips to rest upon it and bent her knees, spreading her legs wide. He'd done this in his mind over and over. Now, it was real, and his excitement threatened to relieve him too soon. That would not do. Calling the consorts' attack to mind sufficed to stall his anxious cock, and he began blazing a fiery trail down the length of her body, from her swollen breasts to the shadowy hollow of her navel to the pubic curls between her thighs.

Parting her nether lips, he exposed her erect nub and sucked it until she cried out, holding his head against her parts, and leaned into his motion as she undulated against the rhythm of his lips and tongue. Simeon raised her hips higher and entered her with his tongue, stabbing in and out as if it were a cock, moving from the hard, moist bud he'd brought erect to the soft throbbing flesh deep inside her, laving her vulva, lapping at the luscious juice of her release, drinking his fill of her honey sweetness with each climactic shudder.

It was beyond his wildest imaginings. She was his. He had drunk her essence, savored the nectar of her release. This was one of the mysteries of the mortal race, one of the curiosities of those that lived above the waves, that had intrigued the creatures of the deep since time out of mind, and he had embraced it. There was no way he could leave her now or ever. He had drunk of the very elixir of her life.

His sex was bursting, his need painful. Cupping the globes of her buttocks, he lifted her to him and buried his cock deep inside her. Clinging to him, Meg called his name as he thrust himself again and again, deep pistoning thrusts that filled her with the warm rush of his seed. It was a rush so heavy she could not contain it and some overflowed and spilled out of her onto the sand.

Crushing her in his arms, Simeon held her against him without speaking, his heart hammering against hers for some time before his breathing became normal and his spent shaft relaxed inside her.

"Y-you will not leave me?" she begged him. "Say you will not leave me, Simeon . . . *Swear it!*"

"I will never leave you," he murmured against her hair. "But I must return to my realm before first light. There are things I must do there before I can resolve what faces us."

"The solstice is only two days off," she said. "They will come for me! They will make me—"

"Sh," he soothed, holding her close. "I know, Megaleen. We celebrate it below as well. You must trust me. We will be well away by the time the ceremonies begin." He rose to his feet and pulled her up alongside him, taking her face in his hands. "I want you to go now, back to the cottage, before someone sees you like this. Meet me here, in this cove, tomorrow night at midnight. All will be well. . . ."

Simeon took her lips in a steamy kiss that left her sagging against him before he put her from him gently but firmly. "Now go," he said. "Let me do what I must do. Until midnight tomorrow . . ."

# 6

Meg followed the lean, muscular figure of the Lord of the Deep with her eyes until he disappeared beneath the waves. Would she ever see him again? She had to believe she would. All at once she was cold. She hadn't felt the chill in the air while she was in Simeon's arms, despite the misty dampness. She shuddered. He had robbed the warmth from her body as well as her soul. She was naught but an empty shell without him.

Hugging herself, she rubbed her arms to prompt circulation. Where had her mulberry gauze kirtle gone? She had no recollection of when she'd parted from it. Simeon was right about one thing: she needed to sneak back into the cottage before Aunt Adelia discovered her missing. It would not do to be caught out naked on the beach again in the dead of night two days before the solstice.

As cold as she was, Meg couldn't return covered with sand and sticky with the selkie's seed. Padding to the water's edge, she scooped up some seaweed stretched out like a ribbon along the surf and bathed her thighs and mons area with it. Plunging deeper, she submerged her body to wash away the sand, then ducked her head below the waves. She broke the surface facing the sea, letting the water cascade over her sore body, which ached from the ecstasy of Simeon's embrace. How good the saltwater felt sluicing over her hot skin, cooling the fever his hands, his lips, his dynamic body had ignited in every pore. Taking a deep breath, she plunged again and rose, sliding her hands down the length of her body, over the swell of her aching breasts and taut hard nipples, down the length of her torso, and over the V of pubic curls between her thighs. Reaching back, she soothed the globes of her behind, then brought her hands around in front again retracing their path to the slender arch of her neck. Lacing her fingers through her long, sun-painted hair grown dark in the water, Meg spun toward the shore, only to freeze where she stood, treading the sandy bottom underfoot, submerged to the waist, buoyed by the swells. She uttered a stifled cry, her eyes flung wide toward Adelia standing at the water's edge, arms folded across her sagging breasts. Meg gasped again: the woman gripped a long willow switch in her hand.

"So, niece, you are found out," Adelia seethed, the willow branch making a formidable whirring sound slicing through the air as she slapped it against her open palm. "Get out of that water! You've had your last midnight swim."

Simeon dove straight for the tunnel that led to the palace. Surging out of the water, he streaked through the chambers one by one, but they were vacant. There was no sign of the selkie females in seal or human form. All was still. Not even the annoying silt roses twittered. Exasperated, the selkie lord sought out Vega. He found him sorting eel skins in the servants' quarters where they were stored.

"Leave that," he said. "We need to talk."

"I'm trying to make you a new eel skin, Simeon," Vega said, his speech more familiar now that they were alone. "You're down to your last one. You have got to stop leaving them about."

"Where are the consorts?"

Vega shrugged. "I haven't seen them since the latest melee," he said. "You really need to do something with that lot before serious harm is done. This last nearly *was* the last. I have never seen Alexia in such a rage. I cleaned up the mess in your apartments, but I won't do it again. I'll let the purists club me first. There was seal scum in the corridors, on the bedstead—on the ceiling vault. I wash my hands of it!"

"You shan't have to worry over that after tomorrow," Simeon said. "We're leaving."

Vega staggered back from his chore, eel skin in hand. "Leaving? Leaving for where?"

"I'm taking up residence at the Pavilion . . . for now. I will need you with me."

"*The Pavilion?*" Vega said, slack-jawed. "That outpost hasn't been inhabited in eons. Father deemed it uninhabitable long before he passed. It's too far from the Isles to frequent them."

"That, Vega, is exactly what I want," Simeon said. "We need to be ready to leave by midnight tomorrow."

"What of the consorts? It is too far for them to travel back and forth. Why, I doubt they could make it there at all!"

"I'm counting upon it! The consorts are over."

"Are you mad, Simeon? There will be slaughter done!"

"Oh aye, and I shall be the one to do it if they dare oppose me. What went on here earlier will not be repeated."

"What went on here occurred because you brought an outsider into the deep—a *mortal*. What could you expect? You have never done that before. You have always confined your mortal dalliances to land trysts."

"This is . . . different."

"Oh now, you can't mean to take the chit with you?" Vega blurted, realization having struck. Simeon would have laughed at his brother's sagging jaw and arched brow if it wasn't such a serious matter. "Y-you *do!*" Vega breathed. "Do you not have enough consorts to keep you sated and more patiently waiting to have their turn? Well, you don't need me for this mad ramble. I'm quite comfortable right here at the palace. Think of all the fun I'll have placating the consorts after you've gone. That Risa is a comely little sea cow. I wouldn't mind her lips around my cock. When did you say you were leaving, 'my lord?'"

Simeon arched his winged eyebrow and gave Vega a withering look. His brother had crossed the line again. "This wouldn't be a subtle attempt to change my mind, would it, Vega?" he said. "Because if it is, you waste your breath. I have taken Megaleen's virtue. Two days hence, she is to yield it to the shaman priest in her rite of initiation to become priestess of the Isle of Mists. When he discovers she is no longer a virgin, she will be sacrificed to the gods instead. I cannot leave her to such a fate, and I cannot bring her here among the consorts. You saw the outcome of that. What other choice have I?"

"Certainly not the Pavilion," Vega said. "It has surely gone to ruin. And if you think to take me along to put it to rights, think again. I am your valet, your horse master, your protector, and your friend—not to mention your brother, though that is best left to speculation in the minds of the masses before we start an insurrection. Nowhere in the long list of my duties do I find the word 'slave' mentioned anywhere. Besides, you waste your time. Judging from your last misadventure, your Megaleen could not live long beneath the waves."

"You saw that then?"

"I see everything that concerns you, Simeon; that is my function."

"You might have intervened."

Vega uttered a wry chuckle. "What? And risk castration or worse at the mercy of those vicious cows? The fog of love has addled your brain."

"When the consorts attacked, fear broke the spell," Simeon said. "That can be remedied. Spells can be countered...."

"And you fancy yourself the sage to take that on, do you? The Pavilion, indeed! You need reining in now and then. I'd hoped you'd see reason. Evidently not. Now you think fleeing to that godforsaken outpost is going to spare you the consorts' wrath? Not that lot, Simeon. You dream."

"I do not need your lecture; I need your help. Who will tend my sealskin? I can hardly entrust it to Megaleen."

Again Vega laughed. He swept his arm wide. "And for the likes of that—a woman you cannot trust—you give up all this!" he marveled.

"You overrate 'all this,'" Simeon seethed, avoiding the first part of the question. "I have known something in Megaleen's arms that I have known in no others'. You call it 'love.' I do not know. Whatever it is, I have not ever known it before, and now that I have tasted it, I do not want to live without it, Vega. She makes my cock sing. She brings me to life in ways I never imagined possible. I have drunk her essence. Hah! You scoff at the Pavilion. I would take her to the ends of the world—to the Netherworld itself—if needs must to keep her."

Vega gave it thought. "I never would have expected . . . this," he mused.

"I tried to do the right thing. I took her back to the Isle. I thought in time she would forget . . . But then Gideon intervened, the gods rot him!"

"The gods have already dealt with Gideon. He has fallen, but he is still what he was, at least in part, despite that he is outcast with his lesson learned too late. I pity him his lonely existence. I cannot imagine it. And you cannot fault him in this. You would have reached this mad decision without his interference. He is not your enemy."

Vega was right, of course. He was always right, and Simeon heaved a sigh. "I need you at the Pavilion, old friend," he said.

"There will be sprites and sirens aplenty to stroke your vanity and your cock, I assure you."

"It's not my cock that worries me, Simeon. Yours, on the other hand . . ."

"Never you mind about me. Make ready. I collect Megaleen on the Isle of Mists at midnight."

It was cold and dark in the bait shack, where Adelia had locked Meg while she went to the cottage to fetch her a fresh kirtle. Why didn't her aunt just take her back to her loft chamber? What was the purpose of barring her inside the smelly little shack naked, in the dark . . . in the cold? Adelia hadn't used the willow switch, except to prod Meg along, but the threat still lingered. Adelia wasn't a cruel woman, just a difficult one. Meg was counting on past performances to prevail, but there was no set precedent for being caught out naked in the dead of night cavorting in the water.

While her actions soothing herself were innocent enough, and quite therapeutic, they could have easily been construed as sexual in origin to one of Adelia's strict sensibilities. Did she know? It was highly likely, considering her aunt's extrasensory powers, though Meg prayed against it while she waited and listened to the squishing sound the horseshoe crabs were making traveling in their sandy compartments in the dark.

Meg wasn't given long to wonder. The rasp of the wooden bar being raised on the shed door outside brought her to her feet as Adelia entered with a rush candle in one hand, an indigo kirtle looped over her arm, and the willow switch at the ready. The old woman's expression was unreadable except for the fury flaming in her eyes. That hadn't changed since Adelia confronted her on the strand. Meg took a step forward, reaching for the kirtle.

"Not so fast, niece," the old woman barked, spreading the gown out on the chopping block. "Climb up, Megaleen."

"On *that?* Why?" Meg asked warily, casting a sidelong glance at the cleavers in their brackets on the wall that glinted in the rush candle flame.

Adelia flashed a smile that did not reach her eyes. "Because I said to," she returned. Setting the rushlight down on a stool nearby, she whipped the willow switch out from under the crook of her arm and swiped it across Meg's bare bottom. "Climb up and lie down. Do it *now!*" she charged.

"W-what do you mean to do?" Meg asked, hitching herself up on the edge of the block. Her bottom smarted from the switch, and she climbed gingerly, a close eye upon the willow, which carved threatening circles in the dank, oppressive air.

"Lie *down!*" Adelia demanded, slapping her own open palm with the willow. "Or do I have to fetch a eunuch from the temple to hold you down?"

Cold chills walked the length of Meg's spine. There was no mistaking Adelia's demeanor now. Her aunt was seething with blind passion, and her wrinkled hand gripping the willow switch trembled with rage. It did not bode well.

A swipe across her breasts with the willow and Meg leaned back. Adelia had always been a fierce taskmistress, but this was frightening. Meg barely fit on the butcher block with her knees bent. Her terror could be tasted, like bile, when her aunt pried her thighs apart with the branch and thrust her hand between them.

Meg fought back, shoving Adelia's hand away, which earned her another stripe, this time on the soft tender flesh on the inside of her thigh. It stung so much her eyes began to water, and she cried out, but to no avail.

"Open your legs!" Adelia shrilled, raising the switch again. "What sort of fool do you take me for? You reek of come. I smelled it all over you the last time I found you naked in the water. What? You think a plunge in that brine out there will kill the stink of it? Harlot! Whore! You've been running with the selkies!"

Meg needed both her hands to fend off her aunt's blows to her head, and though she kicked and screamed and flailed at Adelia, it was no use. The woman was very strong. Seizing the rushlight, Adelia held it high and parted Meg's nether lips.

"You are ruined!" she screamed, probing Meg's vagina cruelly. "Spoiled!"

Meg slapped her aunt's hand away and leapt off the chopping block, clutching her kirtle about her and wriggling into it. "I do not want to hurt you, aunt, but I will strike you if you touch me thus again! You have no right!"

"I have every right!" Adelia shrilled, pounding the block with her fist. "You are my charge and my blood. The future we planned would have saved you. What are we to do now, eh? Whatever possessed you to flaunt your piddling gifts to impress the gentry in the first place? Foolish chit! You cannot go back to the mainland now. Your accusers will kill you. That we took you in has spared you, for they fear us, but your salvation comes at a price. You must become a priestess, and to do so you must be a virgin. Well, my girl, you are no virgin now. You have been spoiled by a selkie seducer. I hope it was worth it, Megaleen, because it is the last you will get. What will I tell your Uncle Olwyn? He has spent the tribute the shamans gave for you. You are bought and paid for, and their coin has bought them damaged goods."

"Aunt . . . I didn't—"

"Can you grow a new virgin skin by Midsummer's Eve?" Adelia railed. "Can you restore yourself as you once were? Can you possibly hope to dupe the shaman, feigning innocence? You have destroyed the only thing that could have saved you! What do you think will happen to Olwyn and me for this, hm? You cannot stay here anymore now, either. Foolish chit, you have doomed us all! Well? Explain yourself!"

Meg chewed her lower lip. How could she explain the passion that had obsessed her? How could she confide that even now her body throbbed for the Lord of the Deep? Her sex ached for him. Her heart quickened at the thought of him. Her fissure moistened just remembering his anxious bulk moving between her thighs, and she stiffened, reliving the pressure of his tongue laving, scraping across her hardened bud, riveting her with waves of wet, icy fire—even now, her flesh still stinging from the stripes Adelia's willow branch had left behind.

"Well?" her aunt barked, her voice hoarse and her breast heaving.

Meg's lips parted twice, three times, in a vain attempt to speak, but it was no use. She had no defense, at least not one Adelia would listen to, much less accept. Should she tell her at midnight on the morrow it would no longer be an issue? She would be away with her selkie lover? She didn't get a chance to decide.

Wailing like a banshee, Adelia wrenched the cleavers out of their brackets and glanced about the shed. Spying a spade, she seized that, too, taking them with her as she reeled out of the little bait shed and dropped the bar, locking Meg inside.

"I know your mind," Adelia said. "You'll not use these to make your escape!"

"Aunt, please!" Meg cried, pounding on the door with both tiny fists. "I beg you, do not leave me here! Let me out! Let me *out*, I say!"

"You will remain right where you are until your uncle returns day after tomorrow on the eve of the solstice," came her aunt's muffled voice from the other side. "He will decide what's to be done with you."

There was no time left. Adelia's footsteps crunching in the sand brought Meg's fists to the door again. "Aunt, please!" she cried. "After midnight on the morrow, I will no longer be a burden to you or Uncle Olwyn, but you must let me out if I am to spare you! Simeon is coming for me . . . to take me away, where we can be together. . . ." The crunching sound ceased, though there was no reply, and Meg went on quickly. "Let me go, I beg of you. I do not want to be initiated into the Order. I want to be with him. Aunt Adelia . . . *please!*"

For a moment there was silence, deadly and deep, the kind that is tasted like death, before the crunching sound resumed and grew distant, carrying Adelia away.

## 7

Simeon tossed beneath the quilts of woven moss and seaweed. Meg was holding him, her tiny hands flitting over his naked skin. She spread his legs and moved between. He could feel her hardened nipples scraping against his inner thighs as she arranged herself in position to take his cock in her mouth. Her fingers tightened around his shaft, stroking, squeezing, bringing it to life.

He tried to open his eyes, but he could not. It was one of those dreams where no matter how hard he tried, he couldn't force his eyes open. He hadn't had one like it since he was a child. He strained and strained, but it was no use. His eyelids wouldn't budge. It almost angered him. He wanted to see. He wanted to watch Meg take him. It would heighten his pleasure to watch her mouth gliding up and down the bulging veined shaft of his cock, flicking her tongue over the burgeoning head, finding the rim of the opening with the tip of her pointed tongue, and teasing it until she'd nearly driven him mad, until the fine, milky pearls of pre-come began to leak from it. His climax was always intensified when he watched his shaft slip in and out between her lips or penetrate her slit like a sword sliding into its sheath.

A soft moan escaped him. His cock was throbbing, his breathing rapid. This was pure fantasy, though his dreams had brought him to the brink of climax. Most of his imaginings had never occurred, but he wanted them to. Oh, how he wanted them to. Meg was an innocent, but not one spoiled by the rigid sensibilities of her mortal existence like others above the waves that he had known. She was possessed of a passion that matched his own. She could have selkie blood for the depth of that passion. He had never met the like among mortals. He had never felt like this before. Could he be experiencing what mortals called *love?* It wasn't practical for a selkie. Where could it possibly lead? Somehow, that didn't matter; neither did the fact that it was happening so quickly. He had to have Meg, whatever the cost. No one would ever satisfy him now, not after her life had made his live. Not after he'd formed her sex into the perfect sheath to fit his sword and made her his own.

Absently, still in the dream, Simeon reached to soothe his throbbing sex. But it would not be soothed. It wanted Meg. *He* wanted her. No other would do. Her beautiful face wandered into the dream, and all at once, it was her hand stroking his cock—her fingers flitting across its aching head—her sultry voice calling his name. His release was a throbbing, pumping explosion that brought his eyes open finally, but she wasn't there. He was alone in his bed made with quilts of woven seaweed and lush aquatic moss as soft as eiderdown.

Simeon groaned. Swinging his feet over the side of the bed, he took his head in his hands. It was no use. It was still hours before dawn and a whole day to get through before his assignation with Meg at midnight. Too restless to sleep, he decided to swim to the Pavilion and assess the damage time had conferred on it before taking Meg there.

Surging to his feet, he left his chambers and went to the edge of the water tunnel. Parting his lips, he shut his eyes and hummed the mantra that would bring his summoner. Vega would be out of earshot and asleep at this hour. The vibrations his voice made reverberating in the water would not rouse him at his distance, but it would bring a creature that could fetch his brother to him. Minutes later, an elegant swordfish broke the surface of the water, leaping and dancing. Then hovering beneath the surface, the great fish awaited instructions.

"Bring Vega," Simeon charged.

The swordfish streaked off, parting the water, and Simeon waited somewhat less than patiently for his valet to appear. It was only minutes later, though it seemed like an eternity, when Vega entered, his sharp eyes dulled with sleep.

"What now, Simeon?" he said, not a little annoyed, Simeon thought, judging from his brother's rigid bearing and tight-lipped expression.

"I cannot sleep."

"Neither can I, so it seems," Vega said caustically. "What is the press?"

"I'm going to the Pavilion to see for myself how badly it is in need of repair before I take Megaleen there."

"Do you want me to come with you?"

"No. It's best that you remain here and keep an eye on the consorts."

Vega loosed a lecherous chuckle.

"I'm not liking their absence of a sudden," Simeon said, ignoring the levity. "They're up to something; I'd stake my life on it. Besides, I thought you ought to know where I've gone . . . just in case. Something isn't . . . right. I can sense it. I can feel it, and I always trust those instincts."

"It's a long distance. Will you be wanting your sealskin?"

"No," Simeon said.

"Your eel skin then? I've fashioned you a new one."

Simeon hesitated, giving it thought. "Yes," he said at last. "It served its former owners well enough for warmth and speed, though I've never used it traveling so great a distance before."

"As you wish, then."

"What?" Simeon said, addressing Vega's clouded expression. Darkly handsome, only subtle differences marked his half brother as older. "I know that look. Out with it."

"Very well," Vega responded, squaring his posture. "Since you insist . . . Do you really think you can keep her under the waves? You certainly have no difficulty breathing while under water—neither do I because I am half selkie. Our bodies are conditioned to breathe in the deep in either incarnation. We have gill cells in our lungs that extract oxygen from the water when we are below the waves in human form, but she does not. She is *mortal*. Why, she—"

"And my breath empowers her with the same advantage," Simeon interrupted him.

"Temporarily," Vega pronounced. "Look what happened earlier. You barely got her to air in time. What happens if you are not there one day when such a situation arises? She would die, Simeon. She would never reach the surface from the deep in time unaided. You will kill the very thing you love!"

There was that dreaded word again: *love*. Simeon heaved a sigh. It must be so if Vega saw it . . . His insights were legendary. Worst of all, he was right. Meg could not exist for long periods under water. She was not a magical creature of the fey. She was a flesh and blood mortal. Somehow, he would find a way, but now the night was passing. He needed to put what was left of it to good use. He needed to spend some of the volatile pent up energy that was ready to explode. He needed to still the anxious flesh of his cock that even now threatened to rise against him. He needed to replace the gloom of utter frustration with the ray of hope the Pavilion offered, and there wasn't much time. Soon the dawn would break. Everything must be in readiness by midnight. There wasn't a moment to lose if he were to do what he planned and return in time to meet Meg on the Isle of Mists.

Simeon shut his eyes, listening to the vibrations in the water. They were strong tonight. He turned to Vega. "Ready Elicorn," he said.

"You *ride* to the Pavilion?"

Simeon nodded. "A storm comes," he said. "The surf runs high. The waves will be capped with white, just as Elicorn likes them. We need to reach an understanding, that waterhorse and I. He nearly killed her, Vega. That cannot happen again. If all goes as planned, she will have to be safe alone with him on occasion."

Vega chuckled skeptically. "I wish you luck," he said. "A waterhorse will do what is in its nature to do, little brother."

Simeon gave a crisp nod. "So will the Lord of the Deep," he said, and said no more.

Meg sagged against the scarred bait shack door and heaved with dry sobs. She was too devastated for tears. Why hadn't Adelia let her out? It was the perfect solution. Praying her aunt would realize that and change her mind, Meg slid down the length of the door to the sand underfoot and slumped against the boards heavy with the sour smell that salt leaves behind over time in seasoned wood. Combined with the stink of tar drifting from the nets piled in the corner and the smell of the horseshoe crabs, it threatened to make her retch.

It was dark as coal tar pitch. She could barely make out the shape of the partitioned bins that housed the crabs, though there was comfort in the squishing sound they made crawling through the sand. It whispered of the sea connecting her to Simeon, but that brought a new terror. She wouldn't be waiting in the cove at midnight. Would he come searching for her? Or would he think she'd given in to the demands of her aunt and gone to the temple to be initiated in spite of her lost virtue?

The temple wasn't on the Isle of Mists, though there was an

order that resided there at the training hall, where she would go to be mentored in the Witching Way to bring out her natural gifts once she'd been installed as priestess. The temple itself was on a little rockbound spit of land connected to the Isle by a stacked-stone jetty that appeared only at low tide just after dawn and dusk. Otherwise, it was sunken too deep to access. There, on what was called Shamans' Mount, the temple stood like an ancient folly, a round stone fortress three stories high hewn of the rock it stood on. If such were to be the case, Simeon would never find her there. None but the chosen were permitted to cross over. Shamans' Mount was impregnable.

All at once, there was a sound. Meg pricked up her ears and listened, scarcely breathing. Someone was coming. Aunt Adelia had relented after all. Scrambling to her feet as the footsteps drew nearer, Meg smoothed the indigo gauze kirtle over her trembling breasts and shook out the hem to loosen the damp sand clinging to it. Dawn had broken. The first bleak rays were showing through cracks in the wall boards that she hadn't even know were there. She could scarcely contain herself until she heard the rasp of the wooden bar being raised outside.

"Oh, aunt!" she cried as the door came open. "I knew you wouldn't . . . !"

But it wasn't Adelia who crossed the threshold and took hold of her, though her aunt was there, barking commands. It was two hulking eunuchs from Shamans' Mount.

"Just take the whore!" Adelia shrilled. "I wash my hands of it! I want shot of the harlot before my husband returns." Then to Meg as they half dragged, half carried her out of the bait shack kicking and screaming, "You brought this down upon your own head, my girl! You could have lived in luxury as a priestess of the temple. See how you like life among the shamans' whores! Take her away and good riddance!"

Adelia said more, but Meg scarcely heard as the two hulking brutes dragged her away. She had heard nothing past, "the shamans' whores." What were the shamans' whores? Meg had never heard of this. All Arcus knew the shamans' took no oath of celibacy. Sexual congress was part of their hushed mystique, never spoken of openly, though all knew and feared them for it. To be called before the shamans for whatever infraction of the Arcan laws was every mother's dread for her female children. If a woman was barren and a shaman was called in, she was soon miraculously with child, and many a poor unfortunate woman called before the shamans was found wandering the Isles stark-staring mad after the interview. These were mysteries never spoken of, though even on the mainland they were known and feared.

But the *shamans' whores*? And she was to become one of them?

Meg fought her captors with all her strength, kicking and biting as the reality of her predicament became clear. She would not be at the cove at midnight, and Simeon would never find her on Shamans' Mount. But her bare feet failed to make a dent in the eunuchs' thick shins, though she drubbed them soundly. All that came of her struggles were smarting toes that tingled with pain while the eunuchs hauled her along the strand to the jetty that made the Mount a peninsula at low tide.

The stacked stones were hard and unyielding beneath her feet as they propelled her along. The Mount was gated, wreathed around by a high stone fortification. The eunuchs hauled her through a gate in the wall that was virtually undetectable to an untrained eye. They steered her inside the round tower, down a steep, narrow staircase chiseled from the same rock as the rest, and into a dank subterranean bathing chamber. Here, they stripped off her kirtle and left her.

Dazed, Meg rubbed her arms which smarted from the eunuchs' grips on them. Her first instinct was to run, but a bolt being thrown above stopped that. It was no use. There was no way to escape, and she hugged herself in a vain attempt to stop her quaking.

Thick steam rising from the center of the room called her

nearer, albeit warily. It was spiraling up from what appeared to be a large round tub sunken in the stone floor. Waving the mist aside with her hand, Meg saw that it was shallow and large enough for several to bathe together. The water looked so inviting, rippling blissfully. How good it would feel on her willow switch stripes and sore feet. She glanced about. She appeared to be alone in the little chamber. What harm to sooth her aching flesh—her feet at least? She padded to the edge of the sunken tub and sat down, dangling her toes in the water.

It felt even better than it looked, and a low moan escaped her lips as she threw her head back, indulging in the luxury of the steamy bath. It felt like silk between her toes, and she groaned again, lost in the delicious fragrance of wild botanicals wafting toward her nostrils from the water. It was like a drug. The rapturous feeling spread from the tips of her toes to the scalp of her head, welling in the deep epicenter of her sex. There was no bathing tub at the cottage. Meg hadn't submerged herself in one since she lived in her home on the mainland. That wasn't so very long ago, but she'd forgotten how delicious it was to sink up to her neck in a scented tub. Her body ached for it. Her soul longed for it. She was just about to satisfy her longing to do just that, when three handmaidens appeared from the shadow-steeped periphery of the room. How long had they been standing there? Had they been watching all the while?

Meg's posture clenched as they approached her. They were scantily clad, bare breasted, and barefooted, wearing only loin cloths of gold tissue between their legs that barely covered their mons area. All three were dark haired, their long tresses styled in elaborate plaits and cascades. One was carrying a cobalt-blue glass jar. The second was laden down with a sumptuous fur rug and a stack of thick towels. The third carried a garment of bottle-green gauze so sheer the woman's arms were visible through several layers draped over them. Meg watched them guardedly, at the same time searching the shadows for a means of escape.

The handmaiden with the towels laid them aside and spread the fur rug behind Meg on the stone floor. The woman with the jar set it down alongside, while the third draped the gown she carried over something in the shadows Meg couldn't see. When all three converged upon her, Meg tried to rise, but they seized her and laid her back upon the thick, white fur.

"It is no use to struggle," said the maid with the jar. She had taken it up again and was dipping her fingers in the pleasant-smelling oil inside. "You must be readied for the shamans. The experience can be as pleasant as you allow, but it must be done. You must be prepared."

"Why? Who are you?" Meg cried, straining against the others' grips on her arms. They were holding them over her head, and she was terrified.

"Does it really matter?" the handmaiden said, her oil-drenched fingers suspended over her. Several drops of the oil dripped on Megs breasts. It was cool, yet the flesh beneath grew hot as it touched her skin.

"It does," Meg said. "Are you priestesses or whores? Why must you prepare me . . . for what?"

"I am called Zeona," the maid said. "My sisters are Isobel and Mariet. Lie *still!*"

"Let me go!" Meg shrilled. "I beg you, turn me loose. I do not belong here. I've been brought against my will!"

The one called Mariet snorted. "You think any of us came here willingly?" she said.

"Then let me go! Why do to me what others have done to you?"

"There is no escape for the shamans' whores," the one called Isobel chimed in.

"You are no better than they to do this to me!" Meg sobbed, struggling. "Let . . . me . . . go . . . !"

"Would you rather the shamans do it, then?" Mariet said. "They will not be so kind. They will be angry, and you will suffer for it—we all will suffer for it. Lie still and submit. One way or another, you will be prepared. Better it should be at our hands than theirs."

Meg sagged against the others' grips. It was no use. They were possessed of uncanny strength. She could not stand against the three of them, and she shut her eyes and called up Simeon's image.

Zeona had begun to massage the oil into Meg's skin. She was a gifted masseuse, taking great pains to rub the ambery oil into Meg's breasts. It smelled of hazelnuts, smoky and rich. It took her breath away. It was like a drug pulling her under, while heightening her senses at the same time. It was passing strange. Every pore came to life as Zeona rubbed and tweaked and circled her tall, erect buds, massaging the oil into them until they glowed. The heat it generated relieved her sore skin. If she only wasn't so dizzy all of a sudden.

Zeona's hands slid lower, following the contours of Meg's torso, working the oil into her navel and along her thighs. Mariet's hands worked her breasts now, and Isobel had parted her legs and spread them open for Zeona to knead the oil into Meg's pubic curls. As dazed as a lord drunk on mulberry wine, Meg fought the waves of vertigo that starred her vision, but it was no use. The pungent scent of hazelnuts threading through her nostrils had rendered her helpless as Zeona spread her nether lips and opened her slit. One—two of the handmaiden's fingers dripping the woodsy-scented oil slipped into her vagina, slathering the oil on her hardened bud, rubbing it deep inside her in circular revolutions that arched Meg's back off the fur rug as if she'd been launched from a catapult. She groaned. Whatever was in the oil had awakened every nerve ending in her body until the tactile element of the massage became a painful experience—an excruciating ecstasy that cried for release. Meg's whole body throbbed with it.

She was slipping further and further away. Subdued by the

drug the handmaidens had rubbed into her skin, she'd become docile, almost semiconscious. "W-what are you doing to me?" she murmured thickly.

"Does it really matter?" one of them said. Meg couldn't tell which one, though their voices were hardly similar. Now, under the influence of whatever they had administered through the oil, the laughter and chatter of all three sounded like it was coming from an echo chamber.

She scarcely felt them roll her over on her stomach. The coarse fur beneath her, rubbing against her engorged bud— grabbing her vulva as they moved her—caused shockwaves of riveting fire to course through her swollen sex. Her nether parts seemed gargantuan, as if the swelling had forced them to turn inside out.

The handmaidens had begun massaging the oil over her back, over the globes of her buttocks and the curve of her thighs. One of them spread her legs again. Another raised her hips, while the third massaged the oil into the tender skin between her sheath and her anus, penetrating it lightly to smear the thick, hazelnut-scented stuff inside the edge of the puckered rim.

Then she was on her back again. The handmaidens had removed their loin cloths. How odd: their pubic curls were shorn. Their nether lips and clitoris were visible, their pelvises as smooth as a baby's bottom. Moving as if time had slowed to a snail's pace, all three handmaidens descended on her, on her breasts, on her navel, on the throbbing, tormented flesh between her thighs, sucking, stroking, laving until she feared she would go mad, helpless to prevent what they were doing to her and to each other.

It went on forever. Weak and wet from involuntary climax after climax and the strange effects of the hazelnut-scented oil, Meg lay helpless while they fondled, stroked and caressed her. Was this it, her preparation? Her heart was aching for Simeon's embrace. Was this some sort of consolation? How could it be, when they knew nothing of her alignment with the Lord of the Deep?

Just when she feared she would die before she could bear more, they eased her into the steaming tub and formed a semi-circular arc around her while they stroked and laved and palmed each other's breasts, then bathed each others' nether parts inside and out in the silkened water.

Had she died? And if so, was this heaven or hell? Still under the foggy haze of drug-induced euphoria, Meg breathed a ragged sigh. Her *preparation,* as the handmaidens had called it, was over at last. Preparation for what was still vague, for it was as if her mind had become unhinged—as if it had become separated from her body—and all that had happened since the eunuchs dragged her through the Mount gates had happened to someone else. At least that is what she thought until a cold draft snaked its way down the narrow stone staircase announcing the arrival of another. The heavy iron-hinged door slammed shut behind the tall, muscular man descending.

He was too attractive for a shaman, though that is what he was—a striking figure with chestnut hair and eyes so deeply sunken beneath the ledge of his brow Meg could not tell their color. He was wearing a long black *cote-hardie,* and he was naked underneath, his thick, bulbous erection exposed, protruding through the opening in front. He made no move to tuck it away, but flaunted it, instead, coming nearer. Nodding toward the cobalt-blue glass jar, he cast a slow blink toward Zeona, who scrabbled up out of the tub and dipped her fingers in the oil. Jutting his shaft, he stood arms akimbo while the handmaiden massaged it into his penis from its root along its long veined shaft to its burgeoning head.

After a moment, he groaned, and turned hard eyes upon the handmaiden. "Enough!" he bellowed, backing Zeona up apace. "Leave us, all of you!"

# 8

---

The three handmaidens fled, and the shaman strolled closer, stroking his penis absently. Meg barely stifled the gasp rising in her throat. His eyes were visible now. They were as black as sin, staring down dilated with desire.

Meg shrank back from the formidable image towering over her. Did her aunt know this was what would happen to her when she summoned the eunuchs? She must have. Would Uncle Olwyn have prevented her? He had been kinder, less rigid, in the short time she'd spent on the Isle. Perhaps that was why Aunt Adelia had given her up.

*And good riddance!* Adelia's parting words ghosted across her memory. And she had said she wanted to get shot of her before Olwyn returned. Could she have been jealous? It never crossed Meg's mind until now, but it was a distinct possibility. It hurt her heart, but it didn't matter anymore. Her fate was standing over her, reeking of stale sweat and strong drink. Instead of becoming a priestess of the Isle of Mists, she was about to become one of the shamans' whores.

He laughed. "Come, come, do not shrink from me," he said.

"It is no use in any case. There is no escape. No one ever returns from Shamans' Mount. I am sure now you see why. But that is of no consequence. It isn't a bad life, servicing us. You shall want for nothing. You shall bathe in the most precious oils—wear the finest silks—eat the most delicious delicacies—live in the most sumptuous dwelling, all for the pleasure of lying beneath us in our turn."

"Please, I beg you, let me go," Meg pleaded. "I have been brought here against my will. . . ."

"It is a privilege to lie beneath us," he said. "It isn't as though you are an innocent. Your virtue has already been taken, elsewise your fate would have been quite different. Now, you have two options. You become a temple whore or a blood sacrifice to the gods of Arcus. I presumed this would be your preference. Have I presumed wrong? Because if I have—"

"I belong to another," Meg persisted. "I do not even know you!"

"That hardly signifies," the shaman said through a wry chuckle. "You didn't know him either, your lover, yet you spread your legs and gave him your virtue easily enough."

"*Gave*, yes," she sallied. "He did not force me."

"I shan't force you, either, little whore. Before I'm through, you will beg me to take you. And since it seems to be a point of contention with you that you must have the intimacy of a name to go with this face, I am called Seth, but you will not call me thus. You will address me as 'my lord.'"

"You have plenty of whores," Meg argued, scrambling out of the tub. "Willing ones. I will never give myself to you of my own free will, and if you force yourself on me, you will be shamed before the others."

The bottle-green gauze kirtle the handmaidens had brought lay draped over a bench in the shadows. She reached it in three strides and wriggled into it. Looking down, her breath caught. She may as well have been naked for the coverage the flimsy thing gave her. It was slit in front to the navel in a wide V that barely covered her nipples. There was virtually no back to speak of in the garment at all. Despite the long flowing sleeves and voluminous skirt, her skin showed right through the gauze. It was sheerer than spider silk.

"I'm glad you're coming to your senses," Seth said, strolling closer, as if he hadn't heard a word. "That gown is much more provocative than naked skin. Wise decision."

"They have taken the kirtle I arrived in," Meg defended. "I have no other."

"Ah, but you will, Megaleen, the moment you accept this," he said, exhibiting his penis. He'd been pumping it since their conversation began—slow, lingering strokes through the ring he'd made of his thumb and middle finger. The engorged shaft was blue with distended veins, the head a threatening shade of purple. It trembled in readiness, wet in anticipation.

Meg backed away. "I told you, I belong to another," she snapped at him. Maybe that would shrivel the menacing penis, reduce it to a flaccid state. But no, it only seemed to grow thicker—longer. She took another step back from him.

The shaman continued to stroke his sex. "The Lord of the Deep?" he scoffed. "The selkie lecher of Arcus . . . Have you any idea how many maidenheads he's taken? And you accuse *me* a whoremaster!" He threw his head back and convulsed in riotous laughter. "You think he will be faithful to you—a *selkie* be faithful to a mortal? Never—not unless she possesses his sealskin, and you do not. Already he strays."

"I am not his whore!" Meg insisted. "And even if I were, he is not a priest of the temple! You are a sacrilege to the Arcan gods you serve."

Again, the shaman flaunted his penis. "You waste our precious time together," he said. "Do you see what I do? My cock is ready. If it comes in my hand and not in you, you will be the worse for it."

Still skirting his advance, Meg ignored him. "How do you know these things," she said. "How could you know so much about me . . . so much that no other knows? How do you know he strays?"

The shaman hesitated. "Tiresome little bitch!" he seethed, seizing her arm. "That's got your attention, has it? You want to see how? Will that persuade you that you are better off right here with me? So be it!"

Hauling her up the narrow staircase, the shaman dragged her out the same way she had entered with the eunuchs, only this time, he took her behind the folly, where an ancient copse fringed the rear approach to the temple complex. How strange, Meg thought, that trees grow here and not on the Isle of Mists proper. But then, a peculiar, mystical atmosphere prevailed about the archipelago. Mainland folk had long since spoken about it in hushed whispers, about the water world beneath the waves that served as the deep lord's subterranean island, and the dark lord's isle, lonely and barren, that none dared trespass; about the enchanted forest isle, home of the Lord of the Wood and the forbidden fire lord's volcanic domain; and in their midst, about the mysterious Isle of Mists, where, like an arm flung into the bay, stood Shamans' Mount, the seat of Arcan clerical power, cloaked by the fogs unless the shamans chose to expose it to mortals, view. Not once since she'd come to the Isle of Mists had she seen the Mount until now . . . when it was too late to be forewarned of the true danger, of the shaman's dark secret that none who ever ventured to the Mount returned to tell.

They started down a narrow footpath through the trees that soon opened to a little clearing, where a rock pool stood. It was small and deep, judging by the color of the water, but that, Meg surmised, could well be from the canopy of pine boughs that let precious few shafts of light through to reach the ground. Instead, an eerie green darkness clung about the place. It was well into the afternoon, and one fractured sunbeam sliced through the haze, illuminating the pool of dark water enclosed in a rock formation that was part of the granite wall at the opposite end of the peninsula. Meg could see it in brief glimpses beyond the thinning trees.

The shaman hauled her along toward what looked like a little raised well at the edge of the pool. A strange green mist rose from it, taking color from the atmosphere in the wooded glade. Fisting his hand in the back of Meg's hair, the shaman propelled her closer.

*The scrying pool.*

Meg's heart leapt. It was! She had always presumed it to be hidden somewhere on the Isle of Mists proper. Giving her hair a jerk, he shoved her closer, and she braced her hands on the cool, smooth stones that edged the pool and peered over the rim. The strange green mist drifted up her nostrils. It was warm, and smelled sweet with the heady, woodsy scents of spring approaching summer. It did frightening things to her equilibrium.

"What would you see first, eh?" the shaman asked. "The past, present, or future?"

"Please . . . just let me go," she pleaded.

"You wanted to know, did you not? Well now you shall . . ."

The shaman swept his hand over the scrying pool, and the mist dissipated, revealing her image and Simeon's during their last embrace in the little cove, where in just hours, she was to meet him again. She gasped and reached toward the water.

The shaman seized her wrist. "No!" he said. "Do not touch!"

Before her eyes, she watched Simeon embrace her—watched him build a little pillow of sand beneath her hips and drink her juices—watched his life live inside her deep, pistoning thrusts that had brought her to ecstasy like no other.

"No more!" she sobbed, trying to turn away, but the shaman held her fast.

"Now the present," he said, passing his hand before the

water in the scrying pool again. "You wished to know how I knew your precious Lord of the Deep would stray . . . Even as we speak, he lies in the arms of another, little whore—*look!*"

The water rippled, then cleared, and Meg stared at Simeon in the arms of his favorite consort, Alexia, their naked bodies entwined. She had hold of his penis and was twisting it erect. They were underwater, beneath some sort of mesh canopy, but the setting was unfamiliar to her. Other consorts were grouped around them. For a moment, they appeared to be spectators, but then they, too, swam beneath the canopy to participate in the coupling.

Tears welled in Meg's eyes. She couldn't bear to look, and yet she couldn't tear her eyes away. Was this something in the selkie nature that couldn't be broken, a drive that not even love could curtail? There was no mistaking what she was seeing. The selkie females were all over him, like a living, breathing quilt of naked bodies. Her heart was breaking.

"No more!" she sobbed, struggling against the shaman's grip. He had hold of her still, but he also had hold of his penis again. He had brought it to life with quick, deft strokes until it had grown longer and harder than before. Evidently the scene in the scrying pool had aroused him. Spinning her around, he leaned her back against the stone rim of the pool and forced his hot hard shaft against the cushion of her pubic curls through the thin gauze kirtle.

"I will wait no longer," he panted. "This is as good a place as any for our first coupling." He began hoisting the skirt of her gown up with his free hand while tethering her with the other. "Do not struggle," he warned. "Struggling only stimulates me." Spreading the *cote-hardie* open wide, he exposed his hard muscled body to her gaze and forced her hand against his engorged penis. "That's right, hold it . . . stroke it . . . put it in you," he charged. "Take me the way you took him. . . ."

Her hand jammed against his shaft grazed his testicles. They were swollen and hard, and Meg shifted position. He was on the verge of climax, and she gave his sex a vicious tug, brought her knee up and delivered a blow to his groin with all her strength.

Shrieking, the shaman let her go and doubled over just long enough for her to shove him away and dart off into the forest.

"Run!" he thundered. "You cannot escape me, little whore. You would have to sprout wings to escape the Mount. I will have you, and when I do, you will rue the day you raised your hand against me!"

As the sun approached the zenith, Simeon reached the Pavilion astride a penitent waterhorse. Much of the distance had been traveled beneath the waves since it was daylight and the course took him dangerously close to the mainland, something selkies rarely risked except at night. Only for brief intervals did he allow Elicorn to surface and ride the white-capped waves as the animal so loved to do, and those occasions were well offshore, out of sight of prying eyes. Now, they had reached the place where bay and sea met in a howling vortex seamed together by seven currents that whipped the seas to a briny froth and lured more than one ship to a watery grave, fair weather and foul. Here deadly waterspouts hammered vessels and their crews into swirling eddies to vanish without a trace, and the sirens' wails from the rockbound shoreline of the mainland alone proclaimed their eulogies.

The undertow was strong and dangerous—too dangerous for the selkie cows to navigate, he was hoping. In their seal incarnations, the females could not stay under water more than an hour or two without discomfort and finally being driven above the waves. Neither could the males, except for himself. The Lord of the Deep could exist in any underwater condition. It remained only to determine if Meg could exist there with him.

The water here was many fathoms deep, with great rocky shelves and underwater caves, many with air pockets. Simeon left Elicorn in one of these to graze and swam below, passing shipwreck after shipwreck all the way to the bottom. Vega was right. Meg would never make it to the surface if her breathing failed. He would have to visit the Waterwitch for a potion or a spell, but that would have to wait. He was nearing the bottom, and the Pavilion, which had once been grand in its day, loomed before him from its subterranean air pocket, draped in sea moss and overgrown with aquatic vegetation. The sea creatures welcomed him, flocking to him in droves. He had not come this way since he was a child, and it warmed his heart that his legend had lived even here, at the edge of the Arcan wilderness.

Sirens and sprites, nymphs and naiads flocked to him there to pay homage to the Lord of the Deep. There was no question that he and Meg would be welcome, and all factions, ecstatic at the prospect of having their prince so close at hand, pledged to restore the Pavilion as best they could—to sweep the ocean residence clean of the death and decay that occupied it now and make it fit for their selkie lord and his bride.

At last there was a ray of hope, and he bade them farewell and started back to the cave where he'd left Elicorn. Time was short. If he was to reach the palace in time to slip into his selkie skin and meet Meg at the cove on the Isle of Mists, he couldn't waste a minute.

Warmed by the music the sirens made proclaiming the news from their rocks along the shoals, Simeon surged through the water passageways that threaded through the maze of underwater caverns, caves, and sunken ships clinging to their ledges toward the surface. Muriel, their leader, was marshalling the legions, and the water rang with their sweet music, calling sea creatures near and far to lend a hand in the restoration.

Simeon had nearly reached the surface when he passed the wreck of a recently sunken barque clinging precariously to a shallow shelf. He was so close to the surface the color of the murky water around him had begun to lighten from the sun beating down upon the water from above. All at once, motion caught his eye but not in time. He felt the restriction before he realized the cause as a large net was thrown over him and tightened in the hands of a half-dozen aggressors.

Caught off guard, Simeon had no time to strategize his escape. He thrashed about in a vain attempt to free himself. The more he fought his captors, the more he became tangled in the mesh of the net. The water around him clouded, having grown murky despite the light streaming down as his efforts stirred long-dormant algae and aquatic debris clinging to the wrecked ship. *Elicorn!* He had nearly reached the cave where he'd left the waterhorse to graze, and he shut his eyes and hummed the mantra, sending far-reaching vibrations rippling through the water that would bring the animal. But when Elicorn pranced alongside, he was not alone. Alexia was mounted on his back.

"Do not struggle, my lord," she said, motioning the others to cinch the net in tighter. "You cannot escape. What? Did you think you could just kick us aside and disappear here at the Pavilion with your mortal whore without a word to us, your loyal consorts who have served you so faithfully? Did you think we could not follow you such a distance? You forget the coral reefs, the rocks along this coast, where a selkie—many sekies—can take refuge. You are a fool, Simeon, to think you could escape us."

"You sealed your fate when you attacked me in my sleeping chamber. You nearly killed Megaleen. Can you possibly imagine such a vicious attack would go unpunished? You do not rule the deep—*I* do. As it stands now, you are outcast. Carry this further, and you leave me no choice. Treason is punishable by death. Now let me out of this before it's too late!"

Fury ruled Simeon's posture as he struggled within the confines of the net. Twisted as he was on his back, it was impossible to right himself and get a grip on the others who had become visible now—female selkies in their human incarnation, their naked skin glowing with underwater phosphorescence.

"You brought a *mortal* beneath the waves!"

"I have had many mortals in the past, Alexia."

"But this mortal is . . . different. . . ."

Even Alexia noticed a difference in Megaleen. None of the others had ever posed a threat . . . until now. "Let me out of this net!" Simeon thundered. "You have no authority over me. Stop this now, while there is still time so save yourselves."

Alexia ranged the waterhorse closer. Anger set the blood boiling in Simeon's temples. How fickle was the beast beneath her to allow such a traitorous assault? The animal was beyond redemption. He would have to set it free. Or it could serve these treacherous cows that it abetted now. A waterhorse was what a waterhorse was—a great deceiver, even of its master. Vega could unwind that coil. Right now, Simeon needed to deal with the situation at hand. He needed to break free from this herd of disgruntled selkies and keep his rendezvous with Megaleen. By the dull color of the water overhead, which not so long ago had seemed brighter, the sun was already sinking low. There wasn't a moment to lose, and he punched his fist through the mesh of the net and seized Alexia's long, black mane.

"Let . . . me . . . go!" he seethed, giving her hair a wrench.

Alexia shrieked. "'Tis enchanted, the net," she cried. "I cannot!"

"I will show you enchanted," Simeon breathed, jerking her hair again. "Loose these bonds!"

All at once the net began to move, taking Simeon with it. Through the bleak, fading light filtering down from above, he watched the wreck slip away. The consorts were dragging the net through the water to a small cave, where the light nearly failed altogether. There, the net was loosened, but before

Simeon could untangle his limbs from it, Alexia had slipped off the waterhorse's back and mounted him instead.

"What can she give you that I cannot?" she purred, tearing at his eel skin suit.

Simeon groaned as the skin ripped. Vega would not be pleased after all his hard work making it, and he loosed a roaring bark not unlike what he might have uttered in his seal form, struggling with her beneath the loose, floating net.

"Enough!" he demanded. "Give it over, Alexia. I do not want to hurt you. You cannot win."

"I have already won," the selkie crooned, ripping the rest of his eel skin suit down the front. She seized his cock. "I have this in my hand, and you cannot tell me I do not still excite you."

He was what he was. A selkie's libido was legend. But even if her touch did arouse him, he wasn't about to give her the satisfaction. He was on fire, but not for Alexia, or the dark young beauty, Risa, or any of the others who had serviced him over the years. His mind, body, and soul burned for Meg with such a drenching, all-consuming passion, it had built a wall of fire around his heart that would admit no other. Even if Alexia were to take him—to drain the seed of his body—there would be nothing but emptiness in it. It would signify nothing more than a mundane bodily function. If this was love, it fostered loyalty—*monogamy*—and that was totally foreign for a selkie and not a comfortable thing. But there it was.

Their bodies entwined beneath the net, Alexia tore the rest of his eel skin suit away and ran her hands over his naked torso. Seizing his cock, she worked its silken shaft in a way that had always aroused him—twisting her hand in a spiraling motion up and down along its thick, veined surface, bringing him to full arousal. Relentless, she twisted it deeper with each stroke, meanwhile flicking her forefinger over the silky smooth mushroom tip in teasing, fluttering passes like the kiss of a butterfly's wing.

With her free hand, Alexia reached between her thighs and spread her nether lips. Finding her bud, she moaned and began fondling it, sliding her fingers along her fissure, slipping them inside her vagina, moving them in and out as she undulated against them.

"Deny me now, Lord of the Deep, if you can!" she triumphed. "Tell me that which I hold in my hand has not come to life for Alexia!"

Simeon loosed a bitter howl. Anger and lust welled inside him. He hated his traitorous member for rising in Alexia's hand—hated the eons-old force that drove the selkie to fulfill his sexual desires. Most of all, he hated Alexia for taking advantage of that inherent drive to serve her own ends. She certainly wasn't serving his. His longing was for Meg, in a way that Alexia could never sate no matter how she took him.

"What you are holding there would come to life in any hand that strokes it, you stupid cow," he gritted out through clenched teeth. "It is the nature of the beast and signifies naught but that it is in good working order. I could have done the same myself—and better."

He had nearly forgotten they weren't alone until the net was lifted slightly and the others began crowding close beneath it. Alexia hissed at Risa like a viper when she attempted to nudge her out of the way, and several of the others wriggled underneath the net. Their hands were everywhere, stroking, mauling, violating. But Simeon had a plan.

He laughed; the sound was so cold echoing in his ears it chilled him to the bone. "You see?" he said. "Their hands are just as effective. You overrate yourself, Alexia."

The net was spread out wide, floating overhead, and he encouraged the others to glide underneath it. Then clearing his voice, he loosed a vibrating mantra into the water, humming what he hoped they'd think was his contentment, while he had quite something else in mind.

Risa's nipple found his mouth, and Alexia slid down his body until his cock rested between her breasts, mimicking the twisting motion she'd done with her hand earlier as she undulated against him. Simeon had reached the point of no return all the way around. His engorged shaft, trapped between the voluptuous globes of Alexia's breasts would not be ignored. It had throbbed to life, but so had the burgeoning seeds of his plan. He bided his time until all of the consorts had crowded under the net. He waited until all hands were stroking him, exploring the hills and valleys, every orifice, every erogenous inch of his hard-muscled body—waited until they began pushing and shoving, trying to usurp one another, vying for his attention, and taking credit for his pleasure-moans.

First he stroked one's bottom, then another's nipples, and another's slit, just long enough to cause contention, and a power struggle soon began as they fought over his sex, slapping and pinching and pulling hair.

Alexia, still in control, raised her body above him with intent to impale herself upon his hot hardness, but Simeon was too quick for her. That he would not allow. Sliding out from underneath the literal blanket of females scrapping like cats over possession of his body, he released one last humming mantra into the water, seized the cinch rope that edged the net, and gathered it shut around the unsuspecting females.

Simeon could not prevent his climax. The minute he reached to soothe his aching, bursting cock, it pumped him dry, but none had the satisfaction of feeling him inside her. He had trapped them with their own device, and no sooner had he tied the knot that secured them, than an army of sirens, sprites, nymphs, and mermaids surrounded them.

"You called, my lord?" Muriel, their leader, said.

"Dispose of these," Simeon charged. "I would see them no more."

"As you wish, my prince," the siren said. "Is there to be an inquisition?"

"If I set eyes upon them again, there will be an *execution*," Simeon said. "It will suffice that they are sent from the archipelago, never to return. There are plenty of islets off the mainland where they can find a home . . . but not with me. I will not sleep with vipers. Take them away. . . ."

"You cannot do this," Alexia hissed, like the snake he accused. "To the others, perhaps, but not to *me!* You cannot put me from you just like that. We are one—we have always been one. Let me out, my lord . . . Let me out, I say!"

Simeon stared at her through narrowed eyes. Around her, the tangled snarl of struggling, shrieking female selkies were thrashing about inside the net, their naked bodies stretching the mesh. "You cannot even be loyal to your sister selkies," he observed. "And you have just demonstrated your treachery against me. Your betrayal has brought you to this punishment." He turned to the siren and her legions. "Take them away."

Offering a respectful bow, Muriel signaled the others, who began hauling away the net filled with shrieking, battling females. But one being waiting on the sidelines remained. From the shadowy depths of the cave, Elicorn pranced forward, bobbing his proud head in what seemed to Simeon a penitent posture.

He turned cold eyes upon the animal. "Well? What are you waiting for?" he snapped. "If I can change my nature—defy what is *in the blood*—what are you that you cannot do likewise? Think upon it, and if you cannot, then you belong with these in their exile. So go, if that be the case, I never want to see you again. Decide! I have no more time to waste on you."

And without a backward glance, he sprang from the shelf and swam off toward the surface.

# 9

Darkness came quickly on Shamans' Mount. The copse was too sparse to elude pursuit for long, though Meg ran the shaman a merry chase. The spirits he'd drunk soon had their way with him, however, and it wasn't long before he tired of the game.

Standing behind a sturdy pine her pursuer had just checked, Meg held her breath, her eyes upon the shaman reeling off toward the scrying pool, certain he could hear her heart pounding; it was making such a racket in her ears.

"All right, little witch," he snarled, waving a wild arm in the air in a rough gesture of dismissal. "I give you over to the mists." His *cote-hardie* was still gaping open in front, and he spun in a staggering circle, exhibiting his flaccid member in a lewd gesture. "It tires of you in any case," he rambled on. "But do not let that give you false hope of dismissal . . . only a reprieve. So! Run your pretty legs off! They will take you nowhere. Like I said . . . you cannot escape the Mount, lest you sprout wings. You cannot scale the wall, it is too steep. It gets cold in the mists in the dark, and you half naked in that rag—you'll come a-knocking soon enough, little witch, and you had best pray when you do that I am still this drunk!" He spun again, jutting his pelvis and exposing his penis roughly. "You will pay for this!" he snarled. "Never doubt it."

Then he was gone, swallowed up in the fog, and Meg sagged against the ancient tree trunk, hugging it as if to absorb its strength into her trembling body. Exhausted, she slid the length of the trunk to the mossy ground and leaned her back against the rough bark. It was running with sap, and it caught on the flimsy gown, but she didn't care. It was long known that sitting thus against one of the ancient trees evoked its spirit to enter the body. If ever she had need of ancient strength, it was now.

It was even said in hushed whispers that the greatest of such trees were able to move about when all was still in the dead of darkness. She dearly wished that the one she leaned on now was not a species of that variety, though a little of such magic would be welcome now, and the Mount was reputed to be magical, after all. If in truth and fact it was, she knew in her heart, though untapped, she possessed the gift to summon it.

Meg closed her eyes, praying it was safe to do so because that was part of the summoning. Taking deep breaths, she intoned the supplication:

> "*Sacred spirit in this tree,*
> *Come forth now and bond with me,*
> *Arise! Give ear! Awaken!*
> *Leave not your servant here forsaken,*
> *Ancient spirit in this tree,*
> *Come forth now and enter me. . . .*"

The rest was prayed in silent meditation. It was only a childhood rhyme, something learned at her mother's knee. But that was where she'd learned of her other gifts, and they were real enough to see her banished from the mainland for evoking them. The Mount was a place enchanted after all. If she only was able to tap into that magic . . .

All at once, the ground beneath her began to throb like a heartbeat. It seemed to shift, like a person turning in bed, and sigh, or was that the wind in the boughs spreading the heady scent of pine? But there was no wind. Was it the tree's sweet breath inhaling life that she felt whispering through her hair, warming her skin beneath the flimsy kirtle? She drank it in deeply.

The mulch of grass, dead leaves, pine needles and boughs peppered with pinecones shifted underneath her as the tree seemed to sigh again. The ground heaved, as long-dormant roots trailing tendrils sprung out of the forest floor like snakes and held her fast. Meg sucked in a hasty breath as the roots crawled over her body. Had she evoked the spirit in the ancient pine and brought it to life? What other explanation could there be? Strangely, she did not fear it. She had conjured it after all. She did not struggle. Sitting very still, she allowed the roots to explore her body.

It began with her tousled mane of hair that drifted about her like a veil, having dried as she ran through the wood to escape her pursuer earlier. A vibration began to hum through her body from below ground. A strange warming sensation accompanied it as the hum spread from the tips of her bare toes to the tips of her fingers. New trails of sensation spread to her breasts, then settled at the epicenter of her sex, causing a quickening of her heartbeat and breathing. Something fluttered through her loins. She was aroused, scarcely breathing, as two of the roots plucked her bodice aside, baring the orbs of her breasts to the cool mist, and twined their tendrils about her nipples.

Meg cried out, unable to contain the outburst as the root tendrils tugged at both her nipples at once. She dared not break the spell. The magic was too great. Break it now, and she would surely shatter. She had heard of such, of trees that took this sort of liberties in exchange for favors rendered. According to legend, only those with the greatest gifts—the truly endowed—possessed the power to entice a tree to bond in such a way, and never was it ever heard of except on the Forest Isle in the realm of Marius, Prince of the Green.

Its touch was sweet torture as the tiniest hair tendrils on the tree's root arms flicked the tips of her hardened nipples. Fisting her hands in the mulch she sat on, Meg groaned. Thick as milk with mist, the very air had a pulse. When one of the roots left her nipple and groped at the hem of her gown, she gasped again, digging her hands deeper in the fragrant mulch at her sides. But another root sprang up from the ground displacing the pine needles, sending pinecones rolling in all directions, and took the place of the other root at the nipple it had discarded.

Inch by inch, the tendrils at her hem began to draw the skirt up along her leg, over her thigh, feeling for her pubic curls. She could have sworn she heard the tree sigh again. She could bear no more, and a troop of orgasmic cries escaped her throat as the tendrils found the bud at the top of her fissure and began fondling it. Ripples of pulsating sensation riddled her deep inside as other roots sprang up, tethering her closer and explored every inch of her, burrowing beneath the sheer gown, spreading her legs, her nether lips—lingering on the edge of her slit, spread open to receive penetration.

Wet with arousal, Meg arched herself to receive one root that had joined with another and twisted into a spiral. The ground beneath her shuddered as the twisted roots moved in and out of her, riding the rhythm of her pelvic thrusts. Overhead, the pine boughs swayed in an imaginary wind that spread their scent. Needles rained down, slick with sap and dripping dew the mist had spent on them. They felt cool against Meg's hot skin, and she groaned again as her hips jerked forward, bringing her release.

Wave upon wave of searing fire flooded her loins with riveting contractions, as the rough textured tendrils addressing her erect bud rubbed and scraped and palpated the tiny erection between her thighs to rock hardness. Shuddering helplessly, she sighed when she climaxed once—twice—as the roots withdrew on the silk of her juices and burrowed back into the ground with the others that gave up her nipples and vacated her hot, moist skin.

Then the forest floor was as it was before she invoked the tree spirit—as if it had never happened. But this was no dream. It had been a bonding. Whatever strength, power—advantage—she had gained from the union would manifest itself in time. Whatever enchantment was afoot would one day make itself known. This, she would not confide in Simeon. It had no bearing on what was between them. It was something magical for her alone to know. A secret she would take to her grave, like touching herself in the dark, for if the mainlanders branded her a witch for looking into people's hearts, they would surely burn her at the stake for *copulating with a tree!* She would be put to death for unnatural practices.

Her eyes were open now, though hooded with the last dregs of desire. Her heart was hammering in her breast, her breath coming short and in spurts. She rotated her hips and squeezed her sex to still the palpitations, only to reach orgasm again. Grown weak and docile, she waited for the searing waves of drenching fire to subside, then straightened the gown around her, covering her flushed nipples, and staggered to her feet using the tree trunk for support.

All around, the little copse was very still. No woodland creatures spoke—no bird chirped. There was no human sound. Ordering herself, Meg thanked the gods that the shaman had tired of the game and gone back to the temple and his real whores—if his parts had recovered from her attack upon them. She glanced in the direction of the scrying pool, where she'd last seen him as he staggered off. . . .

*The scrying pool!*

Could it be possible that he hadn't left her at all—that he had seen what had just happened in the pool. Frantically, she strained the mist with narrowed eyes for some sign of his hulking bulk in the flowing black *cote-hardie*. For a moment, nothing met her gaze, only the swirling, eddying mist that seemed to pick and choose its hollow and had settled in around her. Her posture had barely collapsed in relief when a firm hand clamped around her arm from behind and reeled her along into a little clearing at the edge of the wood.

"So, little whore," the shaman said, jerking her to a standstill. "Did you really think I would leave you out here all on your own?"

"Let me go!" Meg shrilled, prying at his fingers that made deep imprints on her arm—so deep they'd nearly stopped the circulation.

"Gazing in the pool always sobers me," the shaman said, "and after what I've just seen, you have no case to plead." He ran the back of his hand down the V in the front of her gown, over her bare skin, lingering upon the voluptuous swell of her cleavage. "Um," he hummed. "You are like a succulent grape that has just been peeled, all moist and blushed, and aching to be sucked dry of all your sweet juices." Jerking her close, he ground his penis into her groin through the thin gauze gown. "I am the best you'll get here," he boasted. "No dried up prune, this. Accommodate me, and no one need know about the tree. You are not simpleminded. Such sorcery is condemned—even here. You know you cannot escape. This is what must be, and the sooner you accept the reality of that, the better."

His hands were upon her then, pinching, mauling—molest-

ing. Meg screamed as he tried to work his way beneath her
skirt, but he shook her to a standstill. "Open to me!" he thundered, trying to spread her legs apart. "By the gods, I will take
you right here where you stand, and you will know you've
been taken. You are more trouble than all the others in my
household put together but well worth the battle, eh? Open, I
say!"

All Meg could think of was that it was nearing midnight.
Simeon would be at the cove, and she would not be there to
meet him. Anger roiled in her at the circumstance that prevented her from keeping their assignation. She turned it upon
the shaman. With all her strength, she beat him about the head
and face with her free hand, meanwhile raising her knee to de-
liver another blow to his groin, but he was prepared this time
and seized her leg before it reached its mark.

"Let go of me!" Meg demanded.

The shaman shook his head. "No, little sorceress," he
seethed. "You will take this inside you, and it will revenge itself
on you for the swelling in it that is not result of this arousal. Believe me, it will whip you into shape from the inside out!"

Frantic at the rabid passion he exuded, Meg raised her hand
to strike him, but he dropped her leg and countered the blow.
She was just about to strike at him again when a whoosh of dis-
placed air and loose feathers raining down halted her hand midstroke as a winged man descended out of the misty sky and
came to ground frighteningly close beside them.

His eyes, as black as onyx chips, sparkled in the defused
light cast off by the mist. He glanced between them and spoke
but one word to her:

"Decide!"

The shaman's hands fell away from Meg's arms. "What do
you here, bastard of the gods?" he snarled.

"Their will," the winged man responded. He was clothed all
in black in a skin-tight suit that left nothing to the imagination.

A shock of hair the color of raven's feathers combed by the wind fell across his brow. His eyes were riveted to Meg's as he flexed his silver-white wings and said again, *"Decide!"*

There was something vaguely familiar about him. Meg gasped. Could it be the same winged man she saw circling the little skiff? She gasped again.

"You have no jurisdiction here, Gideon," the shaman barked. "Take yourself off and be gone. You are not welcome here."

"Small wonder," Gideon ground out through a wry chuckle, his eyes snapping toward Meg again. "Decide now!" he charged her.

Meg hesitated. She couldn't stay, but how could she go with this creature? Still, he possessed the wings to liberate her, and she ran into his arms.

In the space of a blink, Gideon stretched his wings and soared into the star-studded night sky. "Hold on to me," he said.

Those words were wasted. Looking down at the half-naked shaman railing and shaking an angry fist at them from the clearing below was enough for Meg, and she buried her face in the dark lord's shoulder. She didn't open them again until she felt him touch down on sparkling black sand.

"Who are you?" she demanded. "Where is this place?"

"I am Gideon, a friend," he replied, "and this is my island. I mean you no harm. I am also a friend of Simeon, Lord of the Deep, though he doesn't know a whit about gratitude. But that is neither here nor there. You will come to no harm here, under my protection." He raked her with familiar eyes. "And though you are a sight to tempt a eunuch, you are quite safe with me in that regard. That is enough for you to know . . . for now."

"Th-thank you for rescuing me from that place," Meg said low-voiced, scarcely meeting his eyes in sidelong glances. They were boring into her. Embarrassment flushed her cheeks crimson; she needed no mirror to see it. Hot blood raced through her veins and throbbed through her temples. Could he have seen her bond with the tree spirit? If he had, it was the second time he'd seen her nearly naked in similar circumstances. What must he think of her? She shuddered imagining it.

"The shamans stole that tree when it was no more than a sapling many years ago from the isle of the Lord of the Forest. An ancient sage lives inside it, just as many do on the Forest Isle. By time it was discovered where they'd taken it, the tree had taken root so deeply and grown so tall it was impossible to have it back."

Meg gasped. He *had* seen her . . . Or he could read her mind. She didn't know which was worse.

"I am thinking it is glad for having bonded so sweetly with such a maid after years of being pissed on by drunken shamans. But that is only my humble opinion, and I do not meddle in the metaphysical. I leave that to the gods that have abandoned me. Your secret is quite safe in my keeping. Come," he said, leading her into the petrified wood.

"W-where are you taking me?" she asked him, picking her way through the marshes, following in his footsteps to avoid the soft places.

"To my stronghold," he said, "where you will be safe while I go and find Simeon to see to you."

Meg gasped. "What is the hour?" she begged him, laying a hand upon the wing closest to her to get his attention. It was folded, tucked in at his side until she touched it. The minute her fingers came in contact with the silken feathers, both wings burst into their full span nearly knocking her over.

"Do not touch my wings!" he snapped at her, spinning away out of reach. "*Never* touch my wings . . . Eh . . . They are very . . . sensitive."

"O-oh," Meg murmured, her eyes riveted to the bulk of his penis threatening to burst the skin-tight suit he wore. Had ever so slightly touching his wing caused his arousal? She swallowed the gasp in her throat, watching his hands cover the obvious. After a moment, his wings folded close to his body again.

"What did you just ask me?" he finally said. He seemed disoriented—almost angry now—and while she didn't fear him, she hesitated before speaking.

"I . . . I asked you the time," she said when he jutted his chin to remind her.

Gideon looked to the heavens and assessed the stars in the indigo vault. "It is just past midnight," he said. They had reached a large cave, and he stood aside and motioned her to enter. "Why do you ask?"

"I was to meet Simeon in the cove on the south beach of the Isle of Mists at midnight," Meg said. The words gushed out of her in a steady stream, halting him where he stood.

"Make yourself at home," he said. "I will bring him."

And before she could speak, he had spread his wings and soared off into the night.

# 10

Simeon thrashed up onto the strand on the Isle of Mists in his sealskin a little before midnight. He had first decided to come in human form, but thought better of it, opting for the anonymity his seal incarnation would give him should mortals be about. Besides, once they'd paid a visit to the Waterwitch in hopes of finding a solution that would allow Meg to breathe under water for long periods, he would be taking her to the Pavilion, where they would be safe . . . at least for a time. Until he was sure the sirens and the sprites had carried out his wishes to exile the consorts.

Vega had gone on ahead to the Pavilion make certain no surprises lay in store. Simeon was anxious to show Meg his world, anxious that nothing spoil their special time together, during which he planned to teach her the many ways of making love to him—secrets he'd once taught the selkie consorts that would bring them both pleasure beyond imagining. He would find an islet above the waves, where he could exist in his seal incarnation and she could satisfy her need to breathe the air. Then, they would have the best of all worlds; at least that is how he'd worked it all out in his mind. All that remained was to spirit her away from the Isle of Mists before the shamans cancelled his plans.

The beach looked deserted. Meg was nowhere in sight. The cottage stood in darkness. No light was showing at the widows. That was as it should be at the witching hour, but he would have to get closer to be sure, and he could hardly go exploring in his sealskin. One seal alone would be suspect, since they always traveled with others in a group. Going about naked was not the ideal situation, either, but he had no choice. He shed his sealskin, stepped out of it in human form, and with the aid of a large scallop shell he'd found washed up on the strand, buried the skin in lee of the dune where he and Meg had last made love.

Crouching low, he moved off toward a better vantage to observe the cottage. Why hadn't she come? All manner of possible reasons haunted him. Had her aunt already delivered her to the shamans? Had the woman locked her in the cottage? Had she talked Meg out of the rendezvous? No. That he would never believe, but something had detained her, and he needed to go around to the other side of the dunes for a closer look at the cottage.

It took some time, since he moved with extreme caution, becoming one with the dunes he used as a blind. Something untoward was afoot, he could feel it—he could taste it. The more excuses he dreamed up, the greater his fear that something had happened to Meg. By the time he'd reached the other side of the dunes, his heart was hammering against his ribs. Looking through the tufts of beach grass at the top of the rise, he scanned the cottage with narrowed eyes. No light was showing from the windows. All was dark and still, and he decided to slip back into his selkie skin and wait on the rocky ledge along the shore, where he could observe the beach openly.

He was just about to implement the plan when Gideon touched down on the beach and strode toward him.

"What's happened?" Simeon asked the dark lord, his voice like feet crunching upon gravel echoing back in his ears. His hackles were raised at the sight of the winged prince advancing.

"Much," Gideon replied. Conversing with the dark lord was maddening at best. Gideon was an entity of few words, and what few he spared were oftentimes too metaphorical to be understood. "But take ease," he continued. "She is not here. I have given her sanctuary."

"*You?*" Simeon blurted.

"Her aunt gave her over to the shamans on the Mount. They were grooming her for a temple whore."

"And you got her out?" Simeon said. "I am in your debt, old friend. No one comes back from the Mount . . . But a whore in the temple? I have not heard of this. How did you know?"

"I see much from above, Simeon," Gideon said. "And that is why none return from Shamans Mount. It is their best-kept secret. And I do not know how much of a favor I've done you. The one they call Seth will track her to the ends of Arcus now for what she knows and might tell."

"I will deal with that if it happens," Simeon said. "I knew of the sacrifices, but not this. Did they . . . Is she . . . ?"

"She seems sound enough, though the sight of her would grow balls on a eunuch."

"Take me to her!"

Gideon swung his arm wide. "Hang on," he charged.

Unfurling his magnificent wings, Gideon soared skyward, taking Simeon with him. Simeon hadn't seen the archipelago of Arcus from this vantage in many years. From above, the isles looked like stepping stones laid out in a sweeping arc beyond the coral reefs and the long, narrow barrier beach that bordered the mainland. No doubt this was where the consorts had been exiled. The Isle of Mists was closest to the mainland. Then came the Forest Isle, Gideon's Dark Isle, and like a hand flung into the ocean, the Isle of Fire, whose volcanic eruption had nearly destroyed Gideon's domain so long ago. There was a generous stretch of water between them, which Simeon ruled, and the sea was peppered with many other isles and islets, but from the sky, the whole configuration resembled a skeletal arm with a bent elbow and hand with a pointing finger. Simeon drank in the sight, but it was soon gone from view, swallowed by stubborn mists drifting over the archipelago. It didn't matter. Gideon was an excellent navigator, and Simeon's relief in that he would soon hold Meg in his arms again commanded all his thoughts.

Hidden behind the dunes on the Isle of Mists, Adelia watched the winged prince lift off with Simeon and soar into the night. Still, she waited a moment before stepping out into the open. Just in case.

Megaleen had been truthful about that after all. At first she had thought it Meg's ploy to buy her freedom, but no, the girl had no guile. Still, she'd done the right thing selling the chit to the shamans. Meg was too much of a temptation to Olwyn. She'd glimpsed him ogling the girl. She'd seen him with his eyes halfway down her bodice, drooling over the milk-white expanse of Megaleen's bare skin that spilled over at the neck of her kirtle. The girl had no modesty, going about with the globes of her breasts exposed to the teats. That might be the fashion on the mainland but not on the Isle of Mists.

Yes, she had done well getting shot of the gel and made a tidy sum for herself in the bargain; something she would withhold from Olwyn. It was no more than he deserved. The fates had stepped in and seen him off to the mainland, giving Adelia the opportunity to set her plan into motion. Olwyn was *her* husband after all, and she would keep him. She was too old to go a-hunting for another. Better the old fool should think Meg had drowned in the sea, and good riddance.

What had to be done now had to be done quickly and with the greatest of stealth. Olwyn would return on the morning tide, and he must know nothing of what she was about to do this night. She strained the vault of heaven with narrowed eyes. There was no sign of the dark lord returning. All was still, and armed with the spade she'd taken from the bait shed, Adelia stepped out from behind the dune's rearing head and shuffled around the lee of it. There, she began to dig until she'd uncovered the sealskin she'd watched the Lord of the Deep bury. Evidently worried over why Meg had not come as they'd arranged, the lovesick fool had forgotten to retrieve the enchanted sealskin that masked his true identity. What untapped magic it must hold! And what power would be hers with it in her possession! What might the shamans pay for it? She quickened her steps in anticipation.

It was heavy. She'd never considered that. After smoothing out the place where it had been buried, she hefted the skin and staggered under its weight. Still warm from the heat of the selkie's body, she draped the hind end over her shoulder and dragged it over the dunes to the darkened bait shed, half-hidden in the mist.

Gideon touched down beside his cave, sparing Simeon a trek through the marshes, and there the winged lord left him to disappear in the night. Gideon was like that, appearing and disappearing at odd moments. Simeon had always found it jarring. Still, the dark lord always managed to be where he needed to be for whoever was in need. Whether he disappeared now to give him privacy with Meg, or he had pressing business elsewhere, Simeon didn't know. Gideon rarely explained himself. He moved through the world like a wraith in the mist, and no one—not even Simeon—knew his mind.

Only one thing mattered then: holding Meg in his arms again. Oblivious of the fact that he was stark naked, since it was the selkie's natural state, Simeon sped through the corridors, calling her name at the top of his voice. He needed to see for himself that she was unharmed. When she stepped out of one of the cells on the west side of the corridor and rushed into his arms, he groaned and shut his eyes, inhaling the fresh herbal scent drifting from her hair and the dark, smoky aroma of hazelnuts clinging to her skin.

Her soft sobs bled into his euphoria, and he searched her face, taking it in his hands, gentling the tears from her cheeks with his thumbs. He kissed what remained away. They tasted of salt, of the sea, reminding him of the world of differences between them. But he beat those thoughts back and tilted her head up to his gaze, looking deep into her eyes.

"I thought . . . Never mind what I thought," he said. "What happened? Did they harm you?" He held her away, taking her measure, his narrowed eyes flitting over her body from head to bare feet. They lingered upon the bottle-green gown that barely covered her nipples. They were clearly visible peeking through the gossamer gauze, which was somewhat worse for wear in spots. His gaze slid lower to her belly and the V of pubic curls showing through the fabric, their golden color almost glowing through the glittering green of the gauze. "What manner of gown is this?" he murmured.

"Aunt Adelia sold me to the shamans," Meg sobbed, as the events of the past few hours spilled out of her in a breathless spate. "They took my kirtle away . . . and gave me this to wear . . . They locked me in! I couldn't come as we'd planned. Then *he* came . . . the winged one . . . I—"

"Sh," Simeon soothed, crushing her close. "Slowly . . . from the beginning . . ." Her hardened nipples straining the gauze dented his bare chest. His muscles contracted as his cock surged to life and leaned heavily against her belly, the hard root of it seeking the soft cushion of curls between her thighs to nuzzle.

"Aunt Adelia saw us when you brought me back," Meg said. "She locked me in the bait shed and summoned the shaman's eunuchs to take me to the Mount. . . ."

"Because of us?" Simeon asked. He could not keep his hands from fondling her, from spreading the silky gauze to free her breasts for his hands to palm. He traced the pebbled areola of her nipples, teasing but not touching the hardened tips, delighting in her shudder as he coaxed them taller still.

"She has always been . . . difficult, Simeon," she said. "But after she examined me and discovered I'd lost my virtue, she was like a madwoman!"

In the light of the rush lamp flickering in its wall niche, the stripes on her breasts were visible, and he traced them with his finger. "She beat you?" he said.

"I tried to fend her off, but she's a strong woman, Simeon. I couldn't. She obviously was expecting a great sum from the shamans were I to be trained as a priestess. She would have gotten nothing if they made a sacrifice of me. It would have been considered her duty to turn me over to them. So she gave me over to the eunuchs to make me one of the shamans' whores instead, for a price above gold. I didn't know there were such things. . . ."

"No one does. Well, almost no one. Gideon says that is the reason no one ever returns sane from Shamans' Mount." He took her measure again, his hard gaze lingering on the flimsy gown. "They didn't . . . touch you?" Why did she hesitate? Why were her eyes downcast? Something had happened, something of a sexual nature she feared her eyes would reveal. He was just about to challenge her when she spoke.

"Handmaidens took my kirtle and gave me this"—she flicked the skirt of her gown—"but the winged one took me off the Mount before they . . . before he, the shaman Seth, could do more than maul me. He had drunk much wine, and he was very angry."

"You haven't heard the last from him," Simeon warned her. "You must be very careful when we are apart. He will not let it end here, Megaleen."

She reached for him, and he swept her up in his arms and carried her into the chamber she had vacated. It wasn't a bedchamber, though a low couch draped with fur throws stood against one wall. Rush candles were set about. A jug of wine and two goblets were waiting on a table near a brazier, which was fitted with a chimney that exited through the roof of the cave. Live coals glowed in it, no doubt to chase the chill, for even in summer the nights were cool and damp in the Isles.

Something caught Simeon's eye at once. Neatly folded on a bench beside the couch lay the eel skin and cloak he'd left on the beach in his haste to return to Meg what seemed an eon ago for all that had happened since. Cold chills raised his hackles. It was almost as if Gideon knew he would come to reclaim them.

Setting Meg down, he slipped the gown from her shoulders and let it slide the length of her body to the floor until it puddled at her feet. How exquisite she was with her skin tinted golden in the brazier glow, her tawny erect nipples leaning against his hard-muscled chest. His hands rode up and down her sides, following the shape of her waist and thighs. She was without blemish, his golden mortal lover, and in that moment, there was no Shamans' Mount, and there was no threat of Seth looming over them. They were just two lovers answering the primeval call of passions that had existed since the dawn of time.

That their union was forbidden by both societies held no significance except to quicken desire. In the space of a heartbeat, he had taken her from spark to flame, and she had taken him to blazing inferno.

Seized by an unstoppable desire to know her totally, in a way he never had before, he gripped the globes of her ass, lifted her onto his bursting cock where they stood, and rushed her against the wall. Nothing would cool the fire in his loins but filling her—feeling her milk him dry to the very soul, like no other had ever done before or would again.

Drinking in her gasp, he ground his anxious pelvis against her, leaning into the golden pubic curls that so fascinated him. How soft they were, like eiderdown against his hardness, wet and slick with the dew of her arousal. He thrust deeper into her, reaching for a place he'd never touched, aching for release, yet holding back to make the climax sweeter for them both.

"Do not come yet," he whispered against her hair. "Wait . . . Let me give you this . . . Let me show you what can be. . . ."

He covered her mouth with his own, his tongue reaching, touching hers as it responded, his cock so swollen he feared it would split her in two as he pounded into her with shuddering thrusts between spiraling withdrawals that almost took him out of her. He teased her erect bud with each grinding, twisting plunge.

The sucking sounds of their passion nearly drove him mad. He could see her ecstasy in her hooded eyes that reverenced him. This is what he wanted, to see her come, not just to feel her release, but to see the desire in her eyes, to watch them dilate for him—to feel the tug as her vagina gripped his cock and sucked him dry.

But not yet . . .

Her groan resonated in his body as he stopped midstroke. Pulling halfway out of her, he rotated his pelvis in slow, deepening revolutions as her sex gripped him. Never taking his shuttered eyes from her flushed face, he gloried in the blackness of her eyes, so dark he could see no trace of their shimmering blue. They were glazed with the mindless oblivion of coming, distant in the grip of rapture—rapture he had given her. This is what he longed to see—the very moment when she gave herself up to him. It was close.

"Hold me ..." he murmured. "Tighter, my Megaleen!"

She was already gripping him so hard the pain of her fingernails denting the flesh of his back was riveting. He sucked in his breath. He'd hoped the pain would stall his climax, but instead it threatened to bring him off too soon. Her body heat scorched his flesh. The musk rising from their coupling rushed up his nostrils as her wetness leaked out of her. His thighs were slippery with her precious juices, and he groaned. Pulling out of her, he dropped to his knees and drank, laving her bud until she leaned into the pressure of his tongue, writhing against it.

But still not yet ...

Surging to his full height, he lifted her onto his erection again and plunged into her, crying out as her sex seized his cock. This time, she would not let it go.

"I ... can bear ... no more," she sobbed, tears streaming down. "Now ... I beg you ... *now* ...!"

Her words were the charm, or the curse. He wasn't sure which. Her nipples boring into his rock-hard chest were so hard that their pressure was painful. He looked down, watching his shaft glide in and out of her, then shifted his gaze to the ecstasy in her dilated eyes with their lids, like shutters, closed halfway in mindless bliss. She groaned with each pistoning thrust. An involuntary mantra leaked out on her sweet breath. It spilled from her lungs with the shuddering vibrations of her climax as her contractions seized his cock and sucked him dry of every last pearly drop.

Simeon eased her down on the couch. Their bodies were glowing with sweat, and he wrapped the fur throw about her and pulled her into his arms. "There is so much I want ... no, *need* to show you," he murmured in her ear. "So many delights."

"Where will we go?" Meg said. "We cannot stay here in this dark place."

"No, we cannot. I have made a place below the waves—"

Meg shook her head adamantly. "I have been below the waves," she said. "What of your concubines? They will expect things to continue as they have been. If they do not, those dreadful sea cows will kill me! And I do not want things to continue as they were. I want you all to myself. I am not a selkie. I was not made to share. Mortals are made to love and be loved by one man. It would have been better had they made me a sacrifice, I—"

His kiss cut off her words. Threading his fingers through the silk of her hair, he drew her closer. "The consorts are over," he said, peppering her skin with salty kisses, legacy of her tears upon his lips. "They have been banished." An insatiable hunger overwhelmed him. He marveled that it came upon him so soon after such a heart-stopping climax. All at once he was ravenous again, his cock humming to life between them. It would have to wait. It was too soon—much too soon. Abstinence was the key to the perfection he was seeking. The longer they abstained, the greater the orgasm would be. But how could he keep his hands from fondling her? How could he convince his traitorous cock to wait when every fiber in his selkie being demanded consummation?

"And then there is the matter of my breathing underwater," Meg went on. "I thought I was dying when they forced my head beneath the water, Simeon. I cannot begin to describe to you the feeling, since you have never known it. It is frightening! Water rushes into the throat. It blocks the breathing passage and no air comes through. The more you try to breathe, the more water floods your throat and lungs. You fight, but it is useless. You know you are about to die so . . . horribly! I cannot live with the fear of that happening to me again."

"That is the only obstacle left," Simeon said. "And there is a solution. It calls for sorcery. There is one who can help with this. I have only to consult her. We shall go there now—together. All will be well, you will see. With the help of the Waterwitch, we can have both worlds, Megaleen. The night is warm. We shall bathe in the bay first. Come. . . ."

Maybe a plunge in the bay would tame his member. He almost groaned. That was myth. Water always heightened his sexual experience, and why wouldn't it? He was Lord of the Deep, after all, and that was all part of his legacy.

Surging to his feet, he took her hand, pulling her up alongside, and picked up her dress. A good plunge in the surf would probably shred the flimsy gown. No matter. He would fetch her something more befitting royalty that ruled beneath the waves. The sight of that frock, knowing that Seth and the gods only knew who else had seen her body through it, set his teeth on edge.

Snatching his eel skin and cloak from the bench, he looped them over his arm with her gown, took her hand, and led her out of Gideon's cave and through the marshes to the stretch of black volcanic sand that served as a beach. Tossing their clothing down on high ground, he led her into the water, where they bathed each other, washing each other's genitals in the sighing surf.

But his hands lingered a little too long upon her pubic curls and strayed too quickly to her erect nipples, which begged to be cooled in the brine, to be stroked and strummed and laved as the waves washed over them. And her tiny fingers played too skillfully upon his cock, paying too much attention to the mushroom tip, ridged and hard despite the shock of cold water caressing it.

So much for the martyrdom of abstinence.

Simeon was in his element now—water. It empowered him—fed him—took him to its breast for comfort. Here was his mistress—his consort—his whore. Here was Meg's rival—

the sea. And it was a jealous rival, which he realized the minute he dove beneath the waves.

Diving down through the sheer translucent curl of an oncoming comber frothed with white, Simeon took a deep breath just as he always did, when he filled his lungs underwater. But this time he could not breathe. All that Megaleen had described of drowning he felt now—the terror, the panic, the utter hopelessness of suffocation. He thrashed and flailed and strove to break the waves above his head.

Vertigo starred his vision. Could he be drowning? There was no light in the water, no phosphorescence, only the veil of deepest darkness that accompanies death.

Then, he remembered!

---

## 11

Meg dove beneath the waves as Simeon struggled toward the surface. To her horror, she realized he couldn't breathe. He was drowning! How could this be? They broke the surface together. Simeon crawled out of the surf and collapsed, coughing and sputtering, on the beach. Stunned, Meg stood with both hands over her mouth, watching him struggle to right himself in the wake of the high-rising tide. All she could think of was what a beautiful creature he was, lying in the water he loved, his wet skin gleaming in the moonlight. It was as if the reflection of the low-sliding moon on the breast of the water had formed a shimmering arrow pointing straight toward him. It was an eerie sight made more so because the water he loved—that was his life force—had nearly killed him. Why?

Meg knelt beside him. After a moment, he righted himself on one elbow and gazed into her eyes. The devastated look in them brought tears to her own. "Is this . . . what you felt when you couldn't breathe . . . in the water?" he said, his broad chest heaving as he gulped the salty air. "Is this what . . . *drowning* is?"

Meg nodded, taking him in her arms. She couldn't bear the

horror in his face—the devastation. "What happened?" she sobbed. "How is it possible, this?"

Simeon scrambled to his feet and staggered to where he'd dropped their clothes earlier. Snatching up her gown, he thrust it toward her. "Put this on," he said. "There is no time to lose."

"What is it, Simeon? Please . . . You're scaring me."

"I'm not certain," he said, tugging on his eel skin suit. "Just pray to your gods that it isn't too late."

"Too late for what?" Meg shrilled.

"As far as I know, there is only one thing that could cause what just happened to me beneath the waves. I was so anxious over you that I left my sealskin on the beach on the Isle of Mists. I buried it, but if someone saw me . . ."

"Oh, Simeon! What does it mean?"

"You know what it means. If my sealskin has been taken, I am bound to the land. I can swim in the water, but I cannot breathe beneath the waves . . . like what just occurred." He cupped his hands around his mouth and hummed a mantra that moved her back apace.

"What do you do?" she said, holding her ears, for it was deafening—so shrill the sound waves could almost be seen vibrating in the air.

"I've called Elicorn," he said. "I must return to the Isle. I cannot swim the distance above the waves—neither can you— and I do not intend to let you out of my sight. I can only hope that rebellious waterhorse is repentant enough to help us. His treachery put me at a great disadvantage when I went to prepare the Pavilion for us."

"Pavilion?"

"It is a place where we might have been safe. There is much I need to tell you, and I will on the way. I only pray I still have power enough to command Elicorn."

"Well, *I* certainly do not!" Meg said. "And if you do not, that horse will drown us both!"

"Did you tell anyone we were to meet at the cove at midnight?" Simeon asked.

Meg gasped. "*Aunt Adelia!*" she cried. "She wanted to be rid of me. I thought if she knew I was going away with you she would let me go. I didn't know there was such a sum involved . . . that she hadn't taken me in out of the kindness of her heart. She is my father's sister! We are blood kin, Simeon."

"Gold turns mortals into madmen, Megaleen. We have no such corruption below the waves to tempt the dwellers of the deep."

Simeon cupped his mouth and hummed the mantra again. Twice—three times more he sent out the vibration before the surf took on the shape of the regal white waterhorse prancing ashore amid the crashing foam.

Simeon reached to snatch his cloak from the sand, but Meg's quick hand arrested him. "Wait, there is a rider," she said, backing away from the prancing white stallion coming to shore with the surf. A man on its back bore a definite resemblance to Simeon, though he was older, with angular features more closely resembling those of mortals than the sleek, finely chiseled bone structure of the selkie.

Simeon strode toward the horse, which pawed the ground with unshod hoofs. Meg's quick intake of breath seemed to go unnoticed. Despite that Elicorn had nearly killed her, she was bewitched by his beauty. But then, that was part of a waterhorse's charm, for like the selkie masters they served, horses like Elicorn were skilled seducers.

Simeon had accepted the rider, and Meg ranged herself a little closer. Though he was speaking with Simeon, the man hadn't taken his eyes off her since he came ashore. Those dark eyes, not unlike Simeon's, raked her familiarly. And why wouldn't they, she realized, glancing down at the scanty excuse for a frock barely clinging to her breasts. The fingers of a blush crawled up her cheeks. She was half naked in front of a stranger, and there was no way for her to redeem herself.

Simeon strolled closer and took her arm. "Megaleen, my half brother Vega," he introduced, as Vega sketched a graceful bow mounted as he was. "Not all of my powers have been stripped so it seems if my call has brought him."

"It wasn't your call, Simeon," Vega said. "Your summoner saw what happened and came after me. That swordfish is a loyal subject. He is never far from you in case you have need of him. I wonder if you realize that."

"Elicorn didn't hear my call?"

Vega shook his head. "No," he said. "Elicorn follows the waves. They are running high on the Dark Isle tonight. I intercepted him just in time with *my* call, or he would have drowned the both of you. What has happened here?"

"I do not know," Simeon said. "I left my sealskin on the Isle of Mists. I buried it, but . . . Someone must have found it for this to be. I need to go there to solve this."

"Then, we go!" Vega said, extending his hand toward Meg.

Simeon wrapped his cloak about her and handed her up to Vega, who settled her in front of him. There was no bridle or reins, and sitting sideways instead of astride, she could only fist one hand in the animal's mane, though she was secure enough trapped between Vega's strong arms. Simeon swung himself up behind, and Vega kneed the horse toward the surf.

Meg marveled that they all fit on the animal's back so comfortably, but that was one of the traits of a waterhorse: it was able to stretch its body to accommodate many riders if needs must, for often such an animal would frolic along the strand seducing many before plunging back into the water. The waves were running high, and they traveled against them, but Elicorn leaped over the swells as if they were hurdles on a fairgrounds course.

The Isle of Mists was hidden from view beneath a heavy predawn fog. Meg was glad of it. The last thing she wanted to do was set foot back on that island, so it was decided that Vega would stay astride Elicorn with her at the water's edge, while Simeon went to the cove in search of his sealskin. Something other than the obvious was wrong—something Simeon hadn't confided; she saw it in Vega's eyes.

"This is all my fault," Meg said, forlorn.

"Do not reproach yourself," Vega responded. "If we are to point a finger, my impetuous brother is hardly exempt from blame." He swept his arm wide toward Simeon climbing the dune ahead, visible only in glimpses through the fog blanket. "His mind is no less clouded than this Isle, though with the fog of love. He never would have left that skin here otherwise."

"I never should have told my aunt I was meeting Simeon here at midnight. What will happen if she has taken the skin?"

Vega hesitated. When he spoke, an audible breath preceded his words, riddling her with chills. It did not bode well. "Let's not borrow trouble," he said. "It's lent us enough as it is." Squaring his posture, he made a bold attempt to change the subject. "You are even more beautiful in close proximity than you were viewed from afar," he said silkily.

Meg stiffened against him, and he laughed. "You have naught to fear from me in that regard," he said. "I would never dream of interfering in my brother's . . . affairs. I simply make the observation. It is meant as a compliment and to put you at ease alone in my presence. I see it has had the opposite effect. I am sorry for that."

Meg relaxed somewhat. Was she always to be subjected to the lust of men? She'd seen the same hungry look in Gideon's eyes as well, though he'd never put his obvious thoughts into words. And then there was Seth, the lecherous shaman, which in itself was a mockery, since as far as she knew, shamans were supposed to be above the lure of lust. That myth had been shattered on Shamans' Mount.

Vega seemed a likeable fellow, and he had a pleasing countenance, though there was something . . . different about him that she couldn't help being curious about. "You do not look like a . . . a . . ."

"A selkie?" he concluded for her. "I am what your kind calls a 'half-breed,' My mother was mortal, like you. My father was a full-blooded selkie. He was Simeon's father also, though we do not speak about that for his memory's sake . . . and my safety. Selkie half-breeds are shunned." Meg's jaw dropped as she imagined it. "I've shocked you," Vega said through a chuckle. "That was eons ago. What? Did you think you and Simeon were unique in your . . . association? Much of that sort of thing goes on still, and will till the end of time . . . as long as beauties like you walk the land. Now, if I had seen you first . . . But I did not, so I will stay in my place."

The last was meant to be spoken in jest, though considering her past experiences, Meg found no humor in it, and now he'd said something that disturbed her. "Surely you don't mean 'eons'—not literally?"

Vega nodded.

"H-how long does a selkie live, then? You look no older than forty summers. Why, if that were so, it would mean that selikes are . . . *immortal.*"

"They are," Vega said. "You did not know that?"

"N-no, I never thought . . . I mean, I never stopped to consider . . . But you speak of your father in the past tense. How is that, if Selkies are immortal?"

"There are exceptions, of course," Vega said. "My father was murdered—bludgeoned to death for his pelt on the barrier beach that runs along the mainland below the islands. Ruthless mortals do this to have the pelts to wear upon their bodies. It still occurs today, and when it does, the selkies rise up and bring the storms—fearsome maelstroms that rape the land and wipe out whole islands. There were thousands of isles in this archipelago stretching far out to sea, some as close as stepping stones, when the gods formed the world. There are scarcely fifty remaining. Soon there will be none. They will all have been washed away by the selkies' revenge upon mortal avarice."

Meg was stunned numb. She was afraid to hear more, yet she hung on every word as Vega walked the waterhorse along the edge of the surf, telling his tale. "In spite of the risk of such a death, selkies brave the mortal isles," Vega went on. "It is in our nature to fraternize with mortals. We are a trusting sort. It is inconceivable to us—despite the carnage—that man could do such beastly things to such gentle creatures that mean them no harm. We hope, and we are cautious, but still we come."

"You were not with them that first night under the full moon," she realized, thinking out loud. The reverie harkened back to the moment she first set eyes on Simeon coupling with his consort in the very surf they traveled now as they waited for him. She relived touching herself in the dark of her cottage loft as Simeon seemed to be performing for her eyes alone. She remembered the sight of him naked, driving his sex to the root into the female beneath him as the white surf laved them, lapping at their wet skin in the moonlight. How she'd wished she was the one underneath him, feeling his hard shaft moving inside her.

She saw again Simeon's climax, just as the waves climaxed and crashed on the shore—felt his triumph in the performance—remembered her own release as she played with the nipples she'd exposed beside the fogged windowpane. She relived rubbing the engorged bud beneath her pubic curls as she watched the selkies wild mating ritual. Her clitoris ached with the memory, and she longed to slip her hands inside the cloak and bring herself to climax again. It was a painful fantasy, for she dared not do it in front of the selkie half-breed. From the way he was gazing at her then, he had surely seen her need in the shuttered eyes that couldn't meet his. He had surely heard it in the hot breath leaking out of her in deep shudders. Squeezing her thighs together, she tried to still her need, but that didn't work either. How was it that the mere thought of Simeon—a brief glimpse of her mind's eye—could bring her to a full arousal when she'd come so soon from fulfillment in his arms? He had bewitched her. There was no other explanation.

No, Vega wasn't with them that night beneath the moon. She would have remembered him if he had been, with his different looks and half-mortal bearing.

"I do not run with the herd," he said, in answer to her statement. "Though well I could; my selkie blood allows me. I am privileged with the best of both species you see. But someone must remain behind to pick up the pieces when disaster comes—to warn and care for the others. This is my function, and I am comfortable with it."

"It sounds like a lonely existence to me," Meg said sadly.

"Not at all . . . until I have occasion to encounter one such as you and am reminded of what I've missed. I have lived a long time, Megaleen."

"H-how long a time . . . exactly?" she said. She needed to know, yet she feared the knowledge with every fiber of her being.

"I was born more than three eras ago," he said. "Simeon came later, just before our father met his death."

Meg swallowed dry. She was afraid to ask her next question, though she knew she must. "And your mother?" she said. "What became of her?"

"Simeon's mother was my father's mate," he said. "Her name was Meriwyn. He was with her 'til he died. My mother was called Glenda. She was from the mainland. Father loved Glenda as well, as only a selkie can love—with a passion that consumes, but not enough to give up his immortality for her. No one knows what became of her, except that she seems to have faded into the mists of time. She disappeared before he died. I never knew her. I was raised at the palace. My father may have never acknowledged me openly, but neither did he turn his back upon me. And when Simeon was born, I was made his protector."

"H-his . . . *immortality?*" Meg said, having heard little past that. Her voice was no more than a hoarse whisper.

Vega nodded. "That is the other exception," he said. "Once a selkie gives up his sealskin, he loses his immortality. He will age like a mortal man, and at the end of his days, he will die as a mortal man also. Surely you have seen selkies seduced by mortals who stole their skins and are forced to live upon the land— men and women both. They are quite content to do so, while separated from their skin, but the moment it is returned to them, they go back to the sea that spawned them, leaving everything and everyone on land behind."

He spoke the truth. Meg had seen such on the mainland, selkies who had surrendered to their passion to possess a mortal mate. She had also seen both selkie men and women return to the sea the minute their sealskins were returned to them. She groaned in spite of herself. All at once she felt as if a fist had seized her heart and was squeezing the life out of it. She could scarcely breathe. Had she cost Simeon his immortality? Had she inadvertently condemned him to a life upon the land— taken the one thing he loved most from him—the sea? How could she ever bear it?

"If Simeon's sealskin has been taken . . . There must be something to be done," she pleaded. "He would whither and die without the sea he loves so."

"If such is the case, we will have it back," Vega said. "There is no cause for alarm. All will be put right."

But it wouldn't be put right, not if her aunt had a hand in it.

For all she knew, Adelia had consigned the sealskin to the flames in the old wood stove in the cottage kitchen.

"But if it cannot be had back . . . there is a way . . ." Meg pleaded. "There *has* to be!"

"If there is, the Waterwitch will know of it," Vega said. "Look here, we do not know yet if his sealskin has been taken. Let us wait until Simeon returns before we worry. It does no good to agonize for naught."

But if Adelia had a hand in this treachery, it wasn't likely that Simeon would return. Vega didn't know the depths of her aunt's treachery the way she did. Given that, there wasn't a moment to lose, and she leapt from the waterhorse's back and ran off through the fog toward the cottage.

# 12

Leaving Vega behind, Meg raced along the strand through the fog, for she would have known the way if she were blind, she had traveled that lonely beach so many times since she'd come to the Isle. From a distance, she saw Simeon clawing at the sand beneath the rearing head of the dune where they were to meet at midnight. Just as she'd feared, it was gone, but he didn't stop clawing—flinging wet sand skyward in total aberration—until he'd torn up the dune to the tufts of beach grass that crowned it.

The fog covered him suddenly, and she slowed her pace. Other feet were treading the strand. She could feel the vibrations through the soles of her bare feet. Then there came a sound—a dull thud followed by a groan—and then the ground shook as though something had hit it hard. Meg darted behind a low dune. Her heart rose in her throat, and she opened her mouth to call out, but a hand clamped over it reduced her cry to a stifled snort.

"You can do nothing," a familiar voice whispered in her ear.

It was Vega.

She struggled in his arms, and he pulled her hard against him, tightening his grip upon her mouth. "If you are seen now, they will take you, too. Make no sound. We will have him back another way."

Meg turned her head, casting daggers at him. No mean task, for he held her in a viselike grip. The sky was lightening. Vega's eyes glowed with the first bloodred rays of dawn. They were hard and immutable—his angular jaw set as he shook his head slowly.

"He will flay the skin off my body if harm comes to you, Megaleen," he whispered. "You must let us settle this. We selkies have our ways."

Meg relaxed in his grip. He had by no means convinced her, but she would never escape him while he held her thus. The fog was lifting and shapes were emerging. She picked out Adelia, shovel in hand, standing over Simeon's inert body. She had evidently struck him from behind. The eunuch that had carried her off to Shamans' Mount hefted Simeon over his shoulder, and there was another still hidden in the fog, which was tinted pink in the fiery sunrise—a harbinger of a storm on the way. Slowly the fog drifted inland, and the other's image became clear. It was a tall, muscular man, wearing a flowing black *cotehardie*. Simeon's sealskin was draped over his arm. It was the shaman, Seth, putting coins into Adelia's outstretched hand.

They were taking Simeon to the Mount! How would the selkies have him back from there? The Mount was impregnable. It was her fault. If she hadn't told Adelia about their midnight rendezvous, none of this would be happening. Adelia would never have known where to look for the sealskin, and Simeon would not be draped limp over the hulking eunuch's broad shoulder as the man trudged up the dunes toward the jetty. It would be visible now at low tide, but only briefly. There wasn't a moment to lose.

Convinced that she would have a far better chance of stealing Simeon's sealskin back from inside the fortified Mount's walls, Meg sunk her teeth into the hand Vega still held over her mouth until she drew blood and shoved him with all her strength, putting him off balance as he let her go. Free at last, she ran up the dune screaming at the top of hr voice, waving her arms in wild circles that disbursed what remained of the fog like fleeing wraiths.

"Wait!" she shrilled. "Put him down! Let him go . . . it's me you want."

All three turned toward her.

"See?" Adelia cried out. "I told you he would be the bait to draw her, the little whore—just as the horsefeet draw the eels!"

"So you did, old woman," Seth said, seizing Meg's wrist. He jerked her to a standstill. "We have unfinished business, you and I," he said familiarly to Meg, wrenching her closer. His breath was fetid with mead, or some such strong drink, and mixed with onions and fouled stomach gasses. He stuck out his tongue and licked her face in one stroke from chin to forehead.

"So pay me—cross my palm!" Adelia said, holding out her hand.

"You have been paid, and handsomely."

"That was for the selkie's skin." She made a rough gesture to Simeon's unconscious form dangling from the eunuch's shoulder. "You never paid me yet for him."

"But I have paid you for *her*," Seth reminded her.

"Aye, the once," Adelia said, her sharp eyes flashing. " 'Tisn't my fault you couldn't hold onto the foolish chit long enough to diddle her. I've done twice the work, I'll collect twice the pay, if you please."

"Well, I do not please," Seth snarled, shoving Adelia out of the way with a hand planted firmly on her breast as he yanked Meg along. "The selkie is worth neither pittance nor pother as he is, except for a little entertainment I have in mind, and I soon tire of those dalliances. You've gotten all you'll get, so be off before I change my mind and take you, too." Adelia cowered then, and Seth laughed. "Have no fear, old woman. There's none on the Mount drunk or blind enough to cock a leg over you, but I could use another scullion in the kitchens."

"Please . . . I beg you, let the selkie go," Meg pleaded, digging in her heels. "You just said yourself he's worthless to you . . . *please* . . ."

"Oh, I never said that, girl," Seth responded. "I said I'll not pay for the piddling entertainment I'll get from him. Now that I think upon it, since I have you in the bargain, that little entertainment mightn't tire me so quickly after all. Stop that god-awful caterwauling! The jetty soon sinks below the waves, and there's much to be done before nightfall. 'Tis the solstice! And you've come just in time for the celebration."

As he dragged her off toward the jetty through the last traces of a ground-creeping mist, Meg didn't need to turn to know Vega's eyes were boring into her. He would not interfere. He was outnumbered. He would follow to see where his brother was being taken, she had no doubt, but he would not act alone. She was counting upon that. There needed to be someone out there who knew where they'd been taken; someone they could trust. She was convinced that as long as she and Simeon were together, and the sealskin was in close proximity, there was hope for her to right the wrong she'd done him.

With Adelia's curses ringing in her ears, Meg stumbled across the jetty tethered to Seth just as the tide began to turn. The narrow bridge of stacked stones was slippery with algae beneath her bare feet, and more than once she would have fallen in the churning water if Seth hadn't had a good grip on her arm, dragging her along. Her eyes were upon Simeon, still unconscious, hanging limp over the eunuch's broad shoulder. Once inside the compound, they parted company. The eunuch carried Simeon off toward the rear of the fortress, while Seth steered her inside the round tower, where she had been held before. Hanging back, Meg followed the eunuch with her eyes until he'd carried Simeon around the corner of the fortress's curtain wall and disappeared.

"What?" Seth said around a lewd chuckle. "Did you imagine you two would be housed together?"

Actually, she had. In her naïveté, it never occurred to her that they might be separated. It didn't matter. They were both in the same place, and she would find him no matter how she had to do it. Meanwhile, she was still within sight of the seal-skin.

He did not take her below to the subterranean bath like she thought he would, considering the tattered and disheveled state she was in. He spun her into a chamber on the second level of the tower instead and shut the door behind them. Backing her up against the wall, he tossed down the sealskin. Removing her cloak, he fondled her through the gown beneath, then slid what remained of it over her shoulders, exposing her breasts to his gaze.

He licked his lips. "We have unfinished business," he said, close in her face. "But not yet. I smell him on you, your selkie whoremaster. First we remedy that."

He reeled her toward an elevated canopied bed and sat her down on the edge of it. From the look in his eyes, Meg was certain he was going to fall upon her there, but he did not. Instead, he filled two goblets with wine from a decanter on a small table beside the bed and handed one to her.

"I'm not thirsty," she snapped at him. It was a lie. She was parched, but she wouldn't give him the satisfaction.

"Nor am I," the shaman said, crimping her fingers around the goblet. "This is not for thirst; it's for relaxing, to prepare you for my . . . entertainment. 'Tisn't poisoned. I'm drinking it." He took a rough swallow. "See? I haven't withered and died. Take a sip. I think you will be quite pleased with the entertainment I have in mind . . . at least with part of it. Go ahead—drink! I will stand here until you do, so you may as well humor me."

Meg took a swallow. It was nut-sweet and rich. She took a second swallow. The warmth of it sliding down was pleasantly evocative, the flavor like none she'd ever tasted. It went straight to her sex, igniting a fire at her very core. What had he given her? She longed for more, but dared not take it. It took all the willpower she possessed to set the goblet aside on the table beside her.

Seth drained his to the dregs, crossed to the wardrobe, and took out an indigo kirtle. It was cut low at the neck, with a tucked yoke, and was only semitransparent—quite pristine compared to the tattered rag that revealed her charms now. She snatched it from him.

"Not yet," he said. "This is for after you've been purged of the stink of your selkie lover. Finish that wine; I will return presently."

Striding to the door, the shaman quit the chamber, locking her inside. Meg fell back against the eiderdown counterpane. The silk felt cool against her flushed skin. Had the wine done that? It must have. Lulled by what she'd drunk, by the pleasantly erotic sensations it had ignited at the epicenter of her sex, Meg began to drift off when something struck her like a lightning bolt, and she vaulted upright in the bed. What had happened to the sealskin? The shaman didn't have it with him when he left her.

Meg shook her head in a vain effort to chase the cobwebs from her fogged brain. He'd had the sealskin when they entered the chamber, but he'd tossed it down when he backed her against the wall. It wasn't where he'd dropped it now. He hadn't left the room, and he didn't have it when he locked her in. It had to be somewhere nearby, but where?

Her gaze fell upon the indigo kirtle he'd taken from the wardrobe. *The wardrobe!* Of course, it had to be. Could Seth be so complacent that he'd simply tossed it in the wardrobe and forgotten it? No doubt he thought the influences of whatever was in the wine would keep her subdued in one way and aroused in another. She had to know.

Swinging her legs over the side of the elevated bed, she inched to the edge until her feet touched the platform it stood upon. Her head was swimming. It reminded her of gliding beneath the waves. Just rising to her feet was a mammoth effort, and she had to hold onto the bedpost and opulent curtains for support, at that. The room reeled around her. Why wouldn't it hold still? The wardrobe was only a few feet away, yet it seemed like an unreachable distance. Meanwhile, her loins were on fire. What would have happened if she'd drunk the whole goblet dry? Two swallows and she could barely stand.

Stepping off the platform, she stumbled and fell to the floor. Trying to right herself while tangled in the gown that was barely clinging to her body was impossible. She tried and failed. Time meant nothing then. She would have to stay as she lay, lulled by the gentle lapping of the surf. It seemed to go on forever. Water washed over her in waves. Hot steam rose from it all around her. But this wasn't the sea. The water felt like silk caressing her body. The smoky scent of hazelnuts drifted from it teasing her nostrils. This wasn't a dream! She stiffened, and her eyes snapped open, but to blackness. She groped her face. She was wearing a blindfold, and there was water. She was sitting in it in some sort of elaborate tub, she discovered as her hands flitted over the fluted edge of it.

Someone grabbed he wrists. "Don't!" a hoarse voice whispered.

"What now?" Seth's voice boomed from somewhere nearby. "Get on with it or I shall do it myself!"

Meg heard the sound of wine being poured and the gluttonous sounds of drinking. Seth was filling and refilling his goblet. That struck terror in her heart. Whatever was in the wine obviously aroused whoever drank it. Judging from the amount he'd consumed, Seth would soon be as randy as a ram in rut.

He meant to revenge himself upon her for attacking his private parts by the scrying pool. Someone else's hands were upon her now; large, strong hands. They seemed gentle enough, but she was trembling in fear. It was the blindfold. Why was she wearing a blindfold? She prayed it was a nightmare brought on by the wine, but she knew it wasn't. It as too real; Seth's snorting was too sinister. It was really happening!

The water in the tub didn't reach her nipples. When a hand touched her shoulder, she cried out in spite of her resolve to keep silent.

"Do not move," the whisper came again. She could barely hear it for her thrashing. There was another sound now. It sounded like a chain rattling, and the tub nearly tipped over.

"I told you . . . Do not speak to the whore!" Seth bellowed, his words slurred with drunkenness. "And hurry up. My cock is ready for her. . . ."

More clanking followed, and the tub jiggled as though someone were using it for support. Meg could bear no more. She reached for the blindfold, and the same hand that arrested her before did so again. This time more firmly, though he did not speak.

"Lift that mask and I will have her as she is!" Seth's rowdy voice bellowed.

Meg's hand fell back into the water, and the gentle hand began to rub her shoulder with something that smelled of herbs and hazelnuts—soap. It was *soap*! He was bathing her. As bizarre as it was, she relaxed somewhat. Perhaps it was his touch. It must be one of the eunuchs, and Seth was watching. When his hand approached her breasts, she quickly covered her nipples, but her bather swept her hands away.

"That's right," Seth said through another rough swallow. "Do the teats. I want to see you make them hard."

The bather's deft fingers began soaping the areola around Meg's nipples in slow concentric circles without touching the hardening buds, and she knew. He wanted her to know and not fear him. *I was Simeon.* In spite of herself, Meg gasped. She wanted to reach out and clasp him to her. She reached out to touch him, for reassurance, though she did so with a groping motion so the gesture wouldn't be obvious. Instead of her trembling fingers touching flesh, they grazed cold iron. There was a heavy chain around his neck, and she drew back her hand as if she'd touched live coals and gasped again.

"Sh!" Simeon warned under the umbrella of a sigh.

"Eh?" Seth grunted. "Hurry up, I say! Enough of that. Do her tips . . ."

It was all clear now. They had Simeon in chains, and Seth was making him ready her for sex. Water was a conduit for Simeon. She could feel the ripples of his tension flowing through the bathwater. His rage was like a living entity. It was almost as if it had its own corporeal substance. She could hear it in his breathing and feel it in his touch. It vibrated in the very air around her. Was he stalling in hopes Seth would succumb to the strong drink, biding his time for the right moment to carry out whatever she prayed he was planning? His touch was like a lightning strike then, and she could only pray whatever passion moved him now would not fall upon her later.

Meanwhile, his touch was arousing her. His deft fingers rubbing her nipples sent shock waves though her body that shot through her loins like liquid fire. She longed to hold his hands to her breasts, but she dared not. When Seth's voice broke the awful silence again, she lurched as if she'd been struck.

"Enough! Do her down below!" he commanded.

Simeon's hand glided between her legs, slathering her pubic curls with the soap. Meg spread her legs as wide as the tub would allow. The metal sides were cold against her skin. She scarcely felt it. Her heart was hammering so hard in her breast it made little ripples in the water. Simeon had brought her sex to life as only he could, and she bit into her lower lip until she drew blood rather than let Seth see it.

"Not like that," the shaman drawled. "Stand her up so I can see. Or would you like me to help you?"

Simeon raised her to her feet so quickly water sloshed over the sides of the tub and onto the floor. She heard the chair Seth was sitting in creak with his weight as he left it, then heard it creak again, much to her relief, as he sank back into it.

"That's better," the shaman said. "Continue."

Meg stood while Simeon soaped her. She felt the lather slide down her body, heard it drip into the water. Why was he using so much soap? The water was so slick with it she had all she could do to keep her footing in the tub as he continued to lather her, rubbing his hands over her body, over her breasts, her hips and thighs, and the V between. Parting her nether lips, he exposed her nub, scraping it on both sides with light, teasing strokes, while he continued to lather her with the other hand. His fingers spread her slit and inserted something inside her. It took her a moment to identify it. Lathering had reduced the soap to a cylinder, and he moved it in and out of her creating more lather.

Meg could stand no more. Waves of drenching heat ripped through her loins like firebrands. Her hips jerked forward, and he replaced the soap with his fingers, plunging deep into her as her sex grabbed them. In spite of herself, Meg groaned as the climax riddled her with wave upon wave of spine-tingling sensation.

"Stop!" Seth thundered. "You were not to make her come!"

The chair the shaman vacated tipped over as the lumbered toward the tub. Meg ripped off the blindfold just as Simeon lifted her out of the water and set her down behind him. "Stay back!" he commanded, waiting until Seth had staggered within range of his tether before upturning the tub in the shaman's path.

Hot soapy water flooded the floor beneath the shaman's bare feet. He was naked and aroused beneath the flowing black *cote-hardie*, just as he had been in the subterranean bath when Meg first set eyes upon him. Her suspicions were correct. The shaman's *entertainment* had been to have Simeon bring her to the point of climax and then he would have his way with her.

The rage in Simeon's eyes made her turn hers away as he hefted the tub and heaved it at Seth as he approached. It was a heavy brass and enamel piece. Where Simeon had summoned the strength from to lift it, Meg couldn't fathom. She had heard selkies possessed superhuman strength, but she never imagined anything like this.

Seth was already floundering, slip-sliding in the lather underfoot when the tub hit him squarely in the chest. Simeon had waited until the shaman was close enough to seize. Fisting his hands in the shaman's hair, he drove Seth's head into the leg of the upturned tub until blood gushed from the wound and he'd rendered Seth unconscious. Then he threw the shaman down in the puddle of slippery water that had been the shaman's undoing and turned to Meg.

"Quickly," he said, "the key"—he rattled the chain fastened to an iron collar about his neck—"on his chatelaine—there, with his clothes on that bench by the door. *Now*, Megaleen, before someone comes. That racket may well have been heard."

Meg sprang into action, skirting the sudsy water gingerly, and snatched the shaman's chatelaine from the bench. Her hands trembled as she tried first one key and then another until she found the one that sprung the lock in the collar.

Simeon tore it off and took her in his arms. "Has he harmed you?" he said.

Meg couldn't speak. She shook her head that he had not and clung to Simeon until he held her away. "He is unconscious, not dead," Simeon said. "He will soon come 'round. We must put as much distance between us as possible before that oc-

curs." He nodded toward what looked like as trunk in the corner. "Put your frock on—hurry!" he charged.

The bottle-green gauze gown, her cloak, as well as the indigo
frock Seth had provided lay draped across the trunk, and she
wriggled into the latter, while Simeon hauled Seth's hulking
inert form alongside the tub and fastened the iron collar around
the shaman's bullish neck.

Seizing her arm, Simeon propelled her toward the door, but
she hung back. "Wait!" she cried, "Your sealskin. It's in the
wardrobe, Simeon!"

He stared. "What wardrobe?" he said, clearly nonplused.

Meg spun around and pointed. "That wardrobe there—in
the cor—"

But there was no wardrobe. The light was fading, and still
dazed from the drugged wine, it wasn't until that moment that
she realized with sinking heart that they were in a different
chamber.

---

## 13

"Never mind, we'll find the skin," Simeon said, leading Meg into the darkened corridor. "What ever possessed you to do this? It wasn't me they wanted, it was *you,* and you played right into their hands."

"But they had you and your sealskin," Meg defended. "I thought as long as we—and it—were together, there would be hope of righting the wrong I've done you."

"You've done me no wrong. I never should have left the skin behind. Enough! That's done. What we need to do now is concentrate on getting the skin and getting out of here while Seth is . . . detained. He won't stay that way for long. I'm counting on the solstice celebration to buy us some time. They've already lit the bonfire in the clearing. I can smell the smoke. They were building it when they brought me here earlier. There will be revelry, drinking, and dancing. Hopefully the others will be occupied at that long enough for us to be about our business undetected. They knew Seth meant to have you. I doubt they will disturb him for a while at least. Do you know the way back to the chamber where you saw that wardrobe?"

"It was in the round tower," Meg said. "The second level, I think . . . or the third. I was so frightened for you . . . trying to see where they were taking you, I didn't pay attention. I thought he would take me back to the subterranean chamber where I was held before, but he didn't."

"It seems we are at cross purposes then. Do you know how to get back to the round tower?"

Meg shook her head. "No," she said, "they carried me here unconscious. Whatever was in that wine had its way with me."

"Unless we find my sealskin, we will never get off the Mount," Simeon said. He didn't want to frighten her, but he needed to prepare her for what they were facing. "And we cannot count upon Gideon this time. He will not risk his wings near that fire. By the time it has burned out at dawn, they will have found Seth, and there aren't many places on this accursed isle where we could hide."

"Simeon . . . you cannot breathe under water without your sealskin, but you can breathe in the palace. It's where you live in human form under the waves. Are there other ledges where air pockets exist that you might be safe until we solve this? Because there is a rock pool near the clearing, you could—"

"No," he interrupted her. "I would have to leave you behind, and that I will not do. My breath in your nostrils will not protect you now, and you would never reach the palace without it . . . neither would I, as I am. We selkies are not nearly as skilled in the water without the protection of our skins as we are when in possession of them."

"What about the Pavilion?"

He shook his head. They had reached a turn in the corridor and he flattened her against the wall in the shadows, making certain the hallway was empty before going farther. "It would be perfect, but it is much too far to go as we are," he said, leading her along the corridor again. There was a bend approaching, and he slowed his pace. "We will never find your round tower from inside. This way leads to the courtyard. We will have to chance it. The sun has set. Pull that hood close about your face. If I can find a cloak or a domino to wear, like the others I've seen costumed for the festivities, we will be able to move among them . . . But first, the round tower."

"Suppose it is locked," Meg said.

Simeon laughed. "These rarely lock their doors. They are too complacent. They do not think anyone can storm their bastions. Was the tower door locked when Seth took you inside?"

"Well, no, but—"

"Chances are it won't be locked now, either," Simeon interrupted her. "Walk softly and stay behind me. I may have lost my sea powers, but my strength is still unaltered. Let us hope I do not have to use it, for it will deplete each time I do."

There was no one in the halls. Presuming everyone to be outside for the celebration, Simeon moved Meg boldly through the shadows. How could he tell her he wasn't going to leave the Mount without his sealskin? It was chillingly plain that she had to leave no matter what. Seth had nearly taken Meg down. They would make a whore of her if she remained on the Mount. He had seen the look in Seth's eyes watching him bathe her. The shaman's lust was obsessive. It went beyond desire. There was a fiendish shadow of vengeance in Seth's bearing. Simeon shuddered to remember it. He would have been a captive audience to rape of the woman he loved—yes, *loved,* he finally admitted—but for quick thinking and the wine that Seth had drunk. No, she had to leave the Mount. If he knew nothing else, he knew that.

Another thought rushed at him as he traveled those dark empty halls. Had he lost his immortality when he lost his sealskin? He had no way of knowing. That he hadn't lost his extraordinary strength was cause for hope that he hadn't, and he had to cling to that. But deep down, as he looked into the soulful blue eyes that reverenced him, into the purity of her soul that

lived for him alone, he knew no matter what occurred, he could
not bear to lose her.

The moon shone down through scudding clouds that had all
but swallowed the stars, when they stepped out into the courtyard. He'd read the weather signs at dawn, when the sun rose
bloodred. A squall was on the way, but not the kind of storm
the selkies could bring—the kind he needed. That sparked an
idea, but first he needed to find the sealskin.

A stiff wind was on the rise, spreading the scent of burning
wood from the bonfire in the clearing behind the fortress. Voices
carried on it—laughter and music, flute, drums, and lyre, earthy
and mysterious. The sound of it set his heart racing and sent
hot blood surging to his temples. Not even the cool gusts could
fan the fever that was rising in him, a virtual firestorm riveting
his senses that only Meg possessed the power to quench.

Just as he predicted, the tower door was unlocked, and he
whisked Meg inside and began to climb the narrow staircase
hewn of the same stone as the structure itself. The walls were
bleeding with rising damp. Cold, dank air drifted from them
fanned by their motion. When they reached the second level,
Meg held him back on the landing.

"It was here somewhere," she said. "No, not that way . . . to
the right . . ."

Simeon let her lead him then, and she flung open a door on
the north side of the corridor and burst inside before he could
warn her toward caution. He reached her in two strides. "You
cannot go barging about," he scolded her. "There is always an
off chance that some might still linger here. We cannot afford to
be found out now."

"Look! There it is!" she cried, straining against his grip on
her upper arms as if she hadn't heard a word.

Simeon let her go and she ran to the wardrobe and tugged at
the doors. "It's locked!" she said.

"Stand back," Simeon charged. Two lunges with his shoulder and the door panel splintered. No, he hadn't lost his extraordinary strength. Grateful for that, he tossed the boards aside and groped inside, but it was empty except for several gowns. "It isn't here," he said.

"Let me see," Meg said, rummaging through the wardrobe herself. "It has to be!"

"We're wasting time," Simeon said, turning her away. An elaborately carved chest in the corner caught his eye. The carvings were definitely mystical in origin with triangles and swirls and a very realistic eye decorated the lid. Simeon tried it. It was open, and he lifted the lid to forage inside. "Ah!" he blurted as his hand fisted in something opulent and black.

"You've found it?" Meg cried, hopeful.

"No," he quickly said. "This is a vestments chest." He pulled out a long, flowing *cote-hardie*. "This one is fitted with a cowl. It will do far better than going about as he was in this eel skin." He shrugged it on and arranged the hood close about his face. "Pull your hood thus," he instructed her, lending a hand to the chore. His fingers grazed the soft skin of her cheek. That was all it took to make his blood rise inside, to awaken the images of her lying naked in his arms, wet and warm and open to him. An unstoppable need was building in him, heightened by the danger and by the risk, for it was great. He wanted nothing more than to seize and ravish her right where they stood . . . but not yet. Those feelings would always be lurking just below the surface of his psyche. The longer he suppressed them, the greater the pleasure would be, though he would be tight against the seam until that moment came.

"You mentioned the scrying pool," he said, leading her back into the deserted corridor. "Do you know how to find it again?"

Meg nodded. "There is a clearing behind the temple," she said. "The rock pool I told you of lies at the edge of it. The scrying pool is raised, like a well at the far side of it, and a little copse on the other side of the clearing backs up to the wall that surrounds the isle. You can't mean to attempt to look into the pool with all the revelers about? We would be walking right into them!"

"Dressed thus, and considering that they will all soon be in their cups, that is exactly what I mean to do," he replied. "But there is something else I must do there. . . ."

"You mean to leave me here and return to the sea through the rock pool!" she cried.

"Shh!" he warned her, clamping his hand over her mouth. Her hot breath puffing on his skin and raised the fine hairs on the back of his neck. It was sweet and moist. How he wanted her! "I will never leave you, Megaleen. That pool feeds from the bay—whatever goes into it will reach the sea. A squall is coming, but not in time, and not nearly terrible enough for our needs. I have no doubt that Vega will raise an army of entities from the deep to come to our aid, but one drop of my blood in that water will bring a maelstrom of gargantuan proportions that will help us escape this place."

Meg's jaw sagged. "You mean to cut yourself?" She was incredulous.

"One drop of my blood—*selkie blood*—and a legion of avengers will stir the seas and bays with flesh-tearing winds that will flay the Mount into the bay and drive it down beneath the waves until it is no more. You have no inkling of the power I command as Lord of the Deep or of the loyalty of the subjects who attend me."

Meg dug in her heels and faced him, arms akimbo. "And just how will that help us without your sealskin?"

"It won't," he responded, stopping short of saying that the rain and waves might just put the bonfire out so Gideon could lift her off the Mount like he had before. "But it might create enough of a diversion to keep these occupied while we find the skin," he said instead. It was better if she didn't know what he was planning.

The glow from the bonfire was visible before they'd even rounded the corner of the stronghold. It cast an eerie orange glow over the dark sky. The clearing was swarming with robed shamans and scantily clad temple whores engaged in all manner of ritualistic dancing. Wineskins were being upended. One of the revelers handed one to Simeon. He took a swallow then handed it back, and the young man reeled off and rejoined the throngs. The scene was not unlike that which had occurred on the night of the full moon, when he had come with his consorts and tempted Meg on the Isle of Mists.

His heart began to race. Could this be the same wine Seth had given Meg? He was fully aroused, his cock begging for release. He tugged at it through the tight-fitting eel skin with pinching fingers, but it would not go down. No. It wasn't the wine. He scarcely needed inducement. He was hard before they had ever left the round tower. His need had manifested itself the minute he touched her skin—the instant he felt her warm, sweet breath on his hand.

The pool . . . He had to find the pool. . . .

"There!" Meg said, as if she'd read his mind. "There is no one near it now."

Simeon followed her nod toward the rock pool and the scrying pool alongside. "There's a mist on it," he observed, thinking out loud. "How is that possible with all this wind? And why is it avoided?"

"Aunt Adelia told me the shamans check the scrying pool at dawn and dusk each day. Since they can see the past, present, and future in it, they do not need to monitor it so frequently, I suppose. And Seth whisked the mist away with his hand when he made me look into it."

"You looked into it?" Simeon whispered through clenched teeth as others danced by, in particular what appeared to be one of the shamans chasing a nearly naked temple whore. "What did you see?"

Silence.

"What did you see, Megaleen?" Simeon persisted.

Still she hesitated. "I saw you," she said at last, "betraying me with your consorts. I didn't recognize the place, but you were under the water, and your concubines had covered you like a quilt beneath some sort of net canopy. Seth said it was the present. Did it happen, Simeon, what I saw?"

Simeon felt the blood leave his scalp and drain from his face. He was hoping she would never have to know about that. "It happened," he said, "but it was not what it seemed in that pool. I was set on leaving the Pavilion. What you saw was the reason the consorts are now banished to the barrier beach."

"I saw you come, Simeon."

The scrying pool's accuracy was no longer in question, at least. "And I would have seen you come if Seth had gotten his hands upon you earlier. You would not have been able to help yourself. It would have meant nothing—just as what happened to me meant nothing. But this is neither the time nor place to discuss it. Come . . . and act natural. I must do this before Seth is found and he joins this lot because, while there's hope to elude the others, he will know us despite our disguise."

He steered her toward the scrying pool, swept the mist away, and gazed into it. At first the water was as black as midnight. Then the inky blackness dissolved and an image appeared. Simeon stared, not quite sure of what he was seeing until the image faded and then came clear again.

"What do you see?" Meg said, craning her neck to see also.

"I don't quite know," Simeon said. "There's no time now to puzzle over it. Stay close beside me. I am not liking this. My instincts tell me all is not as it seems here."

The words were scarcely out when a young shaman came running from the stronghold and spoke to two others. All three began to scan the celebration, craning their necks and whispering among themselves.

Simeon seized Meg and spun her around in his arms with her back to the nattering shamans so he could monitor them and stooped as if he meant to kiss her. "They've found him," he whispered in her ear. "Keep your face covered and do not turn around . . . Pretend you're making love with me, like the rest of these."

"What do you mean, 'they've found him?' How could you know that?"

"One just came from the stronghold. He speaks with two others, and they are studying all here. They are looking for us. Act natural . . . Follow my lead, and do not look behind you. What must be done I must do quickly. . . ."

He kissed her in earnest then. Her closeness demanded it. Her scent was like a drug, wild clover and honey mingled with herbs and hazelnuts from the bath. He was undone by it, a captive of her innocent abandon to his ardor. He deepened the kiss and she responded. His shaft shot up, its bulk swelling against her belly through the taut eel skin suit that fitted him like a second skin. It would be so easy to let the rising tide of emotions in him carry him away like the others, but a glimpse of the three men running off in the direction of the stronghold set him in motion, and he let her go abruptly.

"Now!" he gritted through clenched teeth. "Unless I miss my guess, they will soon return with Seth. We must be well away and concealed before then. Look sharp! We can ill afford to be caught out here now."

Leading her past the scrying pool, Simeon moved to the rock pool and began searching the ground.

"What do you do?" Meg said.

He straightened up holding a shard of rock. Digging it into the soft flesh of his thumb, he bore down until a drop of blood welled up, and then another and squeezed it, taking great care that the drops of blood dripped into the water.

"More than enough," he said. Taking her arm, he led her behind the bonfire out of sight of the others, and took her into the grove. By the look of the revelers, there wasn't much chance of generating their interest. Those that weren't besotted with spirits were engaged in orgiastic couplings around the bonfire to the beat of the music that held them enthralled. Had they drunk the same wine Seth had given Meg? By the look of things, he imagined so. The clearing was carpeted with naked bodies entwined, reminding him again of the mating on the strand on the Isle of Mists that had won him Meg what seemed a lifetime ago for all that had occurred since that fateful night. He had drunk none of the drugged wine, except for the stingy swallow he'd taken from the young shaman's wineskin. His passion was pure and would be denied no longer. Having taken her deeply in among the ancient trees, well out of sight of the drunken revelers, he rushed her against the rough bark of an ancestral pine and tore open his eel skin, releasing his throbbing cock.

A terrible thought drifted across his mind as he folded her in a heart-stopping embrace. If all his efforts failed, this could well be their last time together. The strange image he'd seen in the scrying pool was testimony to that. He'd seen himself, but aged slightly, his hair frosted with gray at the temples. Was that the present? Had he seen nothing but his reflection in the water? If that were so, he'd already lost his immorality. Or was he seeing the future in the mystical pool—his future. Either way, it did not bode well, but what mattered then was the beautiful woman in his arms gazing up at him with eyes dilated with desire.

Lifting the skirt of her kirtle, he ran his hands along her sides. How soft she was, her skin like eiderdown. His fingers strayed as they always did to the V of golden curls between her thighs, moistened with arousal. Parting her nether lips, he reached into her, his fingers riding on her warm wetness, like liquid silk inside her. Casting off her cloak, he opened her bodice and feasted upon her breasts with hungry eyes. His hands became rampant, anxious things he no longer controlled, moving over her body as if they were possessed of their own will. Fueled by her moans, he tore at her kirtle until he'd lifted it over her head and tossed it down with the cloak.

Her hands tore at his eel skin until she had slid it down over his torso. He had no recollection of when his cloak fell away. Her tiny hands captured his cock and flitted over the shaft from mushroom tip to turgid balls. He cried out as she reverenced him, for that is what her tiny fingers were doing as they played with him in innocent abandon, exploring, fondling, worshiping—making him harder still.

Swooping down, he took one taut nipple in his mouth and laved it—scraped it with his tongue until she writhed beneath his lips and begged him to take the other. Her honey sweetness filled his nostrils—his mouth—his very soul. He would make this wonder last, and yet every pore in his skin—every cell in his turgid body—cried for release.

The wind had risen sharply, but it hadn't deterred the revelers. Sounds of their lewd antics reached them even deep in the grove. The beat of the strange orgasmic music had risen in competition with the gusts that whistled through the pine boughs overhead spreading their spicy scent. The sensuous rhythm thrummed through his body, igniting the fever in his blood. His whole body throbbed in concert with the pulse in his veins as he drank in the sight of her, with her head thrust back in mindless oblivion against the tree trunk. The moon had disappeared behind dark scudding clouds, the only light a distant glow from the raging bonfire shooting showers of sparks into the sky in the clearing beyond. Flames danced in her eyes and highlighted her hair. How very beautiful she was in surrender. She was his—all his. Oh, how he loved her.

His fingers still moved inside her, riding her wetness. Her swollen labia gripped them in rhythmic contractions, keeping time with the beat of the strange evocative music and the revelers' chanting. He could bear no more. Gripping the perfect rounds of her buttocks, he lifted her onto his bursting shaft and plunged into her in one long, shuddering thrust that siphoned the breath from her lungs. Her groan was bestial—primeval—as he filled her, hammering into her to the root of his sex again and again. He watched her release glaze her eyes, watched them dilate, shining like two glowing coals in the fire-lit darkness. Spiraling in and out of her, Simeon held his breath as he came, his heart hammering against her breasts as he froze inside her, the hot lava rush of his semen spilling into her—out of her. Their thighs were wet with the juices of his palpating climax.

So great an upheaval mounted inside him, it seemed to move the ground beneath them. At first he thought it was his legs shaking with release or the vibration from the revelers dancing which shook the ground, until something tenuous, though strong as steel, crawled up his leg, snaked its way around his waist, and flung him to the ground. He struck the mulch beneath him hard as another vinelike tether sprang out of the ground and seized his cock in a painful stranglehold.

"*No!*" cried Meg, as more roots shot up from the forest floor. One circled her waist, another probed her sex, still more held Simeon down, probing every orifice none too gently.

"What sorcery is this?" he ground out through clenched teeth. The roots had bound his arms to the ground. He couldn't move, though he struggled with all his strength.

Meg sank to the ground. "No! I beg you, stop! Let him go!" she pleaded, embracing the tree trunk. "Spirit, please . . . He is my love . . . *my* roots . . . my home. . . ."

Simeon's jaw sagged as he watched the tree's roots and tendrils stroke her sex and tweak her nipples, exploring her body familiarly. One long, ropelike appendage caught in her hair, driving her head against the tree's bark. Was it embracing her? It certainly wasn't embracing him. It had his penis in a viselike grip. Making matters worse, it had wrenched him out of her before his member could go flaccid, and the way it was moving on him—painful though it was—brought him to the brink of coming again.

"Please, ancient one," Meg sobbed. "He is my mate . . . I beg you, let him go!"

A trickle of sap ran down the tree's trunk, picking up golden glints from the fire glow. Was that its tear? The ground beneath him heaved and settled. The pine boughs seemed to sigh as the wind ruffled the needles. One by one, the tree's roots receded back into the ground, all except the one stroking Meg's nether parts and the one fondling Simeon's erection

Meg crawled to Simeon's side and embraced him. "Do not resist, my love," she murmured in his ear. "It is beyond our comprehending, this, a mystery known only to the Arcan gods. The spirit in this ancient one is eons old and so lonely. These here have stolen it from its home when it was no more than a sapling and treated it cruelly. I beg you, do not harm it. . . ."

Other roots seemed to nudge them closer together. All at once they were in each other's arms as the roots of the ancient tree had their way with them. The ground beneath them seemed to breathe, spreading the heady scent of mulch and pinesap. Simeon could no more prevent the orgasm than he could prevent his next breath. It was a powerful eruption that drained him dry, coming simultaneously with Meg's release. He watched it in her shuttered eyes again and kissed the tears from her cheeks. When had they come streaming down, and why? Were they tears of joy or sorrow? It didn't matter. They were gone now that he had gentled them all away.

Silently, the tree's roots slipped down beneath the forest floor and disappeared as though they had never risen out of the ground. Simeon looked deep in Meg's misty eyes for a long moment before speaking.

"How can this be?" he said finally, brushing her hair back from her hot face. "It is rumored that such things occur on the

Forest Isle, but I have never believed it. *Are* you the witch they accuse? What has just happened here?"

"The ancient spirit in this tree has bonded us. It has given us its blessing, Simeon. It has married us in the ways of the wood on the solstice. There is no stronger bond. We are one."

"We have always been that, Megaleen. We did not need that tree to bind us."

"Shh," she murmured. "Do not anger it. You are from the sea. You know nothing of these mysteries. Take the gift. The giver has the ear of the gods."

A loud uproar rose above the music. Some new merriment was taking place around the bonfire. Scrambling to his feet, Simeon pulled Meg up alongside and steered her to their clothes where they'd shed them on the ground. No mean task, since his eel skin suit was tangled around his ankles.

"Hurry and dress," he charged. "Soon the storm will come, and we must find my sealskin and be away before it does." He snatched up her cloak and slapped the dead leaves from it. She had wriggled into her kirtle, and he slipped the cloak about her shoulders and pulled the hood about her face. "Keep well hidden," he said. "And pray to your gods that Seth is not among these now. He will recognize us both."

The naked revelers celebrating their ritual around the bonfire were being led by one whose chanting rose above the rest. His worst fears realized, Simeon froze in his tracks at the edge of the grove, pulling Meg up short.

"What is it?" she whispered.

Simeon nodded toward the drunken orgy taking place in the clearing. "Seth," he said. "We do not need to search for my sealskin further."

"Why?" Meg said.

"Because he is wearing it!" Simeon seethed.

# 14

"Oh, Simeon!" Meg shrilled. "Suppose he throws the seal-skin on the fire!"

Simeon studied the shaman who flaunted the sealskin draped over his head and shoulders and trailing down his back like a cloak, and gritted his teeth at the sight. "He knows we're here somewhere. He's using it for bait. He wants to ferret us out—bring us into the open. Not all these are in their cups. See"—he pointed to a naked trollop close beside the shaman— "and there"—he gestured toward a robed cleric upending a wineskin nearby—"no doubt there are more." He looked to the heavens. The wind had continued to rise, and the sky was blacker than sin. Dry lightning speared down over the grove. "Come away from the wood," he said, steering her clear of the trees. He knew well the power of the selkie maelstrom. There wasn't a moment to lose.

"The ancient one!" Meg cried, pulling against him toward the grove.

Simeon held her back, shaking a slow head. "It is too late," he said. "Before the dawn, Shamans' Mount will be no more,

Megaleen. The old one evidently knew that when he bonded us. There is nothing we can do for him but pray for a quick and painless death to free his spirit." Still she struggled, and he shook her gently. "Go to him now and you will die with him!" he snapped. "There is nothing you can do."

"He spent his whole life a captive in this awful place," Meg argued. "I cannot bear to see him die thus."

"Tree spirits are the oldest creatures in the world," Simeon reminded her. "As you said, they possess wisdom beyond our comprehending. He did not give us his blessing because we were about to die. What use to marry the dead? He meant for us to live, Megaleen."

Another lightning bolt struck the heart of the grove, and Simeon turned her away. He could have sworn he heard a human cry as the wood caught fire in a hissing, cracking blaze of flame and sparks that raced up tree trunk after tree trunk until the whole wood was ablaze. A great roar rose above the sounds of the fire as towering waves rolled up the granite wall that enclosed the Mount. Giant clouds of diaphanous spindrift rose high into the sky, telling that the waves that spawned it soon would flood the isle. The revelers were running helter-skelter over the clearing, over the courtyard, and through the temple gardens. Even Seth had ceased strutting. He looked bewildered, scanning the devastation that had begun.

"He is falling-down drunk, Megaleen," Simeon observed. "Do you trust me, my love?" His original plan would not work now. Gideon would not risk his wings to the holocaust Shamans' Mount was fast becoming. The alternative was dangerous if it could be managed at all. That would depend upon Meg, and he pulled her into his arms, a close eye on Seth through the rippling heat of the bonfire, where the shaman still staggered in his drunken confusion.

Meg nodded that she did. She was terrified. He could see it in her horrified stare—hear it in her rapid breathing. Her eyes were still fixed upon the burning wood, still glazed with sorrow for the ancient tree.

"Then you must do exactly as I say," he told her. "Seth has drunk much wine. Between that and the blow to his head earlier, I can wrest the sealskin from him easily enough with the help of this"—he held up a rock he'd snatched from the ground—"if I do not have to worry about you. His minions have fled. Once I have it, we must go below the waves. Within the hour, this place will be no more. It will have disappeared and all its evil with it. The sea will merge with the bay. Enormous waves the like of which you have never seen will flood this place, and the rain will drive it down, until all that you see is no more. Come. No matter what occurs, stay close to me."

Except for Seth and a few who had drunk themselves into a stupor lying strewn about, the revelers had all fled to the temple and the tower. Seth was reeling in that direction as well when Simeon confronted him just as the rain began to pelt down on a slant driven landward from the sea. Wrestling with the drunken shaman, Simeon soon won back the sealskin, which he handed to Meg. He did so without hesitation, while he delivered a blow with the rock that brought the shaman to his knees and another with his fist that drove Seth to the ground unconscious.

Staggering to his feet, Simeon took back the sealskin from Meg, who stood clutching it, threw off his *cote-hardie,* and stepped into the sealskin to the waist before turning to her. "Now is when you must trust, Megaleen," he said. "There is only one way out of here. . . ."

"How?" she murmured.

"This is how," Simeon said, and blowing into her mouth and nostrils, he shrugged the rest of the sealskin on. "Hold fast to me!" he charged as he dove into the rock pool and took her down beneath the waves.

\* \* \*

Meg shut her eyes and tried to ignore her terror. That was what had nearly cost her her life the last time Simeon took her below the waves thus. But he hadn't warned her about the undertow being so strong in a storm, and this was no ordinary storm. He hadn't warned her that the heaving swells would dredge up the silt on the ocean floor and make visibility nearly nonexistent. And he hadn't told her to expect bits of wreckage raining down—whole ships and bodies, staved hulls and spars and rigging, with sheets and sails furled fast, as they would be in a storm. But it hadn't been enough to save the ships or the poor souls floating down, down, down to a watery grave.

She shut her eyes, for the fine sand stung them, and clung so fiercely to Simeon's neck she feared her pinching fingers would draw blood. He'd donned all but the head of the sealskin. Otherwise, she would have had precious little to cling to on the seal's sleek body. He was talking to her as they plummeted below, but she had no idea what he was saying. Her heart was hammering so violently in her breast she couldn't hear anything above the noise. His voice was soothing, though, meant to reassure, and she loved him for it.

There was strain in that voice; not the kind that comes from ordeal. Had he noticed her hesitation when he took the sealskin back from her by the rock pool? She thought not then, but now . . . There was something in his bearing that nagged at her, a dull ache that wouldn't be relieved no matter how she tried to convince herself that it was all in her imagination. It was a natural enough reaction after all. Whoever possessed a selkie's skin had him under their spell for life or until he had the skin back. Simeon was under Seth's power until he took his skin back from the shaman. Once a selkie loses his skin he loses his immortality as well. Meg knew that to be so firsthand, for now stains of gray frosted Simeon's temples that hadn't been there before. For that brief time while he was divested of his sealskin, he had become mortal, to live and age and die just as any human being upon the planet . . . Just as she would live and age and die.

Simeon would lose his immortality were she to possess his sealskin, but what of her? Was there a way for her to gain immortality for herself? If there was, she'd never heard of it. She was a witch, so everyone said. Did she have it in her power to cast such a spell, to live in his underwater world with him forever without aging, or was she doomed to die a mortal death no matter where she lived with him? This was not the time or the place to worry over it. Simeon had just loosed a vibrating mantra into the water. Who was he summoning? Her heart leaped. Her breathing became labored. Vertigo starred her vision, and she clung to him with all her strength.

"Just a little farther," he whispered in her ear. "We are almost there. . . ."

He hummed the mantra again and a swordfish appeared, swimming around them in joyful circles. Did that fish nuzzle him? Tears welled in her eyes that a mere fish could feel such joy in the presence of its lord. It spoke volumes to what wonders lay beneath the surface of the man she loved and to what mysteries lay beneath the waves.

"Bring Vega, Pio," Simeon charged the summoner.

In a blink, the swordfish streaked off through the murky waters, and Meg found her voice.

"What is it?" she murmured.

"We are halfway to the tunnel that leads to the palace," he answered. "I need to know if it is safe to take you there."

"Why wouldn't it be?"

"Sometimes in storms such as this, the air pockets flood. It doesn't matter for me, but you need the air until we can sort that out with the Waterwitch."

"And . . . if it isn't safe?"

"Then we must try the Pavilion or one of the outer islands until the storm subsides. Do not worry. All will be well."

"You need Vega to tell you this?" she said.

Simeon nodded. "He will let no harm come to you, Megaleen. He will see you to safety while I attend to this here."

"Attend to what?" she cried.

"Do not excite yourself. It will cancel your breathing!" he warned her. "You saw the dead falling all around us with the wreckage of their ships. They must be respected—prepared for their journey to the gods. This is my responsibility, Megaleen, as Lord of the Deep. No soul that falls beneath the waves must go unreverenced. It has been thus since time out of mind, and it will be so until time exists no more."

"But why must *you* do it?"

"Because I am Lord of the Deep, and I alone have the power to prepare those who die beneath the waves. It is even more important here now, because I am the one who caused their deaths. Who better to make reparation and give them a proper introduction to the gods?"

When he put it to her that way, Meg couldn't very well oppose him. She was fast becoming familiar with new facets to her beloved's persona. She was quickly finding out that Simeon, Lord of the Deep, was deeper than the seas he commanded. This was his world—his very life. How could she take him from it? She was very close to remorse for having even entertained the notion of keeping that sealskin. But then, there was her fierce love of him . . . a love without which she would surely wither and die, old before her time.

Minutes later the swordfish returned with Vega, whose look of relief extended to them both and warmed Meg's heart.

"Thank the gods!" Vega cried. "We thought you were lost—the pair of you."

"We nearly were," Simeon said. "Is the palace flooded?"

"No," Vega said. "But that is not to say it won't. Three vessels are down already; two in the ocean off the mainland and one in the bay."

"We saw many," Simeon said. "I must attend them. I want you to take Megaleen to the palace and stay with her until I return. If it floods, see her to the Pavilion." He turned to the swordfish. "Pio, you will come with me."

The summoner sketched a graceful bow, dipping his sword low. Vega, who was not hindered by his sealskin but wore an eel suit, pried Meg's arms loose from Simeon's neck and moved off in the opposite direction from that which Simeon and Pio had taken without so much as a farewell.

"He cannot bear to part with you even for a moment, much less put the separation into words," Vega said, as if he'd read her thoughts. "Have no fear . . . You will come to no harm in my keeping. Though, I daresay you would benefit from a good trouncing after your behavior on our last meeting."

"Would you have let me go otherwise?" Meg queried.

"Probably not, but only because he would not have wanted me to, and he is Lord."

"He has his sealskin back," Meg reminded him.

"For now," Vega said.

Even if Simeon didn't know her heart of hearts, it was clear Vega knew she'd entertained the thought of stealing Simeon's sealskin herself.

"I had it in my hands briefly," she said, answering Vega's thoughts accusingly. "I could have possessed it easily."

"And yet, you risked your life . . . nearly lost it getting the sealskin back for him," Vega said. "I do not understand mortals."

"You should, being half-mortal yourself," Meg snapped at him. "How do you do that . . . read people's minds like that?" They had entered the tunnel that led to the coral reef shelf and the air pocket, where the palace stood. In familiar territory, she had become bold.

"It is a trait some of us have," he replied.

"Does Simeon have this trait?"

"Sometimes," Vega said. "But you are safe enough. He is too besotted with love for you to read his own thoughts clearly, let alone yours."

"You do not like me very much, do you, Vega?"

He shrugged, causing ripples in the water between them. "On the contrary. I wish I had seen you first," he said through a wry chuckle. "Be thankful, my lady, that you cannot read *my* thoughts."

The rest of the distance was traveled in silence. Soon they reached the end of the tunnel, where it spilled into an underwater ledge with a pool—one of many air pockets, where the palace stood in all its rambling glory, decorated with shells and pearls and gifts of the sea that the selkies gleaned from wreckage after the storms. Great riches lived here, treasures of silver and gold, cloth of silk, wine, and precious jewels. True, it took only three of the steps hewn in the rock to reach the palace, where before it had taken twelve, but it hadn't flooded as Simeon had feared.

Air rushed into her lungs, and she gulped it greedily. It was thick with the taste of salt and went to her head like May wine. She knew the way to Simeon's apartments, though Vega led her there anyway. Meg shuddered, remembering the lumbering sea cows that attacked her the last time she was in Simeon's bedchamber.

"The consorts are not here now," Vega said, answering her thoughts. "They are exiled. You are quite safe here."

Meg glanced around. The silt roses growing along the perimeter genuflected from their coral beds. There was comfort in the gesture, as if she'd been accepted or at the very least recognized, and Vega smiled.

"Fickle creatures," he observed, "but they seem to like you."

"I will never hurt him, Vega," she murmured. His posture clenched, clearly surprised at her words, and she laughed.

"No," she said, "I cannot read your mind, but I can read your countenance. You wear your thoughts on your face and, I suspect, your heart on your sleeve. He is fortunate to have you."

Vega did not take compliments well. He sketched a bow and began fussing with the furniture. He obviously felt out of place chaperoning her until Simeon returned. As uncomfortable as he was in that guise, he would perform his duty to the last detail, keeping watch that the palace didn't flood, staying alert to Pio the summoner's reports, meanwhile falling into his valet's role, straightening and ordering in obdurate silence.

Meg said no more. Vega might not trust her, but she trusted him to stand guard. Exhausted, she climbed onto the opulent bed just as she was—cloak and all—and let sleep take her. At first the dreams were fitful and strange; dark, heart-wrenching visions of the burning forest on Shamans' Mount, of the revelers, and of the towering waves flinging spindrift over the high stone wall that hemmed in the temple fortress all around.

Time meant nothing in that troubled dream state. Exactly how long it was before she experienced the feeling of floating in pleasantly warm water, she had no idea. At first the skirt of her kirtle was billowed about her like a balloon. Then it was gone altogether; so was her cloak. The echo of water dripping into the water around her made a pleasant sound. Someone was holding her. How strong his arms were. The muscles in his biceps rippled against her. His hot breath puffing on her wet skin raised the fine hairs on the back of her neck. His scent ghosted through her nostrils—the tang of salt and the dark, dusky mystery of musky ambergris, sensuous and evocative.

*Simeon!*

Meg's eyes snapped open. This was no dream, and she threw her arms around his neck and clasped him to her with all her strength.

They were submerged in a rock-lined pool of warm, steamy water, surrounded by water lilies, their heady fragrance enhanced by the warmth of rush candles set about in niches carved into the rock. The reflection of the candle flames danced in the water, writhing in the ripples their motion created as Simeon moved her against him, rasping her mound with the hard, anxious shaft of his erection. Merciless pleasure!

"Where is this place?" she murmured between sharp intakes of breath as he ground the root of his sex into her hardened bud.

"Just another room in the palace," he said, nipping at her earlobe. "There are many, smaller air pockets beneath the palace proper, little pools like this one honed out of the subterranean caves by time. Some are inhospitable, but this one is closest to the volcanic flow from the Isle of Fire, so it is heated. Let your feet touch the bottom. . . ." Meg hesitated, and he laughed. "I'm holding you," he said, "Don't be afraid. It isn't deep."

Meg lowered herself gingerly, inch by inch, until her feet touched bottom. Her sex leaped to life as it slid along his rock-hard body, and she undulated against him, relaxing her legs to permit his knee to spread them wide enough for her to straddle his thigh. Her foot touching bottom felt as if a thousand tiny fingers were caressing it. Her posture clenched at the tactile feel of it between her toes.

"Saltwater cress," Simeon said. "Vega planted it when he created this pool; a delight for the senses, like your grass upon the land. Let it relax you, Megaleen. You need this now, else-wise I would have let you sleep."

But Meg could not relax, not while his rigid thigh was moving against her feminine flesh, hardening her bud, making her wet inside and out, leaking her juices into the soothing water rippling around them. Was there no end to the delights she could expect in his arms?

His hot mouth found her parted lips and his tongue tasted her deeply, entwining with hers, teasing the sensitive sides of her lips as he moved her against the curved wall of the pool.

He'd draped her cloak there to protect the tender flesh of her spine and buttocks as he seized them, raising her up, then higher still, until the velvety ridged head of his penis fetched up against the swollen nether lips at her entrance. He hesitated, his dark shuttered eyes gleaming in the candle glow. Meg drank in his smoldering gaze. The heat of his need blazed in his dilated eyes, in the hardness of his shaft, in the persistence of its head pressing against her slit until the ridged tip alone parted her fissure.

Meg tried to envelope it with the soft flesh of her vulva—tried to seize it and take it deep into her—but he held her just out of reach of her desire until she feared her heart would burst through her breast. Exquisite torture! Then she could bear no more. A primitive groan escaped her throat as she called his name, begging him to fill her. Still he hesitated and she pleaded again. This time, the groan bubbled up in his arched throat as in one deep, shuddering thrust, he spiraled into her. Wrapping her legs around his waist, she threw her arms around his neck and clung to him as his hands slid down her sides, grazing her breasts, and his thumbs palpated her nipples.

He seized her buttocks again, matching her rhythm. Water rushed into her with each riveting riposte—soothing, steamy water laving her inner walls, surging over her engorged bud, sparking the friction that triggered her release. It came in waves of unstoppable sensation surging through her belly and thighs, thrumming in her veins, rushing to every recess, every erogenous pore of her gooseflesh-pebbled skin. Every inch of her throbbed like a pulse beat—just as it always did in his embrace.

Staring through eyes glazed with passion, Meg watched his own eyes glaze over as he ground himself against her mound, scraping the sensitive bud protruding from her pubic curls as he pounded into her again and again, spiraling in and out of her until her sex was afire, until her pelvis lurched forward seizing his erection as she climaxed again. This time he climaxed with her in mindless oblivion, the pulse of his seed filling her and making her orgasm again, until, spent, they clung to each other in the curve of the rocky wall of the pool—until their hot joined flesh ceased thumping like a heartbeat.

"Promise that you will never leave me," he murmured huskily, his hot, moist breath ruffling the tendrils framing her face in the steamy atmosphere of the little pool.

Meg crowded closer in his arms. She didn't answer. How could she, when part of her secretly wanted to steal his sealskin to make him her love slave, and another part—the noble part—was entertaining thoughts of setting him free, for that was what truly was needed to put things to rights. She knew it—Vega knew it—even Simeon himself knew it, if only he wasn't too blinded by love to see it, and how could he not? He was Lord of the Deep, Prince of the Waves, Ruler of the Arcan seas, steward of the drowned dead—even the dead of the terrible Shamans' Mount. How could she deny him this? Could she possibly be that cruel? More and more, she was thinking she could not. But how, oh how could she live without him now?

She pulled him closer still and took his lips, anything to prevent him seeing the anguish in her eyes—anything to prevent her from answering that plea.

# 15

"How bad is the devastation?" Vega asked Simeon. They were closeted in an antechamber off the master suite while Meg made herself presentable for their visit to the Waterwitch.

Simeon heaved a mammoth sigh as he paced the length of an Oriental rug that nearly covered the floor completely; just one of the many gifts of the sea over time. "The storm still rages," he replied.

"And the dead?"

"There are many, Vega. I did what could be done. It is up to the gods now to sort the righteous from the heathen. It is not for me to judge, my brother, only to say the words and give the blessing that will lead them home."

"And the Mount? Has it sunk beneath the waves?"

Simeon shook his head. "Much of it has, but not all," he replied. "The temple and tower have crumbled to rubble with all in them dead, as did the forest and much of the wall that surrounds the isle. . . ."

"And Seth?" Vega prompted as Simeon's words trailed off.

"He was not among the dead," he replied, almost sorrowfully.

"Is the Mount inhabitable?" Vega asked him.

"Will it sustain life, do you mean? I think not," Simeon said. "All that remained the last time I saw it was the rock pool, the scrying pool, and a mere spit of land where the clearing used to be. There is no shelter left upon the Mount and no protection with the wall at the bottom of the bay."

"You are certain about Seth?"

"I'm certain."

"He will seek to revenge himself, Simeon."

"I know, but he is not my priority now. I'm taking Megaleen to the Waterwitch. To see what can be done about her breathing under water."

"Simeon, you dream!"

"Then let me dream!" Simeon snapped. "There has to be something."

"Possibly there is, but what of immortality? There is nothing for that. She will age and she will wither and die before your eyes, while you will live on unchanged—just as you are now—until the end of days. That is inevitable. Is that fair to you—or her?"

Simeon reached him in two great strides. Fisting his hand in the front of Vega's eel skin, he yanked him close to his rage. "Do not moralize with me," he seethed. "You do not like her. I can see it—I can *feel* it!"

"That isn't so," Vega defended. "If truth were to be told, I like her far too much, if you must know, but it's you I'm thinking of. How could you bear to watch her age while you stay young and vital? It would break my heart to watch it happen, Simeon."

"Then you had best pray the Waterwitch comes up with a solution, because we both know what the alternative is." He let

Vega go with a rough thrust. "I would rather live and die in mortal years with her than wander through eternity without her. I am in deadly earnest."

The Waterwitch's cave was one of many beneath the waves, where air pockets occurring in the rock and coral formations made breathing possible, like the heated pool beneath the underwater palace. It was, however, not part of the palace complex. It was dangerously close to the mainland at the tip of the barrier beach that edged it.

The storm still raged. The mainland had not escaped its fury. Meg was reluctant when Simeon summoned Elicorn. She did not trust the waterhorse and never would again. The fickle creature would have drowned Simeon in his vulnerable state when he'd lost his sealskin. She would never understand the ways of waterhorses. But one thing was certain: she would never permit herself to be beguiled again.

Still, there was something very sensuous about riding the waves astride the beast. The tactile feel of its sleek white hide scraping against the tender flesh on the inside of her thighs heated her blood. Especially since the bulk of Simeon's genitals straining his eel skin suit was rubbing up against the fissure between her bare buttocks as the merciless horse galloped against the wind, skimming the white-capped combers. Simeon had disposed of the kirtle she'd been wearing, wanting nothing from Seth's domain to touch her skin, and replaced it with a fetching muslin round gown in a soft shade of peach. It was obviously a gift of the sea in a previous storm, as were the other gowns he offered her. Due to the proportions of the skirt, however, it did not lend itself well to riding astride, hence the exposed rounds of her behind. The gown was hoisted up about her waist, and in their haste to reach the Waterwitch's cave before dark, she had forgotten to collect a wrapper. It wasn't really an oversight. The weather was warm despite the storm, and since they would be traveling above and below the waves, a cloak hardly seemed necessary.

"Are you cold?" Simeon said, as though he'd tapped into her train of thought.

"No," she murmured. She was trembling but not from cold. It was hardly that simple. Strands of Elicorn's mane had been plaited into a bridle affair, which Simeon gripped with both hands to direct the horse. Meg held on to it, too. In this position, Simeon's forearms grazed the sides of her breasts, which had grown heavy—aching for his hands to palm them, straining so those rock-hard forearms would graze her nipples. Arousal threatened. Anticipation heated her blood until it pounded in her ears. No, she wasn't cold. She doubted she would ever be cold again.

"I fear the Waterwitch's counsel," she confessed. "What if she cannot help us?"

"One witch fear another?" Simeon erupted. "You must not be afraid of her magic. It is of great benefit to all of us beneath the waves. It is true she has her dark side, I shan't deny it, but she is Queen of the White Water Sidhe, noblest of all the oracles of the deep. She tells us when the worldly storms will come and when to harvest our cress and kelp crops. She foretells the future and casts the spells that ward off danger. She heals our sick and keeps the Scroll of Arcan Rite."

"The 'Scroll of Arcan Rite'?" Meg queried. There was so much she needed to learn about Simeon's water world.

"The history of the deep," Simeon said. "Every truth ever uttered by the gods to those they deem stewards of the word is recorded in the Scroll of Arcan Rite. It is a sacred tome invested to her keeping by the gods themselves."

"Shouldn't you be the one to have custody of such a venerable tome?"

"Vega thinks so, but the Waterwitch predates me. Some say she is a goddess in her own right. I do not know if that is so, but

I do know of her magic. I respect it, I am in awe of it, but I do not fear it and neither should you."

"But you are a selkie, and I am—"

"You are my mate," he interrupted her. "Have you so soon forgotten that the ancient one in the tree has wed us—joined us for life?"

Meg almost had forgotten. Why did that rock her soul with sorrows? Could it be because, for all that she loved him with a passion beyond her wildest dreams and comprehension, she had nearly convinced herself that the only solution for them was for her to leave him to the only world he ever knew and loved . . . the deep? Never had she been more convinced of it than now, delving into the mystical aspect of his domain. It made her piddling claim to witchcraft almost laughable.

"You nearly lost your life," she reminded him.

"But you have given it back to me in the person of my sealskin, for it is a person, just as I am a person. It is part of me—a living breathing part that I alone must possess in order to live."

Meg swallowed dryly. "And where is it now?" she mewed. It was a question she had to ask. Her humanity demanded it. What she would do with the knowledge was another matter. This, she had to know.

Simeon hesitated. "Vega keeps my sealskin when I am beneath the waves," he said. "Why do you ask?"

"Because I do not wish to go through that again!" she snapped a little too quickly. Did he notice? She hoped not, but feared so. It was time to change the subject. "What has become of Seth?" she said. "Was he among the drowned dead you blessed? That would be sacrilege and nothing short of hypocritical, I'm thinking."

"No, he was not."

"Then we are not safe. He will hunt us down until he's killed us both, Simeon. Should we not be concentrating upon that?" It was hard to concentrate upon anything with the thick, hard pressure of Simeon's erection biting into the crease of her buttocks.

The rain had ceased falling, though the wind was merciless and the seas were running high. Simeon reined Elicorn in with a tug of the animal's plaited mane and turned her face toward him.

"Do not sell me short," he said. "I bested and outwitted Seth twice. How he escaped the devastation on the Mount, I do not know. He was in his cups—dazed from those blows to the head—and I was too preoccupied with you to care. He could be anywhere. But if he comes into my domain after what he has done, he will never leave it alive."

Simeon's voice crackled with gritty passion that rumbled up from the depths of him. It sent gooseflesh racing the length of Meg's spine. There was no doubt he meant every word. The hard-muscled span of his broad chest and flexed biceps rippled against her, and she said no more.

They continued on in brooding silence. She could not read his thoughts, and she hoped he couldn't read hers. They had nearly reached the barrier beach when he breathed into her nostrils and took her beneath the waves. This time Meg didn't close her eyes. The coral reef was a breathtaking sight, with its niches, pools, and underwater caves, much the same as Simeon's palace, though the caves were smaller. White and pink coral formed the cave of the Waterwitch. Simeon left Elicorn at the bowerlike entrance beside a pool filled with night lilies, commanding him to stay. The waterhorse seemed content to obey, though Meg didn't miss the seductive twinkle in Elicorn's eye. She couldn't help but wonder if a waterhorse could be tamed and brought to submission by its master. Whether it could or it couldn't, she would be leery of such creatures as long as she lived.

The air pocket allowed Meg to breath naturally as Simeon led her deeply in to the Waterwitch's inner sanctum. She wasn't prepared for the opulence. Many of the sea's gifts had obviously made their way to the Oracle's domain. The walls of the cave were spangled with precious contraband and gold and silver coins glittered from niches in the coral, as if an unseen hand had flung them there. Couches draped with sumptuous furs and cloth of gold defined the perimeter, but a cubicle deeper in behind a curtain of aquatic vines was sparsely furnished and darker. Only one small rush candle lit the area. It connected to a little pool sunken in the rock.

Meg glanced about. The cave was empty. "No one is here," she said.

Simeon smiled. Throwing back his head, he loosed a guttural bark that mellowed into the hum of a mantra not unlike the one he'd hummed to bring the waterhorse on the beach.

"Stand back," he said. Taking her arm, he eased her away from the edge of the pool as the water began to tremble. The vibrations grew stronger, until the whole surface of the pool was atremble with undulant motion.

Meg gasped. Gripping Simeon's arm she crowded close to him as the ripples parted and a creature broke the surface of the water. At first appearance it was hideous, with the head of the ugliest fish Meg had ever seen and a body covered with scales, though it looked human. Meg blinked, and the fish's head transformed into that of an old woman, whose diaphanous gray hair floated about her like a cloud. Oddly, it was dry after coming from the water. It reminded her of Adelia's hair, and she took another step back as the creature climbed out of the pool with the aid of steps carved in the rock under the surface of the water.

The Waterwitch was graceful despite her age, her naked body beneath the scales like that of a woman no older than Meg herself. She made no move toward modesty. Snatching a glittering, transparent cloak from a nearby bench, she tossed it over her shoulders with flourish, hiding nothing, and took her place in an elaborate chair upon what appeared to be a small dais. It was fitted with a canelike scepter capped with a scrying ball, which she lifted from its bracket and leaned on, fingering the clouded crystal. Meg noticed that both the woman's hands and feet were webbed.

"Elna," Simeon greeted, sketching a graceful bow from the waist. "We have come to seek your counsel."

The Waterwitch offered a nod that bespoke royalty and gazed first at him through shuttered eyes, then turned her gaze upon Meg but said nothing.

"We want—"

The Waterwitch stayed his tongue with a raised hand gesture. "I know what you want, impetuous one," she said. How dared the woman speak to Simeon thus? He was the sovereign, wasn't he? "Wait without."

It was an unequivocal command, and Simeon bowed again, cast Meg a reassuring glance, and backed through the aquatic vine curtain into what Meg took to be the parlor they had entered through. The woman had not taken her eyes from her since Simeon left them, nor had she spoken. Was this a tactic on the witch's part to wear her down—to make her prove herself unworthy of the Lord of the Deep? If it was, they were in for a long siege.

Meg squared her posture and stood, spine rigid, facing the Waterwitch's cool glare. There was a strange iridescent glow about the woman's eyes that reminded Meg of the eyes of a cat. Curious, since it was evident she was more fish than feline or human. After a moment, she raised one webbed finger and pointed to a Glastonbury chair in the shadows that Meg hadn't noticed before.

"Sit," the woman said.

Meg sketched a bow and took her seat.

"You do not fear me," the Waterwitch marveled.

"Not you, no," Meg said. "I fear only that you cannot help us."

172 / Dawn Thompson

"Um," the other hummed. "You are a witch in your own right, I have heard. How is it you cannot work your own magic?"

"I do not know that I am a witch," Meg said. "Others say it of me. I have yet to prove it is true."

"You have bewitched Simeon!"

"I am in love with Simeon."

"Is that practical . . . you a mortal, and he a selkie and Lord of the Deep? What can come from such a union but disaster and heartache?"

"We are already joined."

The woman's eyebrow lifted. "Then you have no need of me."

"But I do," Meg insisted. "I cannot breathe for long periods beneath the waves. I . . . We were wondering if you have a remedy."

"Why do you not ask the real question that brings you here?" the Waterwitch said, her iridescent eyes riveting. "The question of *immortality*."

Meg hesitated. The answer to this was her greatest fear. "Very well," she said at last. "Tell it, then."

"Simeon is immortal as long as he is in possession of his sealskin," the witch began. "He lost it for awhile and lost his immortality for a brief time with it—"

"How do you know that?" Meg interrupted.

"The gray at his temples. It is a sign of aging. He did not have it before. He has aged slightly for the loss of his selkie skin. Have you not noticed this?"

"Yes, I have, but his immortality *has* been restored now that he has the sealskin back . . . hasn't it?" Meg begged, hungering for the spoken words that would ease her conscience.

The Waterwitch nodded. "Until he loses it again," she said her voice like a whip. "The selkie's powers of seduction are legend, daughter. They are a lecherous breed, and conquest is all to them. It is not a criticism I speak; it is a madness in the blood that makes them so. It is inherent. They cannot change what they are any more than you can change what you are. I have seen him with mortals before. Seducing specimens of the human race is a selkie's greatest triumph, because they flirt with death when their sealskins are at risk, and that makes the conquest sweeter. It is a cause of much woe beneath the waves. Are you certain what you presume to be love on his part is in reality nothing more than mere lust?"

"I know only what I feel in his arms, ancient one. I cannot speak for him, but—"

"You do not have to," Simeon interrupted, parting the aquatic vine curtain at the door. He strode into the room and raised Meg up in the custody of his strong arms. "I am well able to speak for myself."

"You eavesdrop, impudent one?" the Waterwitch shrilled, banging her scepter on the floor of the cave. "You may be Lord of the Deep, but *I* am the *Oracle*, and you will respect me."

"With due respect, Elna, I do not need to eavesdrop. I have the gift of extraordinary hearing. I do love her, and while I do admit it is not a comfortable thing, it is true."

"It will be the end of you," the witch decreed.

"Then so be it!" Simeon countered.

"No, Simeon . . . Let her speak," Meg said. Something in the woman's cryptic hint of death would not be beaten back.

"She has spoken," he returned. "It is not up to her to moralize with me. That is not why we have come. We came to ask a question—only that." He flashed narrowed eyes toward the Waterwitch. "Do you have a remedy that will allow Megaleen to breathe for longer intervals beneath the waves than is possible now?"

The Waterwitch rose from her chair and moved into the shadows, where she took down two bunches of what looked to Meg like herbs that had been hanging to dry and thrust them toward her. Then reaching into a niche in the coral, she produced a round bottle with a cork stopper and handed that over as well.

"Steep a pinch of each of those water herbs in the boiled contents of this bottle and a pint of water," she said. "Then strain it and take a swallow at will. Take another each month thereafter when the moon is full."

Meg examined the bottle, holding it up to the light. The glass was mottled, cloudy and clear in intricate swirls, quite beautiful, and its contents were the color of amber. "What is this?" she said.

"You would not drink it if you knew," the Waterwitch replied. "Suffice it to say, all things come at a price. With this tincture it is a foul taste, but worth the result."

"Thank you," Meg murmured, sketching a curtsy.

"Um," the woman grunted. "You may rescind that one day, daughter. And now, since your impetuous lover has insinuated himself in what was meant to be a private conversation, let him hear the rest! Drinking that will give you longer times beneath the waves, but *nothing* will give you immortality. If you chose to live in the deep, you will whither and die nonetheless when your time comes, like the mortal you are—nothing can change that—while Simeon will live on through eternity, young and virile, as you see him now. Think upon it." She shed her transparent mantle and padded toward the pool. The minute her webbed foot touched the water, her head became the grotesque head of the fish again—a shock in juxtaposition to the exquisitely formed body beneath it. The perfect breasts, with their large, dark nipples, the thick, hairless slit and exposed nub were the only parts of her anatomy that weren't spangled with scales. Meg couldn't help but wonder who or what creature of the deep serviced her? The Waterwitch grunted as if she'd read those thoughts and turned to Simeon. "And you," she said. "Guard your sealskin well, for more than one covets it, Lord of the Deep, and you are too blinded by *love* to see it."

---

## 16

Elicorn was still where Simeon left him. While Meg waited nonplussed, Simeon collected several vines like those that served as a partition in the Waterwitch's cave, slung them over Elicorn's back, and began plaiting the ends of them into foreshortened makeshift stirrups.

"What do you do?" Meg asked as he tested them, earning him a disapproving glance from the waterhorse.

"For what I have in mind, we can ride bareback, but not without stirrups," he said.

"I don't understand."

Simeon smiled. "You will," he said. Taking the herbs and little bottle of mysterious liquid from her, he wrapped them tightly in a night lily pad and hummed the mantra that would bring the summoner. Always diligent, Pio's sword soon broke the surface of the water beside the cave, and Simeon slipped the parcel into the swordfish's mouth.

"Take it to Vega," he said. "Tell him one pinch of each and the contents of the bottle in a pint of water. He will know what to do."

In a blink, the summoner was gone, and Simeon swung himself up on to the waterhorse's back and lifted Meg up facing him, settling her astride. She sucked in her breath as he lifted the peach muslin round gown over her head and cried out as he tossed it in the pool.

Simeon laughed. "Have no fear," he said. "Pio will retrieve it for you, just as he did that first night. He is ever with us."

So that was how she'd gotten her kirtle back after Simeon tossed it into the bay that fateful night. It seemed like all that had occurred in another lifetime.

Simeon wriggled his arms out of the eel skin suit and opened it down the front, exposing his hot hard shaft and testicles. Meg gasped again as he snugged her up against him. "We will fall off!" she cried.

Again Simeon laughed. The sound warmed her heart. "You cannot fall from a waterhorse, you know that," he said, "not until it drowns you or its master compels it to let you go."

"But is there room?" she said. The words were barely out, when Elicorn stretched his back to accommodate them. "What's happening?" she cried, clinging to Simeon.

"A waterhorse can stretch its body to accommodate many," Simeon said. "Remember when you and I and Vega all fit comfortably upon him? I have seen one stretch its back to fit a dozen unsuspecting passengers before plunging them all beneath the waves to their death at once. It is their preferred method and their most effective. When mortals see one rider upon the horse's back, or two, it gives them confidence to climb on as well. It is all part of the waterhorse's power to mesmerize."

"He won't . . . I mean . . . he isn't going to . . . ?"

"No, he is under my command, Megaleen. He is simply making us more comfortable. You are quite safe."

He ran his hands along her sides, and his thumbs grazed her nipples, which had grown hard in a surge of gooseflesh that rode the thrill of his touch. Blowing into her nostrils, he urged the waterhorse beneath the waves. The water was an eerie shade of iridescent green misted with silt particles dredged up from the bottom by the storm. Meg could scarcely see, and Simeon pulled her close.

"Only for a little," he murmured in her ear. "There are so many things I want to show you . . . so many ways to pleasure you. Tonight . . . We ride the storm . . ."

Meg wasn't sure what he meant, but she wasn't given time to contemplate it. Seconds later, Elicorn was climbing. The water became wild with heaving swells and undulant motion. They broke the waves on a high-curling comber that spilled white water onto the breast of the bay. The waterhorse beneath them was in his element then, plunging and diving through the steamy air that somehow had become warmer despite the storm. Or was it the heat of their passion that warmed her?

The rain had ceased falling, but the wind whipped the water into a wild froth that broke over Elicorn's head, laving Meg's buttocks and rushing up the crease between the perfect rounds as it surged around her, past Simeon, rushing over the water-horse's back. Facing Simeon thus, she could not see what was ahead of them, only what they'd come through—towering waves that raised them up two stories high, then plunged them into valleys of ebb and flow, for they were heading into a wicked offshore wind.

"Touch me," Simeon murmured. His hoarse voice seemed to have a direct link to her sex. It leapt at the sound.

Meg reached to stroke his penis, and it jabbed forward as her fingers ringed it from base to mushroom tip with long, spiraling strokes. Her slit was spread on the horse's broad back, and the leafy vines rubbing against her exposed clitoris brought her to the brink of climax. Some of the leaves slipped inside her, driven by the base of his thick veined shaft grinding against her, reminding her of the roots of the ancient tree that had formed a shaft and moved inside her mercilessly until she came. She was nearly at that point now, and he hadn't even entered her.

"Touch yourself . . . the way you did that first night beside the window," he said gravel-voiced. "Touch your nipples . . . Make them hard for me to suck . . ."

She'd forgotten he'd seen her at her loft window at the cottage, playing with her nipples. Blood surged hot to her temples despite the water crashing over them.

"Not so deep!" Simeon commanded the horse. "Let the water tease our parts not drown them you stupid cob!"

Meg worked her nipples between her thumbs and forefingers, meanwhile writhing against the root of his sex. The whitecaps creaming over her bottom, rolling up her spine like the spindrift had rolled up the wall on Shamans' Mount. Again and again the waterhorse plunged. He was in his element again, riding the waves, his whistles blowing back on the wind, his sleek, wet hide rippling with excitement. Simeon was in his element, too, just as he always was whenever water played a part in their lovemaking; his moves were fluid, like the sea that spawned him—he *was* the sea. But *this* . . . this was unlike anything she had ever experienced before. It recalled to mind that first night, when she'd watched his consort climax as the creaming surf washed over her in Simeon's arms. She remembered how she'd so bitterly wished she were the woman in his strong arms riding the thick hardness of his shaft as the water surged around them. She was that woman now, and every pore in her body ached for him to take her—to fill her with his throbbing thickness.

"We must both come at least once . . . before I penetrate you," Simeon panted as if he'd read her thoughts. "It is . . . too intense . . . I want this to last . . . You will never experience anything like riding the storm. . . ."

Meg scanned the horizon. It seemed vacant of boats, but the

nagging fear that they were not alone out on that turbulent bay would not leave her. "Suppose someone sees?" she said,

"I see no one," Simeon responded, "but the threat that someone might will only add fuel to our fire."

He was right. Meg could hold back no longer. Her release was sweet, pulsating against his shaft until he came in heaving spurts, his hot bulk shuddering against her. But no sooner had he come than his sex grew hard again.

Meg gripped him relentlessly. It was difficult for her to relax for fear of falling off the waterhorse's slippery back. Though she knew she would not from firsthand experience, the nagging fear that the fickle horse would play his Otherworldly tricks and cause her harm would not be stilled. That, coupled with the nagging fear that they would be seen by some ill-fated mariner caught in the maelstrom only served to heighten the sensation that brought her quickly to the brink of another shattering climax. She held back, testing her seat. No, the animal held her securely, just as Simeon said he would. She could move upon the creature's back, but not fall from it. The stark terror and delicious sensation of captivity washed over her like the waves that laved her sex, until she feared her bones would turn to water. He was right . . . there was nothing to compare with riding the storm. Her parts were charged like the dry lightning that speared down all around them.

"It will not harm you," Simeon crooned in her ear. "My blood has brought the storm. It will not harm the Lord of the Deep."

Meg searched his face, ghostlike in the lightning's glare, his eyes like bottomless wells of ink-black water, shuttered with desire. The root of his shaft was boring into her pubic curls, scraping her clitoris. He coaxed her legs around him, seized her buttocks, and lowered her down upon his straining erection, parting her swollen crevice in excruciatingly slow revolutions until he filled her. Her quim seized him. It was a swift, involuntary contraction that thrust her pelvis forward and gripped him hard, wrenching a cry from his lips as he bore down upon the stirrups and raised her up and down upon him.

Oh, how he filled her, like never before, releasing her juices until they spilled over onto the leafy vines beneath her. For all the water surging over their sexes, she could feel the hot, slippery flow of her come seeping out of her nonetheless. Her bones were surely melting. Her heart was hammering so violently her breasts were trembling to the meter of the vibrations. And when his hot lips closed over her nipple and tugged, she came again.

"Do you see what pleasures I can give you?" he murmured huskily. "A lifetime of pleasures, my Megaleen . . ."

Something in the last flagged danger. What was he saying . . . That he would fill her short life with him beneath the waves with such excruciating ecstasy as this? Had he already decided her fate and his? His words nagged at her, but she beat them back. Her need, her blind passion had crowded out all thoughts of future until that moment. Now, they came creeping back like an unwanted guest, but still her need suppressed them. There was more to *riding the storm*. He had yet to reach orgasm again, but it wouldn't be long. He lifted her off his shaft, countering his release, and turned her around to face away from him just as his penis began to pulse.

"Lean forward . . . over Elicorn's neck," he panted.

Meg did as he bade her, fisting her hands in the animal's tousled mane. His hands on the rounds of her wet buttocks, rubbing, stroking, massaging, took her breath away. His hard, hot shaft riding the crevice between those rounded cheeks all but stopped her heart. When he fingered her slit feeling for her opening, she cried out. One finger then two slipped inside her, feeling for her juices, spreading them the length of her quim, along her nether lips to the delicate skin between vagina and anus until she shuddered with delight, raising her bottom even higher. Standing in the stirrups, Simeon wrapped one arm around her middle, while he eased her into position, parted the swollen lips, and slid into her, all the breath in his lungs rushing out of him as he reached deep inside her—deeper than he had ever gone before.

In that primeval position, he touched the magic spot that brought her to climax again. The riveting palpitations rushed through her belly and thighs as the titillating whitecap lace broke over the waterhorse's head and withers washing her parts over and under. It rushed into the crack of her buttocks and laved her anus with cool salt spray that should have calmed her contractions and her ardor. But it didn't.

Meg writhed against him inside her, milking the last shuddering pulse beat of her release. He was still hard. He hadn't come. He continued to undulate inside her, but softly, gently, meanwhile stroking her anus, teasing the tight rosebud open with his fingertip.

"Do not be afraid," he murmured, sliding one finger inside the opening he'd created—then two. Meg groaned, her voice so foreign she scarcely recognized it as her own as he withdrew his shaft from her tingling vagina and slipped it into her tight anal cavity.

The position forced her mons area against the vines beneath her mound. Her breath came short as the wet leaves on the vines scraped her spread vagina, rubbing her erect nub to life again. This time, the orgasm came from so deep inside her she nearly swooned; the little death, when all sanity and reason fled with time and place and conscience. His hands had found her breasts, and his fingers rolled her nipples simultaneously. Her parts convulsed as he deepened his thrusts—slow, pulsating undulations until he came in the turgid confines of her rear, her muscles gripping him relentlessly, milking him of every drop until it rushed out of her and mingled with the spindrift spraying them in diaphanous clouds.

Lightning danced in the water all around them—great snake-like spears of glaring white light raining down, as if the heavens had climaxed also. The seed of the storm; the air crackled with it.

Simeon withdrew himself, leaned back and pulled her back against him. His ragged heartbeat thumping against her back and resonated throughout her trembling body. "My Megaleen . . ." he whispered "You have ridden the storm. . . ."

Cupping her breast with one hand, he reached with the other and turned her head back to receive his kiss, his tongue laving hers, his hand buried in her hair. His breath was hot and salt-sweet as he blew into her nostrils and kneed the waterhorse as they plunged beneath the waves.

Dazed, Meg clung to him as they drove toward the palace. When they reached the cave, he dismissed Elicorn, and the waterhorse rose toward the surface again, where the seas were still running high with plenty of white water to frolic in.

The water hadn't flooded the chambers. Soon the tide would turn and what had risen to challenge the cubicles would begin to subside. The master chamber was just as Meg had last seen it when they entered. She wasn't cold, but Simeon snatched a woven sea fern throw and wrapped her in it before tucking her into bed. Shrugging the top of his eel skin suit in place, he turned to go, but Meg's quick hand arrested him.

"I shan't be long," he said. "I need to see that Vega prepares your tincture."

"What are we to do?" she said.

"Do?"

"About us . . ."

"There's nothing to do. It is already done. It is the reason we went to the Waterwitch . . . for a potion so that you could breathe longer beneath the waves."

"But . . . I cannot stay here, Simeon."

"Where else would you stay? You cannot return to the Isle of Mists, to that woman who sold you to the shamans. You cannot return to the mainland else you be burned for a witch. Where would you go?"

Meg stared. There was hurt in his eyes, but his solution wasn't the only alternative. "I . . . I hadn't really thought," she said. "There are plenty of islands where we . . . where I could make my home, Simeon."

"*I* am your home, Megaleen," he said, thumping his chest. "We are joined. We are one. I have banished the consorts, gotten help for your breathing. Do not speak nonsense. You *are* home, my Megaleen. All will be well. You will see."

Meg never loved him more than she did in that moment while looking into the depths of his silvery eyes, which shone like mercury in the rush candlelight. The hurt in them drove hers away. His love was not in question; it was deep, as deep as the depths he ruled, and as fathomless. Didn't he realize she would not be immortal? Didn't he see she would change with age and one day die, while he lived on, the image of virile youth and Otherworldly beauty? Only if they were to age together would they see each other youthful still until the end. For then, so in love, they would neither mind aging, nor notice it the way they would if one stayed young while the other grew old. And the heartbreak . . . How would she ever bear the heartbreak? How would he?

There was a way for them to do that. If she were to posses his sealskin, he would be under her spell, content to live with her on land, but the moment his sealskin was returned to him, he would return to the sea. It was the way of the selkie since time out of mind and would be until time existed no more. That is what she had been struggling with, what had been prickling like a splinter under the thin veneer of her conscience since she first held him in her arms. Were she to do such a thing, it would mean that he would lose his immortality. That is why she hesitated. That was the reason she'd given back his sealskin in the brief blink of time when she'd held it in her hands on Shamans' Mount.

The terror she'd seen in those mercurial eyes when he'd nearly drowned, his passion for the depths he ruled and for the subjects who adored him, like Pio, the faithful summoner, always at his side, like Vega, his brother who, for love of him, sunk to menial servant's duties—even the silt roses genuflected before their beloved Lord of the Deep—had she the right to strip him of all that—to interfere with a balance eons old to satisfy her mortal passion? Who would respect the drowned dead—lead them to the gods? Simeon was so much more than her lover, Meg was finding out. He could no more live without his first and greatest passion, the deep, than she, a mortal, could live in it with him. There was really only one alternative, if she only had the courage to do what needs must.

She had to let him go.

She had to leave him—give him up to the deep while she still could, before her courage flagged; it was the only way. But not yet, not today, not while his shuttered gaze was ravishing her, not while his evocative scent, sweet-salty musk was on her—in her—all around her. Not while his very presence ignited her loins with liquid fire. Instead, she smiled up at him from the soft warm bed and blinking back her tears as he lifted her hand to his lips, before he went in search of Vega.

## 17

"You are certain you've prepared it correctly?" Simeon asked Vega, holding a glass flask up to the rush candle. He turned it to and fro in his fingers, studying the murky liquid inside.

Vega's arched brow lifted. "When have you known me not to prepare a nostrum correctly, hum? Pio was very specific."

"The gods bless Pio," Simeon said. "Where is he now?"

"Out searching for news of Seth," Vega said. "I assumed you would not be needing him for a little."

"No, I shan't, or you either ... for now," Simeon said. "Once she is rested, we shall test that elixir. I mean to take her to the Pavilion for a sennight to see how she fares. I will need you and Pio for that, so prepare. Have Elicorn ready at the noon hour. I should like to reach the Pavilion by dusk. I need to go in any case. There may be drowned dead to send to the gods there. The storm still rages, though the rain has stopped. I fear more ships than we know floundered in this gale."

"As you wish," Vega said. "All will be in readiness. Shall I bring your sealskin?"

"Yes," Simeon said. "I shall have need of it. It has been too long since I've gone about in my selkie skin as I used to do."

"Has she seen you thus?" Vega asked.

"Briefly."

"I see."

Simeon's posture clenched. The edge on Vega's voice suggested sarcasm, and he rose to the occasion. "What are you on about now, Vega?"

"Only that it may be somewhat of a shock, don't you think?"

"She knows what I am."

"Perhaps it's best," Vega mused. "One of you needs to come to your senses. I am counting upon her. You are beyond hope."

Simeon narrowed cold eyes upon his brother. "If you have something to say, out with it! I've felt an undercurrent for some time between us. So . . . ?"

"I have never seen you so careless before, and it worries me, Simeon. You are besotted with love madness. I fear it will do you in if not gotten in hand quickly. This woman—"

"My mate," Simeon corrected him. "What of her?"

"Your 'mate,' " Vega awarded, sketching a bow, "is *mortal*. How in the name of the gods to you propose to introduce her to our ways? Can you not see there is nothing but heartache in it? You belong with your own kind."

"Who are you to preach that to me?" Simeon thundered. "You, who have never loved a woman in your life! You, who cock a leg over a consort now and again to relieve yourself like you would any bodily function—out of necessity, not passion!"

"I am the *only* one qualified to preach it to you, Simeon, *because* of who I am. I am the spawn of what you are about to commit yourself to, if you haven't already done so—the damned result of our father's weakness."

"You call love a *weakness*?" Simeon was incredulous.

"Love of the Lord of the Deep—a selkie prince—for a mortal female, when he has access to any female of his own race at his beck and call, yes! That is weakness and madness and foolishness, and you must be made to see that, even if it brings about the end of our relationship."

Siemeon stared, his stiff jaw muscles ticking, his broad chest heaving with rage. This was not what he wanted to hear, and if he wasn't very careful, their relationship would indeed be in jeopardy.

"Our father was a fool!" Vega went on. "And I am the result of it—a half-breed, neither mortal nor selkie but a cursed mistake. I have the best of both worlds at my command, I will allow, Otherworldly powers, immortality, mortal good looks, and capability of rational thought, but what good is any of that if neither mortal nor selkie will have me . . . if I am shunned by both races but for servitude? Do you imagine this is a pleasant existence? Well, let me assure you, it is not. You fault me for not having a mate of my own. How can I, when I am shunned by both races and you have banished the only female flesh that will have me, your leavings?"

"Vega, you have never been denied a female companion."

"No, but who will have me? Never mind that now, we digress. This is not about that—about me—it's about *you*. You are my brother, and I love you, but I cannot claim you as such, because the rest would be outraged, so I am your valet. This is what you have condemned your offspring to, Simeon—this is what could already be in her belly—all in the name of *love.*"

Simeon stared at his brother. He dared not speak. He had not been privy to Vega's innermost thoughts before . . . Or if he had been, he'd paid them no mind. What Vega was saying did not alter his feelings for Meg, but it did open his eyes to his brother's pain. They were so close . . . How had he not seen it before? It didn't matter, he saw it now. It had no bearing upon his relationship with Meg, no matter how hard he pled his case. That was in the lap of the gods.

"It isn't too late," Vega said more softly. "Send her back—now, while you still can. Bring back the consorts, you were happy with them, before Megaleen—with Alexia and Risa—you could be again. Or find another among the selkie females to take as your mate. If you must have your mortal, visit her on land like you've done with your mortal lovers for eons, but be true to your race, Simeon. Your subjects expect it—your nobility demands it."

Simeon gripped the bottle containing the tincture with almost enough force to shatter it in his hand. "You have had your say, and now I will have mine," he ground out through clenched teeth. He brandished the bottle. "This will allow her to breathe longer under water," he said. "There really is no other place for her to go. She cannot return to the Isle of Mists, where her own kind sold her for a whore, and she cannot return to the mainland, where she was cast out to begin with. To return there would be sudden death. . . ."

"There are other islands . . . You could visit her. She's going to age, Simeon. You aren't thinking clearly. The contents of that bottle will not give her immortality. If that were possible, there might be a chance, but it is not, and you need to see reason. Keeping her here or at the Pavilion is not the answer. She would be safer among her accusers on land. She will be resented and disrespected at the very least. I shudder to wonder how far it might go beyond that with her at the mercy of the jealous selkies who have set their sights upon you for their life mate. Already there are murmurings. But do not listen to me, with my mortal rationale. See for yourself. I wash my hands of it."

"Are you quite finished?"

Vega nodded. "And I can see I've wasted my breath."

"I could no more sever my ties with Megaleen, than I could sever my right arm. We are one, Vega—joined by the ancient tree spirit in an ancestral pine upon Shamans' Mount on the solstice. That cannot be undone, even if I wanted it to be, and I do not. We are one, and I shan't set her up on some island like a whore or another consort. But there *is* another alternative, you know. I could burn my sealskin and spend the rest of my days as a mortal with her, couldn't I? Which would you rather it be, hm?"

Vega made no reply. It almost seemed as if he hadn't heard a word. He seemed far away of a sudden, deep in thought, and Simeon went on quickly. "No answer? I thought not. Now then, I am going to collect a cake of night lily soap and see to my mate. When I was captured by the shamans, I was chained to a wall and made to bathe Megaleen while Seth watched, playing with his cock, else he rape her before me. I mean to wash those ugly images from her mind with something infinitely more pleasant in the way of a bath. For what it's worth, your views are duly noted. And if you truly want to preserve our 'relationship,' we will not broach this subject again."

Meg was still awake when Simeon reached his master bedchamber. How beautiful she was with her soulful blue eyes that saw only him, that spoke volumes without need of her lips. They were speaking now, proclaiming her love. How could Vega imagine he would ever leave her?

Standing over her as she lay bundled in the sea grass quilts, he held out his hand. "Come," he said. "You need to sleep, but first, something to relax you . . . to relax us both." Raising her up alongside him, he uncorked the bottle and offered it. "Take a swallow," he said. "We test it tomorrow when we go to the Pavilion, but you need to drink some now."

Meg complied, and Simeon set the bottle aside and led her to the subterranean pool where he'd made love to her when they returned to the palace. Stripping away the quilt she'd cocooned herself in, he led her to the edge and peeled off his eel skin suit.

Producing a large oval cake of fragrant soap and a sea sponge, he passed the soap in front of her nose, then raised it to his own.

"Night lilies, dark and mysterious," he said of the scent, "flowers of the night sea. They will soothe and restore you. I am going to bathe you again. This bath is the only bath I want you to remember."

Scooping her up in his arms, he descended into the pool and took her in his arms. The tide was going out, and her feet touched bottom now, where they hadn't before. She squealed as her toes met the rippling cress, and Simeon smiled.

"Your innocence delights me," he murmured against her hair.

"Innocence?" she said. "How can you say that of me now?"

"Because 'tis true," he replied. "Despite the passion in you, the worldly knowledge of your sex and mine, you are innocent still, unjaded by circumstance that should have hardened you, but didn't . . . able to take childlike pleasure in the simple touch of watercress beneath your toes."

"It tickles," Meg said through a giggle. This is what he wanted, to put her at ease. To bathe her as she should be bathed, not as he had been forced to do for the shaman's lecherous pleasure. This was to be his most powerful seduction, for it had to erase all memory of the shaman's lewd foreplay—wipe it from her mind for all time.

"I want you to relax," he said, working up a lather with the soap. The combined scents of night and ordinary lilies wafted through the air on the steamy mist rising from the pool. One fragrance coming from the soap and the other drifting from the lilies floating all around them made each breath an aphrodisiac, each whiff an intoxication. "Put everything from your mind except what I am doing to you, Megaleen, and when I've done, I want you to do it to me."

Working in slow concentric circles with both his hands,

Simeon began with Meg's slender arched throat, slathering on the creamy lather until her skin was white with it. His hands slid lower, capturing her shoulders protruding from the water, and in one motion, he lifted her out of the pool and sat her on the quilt he'd laid at the edge of it, while he continued to lather her arms. When he reached her breasts, her sharp intake of breath excited him, and his erection stirred the water. Taking great care to barely graze her puckered areolae, he deftly avoided her turgid nipple buds, though she writhed under his touch and leaned into his circular strokes. When she reached for his hands with the intent to force his fingers to work the lather into her hardened tips, he returned her arms to her sides.

"You must let me," he said, "all in due time."

Soaping her middle and the small of her back simultaneously, he fitted his hands around her waist, marveling at the way his fingers met in the middle. "So perfect," he murmured. "You are exquisite, my beauty."

Adding more water to the soap until the lather creamed over his wrists, he continued to soap her sides, then her belly and thighs, working from the outside in until he approached the V of golden curls at the top of her mound.

"Lie back," he said, easing her down upon the soft woven quilt. Spreading her open, he began massaging the lather over her quim, over the curls and the hard nub of her clitoris poking through them.

Meg writhed against the pressure of his manipulations. Her pelvis jutted forward as his strokes became more rapid—more urgent. Her breath was coming short as he took up the sea sponge and began stroking her slit with it from the hard feminine erection to the tight pucker of her anus—slow, light strokes at first, then faster until she arched her back leaning into his rhythm.

"The sea sponge is a living creature," he said, "one of the oldest in all the worlds. Mankind dries them for use in mortals' baths and then, of course, they die, but while they live in the water, if you are in tune with their nature, you can feel their pores expand and contract. It is like breathing." He slowed his stroking rhythm. "There!" he cried. "Feel it flutter against your quim? Even this poor creature is enamored of you."

She was almost ready to come when he dropped the sponge and began palming her breasts. The breath left her lungs in one continuous tremor as he squeezed and rubbed and strummed her hardened nipples. Inching closer, he leaned the shaft of his rock-hard erection against her mound, grinding the length of it into her clitoris until she came, her hot juices laving his cock.

Sliding his soapy fingers inside her, he traced the contours of her vulva, penetrating her with his fingertips at first, then to the first digits, then the second, then all the way, plunging them in and out of her until she came again. He could feel the pumping thrusts of her spasms, the involuntary pulse of her release, and the slick silky wetness of her come.

Lifting her into his arms, he eased her into the water and sponged all the soap from her skin, filling the sponge and squeezing the water from it onto her quivering body until all trace of the lather had been washed away.

"I want to see every inch of your beautiful body when you do it to me," he said, his voice husky with desire, as he eased himself up on the edge of the pool where she had lain and handed her the soap and sponge. "Do it," he murmured.

Standing on tiptoe in the water that didn't reach her nipples, Meg reached up and began soaping his chest, concentrating upon his nipples. Simeon narrowed his eyes. He wanted to make this last, but she was so beautiful with the rush candle-light playing on her wet and gleaming, smooth white skin. Her nipples, hard and tall, teased him, peeking out of the water through the ripples her motion created. He fought the urge to reach out and touch them until he could fight no more, moaning as he reached out, working them between his thumbs and forefingers.

Simeon groaned as she approached his groin with the soft, fragrant soap. Leaning on his elbows now, he watched through shuttered eyes as her deft fingers came closer and closer to his cock, and its thick veined shaft reached for her touch. There was no use to prolong the agony, no need to hold back. He would allow himself the sheer pleasure of coming under her touch, of watching his seed spill out of him. The little sorceress would make him hard again in a heartbeat.

"Soap my balls," he murmured.

Her tiny soft hands caressing his testicles made him go rigid. His breath caught as his pelvis jerked forward and his cock began to pulse, spewing his come into the water. Thrilled by Meg's gasp as it spurted out of him, Simeon ground out a guttural groan that echoed through the little subterranean chamber and reverberated off the walls and vaulted coral ceiling, resonating through his body. She had made him come without touching his cock, and he fell back upon the quilt, his arm flung over his eyes, relishing every last moment of his release.

She was touching his throbbing shaft now, squeezing soothing water from the sponge over it. Simeon lay very still while she ministered to him, while she soaped his penis from its thick root to the mushroom tip turned purple where the blood had rushed to it, pumping him dry. She had scarcely begun her ministrations, when it began to grow hard again, just like he knew it would.

"I want to show you so much," he said. "So many ways to give you pleasure. Stroke it, Megaleen . . . Bring it to life for you. . . ."

Her touch worked like magic. The merest caress, the finest butterfly stroke of her fingers, brought him to thick hardness. Inching to the edge of the pool, Simeon lifted her onto his lap, guided her legs around his waist, and entered her in one silken thrust. Her whole body convulsed around him, taking him deeper as he cupped her buttocks and pounded into her—quick, pistoning thrusts that literally took her breath away, snatching it from her nostrils on a long, ragged groan. It seemed to bubble up from the very depths of her soul as she clung to him and gripped his cock with her labia, holding him to the promise of pleasures. But it was she who was pleasuring him now, in mindless oblivion, her eyes a joy to behold, dilated with the darkness of her passion

He could bear no more. He felt her release when he came. It made his orgasm more intense as their juices mingled, as he filled her with the hot, quick spurts of his seed.

*His seed*... All at once Vega's words ghosted across his mind. Was it already too late? Had he planted his selkie seed in her mortal womb? He shook those thoughts free—shut out his brother's augur. He would not hear it—not now, with her body fused to his in perfect bliss. He tightened his grip upon her greedily and beat back those thoughts. His lips found hers, and he took them in a fiery kiss that threatened to arouse him again.

Still inside her, he eased her into the pool. He would take her one more time in the water that fueled his sexual prowess before they slept. One more release, one more little death, for it was like death to part from her even for a second. Her eyes staring but not seeing, glazed over with desire, and he fed on it, bringing them both to the brink with slow, circular revolutions.

She was loving him fiercely, as if it was their last, clinging to him—pouring out all her pent-up passions as if her very life depended upon it, but that would not do. The heady scent of night lilies rose in his nostrils, reminding him. This, he would make last. This was the bath she would remember above all others for the rest of her life if it were the last thing he did.

# 18

Vega approached the Waterwitch's cave while Simeon was occupied with Meg. This was to be one conversation he did not want overheard. The woman's parlor was empty, and he parted the vine curtain and stepped into the inner sanctum. It, too, was vacant, but then it almost always was unless the Waterwitch was summoned. Vega hummed the mantra that would resonate through the water in the pool and bring her, and waited.

There was a brief moment when he almost left with his questions unanswered. What did it matter now anyway? It didn't to him, but this wasn't about him, and when the Waterwitch's hideous fish head broke the surface of the water in the pool it was too late in any case.

She stepped out of the pool, and in a blink, her fish head disappeared, revealing her human countenance, her face old and wrinkled with a nimbus of silver gray hair fanned out wide about her. She was naked but for the shimmering green scales that covered her youthful body except for her breasts and the hairless V between her thighs which protruded like an obscene invitation the way she flaunted it. Vega shuddered. She had the power to shapeshift into many forms. He was not liking this one.

"So, half-breed," she said, sauntering toward the dais. "What brings you to Elna's cave, eh? You have not crossed my threshold in eons." She made no move to cover her nakedness with the robe draped over the back of her chair, but sat in the chair, flaunting her exquisite body.

He sketched a bow and set his tribute, a small sack of pearls, on a low table alongside. "Venerable one," he began, "I seek some truths."

"What truths might those be?" she said sweetly. She knew full well what truths had brought him there, but he would play her game. That was expected.

"I wish to know something of my lineage," he said as casually as he could manage, with her private parts demanding his attention.

"After all this time?" she scoffed. "Why?"

"Does that matter?"

She shrugged. "I suppose not," she said, "but I am curious . . . do tell."

"I wish to know of my mortal mother, Glenda."

"Ah, so," she crooned. "A true martyr was Glenda—gave you up for your father to raise. She had no choice really. Selkie half-breed bastards don't last long on the mainland. They get clubbed to death—or worse. She did you a kindness. Half-breed selkie skins are even more in demand than the common variety, but you already know that."

"Yes, yes, I know that," Vega said. "You are the only one alive who knew her well enough to answer my questions. Was she a full-blooded mortal or a half-breed herself?"

"No, she was full blooded," the woman said. "Why do you ask?"

Vega shrugged. "Just curious. What became of her . . . Where did she go?"

"That was a long time ago, half-breed. Time has forgotten those particulars."

"To be sure," Vega sallied, "but you have not, old one. You were there, and you know. Now you will tell me."

"Oh, so masterful we are . . . so youthful . . . so virile." She got out of the chair with a sinuous motion and sauntered toward him, stopping to open the sack and appraise his bribe along the way. "That which you wish to know comes at a price above these piddling geegaws," she said, letting the pearls slip through her webbed fingers back into the sack.

"It comes too dear if you expect me to cock a leg over you to get it," Vega said through a wry chuckle. "You dream!"

"You could do worse, or not at all," she chortled. "Like now, with the consorts you play with banished to the barrier beach." She changed again, and her wrinkled face became comely, her skin as smooth and white as alabaster, and her hair long, black, and shining like a raven's wing in the rush light glow. "Who milks that cock I see bulging there now, eh? You do, I'll wager, young lordling." She slid her hands over her body seductively. "How can that rough palm of yours be better than this?"

"I know what you really are," Vega said, sidestepping her advance. "Your witch's glamour cannot disguise what lies beneath."

"I am all things to all men, half-breed," she purred. "There is great power to be had for a few brief moments in me. What harm to relieve yourself in this body?" She nodded toward his groin. "Take it out and let me see," she said. "It looks about to burst out of that eel skin suit it is so anxious. Why not let it burst in me, eh? I will not disappoint you."

She floated closer, her fingers tweaking her nipples to hardness. One hand slid the length of her exquisite body to her exposed slit, and she began to rub herself. "You are tight against the seam," she observed, gesturing toward the bulk straining the crotch of his eel skin. "I'll make a bargain with you. Take that out and let me watch you get yourself off, and I will tell you what you need to know."

Her use of the words "need to know," rather than "want to know" told him she knew exactly why he had come. She had the answer he sought, and she was right. His cock was bursting and had been since the consorts were banished and naught but the old sea creatures were left to run the palace.

Selkies had no modesty, they often mated in public, and he was half selkie, so that was not an issue. But he was also possessed of human genes, and the mere thought of exposing himself before the odious crone, much less relieving himself in front of her, brought bile to his throat. Shapeshifters were unpredictable during sex. She may be beautiful now, but he had seen her hideous side, and he hesitated.

"Very well, if you like," he said at last, "but tell me first."

"You do not trust me," she returned, answering her own question. "Your mortal side is strong in you. Selkies are far more trusting, which is why if he is not very careful, the Lord of the Deep will meet his end at the hands of one he's put his trust in now."

Here was an interesting tidbit. Vega lingered over it but only briefly. She was advancing on him. "Stay back, old one," he warned her. "I may not be a trusting sort, but I am trustworthy. Now my question . . . while you perform for *me* . . . to get me in the mood."

She nodded toward his crotch. "That there looks to be enough in the mood to me."

"Yes, well, I am the best judge of that. Touch yourself some more, and tell your tale." He nodded toward the pearl sack on the table. "You can be assured that I shall give you everything you are worth. You have my word. . . ."

She began whirling about, performing a strange dance ritual, jiggling her full breasts and flaunting her sex. How beautiful she was, how graceful, with her slender spine arched back as she swirled. But then all fish were graceful, he kept reminding himself, and she was one hideous, whiskered, snaggle-toothed barracuda in her true incarnation.

"What you seek to know won't help you, half-breed," she said. "It is all in the past—buried in the dust of time."

"Tell it anyway. Where did my mother go after she abandoned me? How did she die?"

The Waterwitch slid a long silk scarf from her chair on the dais and snaked it between her legs, teasing her slit with it as she danced. Her gyrations were making him hot, thanks to his selkie side, but that would have to wait.

"She went to the Isle of Mists, young lordling—"

"Do not call me that!" he snarled. "I am not in line for the throne."

She laughed. "You do not have any idea what you are in line for, but I will not vex you, half-breed."

"Continue! Why the Isle of Mists?"

"Your father paid a tidy sum to the shamans to allow her to enter the nunnery there."

"Nunnery? What nunnery? I know of the training house for priestesses, where the shamans prepare virgins to enter the temple on Shamans' Mount, but I know of no nunnery."

"It still exists," said the witch, "if you know where to find it." She winked and danced closer, grazing him with her perfect breasts as she circled him, undulating seductively as she teased her nipples and played with the scarf between her legs.

"Where?" Vega persisted. He had to keep reminding himself that she was naught but sorceress glamour. She was closing in on him—touching him. When she seized the bulk of his cock, he leapt back. "This was not part of the bargain!" he snapped at her.

She shrugged. "No, but it tells me you are ready to come. I have done my work, but you have not done yours. . . ."

Vega seized her by the throat and jerked her to a standstill. "Oh yes, I have," he gritted through clenched teeth. "You foul, odious creature, I told you I would give you everything you are worth, which I will do—or snap this pretty neck. The choice is yours. Now, tell your tale! Where is this nunnery? My patience ebbs low."

"In the . . . mists," the Waterwitch ground out.

"I gathered as much." He shook her roughly. "Where in the mists?"

"Take care, half-breed, you do not know the consequence of harming me! You risk the wrath of the gods!"

"That doesn't matter any more. The nunnery!"

"You will need a charm." She said gripping his hands clamped around her throat. "T-take one of the crystals in that jar in the table; their magic is universal. Cast it into the mist on the north side of the Isle at the midnight hour, and it will appear to you. You'll never enter otherwise. You'll need the magic. No men— mortal or otherwise—can breech the mists that guard the nunnery; not even you, bastard of the deep."

He put her from him and hesitated over the jar before taking one of the geodes glistening inside and tucking it away inside his eel skin.

"But it will do you no good," she said. Tugging her transparent robe over her nakedness, she sank into her counsel chair on the dais. "The sisters you will find there now do not know the tale entire."

"But you do, and you had best tell it quickly!"

"There is nothing to tell," the Waterwitch snapped. "Like Megaleen, Glenda could not become a priestess; she was no longer a virgin. The shamans would have paid dearly for her if she still had her virtue, for she was very beautiful. She would have become a sacrifice or one of the shaman's whores but for your father, who paid a virtual king's ransom to have her shut up in the nunnery, where she would be safe. That is your tale. Pay, like you agreed, and be gone."

"And she lived there at the nunnery until she died?" Vega persisted.

"Died?" she said. "She lives there still. What? All these years she is but a stone's throw away . . . And you did not know it?" She threw her head back in a burst of coarse laughter.

"Who was to tell me, old woman? Simeon wouldn't know— he came after me—and my father and stepmother have been dead since I'm little more than a child. I'd say the telling of that tale was up to you, keeper of the Scroll of Arcan Rite! It is you who have failed me. How is it possible that she still lives?"

The Waterwitch shrugged. "Some magic of the holy women at the nunnery, for all I know," she said. "Many mortals who are shut up in that 'holy' tomb live long lives, as long as they do not leave the protection of its walls. It is a jumping-off place to the gods, but not *my* gods. I am not welcomed there, with or without a charm. Not that I would court their company, the sanctimonious old harpies."

"How can you be so certain Glenda still lives?"

Again she shrugged. "I keep the Sacred Scroll, do I not? If she were dead, I would know of it. Her page is still unwritten, bastard of the deep."

"You evil old cow! You should have told me all this eons ago!"

"I owe you no explanations. If it was so important, you should have asked it of me eons ago, fool! Now sweeten that tribute and be gone!" she snarled. "I no longer care for this game."

Vega strolled to the table and gathered all the pearls, tossing them to appraise their weight—two dozen in all. Lifting a flawed one of lesser value from the rest, he laid it on the table and tucked the pouch containing the rest inside his suit.

"Here! What is that?" she shrilled.

"More than you are worth, you crone," he seethed, stalking from the sanctum, "and at that you have been overpaid."

Shrieking like a banshee, the Waterwitch left the counsel chair with force enough to tip it over, dancing to a different rhythm now, a rhythm of her rage. Having reached the vine curtain, Vega glanced behind in time to see the hideous fish that was the woman's true form splash into the pool and disappear beneath the ripples.

Livid, having learned what he'd hoped and feared, Vega plunged into the water on the far side of the cave and swam in no particular direction. He needed to think. He needed to sort out what the Waterwitch had just told him. It was true enough. There was no question. He'd seen it in her clenched posture, in her shocked demeanor. Why hadn't he questioned before? He couldn't reproach himself for that. Because his mother was mortal, he had always assumed she'd died as mortals die. If she had not, then there had to be a way for Meg to live on also, but he dared not give her hope of that unless it had been proven. That meant going to the nunnery to see Glenda for himself.

Those thoughts changed his course and drove him toward the Isle of Mists. For the first time in his long, lonely life, Vega would not be at Simeon's beck and call. He would not be there to ready Elicorn and accompany them to the Pavilion. This was more important.

"Something is wrong I tell you!" Simeon said, pacing the floor in his master bedchamber. "It isn't like Vega to fail me he has never done so before. He was to have been here with Elicorn at the noon hour. The sun is already descending. Even if we leave at once, we will not reach the Pavilion before full dark. It is too great a distance."

Meg was relieved. The Pavilion was the last place she wanted to go. It was too isolated and unfamiliar. She could never escape from there, for that is what she had made up her mind to do. If the tincture worked, she could easily reach the Isle of Mists. Despite what Simeon said, there were places on the Isle where she would be safe, at least for now. Besides, she longed to know if her aunt and uncle had weathered the selkie storm. This she could do from a distance, but she needed to know—especially what had become of her uncle Olwyn, who had always been kind to her even if her aunt had not. Despite all that had gone before, they were still her flesh and blood.

Her heart was breaking at the thought of leaving Simeon, but it was the only way. She could not allow him to give up his immortality for her. Neither could she bear to wither and die while he stayed young and virile. She would never be able to stand the look of disgust in his eyes as she aged and could no longer match the power of his passion. It was better to break clean now, to give him back to his own kind, while she still possessed the courage to let him go.

What she needed was an opportunity to slip away, and he hadn't left her side. Making matters worse, the mere sight of him aroused her. Despite her resolve, the bond between them was already too strong to sever casually, and yet it had to be done. Meanwhile, she dared not give him reason to suspect what she was planning, and above it all, she begged the Arcan gods to give her just one more hour in his arms. She was going mad—she had to be. There was no other explanation for the riot of emotions roiling in her then.

"We can go another day," she said. She longed to reach out and touch him as he stomped past, but she dared not. He was very perceptive. He might know. It was torture. Instead, she stood helpless, taking his measure, drinking in the tall, muscular length of him: the sturdy, well-turned thighs and broad shoulders defined beneath the skin-tight eel skin suit that left nothing to the imagination. He may as well have been naked. She couldn't see his eyes, they were so deeply sunken in shadows, but she didn't need to see them to recall their soulful, almond-shaped beauty—the only feature that remained the same whether he was in his human form or that of the great, graceful seal. He was magnificent.

Just when she feared she could bear no more, a strange echo vibrated through the master apartments catching Simeon's attention. He stopped in his tracks.

"What is it?" Meg asked.

"Pio!" Simeon said. "Now we shall have some answers. I shan't be long."

He streaked off toward the tunnel in the direction of the sound, and Meg waited until she heard the splash as his body enter the water before slipping off in the opposite direction toward the subterranean pool, where he had bathed her and made love to her. She remembered the ebb and flow of the tide as it rose and subsided there. It was fed by the water in the bay. It would be easy enough to find the opening.

On her way past the bed they'd just slept in together, the nightstand beside it caught her eye. On it, she spied the flask containing the tincture that would allow her to breathe for longer periods under water. She hesitated, her hand hovering over it. Should she take it with her? She'd already been dosed. If it hadn't worked, it wouldn't matter, and once she'd gotten away, she would have no more need of it. She would not be coming back beneath the waves again.

There was no more time. Retracting her hand, she cast one last glance about the chamber and fled.

## 19

"We may have to postpone our visit to the Pavilion," Simeon said to an empty chamber as he entered the master suite. "Pio has found Seth on the Isle of Mists, and some selkie justice is in order to"—he pulled up short—"see that he never does anything like . . . Megaleen . . . ? *Megaleen!*"

Streaking through the other chambers, he called her name at the top of his voice, bringing a troop of otherwise invisible retainers, mostly older male selkies, who swarmed into the master suite nonplussed at the ruckus. But there was no sign of Meg, and he dismissed them with orders to search every recess.

Raking his hair back with both his hands as if he meant to keep his brain from bursting, Simeon began to pace. First Vega and now Meg had gone missing. He'd sensed something under the surface in Meg, especially the last time they'd made love. It was almost a desperate coupling, as if it were their last. He'd shrugged it off as the heat of passion, but now those fears came crawling back to haunt him. But why would she go and where? She loved him, he knew it. Did she fear the differences between them that Vega was so quick to point out? Didn't she know how much he loved her? Didn't she know he would move the moon and the stars to have her, to keep, and to love her?

His travels pacing the sumptuous carpet brought him close to the nightstand and the tincture bottle standing on it just as he'd left it. The blood drained from his face as if a shade had descended over him, shutting out the light she had lit inside him, and he groaned. She wasn't in the palace. The servants wouldn't find her there. She was gone, and she did not mean to return.

He rummaged through the wardrobe like a man possessed. She had taken nothing from the vast collection of rich costumes and accessories that had been collected over the ages, the boon of shipwrecks, like everything else in the palace. He was certain the exquisite costumes were meant by the fates for Meg alone, and she had taken nothing—not a bauble, not a jewel—only the frock on her back. He couldn't even recall its color or style. Her beauty by far outshone any silk or lace or cloth of gold in the palace, and he had been blinded by it. He had to have her back. Life meant nothing without her—immortality meant nothing. It would be a life of torture. The world and everything in it had no meaning without his Megaleen.

Stomping out of the palace, Simeon plunged into the water surrounding it and swam for the Waterwitch's cave, meanwhile humming the mantra to bring Pio, but the summoner didn't come. Pio, too? What was happening? In all the eons of his life, Simeon had never felt as helpless as he did then, surging through the water alone on the brink of madness.

He surfaced at the Waterwitch's subterranean cave, scrambled up onto the threshold, and burst into her sitting room. As always, it was empty, and he charged through the aquatic vine curtain and entered her sanctum. That, too, was vacant, and he loosed a cry of utter frustration, pounding the chair on the dais with clenched fists. How, in but a blink in time's eye, had everyone abandoned him?

Rage moved him now, and he ground out the mantra that always brought the witch, but it came out more like the roar of a lion. Taking deep breaths, he tried again, and again . . . and again. Nothing. Not a ripple in the water in her pool. Not a sound save the slow, maddening splats of water dripping from chinks in the coral into more water.

How long he stood there, he did not know, only that it was long enough for him to grow hoarse from calling the witch to no avail. Finally, he staggered through the vine curtain into the vacant parlor and dove back into the water. There would be no help for him this time. If he was to have his Megaleen back, he was on his own.

Vega reached the Isle of Mists too soon. He dared not risk climbing out of the bay in broad daylight. He'd swum and swum until he feared his heart would burst through his chest, but it hadn't eased the mortal pain the Waterwitch's words had inflicted upon him or the ferocity of his selkie desire. It was not a comfortable thing.

Through all the centuries of his existence, he'd thought he knew who, and why, he was. Now he knew nothing. In the space of a blink, the Waterwitch had wiped everything he knew and thought and hoped he was away, like the wind carrying off a thistle seed. It would take root elsewhere, but he could not. He was doomed to an existence as foreign to him as his separate races, the curse of a half-breed; not enough of either to be whole.

There were many magical underwater air pockets in the archipelago, where a selkie, or a mortal for that matter, might take shelter beneath the waves. Vega found one close to the Isle of Mists. It was a small, secluded one rising from a little pool filled with graceful sea anemones attached to the coral, where he could rest and think . . . and relieve himself, for despite it all, he was still tight against the seam. Crawling up on a broad flat ledge lined with sea kelp, he stretched out on his back with one knee raised, and opened the crotch of his eel skin suit. Lifting the bulk of his cock out, he groaned as he soothed it—more for relief than release at first, for it pained him so long jammed against the skin-tight crotch of the suit.

He thought of Risa, the beautiful young selkie consort he'd bedded once before Simeon banished all the consorts. That seemed an eon ago. It might have worked between them given half a chance, for Risa was willing, and they had mated well, but that was hopeless now. Still, when he shut his eyes, it was Risa he saw stroking his cock, bringing it to life. It wasn't his roughened palm that gripped it. It was Risa's soft, skilled fingers riding up and down its shaft, her soft quim gripping him, her dewy lips sucking him dry.

His slow, soothing ministrations quickly became rapid and urgent, but he wasn't alone. Vibrations in the kelp bed beneath him brought his eyes open to the sight of a young female selkie, who thrashed up on the ledge alongside him and began shedding her sealskin. Was he dreaming? Vega inched back to give her more room, his hooded eyes following her every move as she peeled the skin away, with painfully slow undulations that revealed her perfect body beneath.

It wasn't the Risa of his daydream, though there was something familiar about her. One of the younger consorts perhaps or one of those hopefuls slated to become a consort that he'd seen loitering about the palace hoping for a glimpse of Simeon. It didn't matter. His selkie side was out of control, just as it always seemed to be when he was overtired.

Her gaze, hooded and sultry, was ravishing him. She's inched the skin down to expose her breasts, teasing him with her hardened nipples, giving him only brief glimpses of their tawny peaks. Just when he thought he could bear no more, she wriggled out of the rest of the skin and knelt before him naked. She was without blemish, her skin like alabaster, her hair gleaming in the defused light with the blue-black shimmer of a

raven's wing. Phosphorescence from the water and light filtering down from above gave her an ethereal look, Otherworldly
and mysterious. It captivated him. Above all, her large, lipid
eyes, a feature inherent in both incarnations, were reverencing
him in a way that made his hot blood sizzle. This was where his
selkie self and his mortal self parted company. This was where
one always gave way to the other. His selkie self had done that
the minute she undulated out of the sealskin. He was pure sex,
as malleable as molten lava in her hands—or any hands that laid
themselves upon him in his selkie incarnation.

Sidling closer, the female fed him one if her nipples, while
she played with the other. Vega saw her through a veil of red
that always obscured his vision when aroused. He had often
wondered if it was the same with other selkies—with Simeon—
or if it was a phenomenon peculiar to half-breeds. He'd never
mustered the courage to ask him. It didn't matter now. Rational
thought was far away. Nothing seemed real, nothing but the
tug his cock felt as he sucked her tit; nothing but the cool touch
of her hand stroking the hot flesh of his thick, hard shaft.

It had been too long since his last mating, and he could hold
back no longer. His release would be strong. It had already
started to pulse when she leaned back from him, her hideous
laughter ringing in his ears. Vega's eyes snapped open to Elna,
the Waterwitch, her gap-tooth grin and wiry white hair looming over him where the beautiful selkie's countenance had been.

"Shortchange me, will you, half-breed?" she triumphed. She
gestured toward his rigid cock. Why wouldn't it go soft? How
could it betray him like this? It should shrivel into limp flaccid-
ity, but there it was, as hard as ever a cock could be! "It can
wither and fall clean off you before I'll finish what I've started
there," she shrilled.

"I would prefer that to relieving it in the likes of you!" Vega
thundered.

"Good!" she snarled, "then this should please you, young

lordling!" Seizing the foot of a green sea anemone from where it was attached to the edge of the pool, she flew at him and jammed the creature's head—tentacles and all—over his erection. "Cock a leg over that!" she chortled, her head thrust back in riotous laughter.

The minute the dozens of stinging tentacles seized his member, Vega came into the flowerlike creature's mouth, the hot rush of his seed riding back up his shaft, coating it—protecting it from the stinging cells the anemone used to paralyze its prey. It would not harm him. They were creatures of the deep—kindred. The Waterwitch hadn't taken into consideration the symbiotic relationship that existed between such creatures and the selkie, and Vega laughed as he took back his cock and returned the anemone to its coral ledge.

"Better than my palm by half, old hag," he said. "And you've nourished the creature to boot! You've done us both a favor."

The Waterwitch's laughter turned to rage. She pounded her thighs with white-knuckled fists and spewed a spate of curses at him. She reached for her sealskin, but Vega was too quick for her. Snatching it up from the kelp strewn ledge, he slung it over his shoulder.

"Oh, no!" he said, "'Tis mine now by forfeit!"

"You give that back!" she demanded, her shrieks deafening.

"So you can tempt another with it?" Vega said. "Never! Where did you get it in the first place? You are no selkie. What poor unsuspecting creature did you steal it from?" His breath caught. "Wait a moment," he said, discovery in his voice. "Is this how you buy your immortality? Is this how you cheat the gods . . . by stealing selkie skins and holding them until the poor creature dies his mortal death? What then . . . you steal another and another, when his days are done? *It is!* And in the meanwhile, you transform into your most seductive incarnation, like you did just now, don the skin, and fornicate among the unsuspecting selkies? I *knew* there was something. I warned Simeon about you eons ago. The Scroll of Arcan Rite in your hands is sacrilege!"

"That is none of your affair."

"No?" Vega seethed, brandishing the sealskin. "I've just made it my affair."

She shrugged. "Keep the skin! I shall only get another."

Vega plunged into the pool. "Well, you shan't have this one! Unless, of course, you want to fish it out of the volcano on Lord Vane's Isle of Fire, because that is where it's going, 'venerable' one, and I would not attempt it if I were you. Once I tell this tale to the Lord of the Flames, you will not be welcome there!" He brandished the sealskin. "This here will become a burnt offering to insure its former owner rite of passage to the gods. See how they welcome you when your time comes, old hag!"

She said more, her hoarse voice crackling over the breast of the water, her fists carving mad circles in the air. Then all at once there came a hitch in her demeanor, as though some fiendish inspiration had struck, and one thing came loud and clear above the rest: "I *will* get another, and you will rue the day you ever touched that sealskin, bastard of the sea! You mark my words!"

Having had enough, Vega plunged beneath the surface of the pool, swam out into the bay, then on to the ocean and the Isle of Fire to keep his word. He didn't linger there. Soon it would be midnight. Whoever's sealskin it was that he'd confiscated from the Waterwitch had been cast into Lord Vane's volcano and was no more. Shrugging off her cryptic augur at the last, he swam for the Isle of Mists and reached it just before the midnight hour. He wasn't prepared for the devastation that met his eyes. The strand was foreshortened by yards. The dune where Simeon had buried his sealskin was gone, so was the little cottage on the rise above it; Meg's cottage. Nothing remained near the beach, and the seas were still running high.

Selkie storms were notorious for their intensity. Much of the archipelago was formed because of them at the dawn of time. It was a miracle that anything remained, considering, Vega thought, since Shamans' Mount adjoining had been leveled to a mere spit of rock and sand. He took that to be an act of the gods' justice.

The night mist had risen over the Isle and cloaked his movements, though stealth was inherent in him. Picking his way to the north side of the Isle as the Waterwitch had instructed, he passed much devastation. What appeared to be a bait shack close to the destroyed cottage had also been leveled. Horsefeet were everywhere, righting themselves with their long sharp tails, clawing their way toward the shore in a mass exodus to return to their home in the sea. Even the babies raised on shore seemed to know this was where they belonged. Vega stopped to help turn several over whose hard, helmetlike shells were too heavy for their tails to flip. All creatures of the sea were kin to the selkie—half-breeds included.

The mists were thick in pockets on the north shore. There wasn't a soul in sight. Glancing about to be certain he wasn't being watched, Vega slipped the Waterwitch's crystal from inside his eel skin suit and turned it to and fro in his hand. *Universal,* she'd said of the charm. How it would be accepted while she was not was a mystery, but then so was the nunnery. He had no choice but to chance it. Murmuring a prayer over it to the Arcan gods of the deep just in case, he cast it into the misty hollow.

For a moment, he felt like a fool, but only for a moment. All at once the mist parted, showing him what looked like an ancient abbey. The Waterwitch had been truthful about that much at least. As he stepped into the illusion, it swallowed him up. Spinning around, he saw no exit. Groping the mist gained him nothing. Searching the ground, he foraged for the Waterwitch's crystal charm and found it. Tucking it away inside his eel skin again, just in case, he turned back to the strange chalk structure before him, which was the color of the mist itself.

Swirling vapors licked his feet as he stepped up to the threshold. To his surprise, the door came open to him before he had a chance to knock, and he faced a short, plump woman garbed in the long white robes of her order, her face all but hidden behind a crisp white wimple. Even the light spilling out onto the sand was the color of the mist. The nunnery was indeed well disguised.

"Good lady," he said, "I am come seeking one of your sisters . . . One called Glenda."

The woman swept her arm wide to signal him to follow and led him to a small cell off the corridor where the light was less acute, then bade him wait. No words passed between them. He understood the woman's meaning exactly. Praying it was not a silent order, he waited somewhat less than patiently for his mother to join him. *His mother!* How could it be . . . and yet it was.

Mercifully, he wasn't left waiting long. He'd just begun to fidget when a tall, handsome woman floated into the room. She was similarly dressed to the other sister, though her headgear was more like a shawl that reached to her fingertips. For a moment, she hesitated, then crossed the threshold and closed the door behind her.

"I am not come for myself," Vega said, breaking the awkward silence. "I am come for my brother, who finds himself in the same situation you did so long ago. . . ."

Glenda heaved a mammoth sigh. "The sins of the fathers," she murmured on the wane of it. How sweet her voice was, and how beautiful she was after all these years, but how could it be? He would not rush right into that.

"I was brought up believing you were dead," he said.

"'Twas best," she returned almost before he'd finished speaking. She could not meet his gaze then. Looking down, her long dark lashes left dusky shadows on her cheeks. It was uncanny. She looked no older than a girl of twenty. This should not seem odd to one coming from his world of immortals . . . but she was his *mother!*

"Why was it best?" he asked her.

"Seal hunters abounded," she began. "Baby sealskins brought high prices. Half-breed sealskins were most prized of all because of their rarity. Many were slaughtered. I could not stay with your father. He already had a mate. You would not have been safe with me alone. I could not have protected you, Vega . . . but your father could."

The sound of his name upon her lips ran his heart through like a javelin. His had been such a lonely life, and now this! He almost hated Simeon then, but he couldn't even do that. They were brothers of the blood.

"So you came here," he said, answering his own question.

"Your father loved you, and he loved me. Selkie men often love more than one woman fiercely. It is the selkie way, and they see nothing wrong in it. Neither do their selkie mates, like Meriwyn, Simeon's mother. She raised you like her own, under your father's protection, and you have grown . . . so handsomely. . . ." There were tears in her voice, though none fell as she took his measure. "They both died by the seal hunters' clubs, but you were older then, and you were spared. The selkie storms that followed their murder changed the face of the archipelago—wiped out hundreds of islands formed by the great cataclysm when time began, and they drove the seal hunters away."

"And Father shut you up in here?"

She smiled. It did not reach her eyes. "Your father gave great sums to the sisters to house me here, where I would be safe."

"But how is it that you have not aged? This is what I must know?"

"Why must you know?"

"Because of Simeon."

"Ah! Simeon . . ."

"And his woman . . . He is so smitten, I fear he will leave the deep to be with her. She might leave her own kind and live beneath the waves with him, but she will age and he will not. I fear that may deter her, and he would die upon the land. When I learned that you still lived—"

"Who told you?" she interrupted him. "How long have you known?"

"Elna, the Waterwitch, told me today."

"Do not trust her! She is an evil, odious crone, Vega."

He ground out a gritty chuckle. "And well I know it, but I am not here about me. You are not selkie, and yet you have not aged. How so? The Waterwitch told me many who take sanctuary here live longer lives as long as they do not leave this place. Is that so?"

Glenda turned away. It was clear she was weighing her answer. Vega did not press her. After a moment, her posture collapsed, then became rigid again, and she turned back to face him.

"Some whom the gods reward with such privilege do," she said, "but I am not among them. They would hardly venerate an adulterer." Again she hesitated. "This is something I would not have you tell Simeon," she said. "It would only hurt him for naught. I must have your word."

"You have it."

She nodded. "Your father has raised you well and taught you honor and loyalty. I have followed your progress from my distance, and I am well pleased. I will take you at your word."

"Please then, how is it that you are immortal?"

She swept her arm wide. "This was only to be temporary," she said. "Even selkie immortals can take sick and die if they contract diseases of the human race. Simeon's mother was such a one. She was sickly, and your father feared that she would one day die of the lung fever that had weakened her. When that day came, he was to come for me and unite us—all three. There was a sorcerer of dubious repute on the Isle of Fire in those days. Your father paid him a staggering tribute for a charm that would give me longer life. That was another reason for incarcerating me here, for if the world at large knew of it, my life would have been in grave danger, as you can well imagine."

"And the sisters took you in."

She nodded. "They gave me sanctuary, yes. It was only supposed to be temporary, and as I said, they, too, were well paid. This is a holy, restful place, not like the evil sham of Shamans' Mount. I have been happy here. So you see your father did not abandon me, and I did not abandon you, not really, Vega, my love child. He meant for us to be together one day, and we would have been, but then . . . he died."

"The charm Father purchased, do you have it still?"

She hesitated. "What sort of person is your half brother?" she asked him, obviously avoiding the question. "His reputation speaks well of him, but is he worthy of a great sacrifice?"

"I would lay down my life for him," Vega said.

"And this mortal woman?"

"If he had not seen her first, I would be inquiring for myself," he confessed. "They are very much in love, just as you and Father were."

There was a long silence.

"Do you hate me, Vega?" Glenda said at last.

He met her eyes. They were glazed now with unshed tears. "No," he said. "I only wish I had known all this . . . before, when it would have mattered."

"One sacrifice deserves another," she said, reaching inside the throat of her habit. Her tiny fingers closed on a silver strand. "Give your brother's lady this," she said, handing him the necklace. "Once she puts it on and accepts the gift, it cannot be lost or stolen. Only her hand can remove it. Tell her to wear it always and it will give her length of days. . . ."

"But what of you?" Vega said, for already her smooth white

skin bore traces of wrinkles. She was aging right before his very eyes. "You cannot do this! There must be another way!"

She shook her head. "I am tired now, let this be my reparation. Your father is dead, Vega. Our dream can never be, but there is hope for Simeon . . . and *his* lady. You must take it. Your father would want it this way."

"You still strive to please him . . . even now," Vega marveled. "Curious." Such a love was incomprehensible to his selkie side, and with no one to mentor his mortal side, it boggled his mind. "But if that is so," he said, "if as you say you are tired of immortality, why did you wait so long to seek the afterlife? Father has been gone for eons."

"I think I was waiting for this night," she said. "for you. Do not let the Waterwitch know of this amulet. She has powers, but they have their limits. She has no access here. Let her continue to think I have gained immortality through veneration among the chosen ones. If she knew of the existence of this charm, she would move the moon and stars to get it, and neither Simeon nor his lady would be safe. Take it, my son, and go. You have given me the greatest gift . . . my peace at last. . . ."

Vega didn't get a chance to speak. She spun on her heels, and in a blink, she was gone.

# 20

Meg found the opening that led from the pool into the bay without difficulty. If she didn't know better, she would have sworn the sea life guided her there, for all manner of fish—large and small—swam with her. As they guided her, their silvery phosphorescence caught glints of reflected light from some unknown source above the waves and reminded her of Simeon's mercurial eyes. Even the underwater plants seemed to point the way, waving as she passed. Her breathing was natural enough, and when she surfaced, she made the transition from breathing water to breathing air as naturally as if she'd done so all her life.

The light source that had silvered the fish had come from the waning moon, which was shining down upon the breast of the bay in all its misshapen glory. There wasn't a cloud in the sky. The storm was over, and though the waves were running high with heaving swells and white-capped curls, their voices were soft sighs now rather than the deep-throated roars she'd heard during the storm. *Their voices.* Had the deep adopted her that she could hear the voices of the waves? It seemed so. A twinge of remorse washed over her, for she had grown to love it, just as she loved Simeon, which was why this must be. Meg needed to keep reminding herself of that, for it was breaking her heart to leave him.

She brushed her long wet hair back from her face, and scanned the horizon, letting the waves buoy her, bellying the skirt of her dove-gray kirtle. Before her, the islands fanned out in a wide, sweeping arc. Which one? It only took a moment to pick out the Isle of Mists. It was the only one half-hidden in the ghostly veils of its namesake, an odd phenomenon when all the other islands were mist free. She started to swim toward it, following the arrow-straight line of moon shimmer on the water that seemed to point the way.

Halfway there, something nudged her under the waves. She ducked beneath the surface but saw nothing. She hadn't swum much farther when it happened again, harder this time, like a kick in the stomach, then something sharp pricked her. It did not break the skin, though it stung, and she cried out as Pio broke the surface in front of her, his long sword gleaming in the moonlight.

"It's no use!" she said. "I have to go, Pio. I have to know if they are still alive."

The swordfish nudged her again, but she paid him no mind. Pushing past him, she continued to swim toward shore, though the summoner swam back and forth in front of her, making her progress difficult. When that didn't work, he broke the waves and danced on his tail on the breast of the water. Meg had often seen fish break the surface and do this, but there was a sense of urgency in the swordfish's antics that almost frightened her.

"Shoo! Go away!" she shouted. "I am going to the Isle. You would have to spear me through with that dreadful sword to prevent me. I have to know if my aunt and uncle live before I leave this place. Then I will be gone to trouble you and your master no more. Now, let me pass!"

If ever a fish could be frustrated, this fish was frustrated now. Meg would have laughed if the situation wasn't so grave. One thing was certain: what she had planned to do had to be done quickly. Pio the summoner would go straight to Simeon with his failure, and he would surely come after her. The swordfish tried twice more to change her course, and when that didn't work, he disappeared.

Minutes later, Meg stepped out of the surf on the Isle of Mists. The moon at her back was barely visible now in brief glimpses through the mist. For a moment, she thought she saw the shadow of a large bird silhouetted against it, but in a blink it was gone. All was still—too still—as she parted the mist and climbed what was left of the dunes toward what remained of the little cottage where it had all begun. As she approached it, waves of déjà vu washed over her like the waves washed over the strand, reeling her back in time to that first night when she'd touched herself in the dark as she watched Simeon performing for her alone with his main consort Alexia—taking her in shameless abandon as the waves crashed over them where sea met seaweed, pebbles, and sand.

How he'd known she was watching that night was still a mystery. There was no logical explanation other than the fact that selkies were perceptive enough to simply know such things—to sense sexual excitement in humans as well as their own kind. He had evidently watched her on the beach for some time from the rocks and boulders off shore where the selkies sunned themselves by day. She'd often watched the seals cavorting there, wondering if the selkie tales were true; secretly hoping they were.

Try as she would to beat those thoughts back, they would not leave her. She remembered how he'd flaunted his engorged sex in the moonlight. How he'd entered the female selkie, impaling her upon that hard, curved shaft as the creaming surf crashed around them. How he'd played with her nipples, teasing, taunting, but not touching the tall dark tips silhouetted against the surf in the moonlight.

Meg's female parts were wet and tingling. It had nothing to do with the wetness of the sea she'd just come from. She was aroused just thinking about Simeon's dynamic body—about her first time in those strong arms . . . and the last. He had the power to bring her to the brink of climax with naught but a memory. How could she ever live without him, her Lord of the Deep?

A captive of the haunting recollections, Meg felt deep spurts, like liquid fire, begin to surge through her moist sex. It was as if she were reliving that fateful night all over again as she had so many times since, only the memory was more acute here, where it all began. Gripping the mound between her thighs with pinching fingers, she tried to no avail to still the scalding heat waves that had drenched her with desire. Not even the sight of Adelia's cottage, ravaged by the storm, standing wounded against the mist could still her need.

There was no one about. If Olwyn and Adelia had survived the maelstrom, they had taken shelter elsewhere. Mindful of her bare feet, Meg picked her way over the debris left by the storm and stepped inside the dilapidated shell of what once had been her home. She turned back toward the beach half hoping she would see Simeon there—even reveling with his consorts, so hungry she was for the sight of him.

Tears welled in her eyes. Her sex was on fire. Staring into the waves crashing on the strand through the drifting mists, she inched up the hem of the kirtle clinging to her body until she'd exposed herself to the midnight damp. Opening the wet bodice plastered to her breasts, she freed them as well, peeling the thin fabric back until her nipples were clear of it, and she began strumming them in concert with the other hand fingering her slit. But it wasn't her hand palming her breast, teasing the hardened bud, it was Simeon's. And it wasn't her fingers parting her pubic curls, exposing her hardened erection, stroking the steely bud to life, parting her nether lips—entering her velvety softness, slick and wet and ready to come. It was the hot bulk of Simeon's anxious flesh—hard as steel—pumping into her. If her mind's eye must conjure him thus to the end of her days, so be it. Apart or together, they were one. There would be no other for her . . . ever.

The orgasm came quickly, lifting her out of herself as if she had wings. She floated in mindless oblivion as the riveting contractions rippled through her sex, through her belly and stiffened thighs. It was excruciating ecstasy until a man's arm snaked its way around her waist and pulled her hard against a real arousal, hard and thick and eager. His warm breath puffing against her ear raised the fine hairs at the back of her neck.

"I knew you would come," he panted. "I knew you would return to me. It was only a matter of time. You've run out of it—time—but mine has just begun. . . ."

It was Seth.

Simeon readied Elicorn himself, which was no great feat, since the waterhorse was already frolicking over the waves, the high seas being the animal's passion. Simeon drove him straight for the Pavilion. Meg had never been there, and even if it wasn't too far for her to reach, she couldn't know the way. But he was counting upon the sprites, nymphs, mermaids, and sirens under Muriel's command, not to mention the mermen that inhabited that quarter and traveled the archipelago, to know if she had come into their domain. Without his faithful Pio or Vega, he had no other alternative. He couldn't sit idly by without running mad.

That she might have died, that she had drowned, was a paralyzing fear for him then. The elixir hadn't been tested, and she'd left it behind. There were so many pitfalls in his water

world that she knew nothing of—that could threaten her life—
he dared not imagine them. He was like a madman as it was.
And then there was Seth.

But for Muriel and her sister sprites and sirens cleaning up
after the storm, the Pavilion was deserted. The trappings there
were even more sumptuous than those at the palace, for it was
larger and closer to the open sea where most of the wrecks occurred. It had been the main residence when his parents were
alive. It wasn't until after the tragedy that they moved to the
palace, where less maintenance and fewer servants were needed.

Simeon found Muriel in the Great Hall sweeping up debris
from the floor with her sprites.

"Did it flood?" he said. "It wouldn't be the first time the
subterranean air pocket has flooded in a gale."

"No, it did not, my lord," she said. "All this is from the
wind. It played havoc with our plant life. We were knee deep in
seaweed once the wind ceased to blow."

"I am come—"

"Forgive me, we know why you've come," she interrupted
him. "She is not here, nor is she among the dead, but we are on
the lookout for her. I doubt she could reach this far, but if she
does, we will know what to do to keep her safe for you."

Simeon climbed the dais and sank into the counsel seat, taking his head in his hands. "She is not among the drowned
dead?" he pleaded.

"She is not among them, though there are many to be respected, my lord, and much salvage to be brought in, though
our men folk are handling that."

"And they will be respected, Muriel, once I have found
Megaleen. She is in graver danger than she knows. At least now
I know Pio hasn't abandoned me."

Muriel smiled, laying a soft hand upon his shoulder. She
snapped her fingers and the others fled. "Why?" she said. "When

you could have had any one of us as your mate, why did you take a *mortal?*"

"I do not know," he said, "except that the madness in the blood the mortals call 'love' has possessed me. It is not a comfortable thing. You have always been a friend to me, Muriel, which is why I can confess it."

She knelt beside the counsel seat, gazing into his eyes. How beautiful she was, with her long spiral curls that shone like polished copper cascading to her buttocks. Her exquisite body was barely concealed beneath the barest of garments as sheer as spider silk falling from one shoulder. Her tawny nipples stretched the cloth across her breasts, and from her position kneeling there, her hairless mound and perfect slit were clearly visible. There was a time when he would have reached beneath that filmy skirt and parted those perfect nether lips, a time when he would have risen to the occasion of her obvious seduction.

Sirens were just as notorious when it came to sexual prowess as the selkies, and they did cohabit. Their Otherworldly presence transcended all worlds in the universe, as did all sea creatures. Arcus had its fair share of them, and many an unsuspecting sailor had succumbed to the sirens' song through the ages. He would not join their ranks. He was smarter than that. He wasn't fool enough to get caught in the siren's snare. He was too drunk with the madness of love and too paralyzed with fear of losing that love to think of anything else.

"What of the consorts?" he said, rising from the counsel seat. "Could they have something to do with this, Muriel?"

She shook her head, rising alongside him with dignity and no loss of stature for the rejection. "No," she said. "They are very closely watched. Whatever you decide, my lord, we are loyal to you, our prince. Nonetheless, the offer had to be made."

He nodded his understanding. "I must go," he said. "There is no time to lose. I will return to respect the dead, and with the help of the gods, introduce you to my mate."

Muriel sketched a demure bow but laid a hand on his arm as he moved past her. "There is one thing," she said.

"Yes?"

"The consorts are content in their exile. Alexia has found a suitable mate among the mermen, as have most of the others, except for one . . . the young consort called Risa. She pines for your brother, and I fear for her health over it, but I cannot let her go without your permission. Will you give it?"

"No," Simeon said. "It is not up to me to speak for my brother. If he does not share her feelings it would be cruel to give her hope. I will tell Vega, and if he is of like mind in the matter, you have my permission to release her to him."

"As you wish, my lord," Muriel said, satisfied.

"If there is any sign of Megaleen . . ."

"You will know of it at once, my prince," she said, with a curtsy. "And she will always be safe among us, you have my word."

That, Simeon believed. Of all the creatures of the sea, sirens were the most patient, willing to wait eons for their heart's desire. It was clear she had set her cap at him, and she would bide her time. He could easily read her thoughts. Humans soon faded into the mists of time. She would wait. She would be there when that time came, with only good and loyal servitude to recommend her. He almost felt sorry for her.

He left her then, and he had scarcely broken the waves astride Elicorn when Pio leapt out of the sea and danced before him, every frazzled scale on his shimmering body trembling.

"Where in the name of the holy gods have you been?" he railed at the summoner.

All voiceless sea creatures communicated with the Lord of the Deep through telepathy, a form of mind-speak that needed no spoken words. Usually, Simeon spoke with his subjects in kind, but not tonight; he was too deranged to still his voice for fear his mind would burst.

"What?" he cried. "*The Isle of Mists?* But you said you'd tracked Seth there!"

The swordfish replied, and Simeon kneed Elicorn ruthlessly. "There isn't a moment to lose!" he called over the voice of the waves. "We must reach the Isle before Seth finds her there!"

*He already has,* said a familiar voice ghosting across is mind. He heard it before he saw its author hovering high overhead.

It was Gideon.

The dark lord swooped down, mercifully where he could make himself heard speaking normally, for Pio's frantic chatter had blocked out all else in the channels of Simeon's mind.

"I couldn't reach her in time," Gideon said, "and he has taken her where I cannot follow."

"Where?" Simeon shouted.

"To the training house for priestesses," Gideon told him. "The passages are too narrow. They will not accommodate my wings."

Simeon felt the blood drain from his face. It was as if his brain had gone numb.

"Leave the waterhorse and let me carry you there," Gideon offered.

"Thank you, but no!" said Simeon. "I have need of him and I cannot trust the beast else I stay upon his back!"

A man of few words, the Lord of the Dark gave a nod and a wave and soared off into the night.

Simeon turned to Pio, who was still breaking the waves in his euphoria. "Bring the others!" he charged. "As many as will come!"

Pio streaked off the minute the command left his master's lips. Plunging beneath the waves, the summoner glided back toward the palace, while Simeon kneed the waterhorse, who had no interest in the situation save galloping with the waves, and drove him toward the distant Isle of Mists.

# 21

"What have you done with my aunt and uncle?" Meg shrilled, straining against the shaman's grip as he dragged her along through the mist. He had evidently fled in naught but the *cote-hardie* he had on when the storm hit, for that was all he wore, and he was naked underneath it, which was evident as it gapped in front. There was no color in him. He was as white as the ghostlike air around them but for a deep red gash on his forehead.

"I have done nothing with them," Seth said. "They were swept away in the storm. You came back here for them, after they sold you like a pig in the market?"

"My uncle had naught to do with my aunt's treachery," Meg defended, digging her heels in. "Regardless, they are my flesh and blood. Let me go!"

"Well, blood or no, they're dead now—drowned in the sea. You've none here to come to your rescue, little whore, and we have unfinished business, you and I."

The mist was so thick Meg couldn't see where he was taking her until a building appeared in their path. It was similar to the buildings on Shamans' Mount in color and shape, though there was no round tower attached to it. Meg knew it at once. She had passed it several times on her solitary walks since she'd come to the Isle. It was the little abbeylike house where novices were trained to serve as priestesses in the temple. The very house where she was to have been prepared what seemed a lifetime ago.

"We shall have the place all to ourselves," Seth drawled. "All else have fled, so we shan't be disturbed."

The sultry tone of his voice riddled Meg with gooseflesh, and she fought him fiercely, digging her fingernails into his hand. When that failed, she swooped down and bit him hard, drawing blood, which earned her a hard slap that would have pitched her over on the sand if he hadn't flung her across his shoulder and carried her the rest of the distance.

They entered through a narrow door and started down a corridor that wasn't much wider toward the back of the building, where a spiral staircase led upward to a small solarium. It was sparsely furnished, except for some gaudy trappings and a mound of pillows on the floor. Seth dropped her there without ceremony and stood staring down, arms akimbo.

Meg glanced about. It looked more like a brothel than a training center for potential temple virgins. The scent of strong incense and stale semen permeated the air. It threatened to make her retch. The room had been used for sex recently. If Seth had his way, it was about to be used for sex again. The look in his eyes was one of deadly triumph, and she shrank from it.

"Not all priestess trainings are . . . successful," he said. He hadn't read her mind, he'd read her expression, which had to be one of disbelief, for she was not skilled at concealing her true feelings. He laughed. The sound raised the short hairs at the back of her neck. "Come, come, you know the chosen among the novices all must know this cock"—he spread his *cote-hardie* and exposed himself—"in order to be installed as priestess of the temple. Those found lacking a virgin skin were made temple whores, without the benefits awarded to a venerated priestess, but there were . . . compensations."

"*Were?*" she snapped at him.

He nodded. "They are all gone—swept away by the storm. Only you remain, little whore, to comfort me in my loss. But be of good cheer. There will be others soon. Meanwhile, I will console myself in you."

Meg's eyes flitted about, searching for some weapon, some means of defending herself against the shaman as he knelt beside her.

Again, he laughed. "It is useless to resist me," he said, crawling toward her like an animal as she shrank away. "This is your destiny—it always has been. Your aunt knew it. She was wise in her decision to give you to me."

"*Give?* My aunt was a poor misguided creature seduced by the lure of gold," Meg corrected him. "I have to believe if she knew—*really* knew—the fate she was consigning me to, she would have never have given in to avarice."

Groping the mound of pillows as she continued to inch away from him as he advanced, her hand closed around a long, slender coffer of carved coral. Hefting it in one hand, she launched it toward him, but his quick hand clamped around her wrist countered the blow, and he wrested it out of her hand.

"Thank you, my dear," he said. "I was getting to that. Thank you for reminding me." He set the coffer aside, unopened, and drew her closer. "We mustn't rush this," he murmured. "The initiation is a thing to be savored, like fine wine. Yours will be a bit more . . . intense, however, considering. My cock still smarts from your assault beside the scrying pool, and you must answer for that. But once you have been humbled, our association should mellow into something quite pleasant for the both of us."

"I do not qualify for your 'initiation,' remember? I am no virgin."

He shrugged. "That no longer signifies, since you are the only female left alive upon the Isle of Mists who isn't in her dotage, and I am sore for wanting. Besides, I need to show you what you've missed."

Meg's mind was racing. She had to get away, not only from Seth, though his advances had paralyzed her with fear, but from Simeon. Pio would bring him, and she needed to be far way from the Isle of Mists before that happened.

She had never intended to remain on the Isle, only to ease her conscience about Adelia and Olwyn before she moved on. She had no idea where she would go. She hadn't thought that far ahead, only that it would be somewhere on land, as far from the sea as she could range herself. She wasn't safe on the Arcan mainland, except perhaps with the bands of nomads who wandered there. If she could join a caravan . . . if some would take her in . . . she might be safe with them in the mountains. Mainland folk shunned the nomads; they feared their mystical powers and strange rituals more than they feared the shamans.

But she had to stay alive to implement that plan. That meant escaping. She could not do that while Seth was anticipating that she would do that very thing. If it meant submitting in order to give him a false sense of security, so be it. Then, once he relaxed his guard, she could escape—with her life, for the venomous look in his crazed eyes then bespoke murder, and she was terrified at the thought of ending her days at the mercy of the lecherous shaman's aberration. She'd almost convinced herself to submit, but he was pawing her, and her posture clenched in spite of her resolve.

The bodice of her wet kirtle was still spread from when she'd opened it to touch herself earlier. She wore no undergarment— they would have been a hindrance under water—and the thin skirt of the dove-gray gown was still plastered wet to her body. Inching it above her mound, he gave a grunt of approval as he combed her pubic curls with his eyes before plowing through them with his clumsy fingers.

"I think I shall have this roughage shorn," he observed. "It blocks my view."

"And who will shear it, with none but you and me in this foul place?" she snapped.

"Shut that acid mouth!" he snarled. "There's a tide pool on this island, where the crabs come in each day at dawn to feed. It's nearly that now. If I sit you in it, they'll make short work of that bush. On the other hand, if you behave, I'll lather that quim with hazelnut soap and scrape the hair clean off that mound with a razor clam shell." He stroked his face. "It works for me, and you are no better, little minx—seducer of selkies—traitorous whore! You might even enjoy it. I know I would."

Meg said no more. Her sharp tongue wasn't helping matters. He had just about relaxed when her outburst lost her all the ground she'd gained. Calming herself with deep breaths, she shut her eyes and did not see the hand that shot out to capture her wrists. By the time her eyes snapped open and the gasp had left her throat, he'd pinned her wrists over her head.

"Do not struggle!" he charged. "Lie still. You might actually enjoy this: many have. It is all part of your initiation. You should feel privileged. You are the last of the old and the first of the new initiates. Together, we will begin anew. We will rebuild the temple. This here will suffice until we can do that, and hopefuls will come from afar to become priestesses under my tutelage. They will pay *me* this time for the privilege. We will call it a tribute to the gods, and the gods will be pleased!"

"You are mad!" she cried, resisting. There was no sense trying to reason with a madman, and he was insane—his wild-eyed stare was evidence of that. Had losing all he'd created for himself driven him so? She had no desire to analyze that, only to flee from it.

She'd forgotten the little coral coffer until Seth groped for it and dragged it alongside. He worked it open one-handed, and when he lifted out its contents, her heart sank. The blood drained away from her scalp. Blinding pinpoints of white light starred her vision as he waved before her eyes what appeared to be a phallus realistically carved of bone. It was long and thick and menacing as he passed it back and forth in front of her wide-flung eyes. Even the veins and mushroom tip had been carved in great detail. It reminded her of Simeon.

"Shall we begin?" he said. "Remember, do not struggle. You might enjoy it. Have no fear. I will be merciful. Since you are the only palatable alternative to diddling myself at the moment, it would hardly be practical for me to administer all your reparation at once. I will enjoy it more drawn out over time in any case . . . That is, unless you anger me, and you are close to doing that now, so take care. . . ."

Meg could not move. She held her breath as he spread her legs and parted her nether lips with the tip of the phallus. It glided inside her on the wetness of her earlier release. Her breath caught in her throat as it filled her.

"Sh," he said. "It is a pleasure tool, not an instrument of pain. What? Your selkie lover has not introduced you to the phallus? How remiss of him. Your innocence excites me. It is almost as if you are virgin still. How delicious. I cannot believe your selkie never showed you this."

"Why would he?" Meg spat at him. "How would he have access to such a thing as that, much less have need of it!" Why couldn't she keep her tongue from lashing out? It would surely be the death of her, but it was the only weapon she possessed. His look alone stilled it.

"Where do you suppose it came from but the selkies, eh?" he said. "Remind you of anyone? I saw your face when you first set eyes upon it just now. Could he have posed for the craftsman who carved it do you suppose, your Simeon, Lord of the Deep? Who was it that got him hard for the artist do you think? Not you. I've had it too long. Did she suck it? Perhaps she straddled him and took it deep inside her. Or mayhap she pulled it into submission with her skilled hand? Oh, I do not mind that it arouses you. It's only a piece of whalebone after all. You really should see your face. How easily you are read. Ah yes, sweet innocence in my arms once more . . . I am going to enjoy your initiation, little whore."

Meg was aroused. Simeon could well have posed for the craftsman who fashioned the phallus. It was as if he were inside her, for she knew every inch of his manhood—every ridge and vein—every curve from mushroom tip to thick hard root. It was torture to think she would never feel him come to life inside her again, and tears welled in her eyes as she remembered all that they had been to each other and mourned all that could never be, for they were star-crossed. No matter which way they might have gone, whether she came to him in his world or he came into hers, her way was the only way to spare him the pain of heartbreak or death. He was Simeon, Lord of the Deep, and always would be. She alone could give him that.

Swooping down, Seth seized her breast and took her nipple in his mouth, meanwhile working the phallus, driving it in and out of her. He had let go of her wrists, and Meg searched the pillows with one free hand, groping for the coffer. Her heart skipped its rhythm when her fingers closed around its hinged coral lid, but she dropped it as if she'd touched live coals when he seized her wrist and forced her hand against the erection poking through his robe. The timing was wrong. Try wielding that coffer now, and he would likely bash her head in with it. She needed more time, but his shaft in her hand told her soon her time would run out. He wouldn't settle. He would want to come in her. She could not bear it.

"There is no reason for forcing," she murmured. "This could be pleasant for us both . . . as you say."

For a moment he hesitated, frozen in place. Nothing moved, not even the phallus inside her. Meg held her breath as Seth slipped it out of her and set it aside. Time was growing short. Any moment, Simeon could burst in on them. Surely Pio would have reached him by now. She glanced up at the domed glass ceiling above. The sky was beginning to lighten. She blinked, and a shadow appeared. At first she thought it was just a cloud, until Gideon, Lord of the Dark, came crashing through the domed glass ceiling of the solarium feet first, his gigantic wings unfurled, and plummeted toward them in a shower of loose feathers and broken glass.

Meg screamed, rolling out of the way as shards rained over them. At first, she thought he was going to seize her, but he did not. Instead, he fastened a white-knuckled fist in the back of the shaman's gaping *cote-hardie* and soared back out through the hole he had rent in the ceiling to disappear in the predawn mist.

He would be back for her any moment, and she scrambled to her feet set to run, but the phallus caught her eye. She snatched it up along with the coffer. If she could not have Simeon, she would have his image, for that is what it surely was, and without a backward glance, she picked her way gingerly, for she was barefoot, over the millions of bits of broken glass, scarcely feeling the ones that pierced her tender skin, and ran out into the narrow corridor.

She was safe there. The confines were far too narrow for Gideon to travel with his wings—even furled—but she wasted no time in any case. Simeon would have no difficulty gaining access to the halls, and she scurried down the back stairs, hardly noticing the pain in her feet, to what appeared to be the servants' quarters below. Trenchers heaped with uneaten food sat eerily untouched on the table. Had the inmates of this dubious place fled in haste when the storm hit? Why? Surely they were safe there. The house was still standing. More likely they had simply fled the shaman's tyranny. Had some escaped alive? She prayed so. Whatever had occurred, the place was deserted now, and she climbed inside a wood box beside the vacant kitchen hearth and burrowed under the wood, praying they wouldn't probe too deeply in their search for her.

## 22

The strand was swarming with selkies when Gideon dropped Seth in a heap on the beach practically at Simeon's feet. Simeon had dismounted. Behind, Elicorn pranced through the surf, frolicking in the high-curling comers, their white froth and spindrift tinted pink by the dawn as if all were well and selkies hadn't just laid siege to the beach on the Isle of Mists.

All around, selkie males were shedding their skins. Some had come from the palace, others from as far off as the Pavilion at their prince's command. Stunned by his unceremonious landing, Seth shook himself like a dog as he scrambled to his feet. Simeon gave the shaman only passing notice as he stalked toward Gideon like a man possessed.

"Where is she?" he demanded.

Gideon opened his mouth to answer, but closed it again at sight of Seth making a dash for the water's edge and Elicorn prancing like a horse performing dressage steps in the creaming surf.

Following the direction the dark lord's eyes had taken,

Simeon made a lunge to follow, but Gideon's firm hand on his forearm stopped him in his tracks.

Gideon shook a slow head. "Leave him," he said. "Let the fates decide. . . ."

Simeon stared after Seth. Other selkies started to converge upon the shaman, but Simeon stayed them with a raised hand. As dawn broke over the horizon in bloodred shimmer, he watched the waterhorse extend one leg and kneel with the other for the shaman to mount. Seth swung himself up anxiously, his robe spread wide on a wind that had risen to chase the mist. Elicorn reared, spun, and galloped into the high-rising curl of a fresh wave racing toward shore, then plunged deeper. The shaman's death scream pierced the still air, then died off to a gurgling as the waterhorse dove one last time and disappeared beneath the waves.

Simeon turned to Gideon. "Is Megaleen in there?" he begged him.

Gideon nodded. "You will have to fetch her yourself."

Simeon stared at the dark lord. "Why didn't you bring her out instead?" he demanded.

"Evil must be dealt with first and foremost," Gideon returned, his voice clipped and strained. "And you must fetch her yourself because she is no longer in the solarium, and my wings prohibit me from the rest of the place. Besides, I wash my hands of it."

The dark lord's handsome mouth had formed a hard, lipless line. He was clearly at the end of his tether. Rage smoldered just under the surface of Gideon's strange expression. Aside from being a man of few words, the Lord of the Dark rarely showed emotion, stoicism being a major part of his mystique. Taken aback by the shocking look of him now, Simeon stared, deciding to force the issue; something he would never have done in ordinary circumstances.

"Why?" he blurted.

"Because she does not want to be fetched, and I must respect that."

"You know that, do you?" Simeon seethed.

Gideon nodded. "I saw her quit the solarium myself, and she hasn't come out, has she?"

"I must have her back, Gideon."

The dark lord gave a crisp nod and unfurled his wings. "Then do," he said. "But I'll not have a hand in it. Unless I miss my guess, she's trying to do right by you. You aren't thinking clearly."

"And she is?"

"Yes," Gideon sallied. "But do not take my word, Lord of the Deep. Go! See for yourself."

Simeon stared, stunned with astonishment. "You're in love with her, too!" he breathed, discovery in his voice.

The dark lord smiled. It did not reach his eyes. "Blind as you are, you do see that, eh, Simeon? You are wasting time. Go if you're going, but take care. You are rid of one enemy, but it's far from over. There is another."

With no more said, the dark lord lifted off and soared into the dawn, leaving Simeon staring after him but not for long. After a moment, Elicorn pranced back up on shore riderless, just as Simeon knew he would. Simeon motioned the others to follow as he approached the training hall. He would have Meg back at any cost. Gideon's sage advice had fallen upon dead ears. Another enemy, indeed! As if he needed more. He shrugged that off and was just about to enter the hall with the others when Vega came running over one of the northern dunes.

Simeon pulled up short. Staring at his brother, righteous passion gave way to unstoppable rage. Where had Vega been? How could he have abandoned him when he needed him so desperately? Vega had scarcely reached him when Simeon drew back a white-knuckled fist and launched it, driving his brother down in the sand with a powerful blow to the jaw.

"Where have you been?" Simeon seethed. "I needed you!"

Vega shook his head and flexed his jaw, wiping blood from the corner of his mouth. This had never happened before. In all the eons Simeon and Vega had been together, one had never raised a hand to the other.

Simeon stared down at his brother sprawled at his feet. He hadn't just struck out at Vega; he'd delivered a blow against the entire circumstance. At Vega for the first time in his life not being there when he needed him. At Gideon—not for his infatuation with Meg; he knew the dark lord would never act upon it—but for always being right. Then there was Meg, for leaving him no matter how noble the reason. And most of all, he'd struck out at himself for not seeing this coming. Had his love for Meg blinded him to all else around him—had he lost her because of it?

He heaved a sigh and extended his hand to Vega. "By the gods, I never meant to do that," he said, hauling his brother to his feet. "I'm half-mad with this. She just . . . vanished. You were gone, Pio disappeared . . ."

"She is here, on the Isle of Mists?" Vega said, ordering himself.

"Yes. The shaman Seth held her captive in the solarium at that accursed training hall. Gideon got him out of there and Elicorn made short work of him just now. The others are searching the hall for her as we speak. She will be frightened. I should be with them."

"Then go," Vega said flatly.

"What are you doing here?" Simeon asked him. The conversation was stilted and strained. He was wrong, and he was sorry he'd struck out at his brother. With all his heart, he wished he could take it back, but that could not be and discussing it then was futile. The look in Vega's handsome eyes speared him like a trident. Hurt, anger, and disappointment lingered there, mirrored in the tense muscles ticking along that angular jawline.

"It can wait," Vega said.

Simeon nodded, clapped Vega on the shoulder, and moved past him to enter the hall. It was too awkward then, and his mind was too full of Meg to do his brother justice. He would not be sane again until he held her in his arms, until he'd settled what lay between them however needs must.

Even though Gideon said he'd seen Meg fleeing the solarium, it was the first place Simeon wanted to look. Bounding up the staircase, he reached it ahead of the others and pulled up short on the threshold. The room was a riot of glass; sunlight streaming through the gaping hole in the glass ceiling bounced off hundreds of glass shards peppering the floor. There was no sign of Meg, though a trail of blood, where she'd evidently cut her feet on the broken glass led out into the hallway. His heart in his throat, he followed it below stairs through the servants' quarters to the kitchen.

Calling her name at the top of his voice, Simeon followed the bloody footprints to the wood box beside the vacant hearth. It was large enough to hold her. There was blood on the edge of it, and on some of the wood inside, which he began tossing over his shoulder in a mad frenzy. He had soon emptied it, and his heart sank as he ran his hands over the bottom of the box. But it was no use. The wood box was empty.

Desperately, Simeon searched the kitchen floor for more tracks, but there were none. Though the blood was still wet on the wood box, Megaleen had vanished.

The sun was high, and Meg had scrambled over the sand to the north side of the island before casting off the strips she'd torn from the hem of her kirtle to bind her cut feet. It hadn't been safe in the wood box. The trail of blood she'd left behind led right to it. Once she'd realized that, she'd bound them be-fore making her escape so there would be no footprints leading away from the novices' hall.

Still, she was out in the open. The Isle was barren of vegeta-tion but for beach grass. There were cottages, like Adelia's, but the ones she passed seemed vacant now. Evacuations were com-mon in storms. Many islanders fled to the mainland during such storms as the selkie maelstrom that had just ravaged the archipelago. She would find no shelter there.

Though the sun had burned off the mist along the strand, there was one stubborn patch in the north where dense vapors still lingered. Deeming that hollow safer than trying to hide in the open dunes, she limped toward it, wishing she could find a tidal pool to bathe her sore feet in, preferably not the one filled with pinching crabs Seth had described.

Meg hesitated at the edge of the mist pocket. There was something Otherworldly about it. For one thing, the wind that had risen chasing the rest of the mist did not blow there. She had never seen the like. For another, there was no logical expla-nation for the mist to even be there that far from the strand. She tugged the cloak she'd found in one of the servant's rooms as she'd fled closer around her. She was cold suddenly, though the day dawned warm. She had no choice. The island was swarm-ing with selkie males. Simeon was among them. She'd come this far trying to set him free; she wasn't about to fail now.

She'd also taken a cloth market bag from the kitchen. It held the whalebone phallus in its coral coffer and some bread and cheese she'd found, but she wasn't hungry. How could she eat when her stomach was tied in knots for fear Simeon would find her? How could she think of food, when, despite her resolve, part of her was praying he would?

Shouts echoed in the distance. Meg held her breath and stepped into the mist. To her surprise, an abbeylike building emerged from it, parting the swirling vapors. This she had not seen before on her solitary walks, but then she'd rarely come this far north. She hesitated. Suppose the selkies were to enter the mist as well. She approached the door, her hand raised to knock. But what kind of place was this? Suppose there were more shamans inside.

The shouts from behind came again. They were closer now, and she knocked at the door. Her knuckles had hardly touched the panel when it came open in the hand of a rotund teary-eyed woman garbed in white.

"You'd best hurry if you want to pay your respects," the woman said, standing aside to let Meg enter. "They have already prepared the grave, and she must be buried before the heat of the day."

Meg had no idea what the woman was talking about, but at least she was inside, out of the selkie's view, and she followed her along the corridor to a room where a bier had been arranged between two tall candle stands fitted with white candles. Others likewise robed in white were grouped around the bier.

"Oh! Too late," Meg's guide said. "They are taking her now. . . ."

Shocked that there were no men, only older women hefting the coffin, Meg gasped. "Have you no men folk to do this work?" she asked.

The woman cast Meg a glance as if she'd suddenly grown two heads. "*Men folk?*" she blurted. "No men folk here—not even the shamans have access to the nunnery. We are a women's spiritual house, my dear. No men are allowed."

"Eh . . . o-oh," Meg said awkwardly. She had never heard of a nunnery on the Isle of Mists. It was passing strange and very mystical. Something very Otherworldly was happening, but it had abetted her escape, and she held her peace.

Meg winced when the women, six in all, lifted the coffin and started toward the door. The woman inside the plain wooden casket was robed in white—at least Meg presumed it to be a woman. The body was so emaciated it was little more than a skeleton seemingly held together by naught but gray dust. A thin veil covered the face of the corpse, but it was no denser than a morning cobweb spangled with dew, and every line, every sunken cavity, was visible through it.

Meg's hand flew to her lips. "What was it . . . plague?" she murmured.

"Oh no," the other said. The pallbearer sisters had reached them, and the woman flattened Meg against the wall in the narrow corridor to let them pass. She motioned the others to stop so Meg could pay her respects before they passed. "How are you related to Sister Glenda?"

"O . . . oh, we are . . . we're not related," Meg stammered. "I am come . . . on another matter."

The woman motioned the others to move on and turned back to Meg. "It's just as well," she said. "You've gone as white as the mist of a sudden. Sit you down and wait. I shall return presently."

She turned to go, and Meg halted her with a word. "Wait!" she said. "H-how did that woman die . . . You didn't say . . . ?"

The woman hesitated. "I suppose there's no harm in telling it," she said. "You wouldn't have gotten in here if you weren't pure of heart and meant us no harm. The doors are never locked you see, they needn't be. The gods protect us. Only good may enter here"—she leaned close, whispering, and winked—"that's why the shamans cannot."

Meg smiled, and the woman patted her arm, discovering her marketing bag. "Can I take that sack for you?" she said. "It looks heavy."

"No!" Meg cried, a little too loudly. "It isn't heavy, really, I can manage." It wouldn't do to have a holy woman discover the phallus.

"As you wish," the woman said. "I'll have to tell it quickly. They'll need me, you know, to say the words. Glenda was a dear, dear friend . . . She was the last of her kind, born during the great cataclysm that formed the Arcan Archipelago—"

"But that was—"

"Eons ago, I know, when the great storms ravaged the mainland and formed the Isles of Arcus."

"Was she a sea creature, then, that she could live so long?"

"Oh no," the woman said. "She was human, like the rest of us here—like yourself—but she was special."

"I do not understand. If she possessed the power to live for eons . . . how did she die?"

The woman's face clouded. "She gave it up, her immortality. Some say it was suicide, but I know different." She leaned closer. "Rumor has it . . . she gave it to another. . . ." Laying a finger over her lips, the woman toddled off then, before Meg could ask her how that could possibly be, and disappeared around a bend in the corridor. It was a strange encounter to be sure, but there wasn't time to analyze it.

Meg glanced about. She was safe. Even though the doors were unlocked, no men were allowed to enter. She would find a corner and stay until there was no more threat of Simeon or the other selkies finding her. Then, when night fell, she would slip away. She would have to cross water to reach the mainland, but as long as she didn't travel *in* the water, she would be safe. A rowboat or skiff would suffice. There had to be one somewhere on the Isle. She would find one. If that poor dead woman could give her immortality away, though her heart was breaking, so could Meg give Simeon his. Leaving him was the only way, and she tiptoed off to a remote corner of the nunnery that didn't smell of funeral flowers, where she found a large cupboard in the wainscoting under the stairs by the rear entrance. Curling up inside, she slept.

# 23

---

Simeon and his virtual army of selkie males searched the Isle of Mists until dusk, but they found no sign of Meg. Finally, vowing to return at dawn and search again, Simeon dismissed the others, mounted Elicorn, and returned to the deep. He'd been on land too long without periods in his sealskin. He could no longer exist comfortably out of the water.

Even though he knew she would not be there, he searched the underwater ledges, haunted the subterranean pools, left no chamber unchecked, but she was not in the palace. It was nearly midnight when he stripped off his eel skin suit and plunged naked into the bathing pool. The fragrant soap he'd used to lather Megaleen and the sea sponge were still lying on the ledge where he'd left them. Simeon hoisted himself up beside them, raised the soap to his nose, and inhaled the intoxicating scent of night lilies. It reminded him of her. She ghosted across his memory just as the scent ghosted through his nostrils.

Simeon soaked the sponge, shut his eyes, and began working the soap into a lather. Rich and thick, it spilled over onto his wrists and ran up his muscular forearms as he squeezed it through his fingers. He soaped his chest, then his taut, hard middle, until the suds slid down his cock. That was all it took. His shaft sprang erect in memory of her hands soaping him there, and he groaned as his fingers closed around it.

He was exhausted, but that was no deterrent. His sexual drive was always heightened when fatigued. He needed sleep if he was to continue the search in the morning. Would release bring it? It was too late to wonder. His cock was hard in his hand, just as it had been in her hand, and the soap as soft as her caress gliding over his thick hardness, over the distended veins and ridged tip, over the swollen balls that ached for her.

Surging to his feet, Simeon stood on the edge of the pool and shut his eyes again, then opened them as if the gesture would materialize her out of the soft, steamy air. But he was alone, overwhelmed by longing, overtaken by the selkie need—a need like no other; all consuming, unstoppable—a palpable—passion that rendered him helpless under its spell.

He groaned, sliding his hand the length of his anxious erection, watching it grow as he soaped it. Slow, lingering strokes from root to tip set hot blood pumping through his veins, rushing to his engorged cock, making in harder still. All he could think of was Meg's gentle hands spiraling up and down, riding on the silky cushion of lather, bringing him to the brink, then halting . . . to make it last.

His heart was hammering in his breast. His moist eyes hooded with mindless desire saw only the ghost of Meg's exquisite body naked in his arms. He licked his fever-parched lips and tasted only the memory of her salty sweetness. His flared nostrils inhaled her scent. Sweet clover and night lilies enchanted him. She *was* a witch, and she had seduced the seducer from wherever she'd gone. Only a sorceress could do that. She had bewitched him!

His erection would not wait. His strokes became rapid, his breathing shallow, his pelvis jerked forward. For a moment, he froze. The minute he moved, it would be over. The minute the fingers frozen on his shaft so much as twitched, he would come. He waited until the throbbing threatened anyway, then pumping his hand in a spiraling motion along the hard bulk of his shaft, he gritted out a guttural moan as he came; the life flow spewing out of him in long, languid spurts. Then he remembered . . . She could well be carrying his child, and he dove headlong into the pool of warm water, loosing a selkie bark that reverberated through the coral dome above and hummed through the water he plunged through, scattering fish and lilies and underwater plant life in his path.

Down, down he plunged with no thought to where he was going or why. It was no good without his Megaleen. Why had she left him? Where had she gone? How could he have let her slip through his fingers on the Isle of Mists? Would she be there still when he returned at dawn to continue the search? It wasn't likely. Spiraling and twisting, he plowed through the water in a blind passion until, spent, he surged back up through the maze of frightened fish and shuddering plants he'd left in his wake and broke through the surface of the pool.

Warm mist welcomed him as he climbed out of the water and struggled into his eel skin suit. Time meant nothing then. How long he'd been in the water, he had no idea, nor did he care. It was his natural habitat after all. He could stay under until the crack of doom if he chose to do so. However long it was, it hadn't calmed his sex, and it hadn't tired him enough to sleep. It was just as well. He had fences to mend, and he stalked off in search of Vega.

There was no reason to light the rush candles. They were in low supply anyway. Vega heaved a sigh. With all the press, he'd forgotten to send retainers to the marshes to gather more bulrushes. That could wait. Vega much preferred the dark, especially now that he had a nasty bruise on his jaw to nurse.

Phosphorescence from the water, a phenomenon of the moonlight above the waves striking the breast of the sea, and a constant flame in a stone basin at the end of the corridor cast enough defused light for him to see by in his sumptuous cubicle. It was more than enough, with his extraordinary night vision, for him to examine the amulet Glenda, his mother, had given him. Withdrawing it from his eel skin suit, he held it up and turned it to and fro in his hand. A sigh escaped him, examining the perfect black pearl dangling from a slender silver strand—a magical collar bought by his father eons ago in the name of love at a price that came dearer than diamonds and gold.

It was all too overwhelming. He should have greeted his mother more tenderly, but he had not, and there was nothing to be done about it now. It was too much of a shock discovering that she lived after believing her dead since a child. How could he have known, when there seemed none alive to tell him the truth of it save herself, locked away where no man could reach her? At first he bitterly resented the abandonment, but no longer. Now he saw it as the sacrifice it truly was then, and was *still*, for she had given up her life for the sake of others. Rubbing and flexing his bruised jaw, he couldn't help but doubt the wisdom behind that decision. But who was he to judge? No one but the bastard of the deep, who, but for Simeon, would have been cast out long ago.

Still, he would never forget the look of his mother when age began to take her. It was swift and painful, he had no doubt, for she could not meet his eyes when it began, and left him at once. She was surely dead by now. It was over. But for him, unknowing, it had been over from the start. All that remained was to give the amulet to Simeon for Meg, hoping his father's purchase so long ago from a wizard lost in the mists of time would continue to reap its rewards. Its secret would die with them and him, for immortality could not be bought except by magic, and if it were known that such a charm existed, their lives would be in the greatest danger from those who would move the moon and stars to possess it.

Vega heard Simeon approaching long before his brother crossed the threshold, and he tucked the amulet away inside his eel skin suit again. He would choose the moment to give it. Taking a seat in a gilded Glastonbury chair half-hidden in shadow, he waited. Simeon's footfalls were heavy and borne down. Exhaustion or remorse? He would soon know.

Simeon thrust a rush torch, which he had evidently lit from the stone basin outside, and Vega shielded his eyes from the unexpected glare. "Put that damned thing out!" He said. "If I'd wanted a light, I would have lit one myself."

"Still angry with me?" Simeon asked, leaving the torch in a wall bracket outside the cell proper.

"You should be sleeping. If you mean to continue your search in the morning, you will need all the rest you can get. You know your strength flags on land . . . unless you're planning to go about in your sealskin?"

"No, I am not," Simeon said. "I cannot sleep. She was there—right there—and now she's gone. Where could she be, Vega?"

"I hardly know," Vega responded. "I didn't see her."

Simeon waved him off with a hand gesture. "I didn't come to talk about Megaleen," he said. "I came to apologize. I don't know what happened. I just . . . snapped. I had no right to take it out on you."

Vega hesitated. Was this the time? Simeon looked so forlorn. Would it help, or would it make matters worse? There was no way to be sure. He had never seen his brother so distraught over a woman, and there had been many. He could give him the amulet and ease his mind, but what if Megaleen was gone? What if she never returned? What good the amulet then, except a heartbreaking reminder of what might have been. Love—all in the name of love! Selkies should have no truck with the emotion. Lust could be dealt with. There was no all-consuming madness of the blood with lust. A man could satisfy his urges, revel in his release, satisfy the demands of his aching cock in welcoming flesh, and sleep at night with lust. Why did Risa's beautiful face ghost across his mind just then? He missed her dreadfully. Their relationship had just begun when Simeon banished the consorts. He heaved a sigh and shifted his position in the uncomfortable Glastonbury chair. He'd grown hard just thinking about her youthful beauty and graceful skill in the art of making love. Was it the lust of his selkie side or the penchant for love his human side awarded that made him hard against the seam? He wouldn't probe that question too deeply. He was afraid of the answer.

"No," he said at last. "You didn't have the right to take it out on me, especially since I went to the Isle of Mists in your behalf."

"In *my* behalf?"

Vega nodded. "And, I might add, at great personal hazard."

"I said I was sorry."

Vega laughed. "You think I'm talking about that piddling facer you planted on me? Hah! I went to the Waterwitch to learn some long-glossed-over points of my existence in hopes of helping you, and I put myself to the hazard. The old hag fed my cock to a sea anemone when I wouldn't pleasure her in exchange for the information."

"Fed your cock . . . Are you all right . . . are you . . . is it . . . ?"

"As congenial as the creatures are, sea anemone do not take kindly to having men's cocks rammed down their throats. Coming saved mine a nasty stringing or worse, but never mind that. I discovered that Glenda, my mother, was still alive—"

"Alive!" Simeon interrupted him. "That cannot be. We would have known? You believed her?"

Vega nodded. "I did," he said. "And more than that, I went to the Isle of Mists and confronted my mother myself! That's where I was coming from when I ran into your fist, brother dear."

"Why didn't you tell me all this? Why did you just disappear without a word? I was half-mad—you were gone—Pio had disappeared. I needed you!"

Vega slipped his hand inside his eel skin suit and withdrew the amulet against his better judgment. "I think you need this more," he said, handing it over.

"What is this?" Simeon said, clearly nonplussed.

Vega watched Simeon turn it over in his hand. "That amulet is what has kept Glenda alive all these years," he said. "Evidently Father wanted to keep her for his consort and paid a tidy sum to a sorcerer for that necklace."

"But . . . I don't understand?"

"Neither do I," Vega said. "Suffice it to say, the magic works. I saw my mother—spoke with her. She was wearing that necklace. The minute she took it off her neck, she started to age. I have no doubt that she has died, for the aging was swift, and I am sure very painful. She gave me that for you to give to Megaleen. She was human, don't forget, and in the same situation you find yourself in now."

"But . . . to give up her immortality . . . ?"

"Our father is dead, and to hear her tell it, she is tired."

"But, Vega . . ."

"Has love so addled your brain that you cannot see?" Vega said, vaulting out of the chair. "Meg loves you just as you love her; I'm convinced of it. I believe she left you because you belong to the deep. You could not exist long upon the land and die a mortal death. She would not do that to you. Were she to come here, she would whither and die before your eyes while you remain as you are, young—virile—ageless. Neither of you could have borne that. Unless I miss my guess, her leaving was a gift—a sacrifice—for you. If I am right, that there in your hand could be the answer."

"Can immortality *be* transferred from one being to another?"

"We shan't know unless we test it, shall we? Simeon, Glenda, my mother, evidently believed it enough to give up her life to prove it. All I know is it worked for her."

"I have to find her, Vega! I have to find Megaleen. Where was your mother on the Isle of Mists? I've combed every inch of those dunes. The place is a wasteland. How could we not have known she was there all this time?"

"Easily," Vega ground out through a wry chuckle. "She was in residence at the nunnery there."

"What nunnery? I know of no nunnery."

"Neither did I, but it's there. On the north shore of the island there's a little hollow that is always thick with mist. The nunnery is cloaked inside that mist. You cannot see it, and no man can enter the sisters' house."

"Then how did you do it?"

Vega withdrew the Waterwitch's geode from his suit. "With this," he said, exhibiting it. "It's one of the old hag's charms."

"So that is where you'd gone. I'm sorry . . . I had no idea. I was half-mad when I found Megaleen missing. I have to go. That nunnery in the misty hollow is the only place we didn't search. We didn't know it was there! If that's where she is . . . if they've given her sanctuary . . . I have to find her, Vega, now more than ever. If you are right . . ."

"Wait!" Vega called out as Simeon darted toward the arch. "Take this—toss it into the mist in that hollow and you will gain access. It is the only way. It is cloaked remember."

Simeon snatched the geode from him. Halfway over the threshold, he paused and turned back. "Oh!" he said. "When I couldn't find you, I went to the Pavilion, hoping someone had seen her, but no. You are to have a visitor soon."

"A visitor?"

Simeon nodded. "Muriel made me aware that Risa is pining away for you, and I agreed to have her—and only her—returned to the Palace if you wished it. I didn't need to ask you. You wear your heart on your sleeve, my brother. I've just sent Pio to fetch her."

Vega's jaw dropped. He blinked, and Simeon was gone.

# 24

Meg stirred inside the cupboard that smelled of cedar wood. Wedge shaped, it was large enough to accommodate her easily. A pile of folded blankets on the bottom of it cushioned her body and sore feet. She yawned and stretched. How long she'd slept there, she had no idea. It had been a deep sleep, a boon of exhaustion, but she'd awakened aroused from dreaming of Simeon. She was safe there, with just enough air seeping in from loose boards at the back of the closet to allow her to breathe comfortably.

She presumed it to be sometime in the night. All was quiet in the nunnery. The sisters had evidently forgotten her presence in the house, what with the press of the old woman's burial, and they did say the doors were never locked. They would have simply assumed she'd left if they'd remembered her at all. These were a trusting sort, without guile. She would wait a bit and then steal away under the cover of darkness to look for a boat to carry her to the mainland. But first, the ache between her thighs needed to be addressed.

She was so lonely for Simeon. The mere thought of him

aroused her. What she wouldn't give to lie in his arms, to feel his hard-muscled body next to hers, bringing her to the brink of ecstasy with his selkie seductions. He had spoiled her for any other lover. From the first moment she'd seen him on the strand performing for her with his consort in the moonlight, she'd known no other would ever satisfy her. Now, she was fleeing from the very thing she wanted most—from the very arms that she longed to hold her for the rest of her life.

Meg seized her mound in a vain attempt to stop the contractions gripping her then—waves like liquid fire that had begun coursing through her belly and thighs. It was dark in the cupboard. Who would see? Just as she'd done on that first night, she lifted her breasts free of her bodice and palmed them. Her nipples were hard and tall, poking through her fingers. She moaned softly as she scraped them, teased them—strummed them until they trembled with sweet sensation.

All at once, she wasn't in the cupboard anymore. She was lying naked with Simeon in a field of fragrant wild flowers, about as unnatural place for him to be as her mortal mind could conjure in hopes of exorcising his image from her mind, from her memory and broken heart, but the image would not fade. He was in her—part of her—as much a part as her limbs or her skin or the nipples she fondled.

Bending her neck with the aplomb of a swan, she raised one breast until her lips closed around the turgid bud, sucking, nipping—laving it with her tongue. But in her fantasy it wasn't her tongue, it was his tongue, salty-sweet, licking the pebbled areola, stopping just short of the tawny nub that had hardened like steel in anticipation of the tug that would resonate in her groin, igniting her with drenching fire.

Meg had reached the point of no return as she courted the little death that would unite her with Simeon, at least spiritually. Rubbing herself through the muslin fabric wasn't enough. Inching up the hem of her kirtle, she exposed her slit and fingered it, parting her nether lips, which were wet with the slick juices of her arousal. She spread the wetness higher to the protruding nub. It was hard and thick and swollen—ready to give her the sensation that would take her out of herself—ready to rivet her with the release that would let her forget for a brief blink in time's eye who she was and what she had condemned herself to for the rest of her life by leaving the man she loved. She stroked it carefully—just enough to excite, but not enough to carry her over the brink.

Then she remembered the phallus. Was it really a likeness of Simeon's erect penis or was Seth mocking her? She plunged her hand into the marketing bag and slipped it out of its coffer. Rush candles in their sconces in the corridor outside let in enough light between cracks in the boards for her to examine the carving. Having seen only one erect penis, it was hard to judge, but she decided it could be. The distended veins were in the right place, the size and shape were accurate, and the mushroom tip was exact. She wasted no more time deciding. Her quim was wet and swollen, aching for release. She slipped the phallus inside her, moving it in and out while she stroked her breasts one by one, scraping the dark, hard nipples, squeezing them between her fingertips as the phallus probed deeper. Her breath caught as it touched the same secret place Simeon had discovered deep inside her. Her pelvis spasmed, jerking as the hard veins scraped against her erection. Her back, arched in an involuntary contraction, booted her mound forward. One long, languid spiral thrust and she came, gripping the phallus with the walls of her vagina, just as it had gripped Simeon's hot hard bulk.

Lost in the exquisite agony of release, she floated as if outside herself and looked down on her ecstasy, on the flushed hardness of her breasts, on their hard dark nipples, on the moist V of her pubic curls between her spread legs, on the phallus still inside her. Writhing against the last delicious wave of orgasmic fire, Meg groaned in spite of herself.

But then her heart sank.

It may be an exact replica, but it wasn't the same. The hard, unyielding phallus was not Simeon's steely yet silky-soft hardness. There was no warm rush of his seed to nourish her. No palpitating, vein-swelling, tip-pumping evidence that she had given him his release. Was this what she had condemned herself to, this turgid coldness?

Tears welled in her eyes as she withdrew the impostor from her flushed quim. Wiping it clean, she placed it back inside its coffer and shut it away in the marketing bag out of sight. Then ordering herself, she made ready to leave. It had to be now, while the house was asleep, when she could slip away without notice. She cracked the cupboard door ever so slightly. The rush candles were still lit in their sconces, flooding the little compartment with lemony glow. That was a good sign. All was still. The sisters hadn't yet risen to begin their day. Her fingers closed around the marketing bag, and she stepped into the corridor.

Her feet stung from the glass shard cuts the minute she put her weight on them, and she sucked in a hasty breath around a grimace. She hadn't taken two steps when the banging began— a loud, constant pounding upon the nunnery door. Meg froze in her tracks. It felt as if her heart leapt into her throat and got stuck as she stood there riveted by that racket, which was as loud as cannon fire. She swallowed dryly. No need to panic. Men were not permitted to enter the nunnery. But Simeon was no ordinary man. He was a selkie, and she'd seen the power of his rage in the storm that had leveled Shamans' Mount and the gods alone knew what else!

Her knees began to tremble. Still dazed from the orgasm, she wasn't at her most powerful. She couldn't see what was happening due to a bend in the corridor, but she heard one of the sisters shuffling along the parquetry, grumbling and complaining, and then her ear-splitting shriek as Simeon, evidently realizing the door was unlatched, burst inside.

"I know she's here!" he shouted, his voice echoing through the narrow corridors. Oh, how it thrilled her! "Young, about so high . . . with hair like spun gold. She has to be here. We have searched every inch of this island—everywhere but here!"

"Th-there was a girl," the woman mewed. "She came in when we were burying one of our own. I told her she was welcome to wait. She looked so . . . distraught. She was gone when we returned."

"You searched to be sure?"

"Well, no, we didn't search. Why would we? This is a holy house, my lord. There are no locks or harsh restrictions here. All who seek sanctuary are given it. She would have been welcome to stay as long as she wished."

"Out of my way, lady," Simeon shouted. "I am Simeon, Lord of the Deep, your sovereign prince of these waters. I mean you no harm, but that girl may be in grave danger—not from me, I am her mate. If she is still here, I must find her!"

Meg heard his heavy footfalls then. The harsh vibrations shuddered through her wounded feet. There wasn't a moment to lose. Spinning on her heels, she raced toward the rear entrance, flung the door wide to the swirling mist, and fled.

Simeon streaked through the corridors like a man possessed. Holy women in their nightrails huddled in clusters along the passages. He scarcely saw them. Calling for Meg at the top of his voice, he stomped through the nunnery, throwing chamber doors wide, with the woman who had let him in following on his heels.

"My lord, I beg of you . . . If she were here, we would know of it!" the holy woman pleaded, tugging her shawl over her nightgown. "Please do not disrupt this holy place!"

"You do not understand! I have to find her!"

The woman babbled on. Simeon scarcely heard. His heart was pounding so hard in his ears he could hear nothing else.

"Selkies are a peaceful people," the woman said. "They do not ravage nunneries and terrorize helpless holy women!"

Simeon stopped in his tracks. "It is true that we are pacifists, lady, but that storm you just escaped here in this hollow was bred of selkie wrath. Being a peaceful people by no means makes us weak. When something threatens one of our own, we are a force to be reckoned with. The great cataclysm that formed the archipelago eons ago was an act of selkie justice, aided by the gods. It will seem no more catastrophic than that piddling mist out there if one hair on that girl's head is harmed. Now let me pass!"

She fell back, though she did not leave him. Protesting all the while, she waddled after him until they reached the corridor that led to the cupboard under the stairs. Simeon was in a blind passion with the search almost complete and still no sign of Megaleen, but something the woman had said earlier ghosted back across his frazzled mind.

"You said you were burying one of your own when you saw the girl I seek?" he said.

The woman nodded. "At first I thought she had come to pay her respects, but she had not."

"The dead woman's name . . . what was it?"

"G-Glenda . . . Sister Glenda," the woman said. "She was very old."

That sank in. Gooseflesh raced the length of Simeon's spine as the pieces fell into place. Vega was right. His mother had died. At least now they were certain of it. She had sacrificed herself for him and for Meg, and for his father. There was no greater love than this. Such a sacrifice could not be for naught.

He said no more. Sprinting along the corridor, he pulled up short before the open cupboard door in the wainscoting. There was blood on the floor beside it. His sharp eyes flashed ahead, where streaks of more blood led toward the rear door, also ajar.

Simeon spun, seized the woman and kissed her on her plump, red cheek. "The gods bless you, lady," he cried. "I trouble you no more. She is found!"

Letting the slack-jawed woman go, he darted out into mist so thick he couldn't penetrate it with his extraordinary selkie vision. It was still dark; the darkness before dawn, when even the mist is sooty-black and the air breathless and still. Nonetheless, he strained to see through it frantically, begging the gods to let him find her. There would be no bloody footprints in the sand. Did he dare leave the mist? He still had the Waterwitch's geode charm tucked inside his eel skin suit if he needed to return. No. Instinct told him she'd left the hollow.

The minute he stepped outside the mist, he felt a vibration beneath his feet. She was running toward the north shore of the Isle. Shouting her name at the top of his voice, he ran in the same direction, bounding over the dunes and clumps of tall beach grass. His heart was hammering against his ribs and echoing in his ears, but he still heard her cries as she fled. Then he saw her. She was tiring—limping. Her sore feet were slowing her down. She stumbled. Then all at once she was in his arms. He was holding her at last. Nothing else mattered. He was holding his Megaleen. Scooping her up in his arms, he laid her down in the sand and fell upon her, pinning her to the ground with his lower body, while he caged her between his outstretched arms.

The look in her eyes—part terror, part despair—misted his own. "Why?" he murmured with a tremor in his deep sensuous voice. "Why did you run from me, Megaleen?"

"You have to let me go," she sobbed. "It is the only way! I

cannot take you from your realm—from the deep you love so—and I cannot join you in yours. . . ."

"It is *not* the only way," he shot back, shaking her. "There is another alternative." He gestured behind. "There is a woman back in that nunnery who gave her life that you might know that alternative . . . Vega's mother. We all thought her dead. My father bought her immortality eons ago from a sorcerer—an amulet. Theirs was a union like ours—he a selkie, she a mortal." He withdrew the amulet from his suit. "When Vega told her of us, she removed the necklace and began to age before his eyes. She has died. We love each other, Megaleen. You cannot let her have died in vain. . . ."

"W-what was the woman's name?" Meg murmured.

"Glenda."

Meg sobbed, throwing her arms around Simeon's neck. "I saw her," she moaned. "It was horrible!"

Simeon handed her the necklace. "You must accept it and put it on," he said. Meg fastened the amulet around her neck, and he gathered her close. "Don't ever leave me again," he murmured, gravel-voiced. "And don't take the amulet off. You need not fear to lose it. It contains strong magic. It will not come off unless you remove it. You will not age as long as you wear it."

Meg nodded against his shoulder, and he tilted her head back and took her lips in a fiery kiss that wrenched a groan from the very depths of him. He deepened it, and she melted against him, clinging to him, her racing heart fluttering against his hard-muscled chest. Breathless and fully aroused, he clung to her, his hand buried in the thick richness of her hair, which was fragrant with the scent of sweet clover and honeysuckle. He inhaled her deeply.

"What of Seth?" she said, leaning into his embrace.

"Seth is dead," he returned.

"Y-you . . . ?"

"Elicorn," he said. "He mounted him in an attempt to escape."

Meg sagged in relief against him, and he scooped her up in his arms and carried her over the dunes.

"Where do we go?" she queried.

"To bathe your cuts," he told her. "There is a tide pool nearby. The water is cool and soothing. It will help you heal."

Meg stiffened in his arms. "Seth said there were crabs in the tidal pools!" she said.

Simeon laughed. "There are," he said. "But they are *my* crabs; my loyal subjects. You forget who I am."

The pool wasn't far. It was small and shallow, edged with shells and smooth stones on three sides, with a flat slanted boulder on the fourth. Simeon set Meg down on the edge of it, stripped naked, and sank into the cool salt water. Crouching in front of her, he examined her feet.

"Some of these cuts are deep," he observed, bathing them gently. The water was cool, but not cold, and she wiggled her toes in it as he examined them for pieces of glass. He found none. His hands inched higher, stroking her ankles, then her slender calves. Her skin was like silk beneath the thin muslin kirtle; it was all that stood between them. Fumbling with it, his elbow grazed her marketing bag at the edge of the pool and it slipped into the water. Simeon dove down, and came up holding the coral coffer that held the phallus.

"What is this?" he said, lifting it out of the little chest. "Where did you get it?"

"S-Seth said you modeled for that," she murmured. "Did you, Simeon?"

He didn't know whether to laugh or scold her. Turning it to and fro in his hand, he admired its magnificence, recalling when he'd posed for the carver who had created it. "A very long time ago," he mused. "It was one of the artifacts stolen in one of the raids centuries ago. Did you enjoy it?" How could he be jealous of himself? But he was. He had to be going mad. She had finally driven him stark-staring insane! Jealous of his own effigy! He didn't give her a chance to answer. "Well, no matter, you'll have need of it no more!" he said, tossing it into the pool, coffer and all.

Seizing her about the waist, he stripped off her mantle, pulled her onto his lap, and plunged into her in one swift trust. Raising the kirtle over her head, he cast it aside. Overwhelmed by unstoppable passion, he let his hands rove over her body frantically, as if he were memorizing every inch of her. They palmed her breasts, and his thumbs scraped her erect nipples until she groaned. They seized the perfect rounds of her buttocks as he surged out of the water and backed her against the boulder, his cock moving inside her—growing—reaching—touching the very core of her being.

Guiding her legs around his waist, he pounded into her, crying out as she rotated her hips to take him deeper still. Her buttocks clenched beneath his grip as the walls of her vagina gripped his shaft. Her hands threaded through his long dark hair, pulling his head down until their lips met, until their tongues merged and their pleasure-moans resonated in his body—in the hot blood thrumming in his veins—in the very marrow of his bones. They felt as if they were melting.

Their first release was wild and fast, his head thrown back, her hands fisted in his hair, the rush of his seed and the wetness of her release spilling over in her. It was like coming in hot silk, for her sex gripped him still, barely giving him a chance to go flaccid before he hardened again. This did not happened to him except in her arms. Selkie prowess was legend. They were the most sexually charged creatures of the deep. But never in his life had he gown hard again in rapid succession after coming, except in Megaleen.

"Never, ever, leave me again," he gritted out through a dry sob as he plunged her back into the water. Moving in and out of her, he let the soothing salt water rush in with his cock and rush out with his seed—let it lave her quim, the tender, engorged walls of her nether lips and the rock-hard nub—as he spiraled deeper, bringing her to the brink once more.

It was still low tide, and the water rose only to his waist when standing. Easing her back until her torso floated in the water, he raised her legs high and gripped her taut bottom again. He was deep into her, touching regions he had never touched before—touching her where she was still virgin, for he knew every inch of her parts. It was dark and mysterious so deep inside her, and it filled him with drenching fire as he watched her hooded eyes glaze in mindless bliss and her lips part, though she didn't speak. For a breathless moment, he let her float there while he ground his pelvis into her, into the fascinating pubic curls that hid her tiny erection as they scraped against the thick, hard root of his cock. How beautiful she was with her long golden mane fanned out wide about her in the water like a siren of the deep. The ripples followed the contours of her curves, like an hourglass, exposing her breasts, following the narrow shape of her waist, welling in her navel, then exposing her belly.

Simeon's breath was coming short. The gentle sounds of the water lapping at her mound, and the sucking sounds his cock was making pumping in and out of her, had driven him to the brink again. Watching his purple-veined shaft spiral in and out of her as he rotated his hips was more than he could bear.

"Hold on to me . . ." he murmured. Lowering her legs, he raised her up guiding them around his waist again as she clasped him fast, and sank back into the water with her. Kneeling on the soft silt bottom, he swooped down to take one hard rosebud nipple in his mouth, then the other, then her lips. Seizing her buttocks, he pistoned into her, drowning in the guttural resonance of her release, in the totality of his own orgasm pumping a stream of pearly come into her and into the water.

His flexed chest heaving, Simeon floated with her in the

water of the little tidal pool until the waves of their release subsided and their bodies became their own again. Dawn was breaking over the pool, which was ghostly pink in the morning mist. The first breath of a breeze sighing over the Isle foretold a fine day ahead. Simeon scarcely noticed. He had his Megaleen in his arms naked, but for the amulet, the rainbow-tinted black pearl on a silver strand resting in the perfect hollow of her slender throat. It had given them their future—their length of days—their immortality, and he was bursting with plans for their future.

When the crabs came with the turn of the tide, swimming all around them, climbing on the boulder, on the shells and smooth white pebbles, Meg squealed in fright. But Simeon only laughed as he hummed the mantra that sent them scurrying to the edge of the pool like spectators in an arena.

Sagging against him in relief, Meg breathed a ragged sigh. "What did you say to them?" she said.

Simeon smiled. "I introduced them to my Lady of the Deep," he said, "Princess of the Waves. See how they genuflect before you? No creature of the sea will ever harm you, once word spreads that you are my mate, and these are just the ambassadors to do the honors."

Surging to his feet, he pulled Meg up alongside him, aroused again as he watched the water trickle down her body in little rivulets, bouncing off her hard, taut nipples and welling in her navel. He watched it drizzle down over her pubic mound, darkening her curls, and drip like pink diamonds over her smooth, flushed thighs, returning to the pool. How very beautiful she was with the first rays of dawn gilding her skin and frosting her long golden hair with copper lights.

He stooped and kissed her softly on the lips, then on the breasts, and finally on the perfect V of golden curls between her thighs before returning to her lips again. "Come, my princess," he said, as the crabs scurried away to form a vacant swath at the edge of the pool for them to climb out. "It is time to go home...."

## 25

M eg squirmed as Simeon probed the cuts on her feet again. He'd removed her dove-gray kirtle and set her down in the middle of his elevated bed. She had finally come home. She could scarcely believe it. There was no other home for her except in Simeon's arms. How could she ever have imagined she could live without him? But she would have, if it meant his immortality, just as he would have given that immortality up for love of her. They were soul mates.

"Am I hurting you?" Simeon said, frowning. How mysterious he seemed when he frowned. Knit brows over those almond-shaped selkie eyes gave him a smoldering, Otherworldly look that thrilled her to the core.

Meg giggled. "No," she said, "it tickles!"

Simeon straightened up and peeled off his eel skin. The sultry look faded from his face and an evocative lopsided smile twisted his lips. It melted her heart. He so rarely smiled.

All at once he was lying beside her, his hard-muscled body naked against her, his hands roving over her body lazily. This was no unstoppable coupling. It was tantalizing and slow. It took her breath away.

"There is so much more I want to show you," he murmured, toying with her nipple, "so many ways to pleasure you."

Meg threaded her fingers through his hair and brought his head down until their lips met. He drew her against him as he deepened the kiss, and her heart leapt, pounding against his rock-hard chest. When their lips parted, she followed the contours of his broad shoulders and the firm, ridged hardness of his middle with her fingertips. Inching lower in his arms, she took his nipple in her mouth and laved it slowly, reveling in his sharp intake of breath, in his clenched posture, in the thick hot bulk of his erection trembling against her thigh. Her hand moved toward it, detecting the pebbled layer of gooseflesh her caress had spread over his skin.

Meg slid lower still, but instead of taking his penis in her hand, she closed her lips around the ridged head and took it into her mouth. Simeon eased himself onto his back and groaned as she took him deep into her in a spiraling motion, swirling her tongue over his hard hot flesh, flicking it over the silken tip ever so lightly, gliding it back down toward the thick root, only to slow the pace the minute he reached for more. She would make it last. He had taught her well.

His hands fast in the back of her hair held her head in place as she sucked him, her lips moving up and down along his thick veined shaft. He rotated his hips, holding her down on it as it grew longer still. Meg thought of that first night, watching his consort Alexia take his penis into her mouth as the surf slammed into them on the shore. Oddly, there was no jealousy. That part of his life was over. He was hers now, but the sight of him thus in her mind's eye, with his sex exposed to the creaming surf—to his consort's eager mouth—sent pincers of searing fire to pluck at her loins, making her so hot she began to tremble.

The surges, like drenching fire, attacking the epicenter of her sex would not be stilled, and she began to touch herself, probing her slit with her fingers, gliding them the length of her fissure to spread her wetness. Her aching breasts scraped against his taut muscled thighs, her nipples grown hard boring into him. She began writhing against the pressure of her fingertips entering her—feeling for the hardening nub that would trigger her release. She moved her fingers lower, then higher, until her pubic curls were drenched in her wetness, and she groaned as thick drops of pre-come salted her tongue.

Simeon groaned. He was watching her touch herself, watching her lips glide up and down his shaft while she stroked herself, watching her tongue peek out as she sucked him, laving the thick, distended veins, from the ridged mushroom tip of his penis to the thick bulk of its root. His thighs clenched. His shaft jerked to full arousal—harder—thicker—more urgent. She tried to hold off his climax, but the opposite happened. Groaning again, he arched himself against her, holding her still, squeezing his hands through her hair as he released.

His hot, salty come rushed into her, the head of his penis so far back in her throat it danced against her palate as she swallowed. Licking him clean, she swallowed again and again. Still he was hard enough to penetrate her.

All at once, his strong hands circled her waist and she felt herself lifted. Spreading her legs, he lowered her onto his erection until he filled her. It slid in easily enough on their combined juices, but he didn't move once he filled her. Cupping her breasts in his hands, he kneaded them, forcing her aching nipples through his fingers, lightly grazing them. Everything below his waist remained still.

"Do not move . . ." he panted, the deep burr of arousal in his voice running her through like a javelin. "Feel how it grows inside you. . . ."

Meg stayed perfectly still. Her breath caught as inside her

his penis began to swell to its fullness. It stretched the walls of her vagina as it grew, touching the virgin place he'd claimed for his own. The groan that left his parched throat then was guttural and primitive. It was a cross between the sound of a barking seal and that of a roaring lion. His pelvis reared against her, and he bit down on his handsome lower lip until he'd bruised it, and he shut his eyes.

"Ride the waves, Megaleen," he murmured huskily. "*Ride the storm. . . .*"

Meg knew what he wanted. Digging her knees into his sides as if she were riding Elicorn, she rode him, taking him deeper with each bounce, her quim gripping him, squeezing him, milking him of every last drop of his seed rushing into her in strong, pulsing spurts, his contractions triggering her release as she ground her tiny pulsing erection into the base of his shaft.

Crying out as the orgasm riveted her, Meg reeled back in time to the night she had indeed ridden the storm, to the lightning dancing on the water all around them, charging the phosphorescence in the water and in the spindrift crashing over them—fusing their bodies—joining their souls. It had just happened again, and she shut her eyes as he rolled her over, still joined, and gathered her into his arms.

Simeon didn't speak. His eyes, still hooded with the blindness of passion, gazed down on her as he took first her lips in a volatile kiss that took her breath away, and then her nipples, still flushed and tingling as he licked them to tall hardness again. She groaned as the laving of his tongue over first one puckered bud and then the other tugged deep inside her groin. White hot ripples, like those that spread when a pebble breaks the surface of the water, radiated out wide inside her. He had grown hard again. It was going to be a long, passionate night.

All was still in the palace, where Vega lay curled in his cubicle in the arms of the young vivacious selkie, Risa. He should be on guard, since the elder retainers, though plentiful and for the most part invisible, were not trusted with guard duty, but Pio was keeping watch. There really wasn't much need for security in Simeon's domain anymore. Once in a great while some young selkie buck would flex his muscle in a vain attempt to usurp the Lord of the Deep, but such insurrections were far between and swiftly quelled. Even the elders in their senility could manage that. Simeon was loved and respected. All creatures of the deep swore fealty to their Lord. He was Prince of the Arcan waters. There hadn't been an invasion from the other side of the continent in eons. And the ever faithful Pio was unsurpassed in his vigilance and devotion.

Vega sighed. Risa always shifted his mortal sex drive into selkie madness—even before they'd become lovers. This was the worst part of being a half-breed. He never quite knew who he was. Selkie or mortal? Right now with the blood on fire in his veins, unable to get his fill of her, he was pure selkie. He had watched her from afar for so long, knowing it was unlikely he would ever claim her as consort. She had belonged to Simeon. All female selkies belonged to Simeon before they were exiled—all clamoring for the favors of the Lord of the Deep. Somehow, Risa wanted *him* instead—was pining for him, just as he had been secretly longing for her. They had only mated once before Simeon had exiled the consorts. Gazing down at her beautiful face so peaceful and pale, he could scarcely believe he held her in his arms.

Her long, dark hair was twined around his arm like a tether, and her pale skin was flushed with the bloom of recent release. His cock was still swollen from the frenzy of her mouth sucking him, from the ecstasy of her silken tongue laving him, and from the sheer rapture of her skilled hand pumping him dry. And that was only the first time!

Yes, he was selkie—pure, seductive, lecherous selkie to the core—and his cock was on fire for more of her, when Simeon's footfalls vibrating through the corridors reached him. Vega met him in his sitting room, where they wouldn't be disturbed.

"You've found her?" Vega said. He could read it in his brother's face, but there was something else there, too, something he couldn't read . . . something that raised his hackles.

"Yes," Simeon said. "Where the deuce is Pio? I knew you'd be abed with Risa, but Pio should be keeping watch."

"He is . . . *was*. I summoned him myself."

"Well, he isn't there now. There is no one on duty out there."

"Settle down, Simeon," Vega said. "All is well here. What? Do you have news of invasion?"

Simeon shook his head and began to pace the length of the carpet. "I felt a turbulence returning. Something isn't . . . right."

"Nonsense! Everything is finally 'right.' Where is Megaleen?"

"Asleep in my bed. She is exhausted. Her feet were cut on the broken glass when Gideon broke through the solarium at the training hall."

"Did you give her the amulet?"

"Yes."

From Simeon's expression, Vega knew he needn't ask his next question, though he would nonetheless. "Glenda . . ." he said. It was still hard for him to think of her as his mother since he'd never known her. "Is she . . . ?"

"Dead," Simeon concluded for him.

Vega nodded. "But . . . to sacrifice her immortality . . . !"

"Imagine her lonely existence shut up in that nunnery," Simeon said. "Father has been gone for eons. She was ready for the afterlife."

Vega nodded. "Which only goes to prove what I've said all along: Selkies ought have no truck with love. It is not in their nature. My mortal logic tells me that. Father succumbed to love, and it was his undoing. Take care, Simeon, that you do not make his mistake."

"I fear it is already too late for that, my brother," Simeon said on a sigh. "I do love her. It is not a comfortable thing, I will admit, and I can only pity father being in love with *two* women. But there's nothing for it. You can rest assured your mother's sacrifice will not be in vain."

"So! What now?" Vega said buoyantly. The subject needed changing. He was beginning to feel a little of Simeon's trepidation. Instinct was strong in both halves of his makeup, and it was screaming in both now.

"That all needs to be sorted out," Simeon said. "The tincture works, and Megaleen has the amulet. It only remains to decide where she wishes to spend her time. If she is content to spend all her days below the waves with me, so be it. If she needs to maintain some of her mortal existence, that, too, can be arranged. I do not think she would want to do that on the Isle of Mists after so much unpleasantness has occurred there. I haven't discussed it with her yet—there hasn't been time—but if that is the case, there are several isles protected by merfolk, where she could visit as needs must if it would make her more comfortable—at least until she adapts to her new life as Princess of the Waves. I could spend time there with her. I need a place in the mortal world to languish in my selkie incarnation, just as I used to do on the Isle of Mists."

Vega nodded. "Well then, will you want the mating ceremony to introduce her as your lady?"

Simeon nodded. "My subjects will expect a grand celebration. I was thinking we could hold it at the Pavilion. Muriel and the sirens have gone through a great deal of trouble making it livable. It would be a nice reward for their efforts. You know, I've been toying with the idea of living there."

"So . . . you mean to abandon the palace, then?"

Simeon stared. "Abandon?" he said. "I mean to give it to you . . . for you and Risa. Yes, I'll visit . . . spend time here on occasion, but I mean it to be yours."

"*Mine?*" Vega said, vaulting out of the chair. It was the last thing he expected. "And who will take on your valet duties?"

Simeon laughed. "I'll find someone. Such duties are beneath you, in any case. If you want consorts, you will have to choose among the new spawn. The others will remain in exile, Vega. From what I understand, Alexia has found a mate among the mermen, as have some of the others. They are quite content as they are, and so they shall stay."

"Well, that's a relief."

"Pio, on the other hand, goes with me, but he will have to do better. I don't know what ails him lately. He usually dogs me like a shadow. It isn't like him to leave his post or shirk his duties. But I will deal with that."

"When will you want to leave for the Pavilion?"

"Tomorrow," Simeon said. "Once I find Pio, I will send him on ahead to alert the sirens that they need to make ready. They will need a few days, and that will give me time to introduce Megaleen to some of her subjects."

"Then you'd best be about it. You will want your sealskin."

"Yes," Simeon said. "It has been far too long since I've put on the sealskin. I'm beginning to feel the effects of abstinence. That may be the reason for my unrest . . . I just don't know. Where are you keeping it?"

"In my bedchamber, in the teakwood chest, where I've always kept it," Vega said.

"I won't disturb Risa," Simeon said. "Fetch it for me. I'll have a turn above the waves while Megaleen sleeps. Then you can mind it for me till morning."

Vega left him and moved through the rest of his apartments. A fugitive wind was blowing through the chambers, stirring the hanging aquatic vine curtains at the archways. It was cold and damp whispering down his neck like icy fingers. He shuddered, thinking of Simeon's unease. He was nearly ready to give credence to the lore of premonition.

Risa was sleeping in nearly the same position as she had been when he left her, curled on her side, her beautiful raven-colored hair fanned out on the eiderdown bolster like a lacy blue-black halo. He wouldn't disturb her, though he couldn't resist stroking a lock of her hair. She didn't stir, and after a moment, he moved away and went to the teakwood chest, only to pull up short. The hasp on the latch was standing straight up. His heart tumbled in his breast. Where was the padlock?

One small rush candle lit the room. It flickered as he threw open the chest and groped inside. But his hands closed only on thin air. The chest was empty. Again and again in denial, he battered the insides of the chest in a frantic attempt to make the sealskin materialize. The racket he was making should have woken Risa, but she remained as she lay, asleep, unaware.

Vega reached her in two ragged strides, knelt beside her and shook her gently at first. When there was no response, he shook her harder, but still she did not wake.

"Risa!" he shouted, lifting her into his arms. "*Risa!* What has happened here? Who was in this chamber?"

There came no reply; she lay as limp in his arms as a rag poppet—so limp that he felt for the pulse at the base of her throat fearing her dead, but she was not. Warm breath still puffed from her nostrils, and her perfect round breasts still rose and fell, but not normally. Her breathing grew rapid and shallow. It was almost as if she were panting.

Rolling back her eyelids one at a time, he saw the mindless stare of one drugged or under a spell. Blood rushed to his scalp like a hundred stinging fingers. Blinding white pinpoints of light starred his always-impeccable vision. He held the young selkie's sagging head to his breast and groaned. She was alive but dead to the world around them, and he laid her back against the bolster, tucked the quilt of woven sea grass about her nakedness, and ran back through his apartments to the sitting room, where he'd left Simeon.

There was only one explanation—only one who could have stolen the sealskin. The Waterwitch! He remembered her cryptic words when he took that other sealskin from her. Her augur on that occasion slithered across his mind like a stinging viper: *Keep it!* she had said. *I* will *get another, and you will rue the day you ever touched that sealskin, bastard of the sea! You mark my words!*

Vega swayed as if he'd been struck, remembering. It nearly cost him his balance as he parted the aquatic vine curtain and burst into his sitting room only to pull up short. The room was empty. Simeon was gone.

## 26

Vega paced the floor of his sitting room like a madman, raking his hair back from a sweaty brow. What was the protocol for this? There was no way of knowing. It had never happened before to his knowledge. When a selkie's skin was taken, it was usually a mortal female who stole it, keeping him on land to do her bidding until the skin was returned to him by hook or by crook; it didn't matter how. As soon as it was in his possession again, he would return to the deep, leaving all that occurred on land behind without a backward glance—even though he may have fathered children—even though he may have seemed content, even happy, on land with his mortal mate. That was the way of it: whoever steals a selkie's sealskin commands him as long as she possesses it—even to the very thoughts he thinks— even to the very breath he breathes. He is a slave to his captor— a mindless, witless, willing slave to her every whim.

That Simeon was gone did not bode well, but where had he gone? Where was the old hag keeping him—on land or beneath the waves? He could not pull the answers out of the air. What was to be done about Risa? Should he tell Meg? His mind was racing. It felt ready to burst. Frantically, he hummed the mantra that should bring Pio, but he had no faith in it. The loyal summoner had gone missing, and unless he was very much mistaken, Pio could not answer. What he needed to petition the gods for now was that Pio was still alive, for Vega knew the swordfish would defend his lord and master with his dying breath.

There was nothing to be done about Risa and Meg then, not until he knew for certain what they were facing. He decided to let them stay as they lay. He summoned retainers to watch after the palace and plunged headlong into the sea, swimming straight for the Waterwitch's cave.

Simeon had heard about the Waterwitch's cages. He'd heard the horror tales of them at his mother's knee, but he'd never seen them, much less ever expected to be held captive in one. He'd never gone past the sitting room and sanctuary in her cave . . . until now. This cubicle lay beyond the sanctuary, a darkened recess, long and winding, where many cages stood along the ledge and in the water of another subterranean pool that ran the length of it. Some were empty. Others contained the parched bones of men long dead. And then there were the ones in the water. Pio was contained in one of those close to the surface within sight. He should have known the faithful summoner had met with foul play not to have been at his beck and call. Simeon's heart went out to the creature. He could hear the frantic hum of Vega's mantra calling the swordfish. Poor Pio had scraped off scales and dented his sword on the bars of his cage, desperately trying to answer that call. Simeon tried with all his might to calm the creature, but to no avail. No longer in possession of his sealskin, he hadn't the authority to be heard below the waves. That was the worst of it. The Waterwitch had hung the sealskin on the wall in plain sight, like a tapestry—like a trophy, for that is what it was. She had stolen the sealskin of the Lord of the Deep. She had made him her slave. How had this happened?

His cage was on the dry ledge. Without his sealskin, he was like any mortal, unable to sustain himself for long periods under water. He had been divested of his powers, and his mind reeled back to the time he'd nearly drowned for lack of them. That brief episode had drained some of the color from his hair at the temples. What would this episode bring? How much would he age this time? Without his sealskin, immortality was lost to him. He would age like any mortal ages, and eventually die.

There were bars on his cage, but it wasn't locked, at least not by conventional means—no padlocks or chains. He had no doubt the Waterwitch's magic was at work here. As her captive, he couldn't leave the cage, locked or not, while she possessed his sealskin. It was a fairly well appointed prison, boasting among other things, a lounge and a few other pieces of furniture. He'd been given plenty of food and drink, but no lamp or candle, though a rush torch in its wall bracket outside cast enough light to see by. The Waterwitch had simply shut him inside, naked, and left him.

His heart went out to poor Pio. If ever a fish could be frantic, this fish was frantic now. Vega's mantra reverberated off the rock and coral walls, resonating in the water, and the swordfish swam back and forth and in circles just below the surface, crashing headlong and sideways into the bars in a desperate attempt to answer the call. Simeon tried to reach the summoner with his mind, but Pio either couldn't or wouldn't listen. How was it Simeon could hear the mantra and not be able to answer it? It was unbearable.

Time passed. Simeon had no inkling how much had slipped by before the aquatic vine curtain at the threshold trembled then parted as Elna, the Waterwitch, entered. Simeon never knew how she would present herself. This time, she was in her sultry guise, voluptuous and seductive, her perfect body naked beneath a robe so sheer it seemed no denser than the air. Open in the front, it parted as she sauntered close, giving him a provocative glimpse of her perfect, round breasts and V-shaped mound, the only parts of her anatomy, except her face, devoid of shimmering green scales. Simeon wasn't fooled. He'd seen her true incarnation—the hideous, bearded, whiskered fish-headed, scaled anatomy too grotesque to look upon. All else was sorceress glamour.

"Well, well, Lord of the Deep," she said, entering the cage. "You have your brother Vega to thank for this . . . incarceration."

"That you have taken my sealskin is no negligence of Vega's," Simeon said. "There is no fault in him."

"Oh, but I am not speaking about lifting it from that chest in his rooms. Your brother stole a sealskin of mine and destroyed it. I've taken yours in exchange."

"What sealskin? You are no selkie. What good is such a skin to you?"

"Ah, but my magic gives me the same properties it gives to you, my prince—length of days."

Simeon wished his mind were clearer. He had lost many of his powers when he lost the skin. He had to fight more loss now with every breath. What was she saying . . . that she had the magic to reap the benefits of immortality from a selkie sealskin? If that were so, he was lost. Without his sealskin, he had no powers to match hers . . . except his wits, and he was leaning heavily upon those already.

"So . . . you have done this before," he said.

"And will do again."

Simeon glanced at his sealskin displayed on the wall. It was so near, and yet it may as well have been fathoms away. There was no way he could reach it. It was torture.

The Waterwitch smiled. It did not reflect in her beady fish

eyes. "You'd like to, wouldn't you?" she said. "Even if I let you out, you could not. I have cast an aura about it, just as I have about this chamber. You are mine, Simeon, Lord of the Deep."

"Where is my eel skin suit?"

"What, a selkie modest in his nudity? I have never heard of it. You selkies go about naked more than you do clothed . . . Interesting."

Selkies had no modesty when it came to their nakedness. Simeon was more at home naked than he was in his eel skin suits but not before the Waterwitch. Her eyes all too often settled on his cock.

"It is mine," he said, his words clipped and edged. "You have taken all else. You might have left me that."

"In due time it will be returned to you," she said, circling him. She carried a scepter fashioned of sea flotsam, which she tapped against her open palm. It appeared to be braided vines crowned with a small pointed shell. Stopping abreast of him, she slid the shell tip under his cock, lifting it for a closer examination. "If I give your eel skin to you now," she drawled, "I will deny myself sight of this magnificence between your thighs. If it is this large flaccid, how large could it be aroused? Let us wake it and see, eh?" She sidled closer. "Will you, or shall I?"

Simeon slapped the scepter away from his penis.

"So! You have spirit!" she said. "Good. I like that."

"You have me," Simeon said. "Let the swordfish go. He is naught to you, and he's beating himself to death caged thus."

"Good!" she said. "That will save me the trouble. I haven't had a good swordfish steak in eons."

"Let him go, I say!"

The Waterwitch's posture clenched. "I give the orders here, Lord of the Deep," she said.

"Very well then, as a favor to me, let Pio go."

"It has a name, your spy, like a pet, eh?"

Simeon hesitated. If he wasn't very careful, the faithful summoner would end his days on the witch's dinner table. "He is no spy, and he is hardly a pet," he said, avoiding her eyes. They had the power to penetrate the soul. "He runs errands . . . and assists the retainers in my home. Let him go . . . as a gesture of goodwill. He is needed now that I am . . . gone."

The Waterwitch considered it. "Perhaps," she said. "But first let us see how well that there wakes up for me, eh? Nothing comes without a price, Lord of the Deep."

Simeon longed to reach out and strangle the woman, but he dared not. Kill her, and he might never be released from his cage. He had no magic to cancel the aura she'd cast about her dungeon.

She sidled closer, like a rippling sidewinder, and seized his cock. Her hands were cold and clammy, and he shuddered at their touch. She was well skilled in the sexual arts, knowing just how to pump him, twisting her hand around his shaft, only lightly grazing the head enough to tantalize.

"Now you," she said, cramming his fingers around his shaft. "Take it. Make it hard for me. Ah! Where is the selkie prowess, eh? Can you do no better than that? It barely stands on its own."

"What?" he said cleverly. "Did you think you could take my sealskin and still have my selkie drive to service you? They are one and the same, old hag; you cannot separate them. Go rub yourself off on my sealskin. That's about as much of a come as you'll get from me unless I possess it."

"You will service me—and well—if you expect to live out normal mortal days, for that is what you have been reduced to, fool! Now pump that thing. I grow weary of this banter." She stepped closer, shedding her robe, and ran her splayed hands over his shoulders, chest, and torso. Simeon stiffened under her touch. A plan was forming. If it worked even for the moment, it would be worth the consequences it might spawn.

"Touch yourself," he murmured, twisting out of her reach.

She purred like a kitten, undulating closer as she ran her hands along her sides, her hips, and her belly.

"Your nipples," he said. "Touch your nipples—make them hard for me."

She cooed like a bird as she cupped her breasts and began strumming her nipples erect. She had chosen an exquisite body to shape-shift into in her sultry incarnation. Most men would easily succumb. But Simeon was no ordinary man. Even as he was, divested of his powers, a slave to her whims with no magic at his command but that which his sealskin afforded, he was *Lord of the Deep,* Prince of the Waves, and he was smarter than she. Besides, he knew what she really was. He had seen her hideous true self. For his plan to work, he would be all right as long as she didn't touch him . . . or he didn't touch her.

The animal sounds she made touching herself were obscene. He blocked them out, shut his eyes, clenched his thighs together and concentrated on coming as he continued to stroke himself to full hardness—envisioning Meg accomplished it. Seeing her with his mind's eye lying naked in his arms—open to his caress, her moist sex quivering in anticipation of his thrusts, brought him to the brink. All went well until he opened his eyes and saw the Waterwitch masturbating, pulling at her nipples as she swayed before him. She pressed closer, reaching for his cock, and he reeled away from the webbed fingers snapping at his shaft.

"Not yet," he said. "I . . . I told you, when you took my sealskin, you took my ability to perform at my most powerful. This is your fault. That being so, you will have to be patient."

"Why can I not touch you?" she pouted. "I could just take you and have done, you know."

"Because this excites me," he said. "And since I am no longer possessed of selkie prowess, I need to work at pleasuring a woman, like the mortal you have made of me. Humor me, venerable one. Touching will come later . . . when I'm ready.

Now see what you've done! It goes down. Show me your quim. Open your nether lips and rub yourself for me. . . ."

Simeon waited, watching the witch sway to her own rhythm, watching her succumb to the fever of her desire. This had to be her fault for the plan to work, if it was to buy him some time. It would work only once.

"That's right," he crooned. "Lie down on the lounge and feel yourself inside . . . Ready yourself for me. . . ."

She flopped down on the lounge, her pendulous breasts jiggling. "Why can't you just come in me and get it over with?" she complained.

"Because, though you are beautiful as you appear to me now, I see you as you really are, and if I touch you before I'm on the verge of coming, my cock will wither and you'll get none. You brought this about. You will just have to live with what you have wrought if you want this cock in you. Do as I say . . . Excite me. . . ."

Rage flared in her, but then she began to undulate, touching herself, spreading her legs for him. Simeon waited until her eyes began to glaze over as she approached release, until her groans became guttural and spastic. She was watching him bring himself erect again. It was time, and he shut his eyes to conjure Meg's image, imagining it was her lips doing the tugging on his throbbing cock instead of his hand. Release hit him hard, his seed coming in spurts, wasted on the cold cell floor. His groan caught the witch's attention. Her eyes snapped open to the blur of his spent seed. Shrieking like a banshee, she vaulted off the lounge and began pummeling his chest with both her balled fists.

Simeon seized her wrists. "This is your fault!" he seethed. "You robbed me of my powers when you took my sealskin. This is all you will get. It may take years to work out the rhythm that will allow me to come in you. You must be patient, Elna."

Wrenching free of his grip, she lowered the flat of her palm hard across his face. "You will rot in here, Lord of the Deep," she shrilled, her harsh voice echoing over the water in the pool. "Humiliate me, will you?" She struck him again. "You will pay for this—never doubt it!"

Screaming at the top of her voice, she shifted back into her hideous, fish-headed natural state, stormed out of the cage, and plunged headlong into the subterranean pool, disappearing beneath the waves she had created.

---

## 27

Vega hid in the shadows of an underwater ledge as the Water-witch streaked past. Following at a safe distance, he saw her head for the open sea. That she was in a blind rage was evident. He picked up the vibration of her mental screams; they were deafening. Hoping she wouldn't be returning soon, he turned back, making his way through the underwater passages that led to her domain.

She had been in such a taking that her bulk in fish form had stirred up the silt at the bottom, making visibility difficult. Practically blind in the sifting stuff, he resorted to the mantra once more, praying Pio would answer. He'd been missing too long. Fears that the summoner was dead had begun to gnaw at his reason. What would they do without Pio? He wasn't immortal, but sorcery and the gods had endowed him with longevity beyond that of other swordfish in order to serve the Lord of the Deep. He had many years ahead of him, or would have had. No! He wouldn't think of Pio in the past tense. He was alive—he had to be! It was then that he heard the swordfish scream.

Swimming blind in the murky water toward the sound, Vega parted the kelp and the sea grass and the muck dredged up from the bottom, to say nothing of the schools of frightened fish darting all about, and came upon the cage with Pio trapped inside. His heart sank. The fish had scraped nearly all the scales off one side of his body trying to fit through the bars. His regal sword, razors harp and deadly, was nicked and dented, and his eyes were bloodred and bulging.

"*Pio!*" Vega cried, "Ah, Pio. . . ." Reaching through the bars, he stroked the frazzled fish, whose whole body trembled. "We have to get you out of there. Where is Simeon?"

The swordfish spun in a circle and sped toward the ledge of the Waterwitch's dungeon, where the cage he was trapped in was hung. Vega felt his way around the cage, and hauled himself up on the shelf. His gaze darted about the dimly lit chamber, and when his sharp eyes spied Simeon's cage, he hauled himself out of the water and ran to him, while Pio spun in circles rejoicing behind, his razor sharp sword stabbing through the bars.

"Simeon!" Vega cried, frantically searching for a lock—a hasp—anything that would free his brother.

Simeon surged to his feet and ran to the bars. "It's no use," he said. "She's used her magic to lock me in here. Megaleen . . . is she all right?"

"She was asleep when I left, Simeon, so was Risa. The Waterwitch drugged Risa or put a spell on her. I couldn't wake her. That's how she got your sealskin out of the chest in my chamber." Just then, the sealskin caught his eye hanging on the wall and he ran to it. "Here it is!" he cried, reaching toward it.

"No!" Simeon thundered, but too late. Vega ran headlong into what seemed like an invisible wall. He struck it hard. Bouncing off it, he was thrown to the floor. "She's cast an aura around it, Vega. You didn't think she'd just leave it there in plain sight unprotected, did you?"

Vega shook himself like a dog. The room spun around him as he staggered to his feet and returned to Simeon in the cage.

"Throne of the gods!" Vega moaned.

"Why do you think I'm still here?" Simeon said. "I would have strangled the life out of that odious hag with my bare hands if I wasn't afraid I'd rot in here. Look at the rest of the cages—*look!*"

Vega did as he bade him. Some were empty, but others held bodies at various stages of decomposition. Most were skeletons, while others were more recent kills. Judging from the look of them, it appeared that some of their flesh had been eaten. He grimaced. Choking back bile, he covered his mouth and staggered back to Simeon. Only then did he recognize the foul stench that hung like a cloud about the place.

"I was afraid if I killed her I would never get out of here— never get that sealskin back. If she dies with the secret of the spells that imprison me here, I will become like those"—he gestured toward the other cages—"and then what becomes of Megaleen—of any of us?"

Vega raked his hair back from his brow and began to pace.

"There isn't time for that!" Simeon said. "Get Pio out of that cage. He's nearly beaten himself to death trying to break free."

"How?"

"She told me she had cast an aura about this chamber as well as my sealskin. You couldn't reach the skin, but you were able to reach me. She must have cancelled at least that part of it when she fled this place. You have to try. He will kill himself trying to break out of there, and if she would eat the flesh of those poor devils"—he gestured toward the cages again—"she would devour him in a heartbeat. She has already mentioned doing just that. Have you seen her?"

Vega nodded. "She was heading for the open sea in a blind passion when I arrived. What happened here?"

"Never mind that now. She could return at any moment. See

if you can free Pio. If you cannot, go and fetch the others to help you; all those who joined the search on the Isle of Mists. You will need to bring them in any case. We cannot do this alone, Vega. And see that Megaleen stays put."

"Where is your eel skin suit?"

Simeon nodded toward a bench in the corner, where it lay folded neatly. "See if you can poke it through the bars."

"Is that wise? Suppose she returns before we do. Won't she wonder how you got it?"

"Hah! Let her wonder. Let her believe I possess a little magic myself. She is obsessed over mating with me. Let us just say I would feel safer robed than naked."

Vega snatched the suit and shoved it into the cage. Emboldened when that worked, he took hold of the bars attempting to free Simeon, but cried out and pulled his hands back as the metal scorched them.

"Teeth of the gods!" he seethed, soothing his burned fingers. "Do they do that to you?"

"No. I do not know what magic holds me or how to fight it as I am. I've lost nearly all of my powers without my sealskin. Never mind that. Just go quickly, and remember what I said about Megaleen . . . Tell her nothing of this, and see that she doesn't leave the palace."

Vega plunged back into the water and examined Pio's cage again. The bars were not as strong as the ones on the dungeon cages. It more closely resembled a large crustacean trap, strongly made, but the bars were not impossible to bend. It took several tries, but it finally bent a little on the far side, in the shadows, where it wouldn't be as noticeable with all the silt clouding the water. Pio squeezed through at once and swam rings around Vega, leaping out of the water until his tail danced on the surface in his euphoria at being liberated at last.

Vega studied the swordfish's antics for a moment, then

raised his hand. "No!" he said. "No . . . I want you to go back inside the cage and wait."

Communicating with his mind, the stunned fish questioned why.

"I do not want the Waterwitch to be suspicious," Vega explained. "If she sees you gone, she may cast another, greater, aura about this place. She is no fool. Besides, I shall need you here to help free Simeon."

Again the swordfish posed a silent question.

"You will know when the time comes," Vega said. "Stay inside the cage unless you are threatened. If that should occur, you are free now and you can easily escape through the rent I've made."

The summoner didn't seem happy with the idea, but that couldn't be helped. Pio would obey. Confident in that, Vega streaked back through the water toward the palace.

Meg stirred in Simeon's soft, spacious bed, which was heaped with quilts of woven sea grass and featherbeds of eiderdown. She yawned and stretched and groped in the semidarkness for Simeon beside her, but the hollow where his body had lain was empty and cold. Was it dawn or dusk? There was no way of knowing beneath the waves. Would she ever get used to it? She smiled at the question. She could get used to the Netherworld—the dreaded Isle of the Dead that lived in the mists of time if it meant having Simeon.

She rose and dressed, choosing a butter-colored round gown from the wardrobe. The low-cut décolleté offset the amulet, the beautiful black pearl, which was radiant with rainbow luster resting in the hollow at the base of her throat. Turning to and fro before the cheval glass in Simeon's dressing room chamber, she admired the way it shone with an inner light against her skin, the patina gleaming in the rush candle glow. It was as if it had been made for her, forged by the gods with her alone in mind.

She was just about to go in search of Simeon when a familiar voice echoed through the chamber. Would she ever get used to having no doors? Vine curtains sufficed for them, and one couldn't knock on those. But then, privacy was nonexistent and nonessential to selkies. There was much she would have to become accustomed to as Lady of the Deep.

"Come," she called.

Vega entered, sketching a bow. "My lady, I have come to beg a favor," Vega said.

"Ask it."

"My lady Risa has taken ill. Would you kindly sit with her while I fetch a healer? It shan't take long."

"Of course," Meg said. "What is her ailment?"

"She cannot wake, my lady."

"But that is serious."

"Yes, my lady, but all will be well. I just do not want to leave her alone should she wake while I'm gone. The retainers are too . . . provincial for such duty." He swept his hand wide. "Will you follow me?"

Meg nodded, letting him lead her.

"Thank you, my lady," Vega said. "We have no females here since the consorts were exiled, save for the very young and the very old. Should she wake, to have a lady close in age to herself for company would be much preferred."

"Where is Simeon?"

Vega hesitated. "I go to fetch him now," he said.

They had reached Vega's rooms, and he stood aside to let her enter. The rooms were small, but well appointed, furnished tastefully with elegant opulence. He led her to his bed chamber, where Risa lay pale and still against the bedding with her long black hair fanned out about her. Meg immediately felt the girl's brow for fever, but it was cool to the touch—too cool—as cool as death.

"I, too, have healing skills," she told him. "Herbs mostly; it was one of the reasons the mainlanders accused me a witch." The look of him then was startling. All color seemed to drain from his face. "Oh, you needn't fear me!" she said. "I mention it only to offer my services." His expression softened somewhat, but there was still unease in his bearing and in his voice when he spoke.

"You needn't trouble yourself," he gushed. "The healer will come directly."

"She has no fever," Meg said, ignoring him. "Yet her breathing is shallow and rapid." She lowered her ear to Risa's breast, and her posture clenched. "This girl isn't ill," she said. "She is under some kind of spell!"

Vega had lost all color. Meg watched it drain away. "The healers will attend her," he said. "If you will just remain with her until I bring them."

Meg nodded. Something was not as it should be. "Of course," she said.

"I shan't be long," Vega returned.

"Where did you say Simeon was?" she queried

"Eh . . . he is with Pio, my lady. I shall fetch him to you as soon as I fetch the healers." He sketched a bow, then, and left her without a backward glance.

Meg followed him with her eyes as he left the chamber. Something in his bearing raised the fine hairs on the back of her neck. She studied Risa so still in the bed beside her. Anyone could have been designated to sit beside the comatose girl. It took only a split second to make the decision. She would summon a retainer to do just that, then follow Vega to find out exactly what was afoot.

Keeping well behind, she followed him as he sprinted along

the corridor to a ledge where dozens of selkies garbed in their sealskins waited. When Vega plunged into the water, the selkies waddled to the edge and slid in after him. Now she was certain. It didn't take a selkie army to bring a healer. Who could have put poor Risa under a spell, and why? There would be no answers standing there, and she slipped into the water and followed them at a discrete distance.

The way seemed familiar, though she was concentrating more upon the swimmers than the water they swam through. She didn't want to lose track of them. She didn't want to be seen, either. It wasn't long before she realized they were heading straight for the Waterwitch's cave. An adrenaline surge caused her to lose her rhythm momentarily. Something was wrong—very wrong. With her heart rising in her throat, she swam on. She couldn't let Vega and the selkies out of her sight.

All at once, for all her diligence, they were gone. They seemed to have vanished into thin air. The underwater steps to the Waterwitch's cave loomed before her, and she broke the surface and climbed up. The sitting room was empty, just as it had been the last time she'd come there. All was still, and she entered the sanctuary half expecting to find the odious crone holding court, but that chamber, too, was empty. The sound of raised voices coming from an inner chamber caught her ear, and Meg crept to the fall of aquatic vines that served as a door between the rooms, just as all the subterranean dwellings boasted, and peeked through the gaps in the hanging curtain.

It took moment for her to take in the scene before her. Her heart was pounding so violently she feared they would hear it. The Waterwitch was pacing before a large cage with Simeon inside. Other cages were beyond it. A terrible stench was coming from them, and she covered her mouth with her hand, fearful she would retch.

"So, Lord of the Deep, you sent for your army, did you?" the Waterwitch was saying. "How did you manage that, eh?"

"I sent for no one, Elna," he returned. "It's only natural they would come seeking me and that this hovel of yours would be the first place they'd look. What have you done with them?"

The crone laughed. "You actually thought that pitiful lot could stand against *me*? You are quite mad."

"Where are they? What have you down with them?" Simeon demanded. "Your business is with me, venerable one, and me alone. You have my sealskin, and you have me. Let my brother go."

"In due time," she purred. "They have come to no harm. They are simply . . . detained. And they will come to no harm as long as you do what you failed to do earlier. You are my slave, Lord of the Deep. You have no choice."

Meg's eyes flashed toward the wall of the dungeon and Simeon's sealskin hanging upon it. Her heart constricted as if a hand had reached inside her breast and clamped itself around it. Unconsciously, she reached to fondle the amulet about her neck. It trembled between her fingers, and she gripped it as if she meant to take its strength within her.

The Waterwitch slithered out of her filmy robe and entered Simeon's cage naked. How exquisite she was with her long dark hair and perfect body, her breasts and sex and beautiful face the only parts of her anatomy not covered in shimmering green scales. A far cry from the ancient wrinkled face she'd last seen the witch wear. She was flaunting her perfection, but not at Simeon; she was facing away from him, toward the vine curtain Meg was peeking through, and Meg's heart all but stopped when she spoke.

"Come, Daughter of the Deep," the crone said. "Do not be shy. Step inside and watch."

Without hesitation, Meg stepped through the vines. Simeon gave a start at sight of her. The look in his eyes was paralyzing. She avoided it, making eye contact with the crone instead.

"I have come to strike a bargain with you, venerable one,"

Meg said as coolly as she could manage, for what she was about to do would change all their lives forever.

"Eh?" the crone grunted. "What have you to bargain with?" She raked Meg up and down and popped another grunt. "Once I've had my fill of him, I will deal with you. No tricks . . . Whatever you're up to, I have magic to dispel it. So beware!"

"I have magic of my own," Meg said, strolling closer. "But my bargain first . . ."

"Speak it and have done!"

"Give me his sealskin," Meg said, "and I will give you this." She fingered the amulet.

"*No*, Megaleen! You cannot!" Simeon thundered. Gripping the bars of the cage, he rattled them fiercely.

Meg ignored him. "This that I wear will give you immorality without a selkie skin," she said. "You will no longer have need of one once I give you this."

The Waterwitch left Simeon's cage and came toward her. "How do I know you speak the truth?" she snapped.

Meg backed toward the ledge, mindful of the pool beneath it as the crone advanced. "You are a sorceress of great renown," she seduced. "Look closely. You cannot take it, it must be given to you, and I will give it willingly in exchange for that sealskin there."

The Waterwitch came closer, scrutinizing the amulet with narrowed eyes. "Where did you get such a token?" she said.

"From Glenda, Vega's mother," Meg said. "She gave it to him before she died. Look closely. You know it is the truth."

"Megaleen, *no!*" Simeon thundered. "You cannot part with that. No, I say! Glenda died to give you that amulet. You cannot give it to this creature!"

"It is mine to give to whomever I please," Meg said steadily, for all that she was in shambles then. The crone was hovering too closely. Her breath was foul, like rotting flesh and dead fish. Pio's image flashed across her mind. Could he be dead? Is that why no one had seen him? She pushed that thought back—steeled herself against the possibility. "Give that sealskin to me, and I will give you the amulet."

The crone came closer still. Reaching with one finger, she touched the shimmering black pearl. No sooner had her fingertip made contact when she pulled her hand back as if she'd touched live coals.

"You see?" Meg said. "I speak the truth." She reached to unclasp the silver strand that held it about her neck.

"Megaleen, *don't!*" Simeon pleaded. "It is our lives you bargain with!"

"Silence!" the Waterwitch shrilled. "You have no say in this, fool. If you were not so drunk with love madness, you would never have lost you sealskin in the first place."

Tears welled in Meg's eyes as she held the amulet toward the witch. Tears for Glenda, who sacrificed herself for naught, tears for Simeon, who could not live above the waves, though he would for her, and tears for herself, for she saw what she would become if she were to stay below the waves with him.

The Waterwitch snatched at the amulet, but Meg pulled it out of her reach. "The sealskin first," she said. "You cannot take this from me. I must give it freely, and I will, but first, the sealskin!"

Sputtering a spate of what could only be a string of blasphemies, the Waterwitch waved her hand toward the wall behind, and the sealskin dropped in a heap on the floor. Meg thrust the amulet toward her, and raced to the wall. Snatching up the skin, she froze as the Waterwitch screamed, and spun around in time to see Pio break the waves. Seeming to dance upon the surface of the water, the battered summoner leapt toward the ledge and ran the Waterwitch through with his long, sharp sword. It speared her, impaling her, piercing her heart, as Pio fell back into the pool, taking her with him.

Meg caught a glint of light as the amulet fell from the crone's hand and disappeared beneath the water. There was no time to mourn its loss. From behind, the rasp of metal against metal echoed. Then Simeon was holding her, his sealskin between them. Clutching the skin, Meg stepped back and made her decision. It was the second time she'd held his fate in her hands—held possession of that sealskin. Looking him deep in his anguished selkie eyes, she handed it to him.

All at once, the ledge was swarming with selkies, some in their skins, some without. Vega climbed up on the ledge, and Simeon thrust the sealskin toward him. "Hang on to this for me," he said.

"You still trust me with it?" Vega replied.

"Of course I do. What kept you?"

"These pools are all crosshatched with traps," Vega said. "She caught us in one of her nets. It fell away the minute she died."

"And Pio?"

Vega shook his head. "I haven't seen him, Simeon.

Vega's words were scarcely out when the summoner broke the surface of the water, leaping and dancing on its surface, the amulet dangling from his sword.

Simeon dove into the water and snatched it from the swordfish who skipped and leapt and plunged back beneath the waves. Climbing out again, Simeon took Meg in his arms and fastened the amulet around her neck again.

"You little fool," he murmured. "You love me that much?"

Meg couldn't speak. She nodded against his shoulder.

"Go with Vega into the water," he said. "I will join you in a moment. There is something I must do here before we go back to the palace." He turned to Vega. "Have no fear," he said. "I think you will find Risa restored when we return," he said. "Take her."

Meg slipped into the pool with Vega, watching while Simeon stalked through the Waterwitch's rooms, scattering her lamp oil, paying special attention to the cages. Then, taking rush candles from their sconces, he tossed them down, stepping back as the rooms burst into flames, and dove into the water.

Meg was in his arms once more, the thick bulk of his arousal leaning heavily against her mound. Those arms . . . Those wonderful arms! She would never leave them again.

## 28

"Do all your residences have such pools?" Meg asked. She was in Simeon's arms, where she had been for the most part since they'd left the Waterwitch's cave. He hadn't let her out of his sight. But they weren't at the palace. This pool was in the depths of the Pavilion. Fed by warm mineral springs on the mainland, the steamy water laved them seductively, lapping at Meg's breasts, barely covering her nipples. It buoyed Simeon's erect shaft, which nudged her as they bobbed with the current. It felt like silk nuzzling her thighs, leaning against her belly, teasing the V between as it nestled in the cushion of her pubic curls.

"Most all the subterranean chambers here and at the palace have such pools attached," he said. "The underwater air pockets were formed when the great cataclysm split the mainland and created the archipelago. You bathe, my lady, compliments of the gods. It is one of the great mysteries of the deep."

"Um," she hummed, crowding closer in his strong arms. "Praise the Powers! Delicious . . ."

Meanwhile, in the Great Hall and above the waves on the

rocks and natural jetties, the creatures of the sea reveled, celebrating the Lord and Lady of the Deep. Merfolk of all descriptions mated, sang, and danced to the Otherworldly music of flute and lyre. Above it all, the voices of the sirens, plaintive and ethereal, drifted out over the water. It echoed all around them, strumming chords born deep in the mists of time. It was an event of lavish celebration, something that had not happened at the Pavilion in eons.

Simeon took the black pearl amulet in hand and rubbed it between his thumb and forefinger. "Elna is gone," he said, "but others will come, Megaleen. It has been thus down through the ages. Vega will keep the Scroll of Arcan Rite, and I must know now that you will not ever take this from your neck again."

"Simeon . . ."

"I must be certain before we can go forward. If I were to lose you again, I . . ."

Her finger laid across his lips stilled his tongue. "I will never do anything ever again that would part us," she murmured. "You have my word. I could not live without my soulmate."

He kissed her fingertips and drew her closer, the hard bulk of his erection anxious against her belly. Meg trapped it between her thighs and clenched them. Simeon groaned, pumping back and forth along the lips of her labia. His hard shaft rode her slippery wetness, unlike the salty mineral water all around them, from the hard nub of her clitoris to the tender skin between her vagina and anus, teasing the tight rosette.

Meg leaned into the friction that sent shivers of pleasure along her spine, trying to trap his shaft and guide him inside her, anything to stop such torturous ecstasy. But he was too quick for her, sinking deeper with each thrust, but not deep enough to penetrate.

"I want you to beg me to enter you," he murmured against her hair. "I want you to ache for my cock to fill you. Then . . . when you are ready . . ."

Meg was ready. Her quim was singing—tingling with the vibrations of her arousal, her hard bud crying for release. Waves like silken fire were riding her sexual stream, just as the little waves they were making in the pool rode their bodies.

"Take me now, my lord," she murmured, gazing into his shuttered eyes. They almost seemed to glow with the phosphorescence of the sea dancing in the reflection of the rush lamps shimmering in them.

Simeon spread her legs and salt water rushed inside her. She leaned closer in anticipation of his rock-hard bulk filling her, but only the head slipped inside. She could feel the pulse throbbing in it, trembling at the edge of her slit—tormenting her. Why wouldn't he give her what she begged for?

Instead, he shut his eyes, his head thrust back, and stood perfectly still. When he met her gaze again, his eyes were dilated black with desire and every corded muscle in him was flexed taut.

"Do you trust me, my Megaleen?" he murmured.

"Yes, my lord," she replied.

"The ancient one in the tree has joined us in the eyes of the gods, but now we must be joined in the eyes of the people for you to rule beside me as Lady of the Deep. Are you ready for the ceremony?"

"What ceremony?" She'd heard no mention of a ceremony, only a celebration.

"Our marriage ceremony, Megaleen," he told her. "I have had consorts aplenty over the years, but I have never married. This union between us is forever. Since time out of mind all Lords of the Deep have performed the ceremony, just as my father did before me. Are you ready to become my lady?"

He could have asked her to walk upon live coals and she would have, and gladly, to join with her soul mate for all eternity. "Yes, my lord," she said.

But then he did a curious thing. While she expected him to pound into her, to give her what her body begged for, he withdrew himself, took her hand, and led her to the stairs hewn of stone leading up to their chamber.

"Where are we going?" she queried.

"To the ceremony," he said.

Meg stopped to pick up her frock neatly laid over a rococo bench.

"You will not need that," he said, leading her into the corridor.

Meg glanced over her shoulder at the frock they'd left behind. "You're used to going about without your clothes," she said. "I am no selkie. I am accustomed to my body being covered."

He laughed, the deep burr bubbling up from the guttural depths of him. The sound of it took her breath away. Simeon had the power to seduce with the sound of his voice alone. "That will change," he chortled.

Diving into the water that surrounded the subterranean cave, they swam toward the surface. Meg was unaccustomed to the terrain at the Pavilion. She had no idea where he was taking her until they broke the waves. It was the midnight hour. Above, the bright misshapen moon beamed down, hung like a lantern in the star-studded indigo vault. It was low tide, and they appeared to be in the center of an amphitheater made of stacked stone benches studded with shells. It was filled with spectators all around, their cheers amplified by the water as the bride and bridegroom approached a large flat rock in the center. It was draped with all manner of sea plants and covered with a bed of sea grass, night lilies, and lotus blooms, their combined fragrances threading through Meg's nostrils on the gentle midnight breeze.

"The ceremony?" Meg murmured.

Simeon nodded. "Do not be afraid," he said, pulling her closer in his arms. "It is a beautiful thing to mate so—to show our subjects that we are one so there can never be a question."

"But . . . in front of all these . . ." Meg said, her eyes snapping around the arena.

Again, Simeon laughed. "Do you remember the first time you saw me?" he said. "Do you remember watching me and my consorts shed our sealskins on the beach on the Isle of Mists and mate before your very eyes? Do you remember how that mating excited you—made you long to be the woman in the waves, the woman underneath me—how you touched yourself in the dark until you came, pretending you were that woman writhing in the surf impaled upon my member?"

"Yes, but—"

"You are that woman now," he whispered, sweeping her into his arms. "You have your wish, your ultimate fantasy, my Megaleen."

Meg said no more as Simeon carried her to the marriage bed and laid her down on it. He was fully aroused standing over her, just as he was when she saw him that first time. Bruised flower petals beneath her spread their scent, and their precious oils caressed her skin as Simeon crushed more, letting them rain down over her, massaging their fragrant dew into her body. He lingered over her nipples, then rubbed the petals down the length of her torso. When he reached the V of pubic curls between her thighs, she groaned and spread her legs for him to work the petals silken magic into her bud and quivering slit, front to back. Rubbing some the length of his hard-veined shaft, he groaned, then brushed them all away, exposing their white bodies to the moon glow.

Mesmerized by the scent, by the sight of him naked beneath the moon, and the sounds of the cheering crowd, Meg arched herself against him. Spreading her legs wider still, he guided them around his waist and slid between them, taking her lips with a hungry mouth. She came the moment he thrust inside her. His skilled fingers fondled her nipples, circling the pebbled areola without touching the hardened buds until she begged him to end the agony of anticipation, and she came again as he scraped those buds against his fingertips.

Still inside her, he rolled on his back taking her with him, and cupped her breasts in his hands, rubbing her aching nipples, pushing deeper into her as she straddled him.

"Ride the storm, my Megaleen," he murmured.

His hands circling her waist raised her up and down, slowly at first, then harder, deeper spiraling thrusts that took her breath away. Her knees bit into his sides as she took all of him, again and again, in mindless oblivion. Milking him of every last hot-lava drop of his seed, she pumped him dry.

Though the spectators were there still, Meg saw them no longer, nor did she hear their cheers. In that glorious moment, she and Simeon were the only two people in existence. They made love until the dawn breeze brought in the tide. They lay enthralled until whitecaps rose around them, laving them where they lay joined together in their conjugal bed, creaming over them like the surf had creamed over the selkies on that first night. The fantasy was complete.

The spectators began to slip away then, leaving them alone at last, all but one. Meg hadn't noticed him until then, and Simeon hadn't noticed him at all, but over her bridegroom's shoulder, Meg glimpsed a lone figure standing upon a tall, phallic stone at the edge of what she now perceived to be a stone garden opposite the amphitheater. Boulders, some low and flat, some tall and sculpted by the sea like round doorways stood there, silhouetted black against the sky as the last of the night's indigo gave way to the dawn. Standing tall on the loftiest stone, Gideon, Lord of the Dark, spread his wings and took flight. He soared off and disappeared in a blink as if he'd never been there. How lonely he'd seemed standing on that towering column apart from the rest, but that was the nature of the dark lord. He was an enigma steeped in the mystery of the night.

But Meg wasn't given long to probe that mystery. Simeon withdrew himself, let all his breath out on a ragged sigh, and pulled her close in the custody of his strong arms.

"Good morning, my Lady of the Deep," he murmured in her ear. The touch of his hot breath puffing against her skin threatened to arouse her all over again. "There are so many delights I long to show you," he said. "So many pleasures I long to introduce you to, my love . . ."

"So you keep telling me," Meg said playfully. "But I cannot imagine how you will ever top this!"

Simeon laughed. "Well, you'll have eternity to see now, won't you?" he said.

And lowering his mouth over hers, he said no more.

Please turn the page for an exciting sneak peek at
Evangeline Anderson's latest novel,

*THE PLEASURE PALACE*

Coming soon from Aphrodisia!

# 1

---

"C'mon, darlin', I jus' wan' a lil' sugar pussy. I'm only top-side on this rock for twenty-four hours. You don't wan' me to go away lonely, now do ya?" He had a thick Centaurian accent and had obviously been drinking all night so the words came out in a drawling slur. Shaina McCullough suddenly found herself pinned against the crumbling gray concrete with the disgusting drunk leering in her face. "Jus' a lil' sugar pussy . . ." he repeated and she turned her head in revulsion as his foul breath, thick with gin fumes, washed over her.

That was it; she couldn't stand it any more. Determined to teach him a lesson, Shaina struggled to get her right hand behind her back and grab the mini-tazer that was taped there. Cursing the stupid skintight design of her skirt that made it impossible to carry anything in the pockets, her fingers wiggled beneath the low-slung waistband of the leather mini, feeling for the small, lipstick-shaped tube. She intended to whip it out and shove it straight into the drunk Centaurian's balls—all three of them. A good sharp jolt in the nads ought to discourage him, since he didn't seem to know how to take no for an answer. At the very least it would teach him not to bother innocent-looking girls who turned out to be Peace Control Officers.

"Hey baby, I knew you'd come around." The drunk had managed to pull the magno-tabs of her crop top apart and was currently trying to get off her demi-bra. His breath was making her want to retch. Shaina fumbled grimly for the tazer. Where was it? She had taped it to the small of her back right before leaving the station, but now her searching fingers found nothing but a smooth expanse of skin—it was gone. The drunk had one hand inside her bra now and was mauling her right breast. Shaina was sure she'd have to take a scalding anti-bac shower that night to even begin to feel clean again.

"Get off me!" she yelled, beginning to feel a little panicky. Okay, it was time to call for backup. The drunk Centaurian might not be the serial rapist she was looking for but she was going to be in serious trouble if she didn't get him off her— pronto. One thick knee was pressing between her thighs, trying to spread her legs as Shaina reached for the autojewel, actually a link to her backup, nestled securely in her belly button. But the drunk's potbelly was plastered against her own flat stomach too firmly to admit so much as a micron between them, let alone her questing fingers. She tried to push him away, but he was all over her, a suffocating, reeking flesh blanket.

Oh, this could *not* be happening after all her careful training and months of preparation for a case like this, Shaina thought despairingly. It was supposed to be her big break. What would Ty think if he could see her now?

As if to answer her question, a deep male voice came from the depths of the alley behind them.

"Hey, buddy, I don't think you're this lady's type. Why don't you back off and get out of here?" Shaina's heart sank. She knew that voice. It belonged to Brent Tyson, the senior of- ficer who had trained her not so many months ago. Damn it all to hell, what was he doing here? She'd almost rather be mauled by this disgusting drunk than have her ex-partner witness her failure.

The drunk in question was paying no attention to the commanding voice behind him. "Find yer own, mister. I was here first," he mumbled, still pawing at her bra. He had exposed both breasts now and he was working on spreading her thighs. Thankfully, the tightness of the micro-mini actually worked in her favor there, making it impossible for her legs to part more than a few inches. Shaina continued to try and wriggle free with no success.

"Fine, we'll do it your way," Ty said pleasantly. Suddenly, the drunk was dragged off her and Shaina was left leaning against the cold concrete wall, gasping with effort and off balance in her ridiculous thigh-high imitation lizardskin boots. Not for the first time, she cursed the stupid costume, which was supposed to make her look like a university student out for a night on the town. She stumbled a few steps and fell to the dirty, gravel-strewn ground, cutting her palms in the process, and looked up in time to see Ty's fist connect with the drunk's face. The punch wiped the leering grin off in a sickening crunch of cartilage and bone. Blood that was nearly black began pouring down the Centaurian's face. He dropped his bottle of gin and cupped his nose, bellowing in hurt confusion.

"Whyth you do that?" he gasped, his eyes flaring orange with pain. "That hurth, you thon of a bith!" He added a few choice words in his native tongue that Shaina couldn't begin to make out, although their meaning was pretty clear.

"Wouldn't have had to if you'd backed off when the lady asked you to," Tyson replied, still in that same, pleasant, no-nonsense tone of voice. He casually smoothed back his thick black hair with one large hand and waited to see if the drunk had had enough. Apparently, he hadn't. With an inarticulate howl, he came stumbling forward, clearly meaning to tackle Tyson and take him to the ground. This time, Ty didn't even bother to punch him. He just stepped out of the way and let the Centaurian run headfirst into the opposite wall of the alley, knocking himself out cold.

Without missing a beat, Tyson turned back to Shaina, who was still kneeling on the ground, feeling stunned. "Upsy-daisy, sweetheart." He hooked one capable hand under her arm and levered her to her feet as though she weighed next to nothing. Angrily, Shaina shook him off.

"Damn it, Ty, what are you doing here?" She gazed at her former partner with disgust. As always, he looked immaculate, as though he was about to attend a meeting instead of punching out drunk Centaurians in a dark alley in the seedy port district. Shaina couldn't stop her eyes from traveling up his muscular legs and thighs clad in skintight black trousers, to the broad chest and wide shoulders in a crisp white button-up shirt. He hadn't even gotten dirty in the short fight, she noticed with disgust. Brent Tyson had a striking, hawklike face and his distinctive amber eyes were glinting with amusement and maybe something else as he stared at her in the dim light of the alley.

"What am I doing here? Saving your sweet little ass, McCullough. At least that's what it looks like from here." He grinned at her. That self-satisfied smirk Shaina couldn't stand, showing sharp, white teeth in the half light of the alley. Ty was half D'Lonian. Usually, aside from the amber eyes and golden-tan skin, you really couldn't tell. But when he grinned like that, it showed. That grin made Shaina nervous because it reminded her of all the rumors she'd heard about D'Lonian males—most of them too incredible to be real and too embarrassing to repeat. All her girlfriends whispered and giggled about it when they heard she was working with a man who was half D'Lonian. People said D'Lonian men were animalistic in their mating habits, that they had uncontrollable, unnatural lust. She tried to push the thought out of her head and concentrate on appearing self-sufficient and professional.

"I had the situation completely under control. There was no need for you to interfere." Shaina lied as forcefully as she could. "This is my case and you shouldn't be here."

"What were you going to do, bludgeon him into submission with these?" Ty cupped her still exposed breasts in large, warm hands and scooped them neatly back into the lacy demi-bra, causing Shaina to gasp. The heat of that brief contact lingered, making her nipples into hard little pebbles as she attempted to close the magno-tabs of her crop top, getting them misaligned in the process. She tried to ignore her reaction to his touch and remain professional.

"No, I was just about to stun him with my tazer before you interfered." She looked up at him defiantly. Even with the absurdly high-heeled boots, he was too tall to meet eye to eye. Smoothing down the crooked crop top, she tried in vain to pull the micro-mini just a little farther down her thighs. Having those smoldering amber eyes on her body always made Shaina uncomfortable for reasons she was unwilling to think about, even to herself.

"Oh, you mean this?" Tyson reached into the righthand pocket of his skintight trousers. Shaina's eyes couldn't help but follow the gesture as she noticed, not for the first time, the thick bulge between his legs. Part of her wondered if it was any thicker at the moment as a result of having his hands, however briefly, on her bare breasts, but she pushed the thought resolutely away. Ty pulled his hand out of his pocket and there, lying in the center of his large palm, was her lipstick-sized mini-tazer. It still had a small curl of Stiksalot—*sticks anything to anything*—stuck to it.

"Where did you get that? I taped it to the small of my back before I left the station." She reached for it but Ty pulled it back, gripping the miniature weapon firmly in his fist.

"And you dropped it about three blocks back. It fell right out the back of your skirt in front of the Green Iguana." He mentioned the local dive the serial rapist was thought to hang out in. Shaina had spent a good part of the night there, letting herself be seen, before wandering slowly away to the darker side streets of the port district, hoping to lure the rapist into following. Instead, she had gotten the drunk Centaurian, who was currently out cold and snoring at their feet.

"You were following me!" Shaina was outraged. "In case you hadn't noticed, Ty, my training period is over. It's been over for months and you're no longer my partner or training officer—you're my coworker. That means we're equals and I don't need you breathing down my neck while I'm trying to work. I don't need you to take care of me anymore." Shaina could feel her pale skin flushing red with anger but she was helpless to do anything about it.

"Well, from what I just saw it looks like you need *someone* to take care of you." His deep voice was quiet and calm, but those wide amber eyes flashed dangerously. "And I wasn't following you. I happened to be having a beer at the Green Iguana when I saw you walk out. I noticed the tazer fall out of your skirt and came along to give it back to you. What would you have done if I had decided to leave you to your own devices and return it tomorrow?"

"I could have called for backup." Shaina sounded sullen, even to herself. Why was it that Ty could reduce her from a grown woman to a petulant child with a few choice words?

"With this?" He stepped forward, crowding her a little, and ran one long finger along the soft curve of her abdomen, indicating the autojewel in her belly button, now blinking red moons and yellow daisies. The brush of his warm, calloused fingertip along her skin made Shaina shiver. "Where *is* your backup anyway?" He smelled like warm male musk.

"They're back a few blocks." She wanted to move away from him, but, once again, her back was to the wall. Her boots grated against the gravel as she shifted her feet; there was no place to go. "I didn't want to scare the guy off. I'm trolling for the Red-Head Rapist; he's been known to hunt in the port district."

"Yes, I know. They're calling him that because he targets redheads, which, I guess, is how you got involved, even though this isn't technically your area of expertise."

Shaina bristled. "I don't want to be stuck in Domestic my entire career. When Tony from Vice approached me about trying to draw this guy out I jumped on it. My hair just made it easier." She flipped her long, silky auburn hair over one shoulder with a defiant little toss of her head, daring him to say anything about it.

"Is that right?" His amber eyes still glittered dangerously. He took another step forward, deliberately invading even more of her space. Shaina held her ground.

"Yes, it is. As a matter of fact, that guy you punched out might be the Red-Head Rapist, for all you know." She gestured at the Centaurian sprawled at their feet.

"You know he's not." Tyson smiled a little, again showing those sharp, white teeth. "He's just a drunk Centaurian out looking for, what did he call it? Oh, yeah—a little 'sugar pussy' I believe is what he said." He leaned in closer, his warm, cinnamon-scented breath brushing along her neck and the tops of her breasts as he spoke, and Shaina felt herself blushing furiously. Goddess! To think he had heard that too . . . it was absolutely mortifying. She was deeply embarrassed—which must be the reason her heart was pounding so hard and she felt like she couldn't get a deep enough breath.

"So you stood there and watched the whole thing. If you were going to interfere, then why didn't you do it in the first place before he started manhandling me?" She fought not to notice how close he was to her. His slim hips were pressed against her pelvis until she was absolutely sure she could feel the bulge of his hard cock digging mercilessly into her flesh.

The heat in his blazing golden eyes was intense and it was all Shaina could do to meet them without flinching. She didn't want Ty to know how nervous he made her.

"McCullough . . . Shaina . . ." He sighed and took a step back. Running one hand through his thick black hair, he shook his head as he looked at her. "I was trying to leave you alone because I knew how you'd react if I interfered with your sting. But damn it—you left me no choice! I couldn't just stand by and watch him rape you, could I?

"I only stepped in at the last minute when it became clear that you weren't handling the situation and your backup was nowhere in sight. I don't see how I could have done anything else. Now, come on." Ty took her small hands gently in his. "You hurt yourself when you fell. I have a first aid kit in my craft. Why don't you come let me bandage you up? Red-Head's not out tonight or he would have taken the bait already. There's no way he could have resisted you." Those frank amber eyes raked over her again, taking in her barely concealed breasts and the too-short skirt, making Shaina feel hot and cold and completely naked all at the same time. She crossed her legs tightly, trying to ignore the throbbing between her thighs. As always, Ty's effect on her body made her feel nervous and angry—out of control.

"I told you, Ty, I don't need you to take care of me anymore. So why don't you do us both a favor and stay out of my life?" She pulled her hurt hands out of his large, warm grip, taking the tazer as she did. Grimly, she pushed past him, fully aware that he was letting her go, the awareness making her angrier than ever.

"Shaina." He grasped her upper arm and swung her around to face him once more. "I admit I've been watching out for you a little bit. You're still a rookie and I get worried about you, especially when you take on an assignment like this. But if that's really what you want, then I'll do it. I'll stay out of your life."

His voice was calm but dangerous; his fingers dug into the flesh of her upper arm like steel pincers.

"Fine." She didn't know why her voice was trembling or why she couldn't look into those golden eyes while she spoke. "Stay out."

"You have my word." Voice cold, he let her go so abruptly she nearly fell again. Stumbling, Shaina got past him as fast as she could, blinking back angry tears as she wobbled in the spike-heeled boots to the end of the alley. She could feel his eyes on her back like laser beams while she walked, and she fought the urge to look back. The boots were pinching her toes and sending spikes of pain through her arches, and every extremity felt frozen solid except her hands—they were still warm from Ty's touch.

Why wouldn't he just leave her alone and let her prove she could do the job right on her own without always swooping in to rescue and criticize her? Shaina knew he had trained lots of other Peace Control Officers, so why did he always single her out, as though her training would never be done?

Well, now at least he had promised to stay out of her life. She wondered how long that promise would last.

As it turned out, it lasted less than twenty-four hours.